TO ANTOINE,

E. J. WIENS

ENDORSEMENTS

We are what we remember. This overwhelming story asks: does Peter Enns dare to remember what he has done and not done, what was done to him by those he loved, or hated; including Antoine, his brother, mentor … his idol. Good reader, dare to follow Peter as he unflinchingly remembers himself. And you will discover the beauty, the guilt, the goodness, the horror of being a human being in the (as he calls it) "demented" 20th century.

Rudy Wiebe, distinguished author

To Antoine is a powerful novel that digs deeply into the lives of Mennonite families and their friends over a 60-year period, from their struggles for survival in Stalin's Russia and Hitler's Germany to their creation of new identities in South America and Canada.

Erwin Wiens, a great story-teller, fills his sometimes noir-ish stories with tension and terror, whether as comedy or tragedy. His narrator is Peter Enns, son of a Mennonite artist and photographer. In 1991-92 Peter, by then in Canada, writes a series of letters to Antoine: Anton Antonovich, a child of former Russian gentry. When Peter was six, Antoine 11, the boys were brought together when Mary Gordon, a Scottish nanny, secretly deposited Antoine with Peter's family. Secrets of Peter's war-time deeds haunt him as he struggles to vindicate himself.

To Antoine, visceral and cerebral at once, is a quest for knowledge and forgiveness. It is a vivid portrait of bit players in the chaos of twentieth-century mayhem: of pragmatism and idealism; of loyalties and betrayals; of opportunism and deceit, complicity and revenge.

Paul Tiessen, Professor Emeritus, Wilfred Laurier University

Erwin Wiens takes us into the lives of individual Russian Mennonites whose communities were destroyed during the communist revolution, who identified with the German forces during their 1941-43 occupation, and who then, in a few instances, became involved with the Nazis and their atrocities. After the war they make their way to Paraguay and to Canada, but they carry their past with them. Wiens' careful research into the historical context, his breakdown of the story into readable segments, and his vivid portrayal of the characters in this cauldron of life and death, integrity and betrayal, courage and opportunism, make this book highly informative, deeply challenging, and hard to put down. The book does not argue for a particular 'verdict of history;' instead, it brings us close to human beings in this heart-rending chapter of Mennonite history, leaving us to also reflect on the similar experience of many others.

William Janzen, former Director of MCC Ottawa Office

Gelassenheit Publications 2022
73 Dufferin Street
St Catharines, Ontario L2R 1Z9

First published in Canada by Gelassenheit Publications
Copyright 2022 by E. J. Wiens

National Library of Canada Cataloguing in Publication

ISBN (pbk) 978-0-9880993-3-3

Title: To Antoine / E. J. Wiens.
Names: Wiens, Erwin J., 1942- author

Identifiers: Mennonite — Russian — Fiction
LCSH: Refugees--Ukraine--Fiction
War crime trials--Canada--Fiction

LCC PS8645.I46 T6 2022
DCC 813./6

Cover design by Elias Mina. Cover photograph: 'Henry and Otto,' by Peter Gerhard
Rempel, appears in *Forever Summer, Forever Sunday* (Sand Hills Books, 1981), courtesy
of John D. Rempel.

To the memory of Maria,
who survived the terrors of both Stalinism and Nazism
with undaunted courage.

BEGINNINGS, NEW AND OLD

September 4, 1991

If, across the low plain you could observe them from a high place, Antoine, they would look like swarms of starlings gathering for a migration. Horsemen, in bands of thirty or forty, sometimes a hundred or more swarming together, a dark mass looming along a distant ridge, suspended there a moment as though uncertain of their purpose, then spilling down the long gradual decline, rising and falling over imperceptible undulations as though buoyed upon waves, they and the wavering grasses the only things that seem to move upon this elemental landscape. Become distinct then as they draw near, man and beast, veer left, right, with uncanny perilous precision, the mounting roar of their hoof beats like a wave breaking upon a beach and tumbling upon some luckless village or sprawling estate. And all is madness now, shooting and shrieking, women running and run down, old men and children, and cattle braying while flames lick the steep roofs of homes and stables.

Then as suddenly recalled from madness, obedient to some wordless command, some brute instinct of the race. They leap again upon their mounts, circle the flames, once, twice, to gather the stragglers, then uncoil like a whiplash across the yielding plain, plunge down a ravine and rise again in disarray, those above kicking rocks and dirt upon those below.

They regroup and veer south along the crest of a shrouded rise, sheered now into a long narrow column silhouetted against a late-summer sunset – like phantoms, weightless on impossibly thin, shimmering legs, and trailing veils of luminous brown dust across a blood-red haze. As much a part of the sky as of the earth below them, a *pas de deux* of horsemen and landscape, a savage beauty in their claim to brute impunity, compared to the calculated terror that came after.

'Go,' said my daughter. 'Maybe you'll find some answers there, before all your people have died.' So in the brief summer of Gorbachev and *glasnost* I summoned what courage I had and went, armed with visas and travel permits, a few small gifts and a hand-drawn map on brittle yellowed paper, and my crisp new Canadian passport. Back to the land that bore me, half a century after I had fled in anger and spite, a land I loathed; loathed, yet drawn to like a dog to a stinking carcass. Did I go to pay homage to the generations of my people who had tilled this land that once held the promise of freedom, then became a prison? Or to give this land a proper burial, to bury it deep in some recess of my mind where it could no longer trouble my sleep?

And once again, an old man gripping an unsteady cane, I stood on that windy crest between two rivers, the Molotchna and the Dnieper, the very spot where you and I once lay on our bellies and gazed down upon a sea of grass and rusty stubble. Saw them all again, those horsemen, not in their flesh but in my mind's eye, and felt, or thought I could, the tremor of their hoof beats coursing through my body. Stories of horsemen, imprinted upon the soft clay of a child's mind, and always in my imagination the sound of doom in horses' hooves, the beginning of the end. So many horsemen, they said, there was no room for them all upon the endless plain but they must scourge and harry one another, so ravenous they must pillage again and again the villages and the wasted estates, then fall upon one another and pillage their pillage, swarm after swarm, till typhus, famine and dysentery exhaust them and make an end. Where they had come to roost the landscape lay in ruin, overturned carts, dismembered orchards, a twisted pair of eyeglasses among charred timbers, and where they passed lay a trail of discarded booty, a mantel clock jolted from its pack, its brass mechanism now spilled like guts upon the plain, a single shoe with a silver buckle, an ivory comb, a tattered dress caught on a broken fence for the curious dogs to sniff. And perhaps the pummelled body of a young girl who wriggled out of her captor's grasp and fell beneath the indifferent hooves. So it was, Antoine, when you and I were born into this mad carnival of a century, then still in its adolescence, still reeling after its youthful adventure in world war and revolution, the ghoulish enticements of the century's maturity still to come.

We didn't stand a chance. We came, head first, puking and wailing into a world already seething. From the Rhine to the Volga, a world in the grip of a mounting fever. Already, deep into the night, hunkered in his Kremlin office one sat brooding how best to fill a Siberian emptiness with corpses. Already, far in the west, in the valleys of the Ruhr, the steel furnaces of Krupp AG were stoked to frenzy by inspired little men, dark specks darting among the flames, their sooty faces glowing in the yellow light. And in the shadow of the Bavarian Alps rose the roar of torch-lit stadiums, bannered and flag-festooned, where a multitude mounted upon a single spot-lit voice. A time when all the moral compasses spun crazily in their binnacles, when the coordinates of good and evil were tossed about in a swirl of rival manias, when Old Europa, senile now, and spiteful of her former beauty, lecherous, with wrinkled dugs and a gummy leer, felt once more a sticky warmth suffuse her loins, and took to bed a pair of hot-gospelers who whispered sweet nothings in her ear – of *Volk* and *Vaterland* and Five-Year Plans – then devoured her misbegotten spawn.

Yet we survived, some of us, caught between the Soviet hammer and the four-pronged hook, the chaff between two millstones, a tattered fragment among Europa's superfluous populations, her Unwanted, refugees, DPs, *Stadtlose*, 'the scum of Europe' – some thirty thousand of us among millions more, *Volksdeutsche,* Ukrainians, Poles, Latvians, White Russians, and God knows what, a tidal wave of human refuse stretching from the Baltic to the Balkans, stumbling westward through *Mittel Europa*, scrambling to keep a month, a week, then a day ahead of the retreating *Wehrmacht*, the boom of Russian artillery louder and louder at our rear, and in the sky the whine of playful Spitfires strafing our flanks for sport – while we, like fabled figures from some distant past of legendary carnage, heaved aching shoulders to the mud-caked wheels of carts and wagons. Lousy, diseased and bewildered, tormented by rumours, herded here, there, by men with guns who shouted gibberish at us, *Achtung! Los! Dowód!* our tongues thick from groping around our mouths for unpronounceable gutturals, our fates hanging on the luck of a nimble lie, or the thump of an official stamp that would authorize us to live. Then camped and decamped, and flushed finally from Europa's fetid shores like so much sewage, to wash up, still blinking and bewildered, on the shores of less fastidious continents.

Forgive me, Antoine, that after long silence I should disturb your peace with the ravings of an old man, here, in my beloved Canada – though I am now anathema to her citizens. But do not wince. I have not summoned you to hear only a litany of griefs and grievances, railing like some self-appointed village Jeremiah against the demented century that has been our allotted time on earth. I see you smirk, no need to hide it. I know how ridiculous I must appear – I, who once trotted after you like a besotted acolyte, who studied the cadences of your speech until I had made them my own, who fluttered around you like a moth around a candle – now plume myself in noisy rhetoric to pronounce my own malediction upon the expiring century. Absurd to strike such postures in your presence. But I need momentum, to keep going, or to conceal myself the better to ambush memory.

How else should I address you? You, Antonii, Anton Antonovich, became Antonio, then Antoine, your name blending with the local patois like a chameleon, polyglot witness to a century's follies. Son of a Russian *barin* and a high-strung German mother not averse to scandal, orphaned before you could walk or talk (or so we thought). A homeless waif, dropped on our doorstep in the dead of winter by Mary Gordon, your *nyanyushka*, your Scottish nanny, to save you from the horrors of a Soviet orphanage for the sons of 'Enemies of the People.' You became my playmate for almost five years – more than playmate, became my brother, my mentor, my idol.

Then she came back, Mary Gordon, and took you away. To Germany, then Buenos Aires, then Paris, and sometimes you mentioned other cities. Lost to me then found again, years later, in war-ravaged Berlin. Wherever people were crawling like maggots upon still smouldering ruins, there you could be found, a faithless pilgrim rooting among the entrails in search of some grim revelation (or so I saw you then), and there you found me, stuffed into a cramped broom closet on an American Army base, hidden among mops, rags and linens, barely capable of garbled speech, my smashed jaw cupped in my bleeding hands. You washed and bandaged my wounds, bound me in strips of torn linen, then carried me like a dumbfounded Lazarus down to that crypt-like basement under the mess hall of McNair Barracks, home of the 6th Infantry Regiment, where you and your motley troop of lumpen intellectuals had burrowed like a subversive sect.

And while I lay convalescing in the snug gloom of the little cell you had made for me, enclosed by tarps and musty US army blankets, I overheard talk like I had never heard before, like the murmur of drunken mourners at a wake, woolly auguries of doom about Dada and Decadence, about *Untergang* and the dying gasps of a civilisation, sometimes in tones of mocking banter, sometimes with table-rapping solemnity. 'When a people kills its gods it is free to begin the pursuit of happiness. Its own happiness. Not the happiness of gods and priests,' said a breezy voice beyond my curtained cell. 'They are like a dog chasing its own tail,' growled another voice, 'till they become dizzy with happiness, or bored with it.' Shadows, cast upon the curtains of my cell by a single bulb hanging from a frayed cord, moved and merged and parted again as the words merged and moved in deeper shadows. 'That's when they become dangerous,' said a third voice, more bemused than chiding, your voice, Antoine, 'All their talk is of the common good, but to their hearts they whisper, *la barbarie plutôt que l'ennui.*' I found no sense in such words, yet in the mists of my fever they fluttered above me like gold-flecked banners in crumbling cathedral domes, scrolled inscriptions on peeling plaster, fragments of revelation among patches of blue and ochre, all that remains of the haloed figures that once hovered above enchanted celebrants.

I opened my eyes. 'You're back,' I said.

'No, *you're* back,' you said. 'You've been delirious for days.'

Seven years, the span of our lives together, a small fraction of a lifetime to absorb the aura of your presence and bask in the glow of our friendship, though there were dark corners that would always be hidden from me. All of us knew, down there in our musty lair under the mess hall of McNair Barracks, that you were marked – not for greatness, certainly not for sanctity, yet something in you smouldered with more persistence than in other men, something all of us knew or felt, pretended not to know or feel yet guarded like temple votaries. You have haunted me through all the intervening years, you have cast a spell on me from which, at times, I tried and failed to escape. Whenever a hand reached out to draw me back into the circle of common affections, I saw your image at my back, peering over my shoulder like a reflection in a mirror. Then the hand withdrew and the circle closed.

Who could have guessed our end from our beginning, when those first incursions of Stalin's terror into our villages began to manifest themselves. You would remember the loveable lad I once was, a prodigy of good cheer bobbing like a toy duck upon the ripples of terror spreading from the centre. Small for my age, cherubic, with an unruly crop of hair that no comb could subdue, a rakish innocence about me. When I entered a room with a boyish swagger and stood squarely, my hands plunged in my pockets, the grief-worn faces of women bent over a steaming kettle would puddle into smiles. If there had been a quarrel its thread would be lost, if there were tears they would be brushed away, even babies with bum rash would stop crying and burble their happiness, I was so winsome. I wanted to be good and saw no reason why I wouldn't be.

And you, both wise and sad beyond your years, an 'old soul,' though the term was not familiar to us then. You had spent the first ten years of your life among thieves and cutthroats in a distant city, a city we could hardly imagine, where your fiercely protective *nyanyushka* had fought, thieved and scrounged to keep you alive – who then entrusted you to the care of my mother when the police in three *oblasti* closed in on her. Mary Gordon, who had been the only mother you had ever known. My hand trembles when I write her name.

Not a happy time, your first few weeks among us. You kept your distance, remained guarded, withdrawn. But slowly you did begin to let down your guard. Among our circle of family and friends you were treated with unfailing kindness, in pity, yes, but more in wonder. To us you were like an exotic foundling and you too knew you were different. You accepted our exaggerated politeness with appropriate deference. My mother adopted you as her own son, and little by little you fell under the spell of her love. You dutifully observed the customs and manners of our people, though you must have found them as strange as we found you.

You remained reserved, but when a sudden smile did leap onto your face its goofiness was infectious.

Yet always there was something about you that could kindle unease among our people. Like your frank steady gaze that seemed to unnerve whomever it fell upon. A neighbour would be expounding upon some trivial subject when he would notice you watching him – and begin to flounder, lose his train of thought, grin sheepishly, and turn aside.

Not me. I didn't flounder. My senses seemed to become sharpened under your gaze, my perceptions more vivid. Me only six years old, you five years older, at that age an enormous difference, yet you allowed me to toddle along at your side and call you my friend. In abnormal times we salvaged what we could of a normal childhood, the two of us exploring our little world together. I was bursting with questions and you patiently provided answers, how pollywogs wriggled into frogs and butterflies burst from their cocoons. Sometimes you would tease me with preposterous explanations, and when my eyes were about to pop out of my head you would laugh and give my shoulder an affectionate punch.

Sunny days, those I now choose to remember. A vast field of sunflowers stretching almost to the horizon, though when you're barely three feet tall the horizon is closer. We made sure we weren't seen, then ducked among the tall stalks almost twice my height, and made our way into the enfolding field, the heavy seed-laden heads nodding above us, a thousand minor suns complicit in our escape. Here we were safe from the gloom of our elders, and from the meddlesome distractions of our schoolmates. You found a fossil and explained that once many animals roamed the world, dinosaurs, but others too, some very small, and now they were all extinct. Not one left.

'Could it happen to people? Extink?'

'It could, it will. Except for you and me, of course. And maybe your mother and sister.' Then you laughed, and I was relieved it was just a joke. Or I would nag you to explain other things. Like girls. How are they different, and you said, 'They are like these sunflowers, and we are like the bees trying to burrow into their prickly centres.'

'Do the bees want to sting them?'

'No. They want their nectar.' That was as graphic as you got.

We would lie on our backs and gaze up at the sky above the nodding flowers, while you told tales of your adventures among strange people in a big city to the south. When there were only the two of us together you would become dreamy and whimsical. I saw a side of you then no one else was permitted to see. You would read to me from a dog-eared novel written in a strange language that you said was English, a gift from Mary Gordon, you said. You would read a passage then summarize it in Russian, and I dreamed that someday we too would perform heroic deeds like those Scottish border people in the book.

The day after two cousins and an uncle had been arrested and banished we were stalking crickets to catch them at their cricketing. We came upon the old church, now a Party clubhouse, where the local *nomenclatura* swilled vodka and eyed one another speculatively, pondering which of them was past due for purging. You whispered instructions to me, then hoisted me onto your shoulders so I could peer through an open window, my fingers gripping the sill, and I shouted in a loud voice what you had told me to shout. 'We have come to report the criminal behaviour of Comrade Thiessen's old dog, Gorki, who continues to mark the fence posts of his familiar fields as though they were his private property.' Then dropped from your shoulders, my feet spinning before they hit the ground, and we ran as fast as we could. Twice I stumbled and fell flat on my face, not in terror but because I was laughing so hard. You had given me a test and I had passed.

I couldn't help boasting about our prank to my mother, my sister, and my Oma Enns, to make them laugh and ease the gloom in our house. My mother clapped her hand over her mouth, to stifle a laugh, I thought, then she turned to you and tried to be stern. 'You were supposed to mind him while we were working. Not get him into trouble,' she said. 'I'm sorry,' you said, and you promised to be more careful. But how could you keep your promise when I was always trotting at your heels like a puppy dog, eager to be patted and praised.

Happy memories, vivid but fragmentary. Perhaps that explains how they remain at our beck and call. Other memories come unbidden. I am tucked into bed on the narrow ledge at the back of our massive clay oven, a hulking remnant of an earlier time. Still standing, that oven, after Makhno's anarchists had burned down my grandfather's house. It now anchored the squat three-room cottage that had been jerry-built around it, its whitewashed hulk towering a full storey above the roof. I lay there with my back pressed against the warmth of the oven wall, at times lulled at times alarmed by the murmur of uncles, aunts or frightened neighbours huddled around an oil-clothed kitchen table on which a single candle cast flickering shadows upon a circle of faces. Who was taken? Who informed? How many? Fragments of adult conversation not intended for a child's ears, and beside me, on a wooden frame next to the oven bench, you, Antoine, holding your breath so you could hear. *Genomeh. Ve'baunung.* Taken. Banished. Words that could not be spoken without a shudder, that hung over our daily lives like a guillotine.

And then another childhood memory usurps all others. The first warm day of your second spring among us, when we went skinny-dipping in the still frigid Dnieper, disdaining all warnings about dangerous currents. We dallied at the edge of the field where the women worked, looking for birds' eggs in the tangled scrub that curled over the riverbank like a shaggy brow, and when we saw our chance we slipped over the brow out of sight, took off our boots and rolled up our trousers because we knew we would sink to our ankles in the mudflat that lay between us and the wide river that only weeks ago had been at full flood. Before us lay an expanse of little mud islands, laced with gurgling rivulets that elbowed their way downstream to join the main current of the wide river that like all wide rivers invited adventure, that scorned the humdrum world on its banks as it drifted toward some more exotic place. We hopped from island to island, those nearer the bank already covered with tufts of new grass, but the grass could not hold our weight. Our feet sank into the cool mud that slurped and snorted like an indignant oldster disturbed in his nap. Then we were there. 'Take off your clothes' you said. 'You first,' I said, but you were already fumbling with your buttons. You found a long, forked stick and stuck it in the mud to hang our clothes on, like a scarecrow, and we lurched into the breathlessly cold water. Then scampered back, hugging our skinny chests and going 'Whoo! Whoo!' Then you plunged back in, 'Come on,' you shouted, and I came on, and then I fell, forward, tripped by something on the bottom and I went under, rose again, tripped again, came up once more gasping, stepped on the thing again which seemed to move under my feet. 'Antonii!' I shouted and you came while I thrashed in the water to get clear of the thing. Then you fell too. 'It's moving' I said, and you reached down, tried to keep your head above water while you groped, and pulled up a muddy brown sleeve with a bloated white hand dripping from it. You held the sleeve while you stared at the hand, touched it with the tips of your fingers, smelled your fingers, then returned the hand to the river bottom.

We thrashed through the water, snatched our clothes from the stick, laboured through the soft sucking mud back to the bank, teetered on one leg then the other to get our mud-clogged feet into our trousers. Turned round and round on the spot where our boots should be, then looked up and saw my sister looming above us, a smug smirk on her face and a pair of boots hanging from each outstretched hand. 'Looking for these?' she said. Sarah, my meddlesome big sister with her haughty airs, ever disdainful of our boyish enthusiasms, the more so because now in her fourteenth year she had become aware she was almost a young woman, and desirable.

We scrambled up the bank. 'Give me my boots!' She held them high so I couldn't reach. Stupid sister, playing silly games at a time like this. 'There's a dead body in the river,' I screamed, 'We saw the hand.' She looked at you. You nodded.

'It's right there! Right there!' I cried, jabbing at the exact spot with my finger.

Again she turned to you. 'Go show me,' she said.

'No,' you said.

'You're both liars,' she said.

'We're not lying.'

'Here. Take your boots, but don't put your muddy feet in them.' My sister Sarah, she alone seemed immune to my charms, could not resist ridiculing my pretensions and enthusiasms, in part, I now think, because I had come into her world as a most inadequate substitute for the brother who had died in the last months of the first famine, whom she had loved. She treated me like a child but she was the silly one. She would hide your cap and we would look everywhere, then there she was, preening in front of a mirror, turning this way and that, with your cap on her head. 'Look, I found your cap,' she would say, 'It's much prettier on me than on you, don't you think?' And I would shout at her, 'You stupid girl. You think we don't know you hid it?' I wanted you to give her a good scolding, but you laughed and snatched at the cap when she tossed it to you.

And now she marched us barefoot across a prickly hayfield, dangling a boot from each hand, to where the women of our village were hoeing sugar beets. I was barely half her height and had to break into a trot to match her stride. We marched past the giant haystacks where the young swains of the *kolkhoz* whistled enticements to her which she pretended to scorn, her long braids swaying above me from side to side like golden banners against the sky.

My mother came running when she saw us, knew by a mother's sixth sense that we had narrowly escaped some sort of danger, and while my sister sneered she clasped us to her body and showered kisses on our foreheads. As the other women grouped around us, Sarah told how she had dutifully kept an eye on us to make sure we wouldn't get up to more mischief, became distracted for a moment, and then we were nowhere to be found. She ran to the river, saw our boots on the muddy bank, scrambled down, then saw our clothes fluttering on a pole and ourselves come splashing out of the water, 'stark naked.'

'Yes, but . . . no, but . . . but . . .' but I couldn't get past the buts. Then Sarah added as an afterthought, 'They say there's a dead body in the river.' She knew how to astound those women with her icy calm. They stared at her, then at us. We nodded. It's true. It's true. The instinctive gesture of each of those women was to cup a hand over her mouth to stifle a cry or a curse.

All except Groote Graeta. 'Is it floating?' she said.

'No,' you said, 'it's got a chain wrapped around it.'

Groote Graeta, until she had formed her judgment, all others held theirs. She, a huge mountain of a woman, her freckled flesh bulging through motley layers of cotton and coarse wool heaped upon her like an unmade bed. On her head an old straw hat, and under its wide brim swirled thick strands of fugitive hair like writhing snakes. Our village fixer and my mother's unlikely soul mate, who could assert her bulk between us and officious Party *apparatchiks*, could give their tortured logic yet another twist so that a few fresh eggs would find their way into our kitchens instead of rotting in a railway car that languished uncoupled on a siding, while Party officials squabbled about the latest policy on poultry products.

I buried my face in my mother's neck but I peeked. Groote Graeta peered across the field where two men were already coming to see what the commotion was about. She raised her hoe high above her head and brought it down with all her strength upon the tender stalk of a sugar beet, then muttered something we couldn't hear. Someone said, 'Is this

another warning to us *Nyemtzy kulaks?*' Someone else said, 'Then why
wrap the body in chains? It's no warning if the body's never found.' Then
a third voice, 'We weren't supposed to know about this murder.'

A quick conference among the women as the two men drew closer.
What to say, or not say? Then Groote Graeta turned to us, two trembling
boys, one of us beginning to cry. She dropped to her knees and held out
her arms, 'Come, my *Lieblings*. Don't cry. Come, come.' She wrapped her
ample arms around us and pressed us to her bosom. I remember the acrid
smell of her sweaty flesh, something like the smell of sourdough, or Brus-
sels sprouts, and I remember its woozy warmth. Then we were whisked
away before the men arrived, to Groote Graeta's cottage, to be coddled
and pampered with glazed sugar buns and sweetened hot milk.

Out in the field, under the accusing eyes of those women, I could
hardly speak but now I couldn't stop babbling. I began to see us in more
heroic roles. We must assemble the whole village, I said, and you and I
would lead them down to the river. I could see it all clearly, there would
be a boat, and men would push it through the mud to the open water and
begin dragging the bottom. Our school teacher would have to be there
too, to record our importance in these proceedings. Also a doctor, and
our local undertaker. Certain proprieties would have to be observed, as
necessary to the occasion as pickles to a picnic. The men would, of
course, find the body exactly where we said it was, then another body,
then another, speculation would grow how many there must be, my
Uncle Knalz keeping a tally, and as each body was hoisted into the boat, a
gasp would rise from the assembled village come to witness the event.
And you and I, Antoine, would nod knowingly to each other.

But none of it happened. For days, almost a week, nothing happened.
Then they came, in a motor car, big men from the city, from Krivoy Rog,
men with tall visor caps and long gray coats with medals pinned on their
breasts. There was no procession, no multitude along the bank. The area
was cordoned off and our village *kolkhozniks* were kept busy at the far end
of the field. Except for my Uncle Knalz who always managed to be where
the action was. They began dragging the river, and when they found three
bodies they stopped.

More time passed. Then at a routine meeting of the *Raion* committee,
Kommissar Kaethler read out the official report in a rapid monotone. The
bodies had been submerged in water all winter, maybe longer, he read,

and their identities might have remained a mystery. But one of them had a metal prosthesis attached to his right arm, with a double hook, which had enabled the NKVD to identify them – three comrades, murdered on November 23, 1929, by Ukrainian nationalists, *narodniks,* recently arrested for other crimes.

Kommissar Kaethler was one of *unse,* one of our people, distant kin to half the village, a Mennonite who had converted to Bolshevism to avenge himself upon neighbours who had never accorded him the respect he deserved. He had wriggled his way up the Party hierarchy to First Secretary of the *Raion* Committee and there his career seemed to have stalled. We thought him cruel but stupid, a squat, bloated man with a fat bulging neck that folded over his collar like dough over a bread pan, the kind of neck that throughout history has always kept its head while other heads rolled. And nested among the folds of his neck sat his perfectly round, close-cropped cabbage head.

We feared his wife as much as him. Quite a handsome figure, she herself might have said, the very model of a Modern Soviet Woman. It was she who would explain to us how fortunate we were that her astute husband had ferreted out the saboteurs and subversives among us, and banished them before they could infect the whole Colony.

As one of *unse,* one of our people, Kaethler had to demonstrate to his superiors that he could be as ruthless as any Jew, Russian or Ukrainian would be in his position, and that his knowledge of our Mennonite 'ways' made him more effective at discerning Enemies of the People among us. He would know, better than any Jew, Russian or Ukrainian would know, which of our elders would have to be liquidated, and which could be cowed into publicly denouncing those who had been liquidated.

No one believed the report he had read to the *Raion* Committee, least of all our Uncle Knalz – one of my mother's many cousins, but from a less proud branch of the family. Always squinting because he was nearsighted, mocked as naively credulous by some and suspected of devilish cleverness by others, who could trace a labyrinth of conspiracies, real or imagined, where others saw only random cruelty. He held a 'management' position on the *kolkhoz,* a Brigade Leader, of the livestock brigade, and as such he was privy to certain information that he would confide to a few trusted friends and family. So once again they were gathered around our kitchen table where a single candle cast flickering shadows upon a circle of faces.

They had come singly or in pairs under cover of darkness – Uncle Knalz and his wife, Groote Graeta, my Taunte Liese and her husband – maybe you remember others whom I've forgotten. And now he leaned forward on his elbows so that he wouldn't need to raise his voice above a whisper and began to unravel the web of fiction and half truths that Kommissar Kaethler had woven together. His wife sat silently beside him, arms crossed, casting her eyes around the table to ratify, with a curt nod, each twist and turn in her husband's story.

So who were they, those three dead men, wrapped in chains in the mud of the Dnieper? 'Who knows?' said Uncle Knalz, but Kommissar Kaethler had been busy crisscrossing the *oblast,* calling in old favours and lining up 'witnesses' to support the official version of the story. One of Uncle Knalz's nephews at the Tractor Station in Zaporozhye had told Uncle Knalz he had seen Kaethler in Dnepropetrovsk, schmoozing with the First Secretary of the *grodkom*. And one of Uncle Knalz's old comrades from the forestry service reported that Kaethler and two NKVD agents had paid a surprise visit to the director of a transit prison in Kubyansk, involved in some kind of under-the-table *blat* with the *obkom*, and . . .

'Enough already,' said Groote Graeta. She alone had the cheek to cut the thread of Uncle Knalz's musings in mid sentence. 'You're talking in circles, Knalz,' she said. 'They shoot people all the time. Then they make propaganda to warn us what happens to saboteurs. So why, now, these three bodies in the river, and nobody was supposed to know?'

Uncle Knalz sighed. He had barely begun to give an account of his diligence. 'Because these murders seem to be a personal matter,' he said, a local settling of accounts, not on orders from higher ups. Maybe some *apparatchik* had taken 'local initiatives' to rid himself of his rivals, maybe an eager youngster tried to do a favour for his Party boss. Who knows. All he knew for certain was that Kaethler seemed more agitated than usual. And more unusual still, there had been a big falling out, he said, with that Doktor Walther, from Krivoy Rog, one of our people, who had gone to Germany to study medicine but came back when the Great War started.

'More Prussian than the Kaiser, when he came back,' scoffed Taunte Liese, my aunt on my father's side, who like my father had a sharp wit, honed by petty scandal.

That was true, said Uncle Knalz, Doktor Walther could put people off with all that German *Ordnung* stuff. But he was a good doctor, saved hundreds of lives during the civil war and the typhus time. No love lost between them but Kaethler had 'information' on Doktor Walther that could put him away. So when he needed a doctor to endorse his 'medical report,' he had sent for Doktor Walther. A routine procedure, done it many times before, but for some reason Doktor Walther had thrown Kaethler's report back in his face. Very odd. Very risky, for both of them. But for the time being, said Uncle Knalz, we were probably safe. No one seemed to want to make propaganda out of the incident, least of all Kaethler. Then he folded his hands tight and they all prayed for God's guidance and mercy in the days to come.

And you and I, Antoine, how did we who had started it all come off? More bound to each other than ever, with a vague fear we had stumbled upon a secret no one dared to probe. Only now that I've returned from Russia do I have an inkling who those three dead bodies were.

September 15, 1991

Ten years in the Paraguayan Chaco, then thirty-three years in this
small town on the Canadian prairie. There you have a rough outline of
my pilgrimage upon this earth since I last saw you in Berlin. You would
find me now on the secluded park bench that has become my daily retreat
from the world, my eyes fixed upon phantoms from my past, hands
folded on the same cane that failed to steady me on that ridge between
the Dnieper and Molotchna Rivers, my dog Butzie curled at my feet. An
old man taking inventory of accumulated griefs and failings, fanning
smouldering memories, picking among the ashes for scraps of vindication, something to settle the heave in the pit of my stomach. I come here
in all weather, oblivious to the chill in the air as the months slip by
toward winter. Sept*ember,* Nov*ember,* Dec*ember,* those embers of the dying
year. Twilight comes early now and mothers strolling their toddlers have
long gone, the dog walkers, gaggles of students, clerks, shoppers. Beyond
the trees looms the skyline of our prairie town, such as it is, the glass
facade of the Royal Bank set ablaze by the last rays of the setting sun, our
tallest building since they demolished the grain elevators. At the southern
edge of the park, willows mark the course of the river and obscure it from
my view, their small yellowed leaves still clinging to the twigs that once
gave them life. Beyond the town lies the prairie itself, hiding nothing,
neither its beauty nor its changing moods, exposing its furry belly like a
pet cat demanding to be scratched.

A woman pushes a loaded grocery cart along the path that cuts diagonally through my park, two complaining toddlers stumbling along behind
her. Young, thin and angular, a little too rakishly dressed for a trip to the
supermarket, shiny black leather skirt and high platform shoes that make
her walk as though she were on ice. It offends me, these people who use
their grocery carts to truck their shopping to the low-rent projects then
dump them at the curb.

A trivial annoyance, this woman, but she triggers an image of two
others with their grocery carts. It was the last week of August, soon after I
returned from the Soviet Union, reeling from the experience, to find
myself in public disgrace. These were not women from the low-rent
projects. These were well dressed in casual chic, appropriate for an outing
to the supermarket, and they hardly bothered to restrain a delicious gush

of horror when they spotted me. At the far end of the Coffee-Candy-Fruit Juice aisle, they back up their grocery carts to get a second look, one of them pointing me out to the other, 'Yes, yes, that's him. There, see? His little goatee, and that silly hat? Just like the picture in the paper.' They roll their eyes at each other and pass on.

True, from where I stood I couldn't hear what they were saying, but what else would it be? We have had a Royal Commission in my country, and they have discovered 158 'potential' Nazi war criminals may be living among us, posing as respectable citizens. Four have now been stripped of their citizenship and deported, to be tried where the crime was committed. Against 20 others there is *prima facie* evidence. The names are not public, we do have a Charter of Rights, but a local rookie reporter has done some 'investigative journalism' and found evidence that my case 'continues to be of interest' to our national police. I had to resist a lunatic urge to run after those women, and shout at them. 'Yes! It's me. Here, look! Under my arm, my *SS* blood-group tattoo.'

I struggled to subdue my shaking, the throbbing in my temples. At the checkout counter, the girl, dutifully cheerful to the shopper ahead of me, counts out her change then turns to me and pauses before dispensing her usual greeting. I half expect her to say, 'Sorry, we don't serve people like you here,' but she recovers. 'Hi. And how are we this evening?'

At first my townsmen recoiled from my presence. On the street, at the post office, conversation stopped. They quickly collected their mail and left. Young mothers gave me a quick glance, then corralled their children and herded them to the other side of the street, and hissed at them when they looked back over their shoulders. But with time my townsmen have learned to ignore me, like an eyesore on the landscape you become accustomed to. I am like a ghost among them, but my presence does not haunt them. I am just some sordid business from the past for the proper authorities to deal with. I scorn their judgment, but unless I be judged I am nothing. So I take pen and paper and turn to you, Antoine.

I grope for a beginning and in the beginning there was an ocean of steppe, then there were villages – archipelagos of clustered boer *Wirtschafts,* proud farmsteads with barns and houses joined at the hip in the Dutch style, whose tall, gabled fronts calmly regarded one another across a broad avenue, pleased to find there reflections of their own civic rectitude. Villages of the fertile plain that modestly asserted their colonial

dignity, burrowed so deep in the black soil of the Ukraine you'd think
they were as enduring as the steppe itself.

These were not like the villages further south and east, the villages of
the Kuban, or the picturesque villages of the Caucasus that spilled down
from their narrow mountain valleys onto the broad plain below as from a
great horn of plenty, where wild men on horseback were as common and
as natural as the changing seasons – splendid barbarians, proud remnants
of the Golden Horde, magnificent in their blousy tunics and blue
pantaloons, each with a furry moustache saddled on his upper lip like a
pair of plump steppe mice, nose to nose, their tails curling into scarred
and weathered cheeks. Still calling Hei! Hei! as they rode to battle, their
sabres flashing in the sunlight. Figures of romance, fit matter for verse by
Pushkin and Lermontov. So it ever was and so it continued, from century
to century, ever since the waters ebbed from Ararat. No need, on that
account, to trouble their souls.

Not so the villages of the plain, settled by Mennonites from Holland,
Danzig, and the Vistula delta when Great Catherine, with a wave of her
hand, allotted them a tract of land deep in the hinterland of her
Imperium. Descendants of a stubborn sixteenth-century brotherhood on
the fringes of the Reformation, forged in the heat of movements and
counter-movements, who as best they could in a fallen world tried to live
as it would please God, in cloistered colonies. What had Mary Gordon
told you about us, Antoine? Another failed utopian community like scores
of others, destined for the dustbin of history? You found us strange but
you were intrigued enough to ply my mother with questions. No
cassocked priests or robed magistrates? No icons? No plaster madonnas?
A people with their own low-land Germanic language, their own modest
rituals? Yet they survived, even prospered. Survived four centuries amid
the national and imperial deliriums that raged around them, till Soviet
communism threatened to crush them. When their peace and prosperity
had come under threat they convened not a party of young warriors but
an assembly of elders, and from their number chose a delegation of three
or four respected *Ohmtjes*, provisioned by their practical *Mumptjes* with a
thick slice of ham and a basket of *tvebak* wrapped in white linen. Then by
train to St. Petersburg to plead their case before the Tsar, waited for an
audience in some muffled anteroom hung with enormous portraits, for

days and weeks if need be, confident in the justice of their petition if not its outcome.

And then there was no Tsar. Then there were those horsemen. In the villages they all knew them, knew them by their colour, the black anarchists of Nestor Makhno, the Red Cavalry of Leon Trotsky, the White Army of Anton Denikin, and knew them, or thought they did, by fine gradations of ferocity among them. You could feel the tremor of their hoof beats before you heard or saw them. Quick, shoo the children from the street, hide the women, bolt the doors and shutters. In the brief moments before the crescendo of hooves there will be fragments of faces, flat, one-eyed, peering through the broken slat of a shutter, like the fragments of flat, one-eyed faces in a Picasso painting. Later in the night sky there will be a dull red glow, and before the flames are reduced to lazy wisps of smoke men will arrive from neighbouring villages to salvage what they can of the disaster and the lives that are left. A disaster like none there could have imagined, yet it was less than they could bear. They would bear more.

Now in my old age I imagine these *Ohmtjes,* these practical boers, rooting under their caps with calloused thumbs, muttering 'What's going on here?' Some read the times, sold their *Wirtschafts* and packed their bags. Others hesitated. Proud, stubborn women would mock the desperate thoughts of their husbands. Emigrate? Never. To start all over, from nothing? Spend our last days in some godforsaken wilderness fit only for painted savages? Like them, live in a one-room sod hut, half in, half out of the ground, stuffing food into our mouths with dirty fingers? No! Madness. If we now must die, then let us die in our once beautiful Russia.

Among others the roles would be reversed, the men wilfully blind to the fears and tears of their wives. This is no time for rash, hysterical action, they say. These troubles must run their course, then cooler heads will prevail. They must, always have. Even among this *Russe peeble*. What they burn we can build again, bigger and better than before. But the land! The land! Where in the world would we find again such rich black earth? Grind a seed into the ground with the toe of your boot, turn around three times, and there's a tiny new shoot smiling up at you. To leave this? For some rocky, scrubby wilderness, land fit only for grazing caribou? And who now would give us a tenth of what our *Wirtschaft* is worth? Four years ago, maybe. Two years even, you could still get a price. Not now. Now is the time for steadfast courage. Let it never be said, they say, that under my stewardship the labour of five generations was squandered in a moment of panic.

Not easy decisions. How long before one's brain must believe the evidence of one's eyes? Then it was too late. The borders closed, and this tattered remnant of my people were left behind to endure two more decades of terror.

Why am I telling you this, Antoine? Why now, in my old age, would I blow upon the embers of that long-lost time and fan them into flame? Do I imagine I can still be warmed by them?

Revolution, civil war, then communism. After the Reds had routed the Whites and purged the *Makhnovtze* from their ranks, after the first famine and after the typhus, some of our people had become hopeful again. The mid 1920s, the NEP time. The Colony had begun to rally, begun to rebuild. They formed an association, the *Menno Verband,* a producers' co-op, and Uncle Knalz was employed as a bookkeeper. The *Verband* rapidly grew to become the de facto government of the Colony, education, health care, land distribution, all under the approving eye of the local Soviet *apparatchiks,* and Uncle Knalz's duties grew to include some of the functions of a mayor. In more formal company he was known as Cornelius K. Reimer. 'K for Klaassen on the *mutta kaunt'* – on his mother's side, he explained. Most unusual, in a country awash with patronymics, for a mother to saddle her son with her maiden name, but she must have read somewhere that's how it was done among your better families in Germany, back in the days of Kaiser Wilhelm. It seemed to embarrass him a little, but to honour his mother's memory he bore her pretense with stoic pride, and never failed to introduce himself as 'Cornelius K. Reimer, K for Klaassen on the *mutta kaunt.*'

Then in 1927 the *Menno Verband* was declared illegal, accused of counter-revolutionary agitation, and Uncle Knalz was arrested. He spent three days in a filthy overcrowded cell, then a guard took him to the examination room, sat him down in front of a big desk littered with stacks of paper, and told him to wait. He waited. Two hours, three hours. Then his magistrate arrived, his *sledovatel,* a big, puffy, blond fellow, with sleepy eyes that he had trouble keeping open. He hardly looked at Uncle Knalz as he settled himself behind the desk. He took a sheaf of papers off a pile, leafed through them, tossed them back on the pile, picked up another sheaf. He seemed bored and distracted. 'Cornelius Klaassen Reemer?'

'Reimer,' corrected Uncle Knalz.

The magistrate verified all the details, date and place of birth, married, two children, etc., then he leaned back in his chair and sighed. He apologized for the long wait. It must be very embarrassing for Uncle Knalz to find himself here, he said, an educated man, respected in the community. But his name had come up in the confession of one of his former colleagues, at that *Menno Verband*. He picked up another sheaf of papers and glanced at the first few pages. 'Peter Yacov Wievye. You know him?'

'Wiebe,' said Uncle Knalz. 'Yes, I know him.'

He went through it all again, Peter's date and place of birth, married, three daughters, Anna, Martha, Elizabeth, and one son, also named Peter. 'Is that correct?'

'It's correct.'

'Hmmm. This Peter Yacov . . . Wievye? Wiebe? – He says you were his colleague for three years, March 14, 1923 to April 8, 1926.'

'We were both bookkeepers, and yes, it was about three years.'

'Says here, in his signed confession, that this *Verband* worked with foreign political organizations. In Canada and America. Organizations known to be hostile to the Soviet Union. Spreading anti-Soviet filth in their capitalist journals. Did you know that?'

'I don't know why Peter would say that,' said Uncle Knalz, 'Yes, there was some contact with the Mennonites over there, but nothing political.'

'Says here that one of those foreign organizations is called *Mennonite Central Committee*. Central Committee? Sounds political to me.'

Uncle Knalz said he had tried to laugh at that. 'No, no,' he said, 'that's just a small relief organization, run by the churches over there. They sent some food and clothes to their relatives here. They'd been told we were all freezing and starving. Capitalist propaganda. I heard the clothes were all of inferior quality.'

The magistrate thumbed through a few more sheets of Peter Wiebe's confession. 'Says here this . . . Central Committee . . . worked with the American and Canadian governments to help refugees fleeing the Soviet Union. Who were these so-called refugees? Was this Central Committee organizing the escape of Soviet criminals?'

'I was just a bookkeeper. I put numbers in columns and made sure they balanced.'

The magistrate pulled out a notebook from under a pile of papers. Uncle Knalz recognized the cover. The magistrate began to leaf through it, casually, as though he expected to find nothing of interest there. Then he paused and raised his eyebrows. 'There's a whole column here. Receipts, it says. It shows 6,014 American dollars, from this . . . Mennonite Central Committee. Is this your handwriting?'

'It is.' If Uncle Knalz had denied it, his magistrate would have asked whose handwriting it was, if not his. He would have demanded a name.

He was arrested and banished, but released after serving only eight months of a five-year term, and allowed to return to our village. Remarkable, unheard of, and rumours began to swirl around him. While others were banished and never heard from again, here he was, 'as smooth and glossy as a well-licked tomcat.' It was rumoured that his cousin, Kommissar Kaethler, had pulled a few strings, and 'traded' someone else for his release. And now he kept Uncle Knalz on a short leash like a trained dog, to cow or cajole us into submission. It was whispered in some circles that Kommissar Kaethler would show him his list of names, of men slated to be banished when the Black Raven vans came to collect their quota of *kulaks,* then he would sit back in his chair, fold his hands on his stomach and smile – while Uncle Knalz pleaded that this name or that name should be crossed off the list, knowing Kaethler would substitute other names. Others feared that Uncle Knalz's days among us were numbered because of the dangerous game he was playing. Among us, his nearest kin, it was known that he kept a small bag packed, ready to go when his time came. A change of underwear, a clean flannel shirt, a pair of heavy socks, some dried fruit and nuts.

You never had a very high regard for Uncle Knalz. To you he seemed little more than a bungling buffoon, a nervous busybody. You were polite and respectful in his company but when there were only the two of us you would mimic him – how he would squint through his short-sighted eyes, how he bobbed his head in greeting when he passed someone on the street, how he would fold his arms and rub his elbows while he talked. We would see him on the street in deep conversation with someone but it was never a face-to-face conversation. He would shuffle around till he stood beside his companion, elbow to elbow, tip his head to the side and talk in hushed tones while he squinted at some undefined object in the distance, and occasionally he would cast a quick glance over his shoulder. His companion would have no choice but to do the same, tip his head and stare straight ahead while he listened, then nod or shake his head whenever Uncle Knalz came to a ponderous pause. Many times I was doubled over with laughter, watching you mimic him, and I would try to mimic him myself. It is normal for young lads to mock their elders.

Now that I'm old they gnaw at my mind, all those people whose claim upon me I had disavowed with youthful bravado. Their names tumble over one another, fragments of lives now scattered over three continents, memories of old women in black kerchiefs, sitting on backless benches in the shade of an adobe hut built by their own hands out of Chaco mud, fanning the Paraguayan heat from their faces. Leathery old crones, still clear-eyed but hobbled by stumpy, swollen legs that once carried them and their mewling offspring across half a blood-soaked continent, and images of tormented old men who had struggled to make choices they could live with. I would summon them all and stand before them in aching fraternity, these people who now loom large as myth in my mind.

Stories of loss, treachery, or courage, memorialized in each retelling. They can lay a heavy hand on young shoulders, whether told to inspire, chasten or hold our lives in orbit, and decades later it's still not easy to brush off that hand. Stories about my own father, a celebrated painter and photographer, who fearlessly mocked our Bolshevik masters till they could no longer endure his presence among the living. He escaped before they came for him in their Black Raven vans but he was never seen or heard from again.

And blind old Ohm Isaac, distant kin on my mother's side, whose former wealth and learning had been the stuff of local legend – marvellous autodidact who knew by heart all sixty-six books of the Bible, in two languages, some people said, plus other tomes besides – who then became a figure of legendary suffering, installed in a crude cottage at the south end of our village, built there in former times to house the village cowherd, its ragged thatched roof barely visible above rampant weeds and brambles. Ohm Isaac, our holy fool, driven half but not wholly mad, who would call his daughter to him – she as mad as himself – and by candlelight behind closed shutters he would command her to read to him through half the night till she too was almost blind. She, reading dully and indifferently for hours, so the story goes, whether in her mother tongue or in languages of which she understood not a word, stumbling through the text and mispronouncing horribly – while he, cross-legged on his cot like an emaciated Buddha, would murmur softly as she read, repeat each word of the mutilated text, would take her words into his own mouth and restore them to eloquence, then launch them again like little ships upon the seas of learning. Ohm Isaac, who had left our Colony to seek his fortune in the wider world, had sought and found it, but whose wealth and learning then made him a prized target of the Bolsheviks. Too big a catch to be left to local bunglers, so they dragged him to Moscow to be broken by professional interrogators in the cellars of the Lubyanka. When they scoffed at his childlike faith he would quote whole chapters from the wisdom of the Prophets, and when they lectured him on the ideology of the Party he quoted Marx at them, chapter and verse like the devil quoting scripture, mocking their ignorance – until one, a seasoned torturer with countless confessions to his credit, grabbed a dinner fork and gouged out both his eyes. 'Let the bastard go,' he muttered to the *urkas* who held Ohm down.

He was found lying in an alley by a wild child, a *bezprizornye,* one of the thousands of waifs abandoned or orphaned by the first wave of purges, who now prowled Russia's streets and ravines in packs like feral dogs, thieving what they could and defending their paltry spoils with knives and shards of glass, who would cast dice to see which of them would slit an old woman's throat for the few kopeks in her pocket, and who, owning no currency but cruelty, would bet their own fingers, nose and ears on a pair of aces. Found by one whose savage soul, it seemed, had been pierced by Ohm's hollow sockets and made mild, who lent him the use of his eyes and led him back to our village, Ohm stumbling behind the boy, one hand on his shoulder, in the other a thin stick to help him feel his way. The *bezprizornye* grew to a big, strapping youth and served Ohm Isaac like hairy Esau once served his sight-dimmed father, bringing him such game as the famine-ravished land afforded, till they banished him for poaching Soviet geese and selling them for profit. And since Ohm's daughter was too mad to chase a mouse off the table, it then fell to me to be Ohm Isaac's eyes.

The *krasnyi ugol.* You would know the term, Antoine. In our time no longer a common fixture but in former times when there was still a tsar in Russia you would find one in the home of every Russian peasant, however mean or squalid – a little sacred place just inside the door, where a constant candle kept watch upon a small table covered with a red silk cloth. Their 'beautiful corner' – where they kept the family's icons. These men and women of whom I write, however unworthy they may be of veneration, are my *krasnyi ugol.* These are the images I have *shored against my ruin,* a vain attempt to mute, for a time, the hiss of my accusers. Let them wait awhile, drumming their fingers on my fat dossier, till I have done.

September 22, 1991

Getting through customs at the Moscow airport had been less aggravating than I feared. The visas and travel permits I had secured in Canada were all in order, but at the train station I was grilled again, this time by a sullen ticket agent, a young woman in a military-style uniform, topped off with a visor cap two sizes too big for her head, her hair tucked under it to keep it perched on top of her head instead of resting on her nose. The sign above her wicket said 'English,' but she clearly held the language in contempt. Zaporozhye? Not an accredited tourist destination. What was the purpose of my visit? How long did I intend to stay? Who would be meeting me there? When neither she nor I could make ourselves understood in English, I ventured a few phrases in halting Russian. I did not want to sound like a native. In this country I was still a traitor, so I kept smiling and repeating the answers I had rehearsed. She stuck out her lips, studied my documents again, turned each sheet over to see if anything was written on the back, then scooped them up and passed me on to her supervisor. He made me wait for almost an hour then asked the same questions.

In Zaporozhye it took a full day before I found a driver who agreed to take me to the former Molotchna Colony. He assured me he could find the places marked on my yellowed hand-drawn map but it wasn't easy. All the towns and villages had been renamed at least once, and every vestige of a Mennonite presence had been erased. Again and again my driver had to ask people for directions, and the closer we got to our village the less helpful they seemed to become.

But we did find our village, Antoine, what was left of it. I looked for landmarks, our school, our squat little cottage with its hulking chimney, the *raion* office where Kommissar Kaethler had wielded his authority over us. All gone except the concrete commissary with its small barred window, where we used to buy our provisions, whatever happened to be available. So in my rusty Russian I accost people on the street and ply them with questions. I name names, describe landmarks, and ask the same question, over and over, 'Are there any old ones still alive who might remember?' – and I'm met by a wall of blank faces. Then a toothless old crone lisps my grandfather's name and points to a patch of weeds. I borrow a blunt, stumpy spade, take off my jacket, roll up my sleeves, and with quick, eager strokes I peel back a thick mat of sod. Under the blank gaze of the assembled villagers I work like a madman till I expose a perfect rectangle of flat stones – a grim record that nothing rests on firm foundations. Tears in my eyes, hate in my heart. Where now, the tall gables? Where, the proud troikas in their polished harness? Where, those ample *Mumptjes* and *Ohmtjes,* all in a row in their best black, staring directly into the camera?

> *Tell of it, you who sit on rich carpets,*
> *and you who walk by the way,*
> *to the sound of musicians at the watering places.*

If, then, there were one, Antoine, one only in the world – moved by whatever motive, *Lebensraum* or *Blut und Boden* – who would reach his hand out to us, would remove at long last the Bolshevik boot from our necks and restore us a free yeomanry on our beloved steppe, who of us would not, in gratitude or desperation, grasp that hand?

'What did you do during the war, gran'pa?'

'It was war. I did what men do in war.'

An Englishman, or an American airman, can answer thus and leave it at that, his medals and insignia displayed above the mantelpiece. But not one who voluntarily donned a Nazi uniform, one who believed in the cause. What could I have said to my six-year-old grandchild, my little Sara, curled on my lap, newly bathed and smelling of Ivory soap, heart-breakingly beautiful in pink pyjamas bordered with sleepy sheep?

'But what did you *do?*' She knew more about war than most children her age. War was the reason she was on my lap. The Vietnam War. Her mother had left her with my wife and me for the weekend, while she and her cohort of aging hippies piled into a VW van to join an anti-war rally in Minneapolis. 'I tried to escape, under cover of an army that was running away,' I told her.

'Weren't they brave?'

'Some were very brave, and many died. Not only those who win wars are brave.'

'Were you brave too?'

'No, not very brave. Your grandmother was brave,' I told her. 'All those women were brave. Not the kind of bravery that comes with drums and guns. Not with a gun but with a child on each hand.' This is true, but it is an evasion. I know it, she knows it. Knows it clearly enough not to press the issue. Perhaps this is her first inkling that on some subjects adults are allowed to lie. I could have told her the story of a Soviet sniper, a young woman, pretty, who faced a firing squad of six German corporals. 'Ready! Aim!' and I jumped in front of their guns, screaming – 'No! No!' – waving my arms, confounding the order to Fire. Then there was a man in zebra-striped prison clothes, high up among the steel girders that spanned a cavernous railway station. Another man took aim to shoot him down and I rammed the butt of my rifle into his neck, spoiling his shot. Perhaps that was brave, but they all died anyway.

What is it that makes first-time grandfathers go gaga with love, Antoine? Do we see in our grandchild some sort of vindication after the mess we made of our relationships with our own children, demanding that they do us proud, that they not disappoint our sacrifices and our ambitions for them? Do we understand, finally, that our grandchildren owe us nothing? And they ask so little of us. Our middle-aged children demand we be always cheerful and 'active,' take our pills, and adapt to the 'times,' their times. Our grandchildren are more forgiving. They are not embarrassed by our accents, or how we dress, do not measure our decay by every lapse of memory, or our indifference to a wayward wisp of hair. To them our shrunken bodies are quite appropriate for someone who is old. Whatever the reason, our love for our first grandchild is fierce.

Time passed, and again she is curled on my lap, snuggling to get as close to my body's warmth as she can. A little older now, a lapful, and she has to put an arm around my neck to keep from sliding off. These were moments when I thought I could shield her against the slings and arrows of a cruel world, when I thought I could ease her way into a world that was now safe from the past. And in this world I would watch her bloom, petal after petal unfolding before my eyes, an infinite flowering without ever diminishing the bud.

But she is eager for more stories, so I tell her about the war that happened before I was born, when bad men raided our villages during the civil war in Russia. I tell her about the *Makhnovtze*. (It takes practice to get the pronunciation right.) And I tell her the story about my brave father,

her great-grandfather. I tell the story like it would be told in her picture books, where the good people always act admirably and the bad people get their just deserts. Or failing that, I try to make them more laughable than frightening. I am careful to exclude any detail that might provoke a nightmare, but already she begins to sense gaps in the narrative, and wants them filled. 'But why did they want to shoot him? Were they just . . . bad men?'

'They lived in a bad time. In a better time they might have been better men.' I cannot see her face, curled under my cheek, can't see her little frown but I know it's there.

'Can't you be good in a bad time?'

'Yes, you can,' I say. 'Always there are some who are good when times are bad.' I don't tell her that those exceptions put the lie to all my evasions. 'Some wanted so much to be good they became bad,' I tell my little Sara. 'They saw Freedom like a beautiful woman, mounted on a white charger and wearing a brilliant blue cape. As she rode by she cast them a look over her shoulder and winked, and they fell in love with her before they knew her. They didn't know she would exact a promise of blood as proof of their devotion, didn't know that too soon she would grow mean and ugly, become bored with her admirers, demand for her entertainment the heads of rivals on a platter, a broken back for a footstool.'

'You're being silly, gran'pa,' she giggled. And so I was.

More years passed, too quickly. She is about to enter puberty and she comes with her mother on a bitterly cold day in February, February 14th, St. Valentine's day. The kind of day when you come in quickly and shut the door, stamp snow from your feet, unwind the scarf around your head and feel the warmth of an open fire flushing your face, and the warmth of an effusive welcome, feel as though you've come in from an adventure and start babbling excitedly. Offers of hot chocolate, warm socks, a seat by the fire. But my granddaughter is sullen, refuses the hot chocolate, slumps in the chair, feet straight out, arms crossed, and stares at the fire.

'Don't mind Sara,' says my daughter, 'she's in one of her moods.'

'Everybody's got moods,' I say, undaunted, confident that in a few minutes I'll have her laughing again and chattering. I marvel at her new haircut, pretend to be shocked by her newly pierced ears, talk to her as though she is still gran'pa's little pet. Has she brought me my valentine? She had brought no such thing.

There had been an incident at school, after her 'oral presentation.' Her teacher had encouraged her to talk about her family, tracing our journey from Russia to Paraguay to Canada. Multiculturalism was the flavour of the month, and here was a living example, right on our doorstep, of a family that had made a positive contribution to the Canadian mosaic. No doubt Sara had embellished some of the stories I had told her, which I had already embellished, and finally a precocious *Kanadier* girl who had been eavesdropping on the gossip among her elders could take no more of this shameless lying. She had leapt from her seat and shouted, 'Your grandfather was a Nazi. He was *SS!*'

There had been a fight, scratching and hair-pulling, and now in response to my request for a valentine, Sara aimed her swollen eyes at me, 'You . . . you lied!'

A painful afternoon while Sara and I avoid each other's eyes, a more painful dinner that should have been a celebration. Then I put on my coat and boots, pull my fur hat over my ears and slink out the door into the bitter cold night. I tramp along the deserted streets of my neighbourhood, past the rows of huddled bungalows, a cosy yellow glow seeping through the curtains of their picture windows, telling of warmth within, the kind of warmth from which I've been banished. I don't remember feeling the biting cold. I remember only the brittle snow creaking under the tread of my feet, and each creak an echo of Sara's accusation.

I had not wanted to emigrate from Paraguay to Canada. It was 1958, just over a decade since I'd arrived, and I had begun to feel an attachment to that cluster of mud huts. And to some of the people who lived in them. On that near-desert plain west of the Paraguay River, in the desolate hinterland of an obscure country, in the middle of a remote continent on the underside of the world, I had found a refuge among my people, not least from myself. I did not know there were other reasons to feel safe in Paraguay, that the whole continent had become a refuge for scores of Nazi war criminals, including the infamous Eichmann and Mengele. But in the late 1950s emigration fever spread among our villages like a virus, a last chance for a better life.

I hadn't wanted to leave Berlin either, to go to Paraguay. You would remember how my conflicting loyalties tormented me, Antoine. But I went. Uncle Knalz and his family, Groote Graeta, Taunte Liese, and also my mother (I thought) had sailed a year earlier, on the *Volendam,* a Dutch ship chartered by American and Canadian Mennonites at great cost. I sailed on the second ship, the *Heintzelman,* which left the port of Bremerhaven on February 25, 1948. It was chartered by the IRO, the UN refugee organization. By 1948 the American and British Military Administrations in Germany were desperate to be rid of us refugees. If Paraguay would take us, *Bitteschön!* Paraguay could have us! Tuberculosis? Trachoma? *SS* blood group tattoos? No problem. Paraguay asked no questions, not like Canada. Good riddance. Let that Mennonite organisation, their MCC, worry about keeping us alive in that godforsaken Paraguayan Chaco.

The skyline of Buenos Aires beckoned as the *Heintzelman* entered the harbour, Beaux Arts vying with Greco Roman, glittering domes rising above wafting palms and flowering jacarandas. A relief from the rubble of Berlin, but after Buenos Aires the landscape rapidly became less enchanting. A cruise ship took us up the Paraná and then the Paraguay River to Asunción where we were duly processed by the MCC, then loaded onto smaller river boats to continue our journey into the desolate heart of the continent. Our rusty asthmatic steamer had begun life as a pleasure boat but in its old age it seemed to despise all notions of pleasure, determined to make a virtue of discomfort, clatter, and blocked plumbing. The villages along the bank became more and more primitive – rusty corrugated tin roofs supported by fragments of mud walls and crooked poles, chickens, goats and cows wandering among the scattered structures at will. I couldn't tell which of those structures were for human habitation, which for chickens or cows, or if such distinctions even applied. Then no more villages, only a few indigenous encampments of four or five families, their naked children watching us from the muddy bank. I waved but they made no response. The steamer's engineer told us they were Guarani, a docile tribe, not like the Moros further north and east. Then nothing. Only scrub bush, reddish sand, and patches of dull green spiny grass that no cow would deign to eat. Everything was dry, spindly and thorny.

I arrived there in shame, like the prodigal son returning to his people after he has squandered his birthright. I had expected to find my mother among those who had come on the *Volendam,* and I came ready to fall on my knees and plead for forgiveness – but she wasn't there. Does that shock you, Antoine?

The 'village' was little more than a clearing in the scrub, with a wide dirt street between two rows of adobe huts. A pitiful parody of Mennonite villages in Russia before the Revolution. Some of the huts had just recently been built by the *Volendam* group to house us, the new arrivals. They were all assembled there to welcome us, and as we approached I scanned their faces, looking for my mother. I was embraced by Uncle Knalz and his wife, by Groote Graeta and Taunte Liese, then they stepped back and looked around, scanning the faces of the new arrivals. 'Where is your mother?' they said.

'She's here. With you. Why didn't she come? Is she not well?'

The last they had seen or knew of my mother was that a man had come to the refugee centre in Berlin, who had told her he would take her to a house where I was waiting. Why should she doubt him? I had told her what you and your doctor friend had told me, Antoine, that the MCC had been duped by the American and Soviet administrations. They would not be taken, as promised, through the Soviet Sector to Bremerhaven where a ship was waiting to take them all to Paraguay. They would be put on a train and sent to some desolate prison camp in the Soviet Union. So how could those people now gathered in the village to welcome her come to any other conclusion – that I had abandoned my mother in Berlin?

I wasn't shunned but I felt their reproof. As much as I could, I kept myself apart from them, and for the next eight years I wrote letters, in three languages, English, German and Russian, hoping for some news of her. I wrote to every military branch and refugee agency in Germany, all to no avail. I let the rags I wore become more ragged and spent my days in solitary rambling, walking indifferently in my bare feet through thorny snake-infested scrub, mumbling incoherently to myself. Sometimes I did lend a hand to a woman struggling with a plough or an axe, and was given some bread and milk in return, and sometimes Taunte Liese would send her little girl to my hut at the edge of the village with a hot meal. Eventually my grief and my desperate letter writing did earn their pity. Then I fell in love, married, fathered two children, built a two-room house, cleared land and planted peanuts and cotton. Can you imagine that, Antoine?

Children were the agents of my recovery. Taunte Liese's little boy and his mates let curiosity get the better of their manners and began to follow me on my solitary tramps, furtively, then more boldly, until they became a familiar cohort. 'Is it true that you have gone mad?' said Taunte Liese's boy. I made a fierce growling noise and contorted my face, pretended to be madder than I was, and that made them giggle. And this led, quite naturally, to teaching. I pointed out the features of the local flora and fauna to them, at first grudgingly, but they were undeterred. I was surprised by their eagerness to learn and they soon broke down my defences. I explained how flowers became seeds and demonstrated how the earth spins like a top while it moves around the sun. I made one of them stand still while another circled him, spinning round and round till he got dizzy and fell down. Then I found some boards, made a crude table and a bench, and began to teach them how to read and write, do fractions, draw pictures. More children came, and when the suspicions of their parents began to wane – and when they considered I was of no other use to the colony – they built me a one-room schoolhouse and voted me a small salary, barring a crop failure. Uncle Knalz wrote letters, then a package arrived from America, with scribblers and German readers.

Most of my pupils were between five and twelve years old, and their school day started at eight and ended at noon. I was about to dismiss them when two older girls poked their heads through the door, one was sixteen the other eighteen. They said they were curious to see if their stupid young siblings were learning anything. After I dismissed my pupils, they stayed and talked. They said they had to spend most of their time in the fields, and if not that then doing laundry or sewing patches on the clothes their little brothers and sisters had worn out. So there was little time for anything else. But they weren't totally ignorant, they assured me. They'd had some schooling in Russia, then in refugee camps in Germany. Did I have any books they could borrow? I gave them a thin volume of Goethe's poems and a collection of Tolstoi's short tales. And that is how I met my wife, my Helena.

It begins innocently enough. They come back and you give them more books. They have questions, you pretend to have answers. They stay longer, an hour, then two hours. Then the older one comes by herself, at noon, almost every day. She tries to be coy, then words and laughter burst from her face. She has devoured the standard 'classics' that others in the colony have schlepped out of Russia, so you give her a 'difficult' modern novel. You try to caution her that the theme may be a bit mature for someone her age, but she comes back, demanding more. And you begin to think what a pity, that this exquisite creature is doomed to be mated to one of our village lunkheads.

Did I dare hope? I could no longer pretend it was only a wistful pleasure I felt in her company, but the feeling came beset by surely-nots. Surely this cannot be happening to *me*. Surely I don't think this bold, innocent girl can rekindle long-lost feelings. Surely this fresh, vital creature could never love a world-weary husk like me. Surely it is nothing more than a teacher's pride in his brilliant student. Surely that is it and nothing more.

But the flesh, or the heart, makes a mockery of our evasions. You shamelessly rest your eyes on her, let yourself be lulled by the sound of her voice. Some of the children begin to notice, linger outside the classroom after you dismiss them, poke their heads through the door and giggle. Your rebukes have no effect, and less conviction, but for another month, and another, you resist. Then the first kiss, the second, third, fourth, fifth, no stopping now. And you know the world has changed. You still try to hold back. There is something here you must be careful not to break, and she so reckless, so much in a hurry. But it was I, not she, who was fragile.

Then harvest time. School's out, and long days of back-breaking work. Children, lovers, even hobbling old *Omas,* all must now to the fields. And when it's time to rest, to sit down and have a bite to restore us, Helena and I try not to rush toward each other, try to appear surprised to find ourselves sitting on the ground next to each other, try not to touch but touch anyway. Now it was our elders, not my pupils, who began to snicker, nudge each other and roll their eyes.

By the time the harvest was in Helena and I were old news. Time now to rest weary bones, and under a big starry sky the whole village had gathered around a bonfire to give thanks and sing, accompanied by two guitars and a zither. We sang German songs, Russian songs, sang ballads, hymns and nonsense ditties, while the happy bonfire licked bright notes off our darkened faces. And my tenor voice, inspired by love, rose above them all.

. . .

No sooner were our two children old enough to go to school than Helena began to worry the issue of emigration. And again I was torn. I had changed, Antoine, you would not have recognized me. In the course of ten years I had remade myself. There were still lapses but I had become a loving, devoted husband and father, and a respected member of the community, of the 'brotherhood.' I had even begun to go to their squat adobe church every Sunday, sang hymns and tried to stay awake through the rambling sermons of our *Praedjas*. I did it to spare my wife and children from embarrassing, prying questions. I was responsible now for the happiness of others, and if that required a little hypocrisy on my part, so be it. The singing and the ritual gestures came easy, and if the sermons rarely stirred me some of the readings from the Psalms and the prophets did, and I would have to sternly remind myself that I was not a believer. I was among people who knew me, and some loved me. Not easy to leave that behind for the promised rewards of modern amenities.

So, 'for the children's sake.' That is the emigrant's mantra. Our own lives, if we must, we are willing to write off. But the children. They must have 'a better life.' By better we mean safer and easier, no back-breaking toil that makes you old, sexless and decrepit by the time you're forty. In these circumstances they are not mean aspirations. So I went through the motions, made inquiries, wrote letters. 'Isn't there a brain doctor in Canada, a Mennonite, whom you knew in Berlin?' demanded my wife. Yes, there was, but how could I tell her I could never write to him? 'We were never what you'd call friends. We haven't kept in touch,' I said, 'and Canada is a big country.'

Yes, him, Antoine. Your old Berlin 'friend,' who would occasionally drop in on us down there in that sprawling basement under the mess hall of McNair Barracks, to 'talk business' with you. Doktor Vik, we used to call him, not always with affection. You were the reason he bothered with us at all, though you rarely seemed overjoyed to see him. He let us know the two of you went 'way back,' back to your student days in Heidelberg, 1938. 'Exciting times,' he told us. 'And we were in the thick of it, Anton and I.' I didn't ask what that meant but I might have guessed. How could I now ask for help from someone who had made no attempt to hide his dislike of me, and sneered at my presumption of your friendship. Still, no harm in trying, said Helena. She would write to her cousin in Winnipeg, who would ask around. 'Can't be that many brain doctors in Canada among our people.'

No, there weren't, especially not of Doktor Vik's renown among Manitoba Mennonites. So here's his address. Why haven't I written? 'No point just puckering your mouth, you have to whistle,' she said. 'Good heavens, we're not asking for charity, just for some information about the paperwork, and how to find jobs.' So I wrote, with apologies for intruding upon his time. He wrote back. Enthusiastically. He would be our sponsor, would be honoured to be our sponsor, we need only sign the enclosed forms. Loans were available to pay for the airfare, and a job would be waiting for me upon our arrival. He had 'pulled a few strings,' he wrote, leaned on the 'Christian charity' of some Mennonite businessmen. They could hardly refuse. 'Heaven forbid their Christian charity should be shamed by a godless atheist.' Then he added, 'Don't get into long conversations with the Immigration people at Asunción, or when you get to Toronto. Just say that at the end of the war you were a refugee from Soviet Communism. You were afraid you'd be sent back there, so you fled to Paraguay. That's all true, and it's all they need to know.'

My wife and children were keen but for me it happened too fast. I did not want any more painful farewells. Uncle Knalz and Groote Graeta had grown old, and there were others whom I felt I was deserting, like Taunte Liese. Also my new friend Alvaro, one of the native Guarani who sometimes came down from the north to help with the cotton harvest and they, in turn, had taught us how to grow manioc. Like most of his race Alvaro was a small man, no bigger than I was. He had an easy laugh and so we learned to tease each other, mocked each other's quaint customs and taboos. I mocked his pagan superstitions and he mocked how we prayed and sang our hymns, belting out our praises to the Lord while we stood ramrod stiff, ranged in rows. We spoke the Low German patois that the Guarani had invented, an ingeniously simplified language, yet remarkably versatile. But the day before our departure he presented himself more formally than usual.

Miena diena frind, he said. I was his friend too, I replied, and clasped his hand.

Miena diena seha goot. Diena miena uk goot?

I told him I too was fond of him, yes, that I loved him. Courtesy demanded no less.

Diena haft schvoa. Diena nich schaftig, he said.

Yes, I was sad, I said, sad to be leaving friends like him.

But he shook his head. He looked around, as though searching for words to make me understand. Then he blurted out, *Diena haft schlaejta schinda upe ridje.* He reached over his own shoulder to show me exactly where wicked devils rode upon my back and tormented me. *Viet vaech laund, schlaejte mensche doah, deena nich goot. Diena velle doot moake,* he said.

This sounded more like a curse than a sad farewell. A devil on my back? Bad people, in a faraway land, who wanted me dead? *Diena vaeht nuscht,* I scoffed.

Miena vaeht, he said. Then he produced a small stone flask, about three inches high, squatted down on the ground and removed the stopper. He poured out what looked like three little reddish berries, fuzzy, like burrs. This was unexpected but not the first time Alvaro had urged his tribal medicines on me. When I was writhing in pain after I fell off a wagon stacked high with cotton bales, he made an analgesic tea for me that gave me almost instant relief. And once he gave me hallucinogenic leaves to chew on when I was down in the dumps.

Diena nem met, he said, *Em viet vaech land.* He scraped the three berries back into the flask with a twig, careful not to touch them with his hands. Then he tapped the stopper in tight, bowed, and handed me the flask, cupped in both hands.

Now I was embarrassed by my rudeness. This must be their custom, a ritual farewell gift, like a talisman, a token of the power of friendship to transcend great distance. I sincerely thanked him and formally accepted the flask in both hands.

I did not declare the flask when we went through Customs and Immigration. I had quite forgotten about it by then. If it had caught the attention of customs officials rummaging through our luggage, how would I have described the contents? Three dried berries with magic properties to fend off evil spirits? Or evil people? I had real evidence of evil to conceal, like the SS blood group tattoo under my arm. But no one asked me to roll up my sleeve.

There was the usual immigrant awkwardness and confusion at the Toronto airport. Stick together. Don't get lost. We find the departure lounge for our connecting flight to Winnipeg, and while we waited I had a chance to observe my Helena. She could see that she was the only woman there who wore a kerchief, that her shoes, laced up to her ankles, looked clumpy compared to the minimal footwear on these Canadian feet, and that her skirt was at least a foot longer than any of these women seemed to think necessary. She could see how confidently they strutted across the room, click-clacking on their high heels, their perky breasts raised, boldly pointing the way. I thought she might be cowed by this scene, keep her eyes lowered, but she held her head up and let her eyes roam freely around the room, and she did not flinch when other eyes met her eyes. She appraised these confident Canadian women with a dispassionate eye, as though she were trying to assess what kinds of changes she would be required to make in this country, and whether she liked the person she would probably become.

Viktor was there to greet us when we arrived in Winnipeg. Still the dapper dresser, casually ruffled, still the same hail-fellow-well-met manner, tall, trim, only a little greying at the temples. Distinguished looking. He shouted my name above the din and instinctively the crowd parted to let him through. He embraced me as though we had been best of friends in Berlin, and had stayed in touch through the intervening decade. I smiled when he embraced me, and I smiled when, with a little more restraint, he took my wife's hand in both his hands, looked deeply into her eyes, and in comically laboured Low German bid her most welcome in Canada. And I smiled again when he leaned down to the level of my children, put an arm around each one, and promised they would have lots of fun together. Yes, I see you shaking your head, Antoine.

He explained that the job he had arranged for me was at a printing firm in a small town south of Winnipeg, and when we arrived we would be met by a Mennonite church group, all women, who would take us to the apartment they had already furnished for us. 'They'll probably give you no rest before they shove a bunch of papers under your nose, for you to fill out and sign – about how to get the kids enrolled in school, and all that kind of stuff.' Then he smirked and added, 'They'll also point out which church they expect you to attend.'

Not long after we were settled in, he drove down to see how we were getting on, and to take Helena and me out for dinner. There was a new 'family restaurant' in our town but he disdained it. He said he preferred a restaurant in one of the French towns across the river, where we could talk more freely, and where we could have wine with our dinner. 'Just a half-hour drive east of here,' he said. The restaurant looked more like somebody's living room, and when we were settled into a cosy nook he leaned forward on his elbows and grinned. 'So how are the brethren treating you, down there in that Mennonite *shtetl?*'

Helena and I gushed about the nice bright apartment, fully furnished, about the helpful school teachers and my agreeable co-workers in the printing shop. But that's not what Doktor Vik wanted to know. 'Have they made a God-fearing Christian of you yet?'

I laughed, but it was a hollow laugh, and Helena was taken aback by his derisive tone. I had not explained to her that although he had grown up in one of these Mennonite towns he had nothing but contempt for the 'tribe.' When we first met in Berlin you had mischievously introduced me to him as a 'fellow Mennonite,' and I had stupidly assumed this would strike a chord of kinship between us. He quickly disabused me of that notion, and I had tried to assure him I too had long ago disavowed any affiliation with the 'tribe.' He now expected me to mock these people who had been kind to us, but he too had been kind, and it seemed churlish to disappoint him. I said we Paraguayans knew we were on a kind of Piety Watch here, that we had to show ourselves worthy of the help we had received from our Canadian brethren. But we had expected that, I said. During those first difficult years in Paraguay the Mennonites in Canada and America had sent us ploughs, wagons and seed to get our cotton and peanut ventures started (for which we were deeply grateful), and since our spiritual guides in Russia, our Elders and *Praedyas,* had been banished or shot, they also sent us 'missionaries' (for which we were not always grateful). Some of those missionaries were particularly appalled to find men and women living common-law, often with 'blended families.' I explained that those whose spouses had been banished to the Soviet gulag, and were known to be dead, could be legally re-married, and many of them had been. But those whose spouses might somehow still be alive in Russia could not remarry, and some of them now 'lived in sin.' One of those missionaries had felt it was his sad duty to publish reports of these 'polygamous common-law arrangements' in *Der Bote,* one of the Mennonite weeklies in Canada.

'Bigoted bastards!' said Doktor Vik. 'Though I can't say I'm surprised.'

I could feel my face redden, and though it shamed me to pander to him I told him about the Kansas missionary who had come to our Chaco colony looking for a wife. A scrawny fellow in his early thirties, with the pimply face of a teenager, close-cropped corn-coloured hair and a stubby little nose that seemed to be attached to his face like a suction cup, with two little holes in the nipple. He always had an oversized Bible tucked under his arm, with bits of ribbon sticking out of it to mark the most severe injunctions against the sins of the flesh. I tried to sound glib and witty. I said this fellow must have known he stood little chance of winning the heart of a flighty Kansas gal, but in Paraguay, among all those desperate young widows, who knows? A woman struggling to break ground with a team of oxen could be tempted by the prospect of a nice little parsonage in Kansas, freshly painted, with indoor plumbing and no snakes under the bed. And all he would require of her was to serve tea to the respectable matrons in his congregation and occasionally organize a quilting bee. At night? Well, it would be dark. She could use her imagination.

It was rumoured that he had sampled what was on offer in the bedrooms of our neighbouring village, which consisted almost entirely of widows with young children. Might not be true, said Uncle Knalz, but there was no doubt that he liked to sample what was on offer in their kitchens. Every day, at dinnertime, he would patrol the village from house to house, his keen little nose in the air to catch a scent of what might be cooking inside. Then he would choose the most aromatic house and pop in for a pastoral visit. And so, when Groote Graeta came in from the fields a little earlier than was her custom, she found him bent over the pot in her kitchen, sipping soup out of the ladle. So engrossed he didn't notice her, she said, even when her huge bulk in the doorway had darkened the whole room. 'Drink, and I will draw for your camels also,' she had said.

He would have caught the biblical allusion – a sign from God that Isaac should take Rebecca to be his wife – but apparently he missed the sarcasm in her voice. He seemed to think Groote Graeta was offering more than just soup. He looked her up and down, still holding the ladle in his hand, then shook his head and replaced the ladle. He tipped his hat, stuck his little nose in the air, and left. 'I was just too big,' she said.

Doktor Vik slapped the table with the palm of his hand and let fly a gleeful guffaw, 'Bloody hypocrites!' I was embarrassed that Helena had witnessed my pandering performance, and relieved when she scolded me in a joking manner. When we had finished our dinner I turned to the subject that was most on my mind. I said my mother had not been waiting for me when I arrived in Paraguay. And I was told she hadn't been among the Berlin group when they were all loaded into American troop carriers in the middle of the night and taken to the train station in Lichterfelde West. None of them ever saw her again, not on the train through the Russian Zone, or on the ship.

I waited for Doktor Vik's reaction. Would he be shocked? He took the napkin from his lap and dabbed his lips. 'Hmm. That must have been devastating,' he said.

I said those who had last seen my mother had told me a strange man had come to the refugee centre on the Ringstrasse, where they were all anxiously waiting for news of their fate. This man had asked to speak to my mother. Told her I had sent him. Told her she should follow him to a place where I was waiting for her. Told her I had made arrangements for our escape through the Russian Zone, then to Bremerhaven where the ship was waiting. They said my mother had packed her belongings, said her good-byes to the others, and followed him. She and another woman, Katya, who never left her side. 'Do you have any idea who that man might have been?' I said.

He shrugged. 'How would I know?' Then he called for the cheque. He said, 'Somebody was probably trying to get at you, not her. Thought they could use her to flush you out. How many of those people working at the base, at McNair Barracks, knew you'd been *Waffen SS*?'

'I doubt there were more than three or four. None of them seemed interested in that.'

'They'd be interested if there was money in it,' he said. 'The American Jews were already busy looking for *SS* people, and the Russians were looking for traitors, like you.'

'I was small fry. I wasn't worth anyone's trouble.'

'No fish is too small if he's easy to catch,' he said.

Then he changed the subject. He said he had written to the dean and the heads of the Russian and German departments at the University of Winnipeg, recommending my admission as a part-time student. What should I have said, Antoine? No thanks, I don't want any help from you? I can make my own way in this country? I said, 'Is there a chance they might accept me? Me, with my nine years of spotty Soviet schooling?'

'No problem,' he chuckled, and I glimpsed the flicker of a sneer on his face. Had he noticed my hesitation? 'This Sputnik thing is still in all the papers,' he said. 'It's put all our educators on edge. They're afraid we're losing the space race because the Russians have a better education system.' He said he'd laid it on a bit thick to the dean, that my nine years of Soviet schooling were easily the equivalent of grade twelve in Canada. And he'd already arranged an interview with the dean and the head of the German department. 'Just tell 'em in the Soviet Union you'd be sent to the salt mines if your marks weren't up to scratch.'

The interview was more gruelling than Doktor Vik had led me to believe but I was accepted, and my employer, pleased to see an immigrant eager 'to make something of himself,' let me hitch a ride to Winnipeg every Thursday in time for my evening class, and allowed me four extra weeks' holiday to squeeze in a six-week summer course.

The first time I set foot in the university library I wandered among the stacks in solemn silence, letting my hand sweep across the spines of books, row on row. I took one off the shelf, opened it at random and read. Something about ancient Egyptian metalwork. I put it back and wandered to another section. Then another. Old books, new books, on all subjects. To a young Canadian student such libraries are a birthright. They can be taken for granted. To me these books were a painful reminder how much of my life had been stolen from me. They taunted. I could never read them all, but I vowed I would read enough to feel at home among them, and little by little the names I once heard casually fall from your lips began to speak to me in their own voice.

I became a teacher again, in a larger town further north, not a Mennonite town, myself and the old school janitor were the only ethnic Mennonites. My principal was an Englishman, Percy Wearing, from an old military family, decorated and twice wounded during the war, but after the war he had found his duties in occupied Germany beneath the dignity of a soldier – herding refugees and Soviet POWs onto waiting trains, to be dumped somewhere in Siberia. So he resigned and emigrated to Canada. 'I dare say, I could have had my pick of the litter. Headmaster at one of those posh schools in Ontario. Even stuffier than the English schools. No thanks.' So he lit out for the territory, he said, and settled here, 'on the doorstep of the best bloody duck-hunting country in the world. Quite unspoiled.' That he and I had fought on opposite sides during the war mattered less than the fact that we had both seen action at the front. He had nothing but respect, he said, 'for the discipline and courage of your common German foot soldier.' He helped my wife and me find a house, and to increase my starting salary he counted my teaching career in Paraguay as bona fide 'experience.' I was hired to teach German and Latin. I had hoped for German and English, the subjects I had studied at university, but there were already two people on staff to teach English. I knew very little Latin, but never mind. I knew enough to keep a day or two ahead of the students.

Helena's first job was in a factory that extracted oil from sunflower seeds, smelly, tedious work, but as soon as I was settled in my new career, it was her turn to improve herself. She became a potter, and entered into a successful partnership with an *Englända* woman whom she had met in one of her art classes. Helena's designs and colours were inspired by the ceramic work of the Guarani in Paraguay, and when the *Englända* woman recognized her superior talent, she became Helena's agent, and opened a gallery.

My wife and I must forever be grateful to that *Englända* woman but I never liked her. She is one of those who prides herself on her infallible sixth sense that enables her to distinguish at a glance 'the real article' from a cheap imitation, whether it's pottery, poetry, or music. 'I just have to open a book at random, read a sentence or two, and I can tell if it's the genuine article.' She expects others to have equal confidence in her sixth sense and is easily offended by even a mild quibble, especially from a third-world Paraguayan immigrant who is expected to know more about burros than art. She finds me opinionated.

So we made it, Antoine, from poor immigrants to respectable middle class in one generation, and all thanks to Doktor Vik. I stopped being wary of him. Yes, we became friends, as much as it is possible for an eminent psychiatrist to become friends with a raw immigrant from the Chaco. I began to feel privileged, even flattered to be included among some of his cultivated 'social set.'

I might have fooled myself but I didn't fool Helena. 'Why do you dislike Viktor so much?' she asked, when I returned from one of his dinner parties, and began mimicking him. 'I don't *dislike* him,' I protested. 'Maybe I sometimes find his childlike egotism amusing, but, dislike him? After all he's done for me, and for my whole family I would be a cad if I were anything but grateful,' I said.

October 4, 1991

When we arrived in Canada my daughter was eight and my son six. In Paraguay my pet name for her had been Kjleene Graet, to distinguish her from her big namesake, Groote Graeta. She was daddy's girl. I had begun to teach her to read German when she was four, and when she was seven I added a little Spanish and English. She was bright, and now in Canada the whole world lay at her feet. I wanted nothing to stand in her way. Not me, that caricature of the scowling, bearded patriarch demanding observance of old-country manners and mores, especially those I was not observing myself. I now called her by her English name, Margaret, and I entertained her new friends with stories about Paraguay, about our mischievous parrot who would repeat scandalous gossip at embarrassing moments, and scary stories about snakes nuzzling bare buttocks in our outdoor privy. They shrieked in terror, then begged for more. Margaret pretended to be embarrassed by my stories, but I knew my popularity among her friends pleased her. Helena was less pleased. 'They take those stories home, you know. And repeat them to their *Kanadier* parents – who need no encouragement to think we all lived like savages down there.'

'What do these proper *Kanadier* know about savagery,' I said. 'It wasn't in Paraguay that we had to live like savages.'

It was known that I had spent the last months of the war in a Nazi uniform, but everybody knew there had been thousands of men my age who had been conscripted against their will. It was assumed I was one of the lucky ones who had survived. And until the Eichmann trial in the summer of 1961 hardly anyone in Canada or America seemed eager to talk, or write, about the Holocaust. Then his trial and the details of his capture in Buenos Aires were in the news daily. I felt a chill, and felt it most keenly when I began to notice my daughter staring at me. 'What?' I said. 'Nothing,' she said, and turned her back.

In her second year at university she plunged into the counterculture of the 60s with a vengeance – pot, protests, and peace marches. She became an activist in the Student Movement – and when she now brought her friends home on weekends, I had to bite my tongue when I heard them casually talking Marxist cant as though it were something learned of long reflection and personal experience.

Neil is his mother's son, an amiable, easygoing lad, and if he rebelled in his teens it was against his big sister. There had always been an ascetic element in Margaret's rebellion. She was prepared, in fact eager, to suffer for her political opinions, but Neil couldn't see the point, or pretended not to. It was the hedonistic side of hippie culture that drew him, the dope, the music and the sex. Margaret thrust placards into his limp hands and gave him his marching orders but he became more and more adept at evading her. Then, at Christmas, during his last year at university, he arrived at our door having shed both his long hair and his blue jeans. He now wore neatly pressed grey trousers, a black turtleneck, and a well-fitting blue blazer. Margaret bristled. 'Looks like you've changed sides,' she snarled.

'*The times they are a-changin,*' he teased. 'Wake up, sister, look around you. The Movement's gone the way of the dodo bird.'

Neil has done well, as they say. He fled to the furthest corners of the world, Tokyo, Hong Kong, Shanghai. International postings with various corporations, a fat salary, but we rarely see him. We tell our friends he is very busy, and it is understood that when you've been entrusted to move millions of dollars into and out of certain people's pockets, filial duties may have to come second. I know Helena must blame me for losing him.

Yes, Margaret was 'idealistic,' but her zeal for The Movement proclaimed to the world, and to herself, that she was not contaminated by her father's Nazi past. In the spring of her third year, she brought her new boyfriend home to meet Helena and me. He arrived with a heavy backpack and a big chip on his shoulder. He had 'dropped out,' he said, and was hitchhiking to B.C., where he knew people who had started a commune. He would check it out and if he approved, Margaret would join him later. I tried to seem interested, asked what kind of crops they would grow, were they into beef cattle or dairy, but my questions showed I didn't really understand what a commune was. I shouldn't have called it a *kolkhoz.*

'Margaret tells me you signed up to fight for the Nazis during the war,' he said.

I resisted the impulse to glare at her. 'I was younger then than you are,' I said, 'and after the Famine and the Great Terror, the Nazis were our chance to escape Soviet communism.'

'So you'd rather be a fascist than a communist.' He looked at Margaret, grimaced and rolled his eyes. Her face reddened.

'You've got a long way to go,' I said, 'Best you be on your way. Margaret will drive you to the highway.'

For the next four years we saw little of her, though she never did join that boyfriend in B.C. There were other boyfriends, and when she became pregnant she was married in a civil ceremony, to which Helena and I weren't invited, of which we were informed two months after the fact – when we also discovered the groom's parents had been in attendance, and had thrown a little party for the happy couple. I would gladly have given my paternal blessing to their union, but how can you bless when your blessing would be deemed an affront?

A year after little Sara was born their marriage broke up, her husband moved to Ottawa to take a job in the Department of Justice, and then we began to see more of her again. She put Sara in a daycare during the week, and dropped her off on weekends to stay with Helena and me. We spoiled her as only doting grandparents can. Margaret had named her after my sister Sarah (though for some reason she dropped the 'h'). The stories I had told her about my strong-willed sister had cast her as a proto-feminist in Margaret's imagination (which she probably was) but Margaret also sensed there had been some sibling rivalry between us, and knew how to turn her admiration for Sarah into a taunt.

After that cold winter day when little Sara had accused me of lying to her, there followed a long and arduous reconciliation. She loved me, she wanted to believe I was a good man, she demanded explanations and I tried to measure them out as she grew older. She was often caught in the crossfire of the arguments between her mother and me, and she would cover her ears and shout at us to stop, just stop. As she grew older tensions developed between her and her mother, and she began to side with me. Margaret felt betrayed and accused me of turning Sara against her, and warping her mind.

I lost them both, son and daughter. Unlike Neil, Margaret became a social worker in Winnipeg, and stayed close enough to keep the tension between us humming. In reparation for the sins of her father, she doggedly stuck with The Movement long after most of her old friends had become successful lawyers and civil servants. She would still drop off little Sara for the weekend, then she and her diminished troop of faithful diehards, all of them now well into their thirties, would pile into their VW van and crisscross the country to wave placards in front of TV cameras, and scream obscenities at policemen and politicians.

> *The fathers have eaten sour grapes,*
> *and the children's teeth are set on edge.*

I found an unlikely friend in our town. For most of a decade I shared my park bench with Seymour, but since my public disgrace we now take care to avoid each other. Remarkable that we ever became friendly at all – he a third generation immigrant from Rumania (yes, a Jew, Antoine), owner of Herzog's Hardware and Appliances, and twice the losing candidate for the CCF in federal elections. And me a high school teacher, German and Latin. I didn't flaunt my *volkisch* Germanness but I didn't try to deny it either, with my serge *förster* jacket and green felt fedora, a discreet little feather tucked in the band, *Tyroler* style. We would never have spoken a word to each other had it not been for our dogs, his a handsome boxer named Winston, mine a shepherd-collie mix I call Butzie.

Embarrassing, our first encounter, two elderly gents in a public park, trying to look dignified while their dogs strain on their leashes, yapping and lunging at each other like old playmates who haven't seen each other all winter. What made it worse is that Seymour uses an 'extend-a-leash' that spools out to about twenty feet, so his Winston charged to the limit of his leash while he stumbled after him, scowling and scolding. The dogs ran circles around each other, and around us, while Seymour and I passed our leashes over each other's heads and behind each other's backs to avoid getting tangled up together. We tried not to touch, shouted contradictory commands at our dogs, ducked under each other's arms and lifted our legs high to step out of the tangle of leashes, tottered, cursed, and muttered apologies for our stupid dogs.

A few days later the same again. Our dogs yelped and lunged, indifferent to our commands. So we gave up and let ourselves be ruled by our dogs, unleashed them and let them play, while we sat down on our bench to catch our breath. It became a daily routine. The dogs played and played, and when they had exhausted themselves, their tongues lolling out of their mouths, one of us would give them water and the other a biscuit. Then they would lie down and look up at us over their shoulders.

'Ain't we just a pair o' characters?' Annoying in people, such smugness, but endearing in dogs. How could we deny them their pleasure?

Did I regard these daily encounters with Seymour as some sort of penance? Offering myself to be flayed and spat upon? No. I was not spat upon. I was treated to endlessly entertaining conversation. We both affected a quaint 'olde worlde' manner, both of us a little vain about our claim to 'kulchah,' convinced we were probably the only two people in our town who could be expected to know the difference between Grünewald and Grindelwald. We chided, we harrumphed, we complained and pretended to find our complaints witty. We disagreed about many things, about modern art, the power of trade unions, about various breeds of dogs – agreed about others, that French cuisine was overrated, East European cuisine underrated, and that no American beers could compete with ours. But agree or disagree made little difference to the development of our friendship. We were never in each other's homes and never had to explain our friendship to anyone, yet I began to feel more relaxed in Seymour's company than among middle-class *Englända* for whom, before my disgrace, I was just a typical refugee from communism, grateful for a chance to be a consumer. And more relaxed than among my fellow Paraguayans in whose company my university education was like a big birthmark on my forehead, that they pretended not to notice but couldn't help staring, while I pretended not to notice that they stared.

I don't know why Seymour indulged *my* company. Maybe it was the example of the dogs, who needed no excuse to find each other agreeable. He was not shy about flaunting his Jewishness, but there seemed nothing reproachful about it. He simply regarded his people as a quirky, fascinating bunch and assumed I would too, and I did. I was a good listener.

As a recent immigrant I needed help, in his opinion, to navigate the maze of popular Canadian culture, and he was pleased to provide it. Summer cottages. The Beatles. Disco.

Cheerleaders at football games?

'Goes back to the ancient Greeks,' he explained. 'The maenads. You know, those ecstatic nymphs of Dionysus. Dancin' in drunken frenzy at religious festivals. But our modern maenads are more practical. They're lookin' for a TV contract.'

Then I told him one of my students was the lead singer in a 'rock' group. 'Stations of the Crotch' they call themselves. Sweet kid, I said, but not too bright, and when he offered me a copy of their new video for ten dollars I felt obliged to buy. 'Cost yuh twenty bucks downtown,' he said. I told Seymour I had dutifully watched it, and there they were, in their studded leathers, spiky hair, their pelvic gyrations amplified by the metronomic beat of the bass, accompanied by a steady stream of fuck-babble. I said I could understand the rebellion of the hippie generation but this seemed pointless.

'*Mishegoyim!*' he said. 'All of a sudden there's millions of bored middle-class kids with money to spend. So there's a market. Used to be you'd tell your kid, dress like a *Mensch* an' talk like a *Mensch,* an' you'll be treated like a *Mensch.* But now? This baby-boomer generation is feelin' guilty. Cause they sold out. Became yuppies. But they don't wanna be like their own parents – an' make their kids *conforrrm*. Be creative, they tell 'em. Wear funny clothes with holes in 'em, put rings in your nose, give offence. *Azoy geyt dos.* But never mind the kids. It's those *alte kakers* that make me a pain in the ass. You open the *Times,* an' some *alte kaker*'s written a review of the latest rock video. They even got a picture of the aaahtist. *Oy gevald,* she's a sexy one already. A blond *bubele* with puffy lips, squeezed into a teensy leather skirt that barely covers her triangle. But these *alte kakers?* Nooo, they're goin' gaga about the *moosik,* like it's the greatest thing since Beethoven. Back in Montreal, we were horny little buggers too. Used to go to the girlie show at the Gayety. But *oy gevalt,* we didn't pretend we were there for the moosik!'

On the subject of Quebec separatism he became more passionate. He had grown up in Montreal, still had some family there, and his analysis was liberally sprinkled with Yiddish expletives. *Mishegas! Geharget! Kush meer in toches!*

Then I told Seymour about my strained relationship with my daughter, how she would shout Marxist slogans at me, make excuses for Stalin's brutality, and shove Chairman Mao's *Little Red Book* under my nose. And how she and her boy friend had sneered at me. 'It's just a phase,' he said. 'We were all ignorant idealists when we were young. She'll grow out of it.'

'You have a son,' I said.

'I have a son.'

'So what would you do,' I said, 'if your son became a neo-Nazi skin-head, came home from college at Thanksgiving, his head shaved and a swastika tattooed in the middle of his skull? Then shoved his face into your face and started quoting juicy passages from *Mein Kampf* at you? Just youthful idealism?'

'I'd tear the skin off his scalp, then I'd take a pair of pliers an' pull out his tongue. But it's not the same.'

I did not insist that it was.

Although Seymour and I saw each other almost daily, we skirted the huge subject that hung between us. He had lost uncles and aunts in Romania but he spared the details, and he told me he'd married a *shikse*. Though she had converted, and was more observant than most of his own family, they had never quite forgiven him for it. I told him about the trek, then ordered to report for military training, deserted to avoid capture by the Russians, then made my way to Berlin and got a job washing dishes at an American Army base. He didn't press for more details. I felt honoured that this garrulous, big-hearted old Jew should extend to me his ungrudging courtesy. At other times I bitterly berated myself for my cowardice and hypocrisy. Then I resolved to tell him all, spare no details, but I could never summon the courage. Or presumption. Whichever it was.

Then one day Seymour announced, 'I know a joke, a Jewish joke.'

I said nothing.

'A Jewish businessman makes a trip to Germany. The country still makes his skin crawl, but it's been forty years, he's gotta get over it. So he's on a train, Frankfurt to Bonn. Finds an empty compartment, at least he won't have to make conversation. But *oi vey*, here comes one, huffin' and puffin'. He settles in, an' he's a talker. Knows right away he's talking to a Jew. He can smell it. It's all that pickled fish an' smoked meat. But he's not prejudiced, not him. *Ach, mein Freund,* he says, such a shame – that terrible Nazi time. Puts everything out of perspective. A mere twelve years! An aberration. What's twelve years compared to the centuries when Germans and Jews all lived together in harmony? Before the Nazi time, Germans were not anti-Semites. OK, maybe a little – back in the middle ages. But the Czechs? Poles? Much worse, much worse. Let me tell you something, *mein Freund.* You want to know who we really hated, we Germans? – He checks the door of the compartment to see if anyone's listening, then leans in to the Jew and whispers, We hated the French! They screwed us. After the First War. Treaty of Versailles, then Reparations, down on our knees, to kiss their dainty tush!

So why didn't you exterminate the French? says the Jew.

The German looks at him. He can't believe this imbecile. Huh! he snorts, England and America would never allow it.'

I could have hugged Seymour, right there on a public bench. We laughed, shamelessly, till we could laugh no more, then we wiped our tears and laughed again. We laughed out of all proportion to the feebleness of the humour. Forgive us, Antoine, but we needed that laugh, that purging convulsion, the quick gasp like a man choking, then the letting go, the moment when forbidden thoughts tug at our sleeve and wink, when the evil that bedevils us slinks into a corner and sulks. So what if we lose all judgment? So what if we become careless and heedless and laughingly consign ourselves to the whims of chance? When we weep we bewail the monstrous finality of chance – we weep because what has chanced can never be changed. Out of infinite possibilities, *one* has happened for ever. But when we laugh, a word or a phrase turns the world topsy-turvy. And so we laughed and wept, Seymour and I.

October 12, 1991

Back to the beginning of the end, the Civil War, April 1918. The year before you were born, Antoine. I have a photograph, dated, from a negative etched on a glass plate, 6" by 9" – your father's estate before the house and barns became a pile of rubble. The photograph shows a manor house in the Palladian style – a grand stairway ascends to an imposing second storey above a squat service floor, tall windows framed by fluted pilasters with Ionic capitals, a low slate roof with stone finials at the corners. The photo can't show the lofty hall inside that row of windows, but those in our village who said they had seen it recalled walls hung with Gobelin tapestries, polished marble floors with geometric designs done in aquamarine, and a high coffered ceiling where four chandeliers of Bohemian glass doubled the candles' power.

In the foreground, to the right, four horsemen stand in line facing the camera, under the projecting portico of the stable. Provincial gentry, *barins*. A few paces back stands a fifth, clearly a serving man, holding the reins of two more horses, one saddled, the other laden with bulging packs wrapped in sheepskins. Three of the horses are standing at ease, their heads just above the level of their shoulders, the fourth, counting from the left, is brilliantly white. His head is thrown back and there is a blur where the forelegs should be, apparently because they are pawing the air. The rider's mouth is puckered into a stern 'Whoa.' He is younger than the others and wears a prim military coat, with epaulettes, and a tall, black sheepskin hat. The other riders wear nondescript jackets buttoned to the throat, and on their heads somewhat lumpy looking *ushankas*. The two riders on the left have their heads turned toward the pawing horse but their eyes are on the camera, giving them a rather shifty appearance. The third rider presents a stern profile to the camera, his head turned squarely toward the young cavalry officer, and he seems to be addressing him. 'D'your man put a burr under that saddle?' or some such mocking jest. He is your father.

Behind one of those tall second-storey windows I imagine but cannot see your father's young German wife, and looking over her shoulder another woman, Mary Gordon, your mother's lifelong companion. She had been the family's Scottish *au pair* in Germany, then followed your mother to Russia when she married your father, her Presbyterian contempt for the rites of the Orthodox Church mistaken for salt-of-the-earth radicalism. I imagine your mother in a foul mood, scornful of this male foolishness that would take her husband from a warm bed on a damp, cold April morning to go soldiering, for this is what they are about. They are off to join General Denikin's White Army and put a stop to the recent civil disorders.

A year ago, ten years ago, they could all see it coming, the catastrophe, outdid one another in gloomy predictions, taunted one another with lurid images of anarchic violence, with gossip from the Capital, murder and mugging in broad daylight, mothers drowning newborn babes in the Neva, on and on, stopping just short of fire-breathing lions prowling the Prospects and equestrian statues leaping from their pedestals. The natural omens had been clear enough – corruption at court, rioting students, the assassination of Stolypin – but now that the end is upon them they can't, or pretend they can't, believe it. The work of a few Jewish Bolsheviks, they say, who need a good lesson in front of a firing squad. Now they outdo one another predicting a bloody but quick end to all this agitation.

Similar scenes would be staged on countless estates all over Russia, usually with grander gestures, but here the photographer has eschewed any operatic display. He could have asked them to wave their sabres or carbines above their heads, but instead they look like a not very enthusiastic hunting party. Perhaps they have an inkling of the futility of their action, or perhaps it is the photographer who sees its futility. He is my father, and this is his last surviving photograph.

On this estate you should have spent a privileged childhood, unthinkable, back then, that the son of a *barin* would end up in a Mennonite village. But your pedigree was dubious. You never knew your father, and came to know your mother only years later after she had gone mad, but Mary Gordon would have told you about the brilliant young men who were regular guests at your mother's 'salon,' who came all the way from Petrograd, some from Germany. In our villages it was your father who was then held in high regard, a model manager of his estate, who demanded and got an honest day's work from his peasants, and rewarded them accordingly. 'Very advanced in his farming methods,' they said, always the best and latest machinery, imported from Germany.

The estate bordered our Molotchna Colony to the south, and on a brilliant summer day during our school break we went, you and I, to see

the ruins, a three hour walk. Two of the peasant cottages were still standing, all that remained. The house and stables had been reduced to piles of
rubble, overgrown with weeds. I found a long cut stone with parallel
grooves carved into it. 'Look, look,' I said, 'this must be from the big
house.' You stood apart, with your hands in your pockets, kicking at a pile
of broken bricks. You glanced over and nodded. Then I ran to another
pile and found a big stone block with a smooth bowl carved deep into it.
'This must have been for water. For a horse,' I said, and again you glanced
over and nodded. Do you not remember any of this, Antoine? Perhaps
not. You never seemed interested in the stories my mother and others
told you about your parents and their life on their estate before you were
born. And later, after you had left us, I heard stories they wouldn't have
told you.

Even before the troubles began your father and mother had become
fodder for the gossip mills. They were mismatched. He, a provincial *barin*
of the 'old school,' accustomed to wielding authority, she, a woman of
spirit who bitterly felt the sting of her isolation. When your father left to
join the Whites he had ordered his wife and Mary Gordon to go to
Odessa to stay with his niece – the black sheep of the family because she
had married a Jew, who could now be prevailed upon to provide a refuge
until this trouble passes. But your mother will not be cowed. She is not
altogether displeased to be living in interesting times. Some of those now
plotting a brave new world in Moscow and Petrograd had been among
the guests in her salon. Had she not laughed with them and with them
proposed toasts to the Future? Had she not gloated over her own scandalous reputation? What else was she to do in this Asiatic backwater, she
a modern woman, educated in the hothouse climate of *fin de siècle*
Europe? She remembers, racked with fury and humiliation, how her
husband, after his annual hunting trip, had come home and thrown out
her brilliant, dissolute guests – switching his riding crop across their
bums as they fled out the door – and installed in their place his own
cronies, stinking of sweat and roast boar and stale ideas. She will not
leave.

Most unusual that anyone in our Mennonite villages would be wined
and dined on a Russian estate but my father had been a frequent guest in
that house, then at the peak of his short career as a portrait painter and
photographer, to both the new Mennonite plutocracy and the local

Russian gentry. Years later, when I was old enough to understand such things, Uncle Knalz explained that it was not uncommon, before the Revolution, for our people to send a bright young man to Germany to study theology or medicine – but not art. People had heard about those 'bohemians' and 'free thinkers' in Paris and Munich. No place for a young, upstanding Mennonite, let alone one not so upstanding, 'Like your father.' But his talent had caught the eye of one of his teachers who persuaded a group of rich *khutors* to establish a fund for art students, so off he went. When he returned, his studies cut short by the outbreak of the Great War, his work was much in demand among the *khutors* who had sponsored him, but among the more pious groups it was rumoured that he had lost his faith, that he'd become a convert to some of those godless philosophies. Nihilism. Anarchism. The anarchist bombings in Paris were much in the news then, said Uncle Knalz.

My father had laughed when he told him what people were saying. 'In those days,' he said, 'you'd have to be a dull fellow indeed not to get caught up in the excitement.' Every day a new Movement and new manifestos – communists, syndicalists, and yes, anarchists, both the violent Bakunin kind and the pastoral, pacifist kind espoused by Tolstoi and Kropotkin. Fierce rivals, all of them. But no, he chuckled, he'd never joined any anarchist group, 'unless you want to call Mennonites anarchists, of the Tolstoi/Kropotkin kind,' which, he said, in some ways they were.

Uncle Knalz said my father did not entirely approve of your mother's 'progressive' ideas but he could mock her ardour with enough wit to make him a welcome guest, a wry raconteur, full of entertaining gossip about the painters and poets who had haunted the coffee houses of Munich and Berlin when he and your mother were both students there, though they had never met. So when the old priest died for whom your grandfather had built a pretty cottage next to the family chapel, your mother proposed that my father move his family there and convert the chapel to a studio, and to everyone's surprise, your father consented.

My mother had been a less frequent guest but not unwelcome – surprising, because she spoke ill of no one and could be deeply saddened by the banter among your mother's coterie, mocking beliefs she held dear. But she could not be scandalized, not even by your mother, who seemed to find her company calming when she needed relief from the conflicts among her guests and her husband's household. My mother had never ventured far beyond the confines of our Mennonite colony yet seemed to sense the tensions tearing at the world of those around her. In my father's many photographs of her she has a serene, almost other-worldly beauty, and people who hardly knew her would tell her things that until that moment they might not have confided even to themselves. When people first met my mother, said Groote Graeta, their first impulse was to sigh, their second to talk. 'She was like the still point in the eye of a storm. Lives whirled around her, but her stillness couldn't still their whirling.'

The first time the *Makhnovtze* attacked your father's estate, your mother and Mary Gordon escaped by cowering in the cottage of a loyal peasant. They pillaged the house and emptied the stable of your father's purebred Arabians, then a small band of them came to the old priest's cottage where my father had moved his young family. My sister was only four years old then, my brother two years older – the brother who died before I was born. They came by stealth, my mother told us, not like the brazen hordes that came later. The sound of running feet, muffled commands, then a face at the window and the sound of breaking glass. My father shouted, 'Who are you? What do you want?' and a voice answered, 'Open up or we'll burn you out.' My mother said there had been only six or seven of them, but in those first moments there seemed to be twenty. Two of them were older, one with a jagged scar on his cheek. The others were young boys, perhaps on their first or second raid. They were frightened and jumpy, had to shout and smash things to build up their courage. They smashed crockery and cabinetry with more vehemence than necessary, as though dumb inanimate objects must also be taught a lesson. They tore up dresses and linen with a fury that was its own reward. One thrust the butt of his rifle through the face of a mantel clock, then turned and leered at my mother. He wanted her to know, she said, that what he had done to the clock he could do to her face, and would, that he was almost ready now, almost primed.

Then their leader, the one with the scar, shouted something and they fell back. He strolled around the room, taking a mental inventory of its contents.

'What's that thing for?' he demanded.

'It's a camera. I'm a photographer,' said my father.

'Did you make all these?' He gestured at the photographs hanging on the wall and standing on the shelves. He studied one more closely, then looked at my mother, my brother and sister, back at the photograph, to match the image with the living flesh. I had to wait till I was older to get the grittier parts of the story from my Oma Enns. She said the man with the scar had seized my mother and held her, with her back pressed to his body. He had ripped open her blouse and cupped a hand under each breast. 'Here, comrade, make a picture of this!'

'I can't,' my father had said, 'I have no plates, no chemicals. Nothing. Here. Look.' He opened the back of the camera, still mounted on its stout wooden tripod. They had already torn off the black hood. Scarface tipped his head to signal one of the young ones to take a look. He looked. 'It's true,' he said. 'Nothing in there. Just a black box.'

'*Blyads!*' Scarface brushed some debris off the table, wrestled my mother onto it and swung his leg over her while he tore open her dress. But before he could mount her, said my Oma, my father seized the tripod, with the camera still attached to it, and with all his strength struck him, in his neck and shoulder. His comrades knocked my father down, kicked him into a foetal position, and smashed his jaw with the butt of a rifle. My brother ran and covered my father's body as best he could with his own. Then they shot my father, once in his thigh, once in his shoulder. 'He was a brave boy, your brother,' said Oma Enns.

The man with the scar had made a terrible noise when my father struck him, cursed and howled, fell to the floor, tried to get up, fell again. Two men dragged him out the door, another took a lamp from its hook and threw it onto a rug, then he too ran out. My brother, still lying on top of my father, had jumped to his feet and dragged the burning rug out the door. Someone shouted, 'shoot the kid' but no one bothered.

My father survived, though he had a broken jaw and nose, and lost three teeth. The bullet in his shoulder was later removed, the one in his thigh stayed there. Months later, his jaw was still supported by a sling around his head.

The family moved to my grandmother's village, where they came again, the *Makhnovtze*, in the fall of 1919, now flushed with victory. They expected no resistance. They approached at a leisurely trot, about thirty of them, followed by a wagon loaded with plunder from their last raid.

Three of the riders, including their ataman, each held the limp body of a woman in front of them, bouncing along like a rag doll, skirts and petticoats billowing in the wind.

Every window of every *Wirtschaft* along the whole length of the street was shuttered, no sign of life, not even a dog barking – except for one solitary figure, standing in the middle of the wide street, bareheaded, in dark trousers and a white shirt, a little unsteady because of the pain in his leg, his jaw still bandaged in white gauze. My father. They would have run him down had he not raised his hand and greeted them with one of their own anarchist slogans. '*Khleb i Volya*,' he shouted.

'*Chernoe Znamia*,' replied the ataman. 'Death to the bourgeoisie! Death to tyrants!'

'Death to slavery,' parried my father, slogan for slogan.

The ataman looked over his shoulder at his men and pointed down at my father. '*Nyemtzy anarkisti*,' he sneered, and they all guffawed.

'We have nothing left,' said my father. 'First your *Makhnovtze*, then Reds, then Whites. They took everything.'

'Took? Took, or you gave? All you *Nyemtzy* pigs support the Whites!'

'They took.'

'Ha! So why didn't they shoot you?'

'They did.'

'In the head?'

'In the leg. The bandage is just the latest bourgeois fashion.'

The ataman glared down at my father and spat. Then he laughed. 'A funny man, this *Nyemtzy anarkist*,' he shouted to his men. 'Should we let him live?'

A mixture of yeas and nays. Then the woman slumped across his lap seemed to come to her senses, opened her eyes wide, and croaked my father's name. He made a move toward her but the ataman turned his horse to block him. 'What? You want my woman?' Then he turned to his men, 'A horny bugger, this *Nyemtzy anarkist*. He wants my woman.' They laughed.

The ataman released the woman from his grasp and threw her onto the ground at my father's feet. 'So you're an anarchist? Just like us?' he sneered. 'Show me. Fuck her.'

His men craned their necks, the better to see the entertainment.

My father knelt down and cradled her head in his lap. 'I can't. She's my sister,' he said.

An inspired lie. There was silence. Some taboos are more taboo than others. My father knew her, but she was not his sister. She was your mother, Antoine. The ataman spurred his horse as though he would trample them both, then pulled back, the horse rearing above them on its hind legs. 'Well, she wasn't *my* sister,' he shouted, and rubbed his crotch. More guffaws from his men, then they charged out of the village, shooting randomly at the shuttered windows as they passed. Then people spilled out of their houses, onto the street. On that day, my father was a hero. Everyone said so.

Your mother stayed in my grandfather's house throughout the winter, under my mother's care, and under the disapproving gaze of half the village, in whose eyes her scandalous reputation deserved little kindness. One of the two other women with the *Mahknovtze* had been Mary Gordon. She escaped or was abandoned by her abductor, the accounts varied, and some of our people spread a rumour that she had driven a tent peg into the temple of her sleeping captor, before she made her way back to our village to find your mother.

Soon after Christmas it was obvious your mother was pregnant, and in the spring, after the White Army had been routed, your father came for her, he and his trusted steward, Sergei Ivanovich, both disguised in ill-fitting civilian clothes. They had gone first to his former estate and found it a charred ruin. The few peasants who remained in their cottages gave lurid accounts of what had happened, then told him where he could find his wife.

A group of village elders had gathered in my grandfather's house when your father burst through the door. Was he overcome with relief to find his wife alive? With gratitude for those who had saved her? Those who years later recalled the scene said he had pointed at her swollen belly like an imbecile, and looked around at those gathered there as though they were all complicit in this outrage. He was a changed man, they said, hardly recognizable, neither his scruffy appearance nor his manner. He began shouting. Why had the men of the village not armed themselves against those *Mahknovtze* savages? Then he turned to my father. 'And you, you! Cracking jokes with the ataman, my wife slumped across his lap.

Why didn't you shoot the bastard out of his saddle, like any decent man would?'

'And you?' said my father. 'Like any . . . decent man . . . you'd run off to play soldier with the Whites. Attacking defenceless Jewish towns. Looting and raping, no better than the *Makhnovtze*. Your fly unbuttoned, ready for action before you leapt off your horse.'

Your father drew his pistol and held it inches from my father's face. 'No!' shrieked your mother, 'Here, shoot me! Shoot *it* – if you think it's not yours.' And she offered her swollen belly for your father to shoot. Her swollen belly with you inside it, Antoine.

My mother stepped between them, placed her hand on the arm that held the gun, and slowly lowered it. 'Whose honour would you save by more killing?' she said. 'Yours? Your wife's? The child's?' People said they were afraid your father would strike my mother, but his rage seemed to wilt. He staggered, his lips began to twitch and his breath came in short gasps. He turned and strode from the house, mounted his horse and left the village. When he returned he was more like the man they remembered. Calm, decisive, one accustomed to exercise authority. He said your mother and Mary Gordon must do as he had ordered when all this trouble began, and Sergei Ivanovich would escort them by train to Odessa. He held a saddle bag in his hand and politely asked that my mother pack a lunch for him. Women scurried to fill the bag with whatever they could find. He thanked them, then he again mounted his horse and rode off, alone, to rejoin a rabble remnant of the White Army.

He was never seen again, though there were rumours that he now led a band of 'terrorists' in the Caucasus mountains, who continued to raid Soviet border installations, who murdered 'heroic Party workers' and displayed their severed heads on stakes along busy thoroughfares.

You would have heard more stories about *my* father than about your own, Antoine. Everybody could tell the story of the 'sabotaged' poster. In the mid 1920s the Party propagandists stepped up their anti-religion campaign, and troops of students toured the countryside, performing little skits depicting lecherous priests and nuns, and in every *oblast* they had distributed large lithographed posters satirizing biblical figures. Kaethler had dutifully mounted one such poster on the door of the church that was now a Party clubhouse. It had been cleverly done by someone with wit and skill. It showed a very pregnant Virgin Mary, blushing sheepishly under her halo, her hands resting on her swollen tummy. The caption at the bottom of the poster read: *'Hey, tovarish. Which way to one of your modern Soviet abortion clinics?'*

Then there was muffled excitement in the village. Someone had sabotaged the poster. With a few skilful brush strokes he had turned the Virgin Mary into Mother Russia. Instead of the halo, the figure now wore the traditional *kokoshnik*, and the saboteur had mischievously parted Mother Russia's robes to reveal a pudgy foetus with an oversized head in her pregnant belly. A head with a big black moustache. Stalin's head. And peeking around Stalin's plump buttocks, another little foetus, with Kaethler's unmistakable cabbage head. The caption at the bottom of the poster remained the same.

My father escaped before the GPU came for him but he too was never seen or heard from again, though there were rumours. Someone reported he had seen my father in Pyatigorsk, waiting on a railway platform with another woman, carrying a small child. 'Rumours planted by Kaethler himself, to torment your mother,' said Uncle Knalz.

This was the brave father who held sway over my boyhood imagination, from the time I took my first baby steps till I became a young man. The father I never knew, of whom I had only a haunting image, slender, with black hair and hazel eyes under heavy brows, the father I knew only by the stories my mother and others told of him, of whom I thought I must prove myself worthy.

October 26, 1991

We've had the first snowstorm of the season on the Canadian prairie, hardly a blizzard but enough to trigger my memories of the night you entered our lives, Antoine. It was the last week of January by the Julian calendar, 1931. I was only five years old but I remember everything, the wind shrieking in the eaves, straining the rafters, snowdrifts piled above the window sills. The kind of night when people swear they heard the howling of wolves where no wolf has been heard or seen for over a century. I remember the knocking on our door in the middle of the night and my mother lighting a lamp, my Oma Enns gathering my sister and me in her arms and whispering sssh, sssh, be quiet.

Mary Gordon was seen first by a man who lived alone at the end of our village, wakened by the growling of his dog, he said. He blew a peep hole through the frost ferns on the window and saw a black hulk with a big hump on its back, fading in and out of view between sheets of blinding snow. He could see a figure lean into the wind, heave its leg out of the deep snow and swing it forward, the whole body leaning, tottering, then standing steady a moment before it heaved the other leg forward. He said he would have gone to her aid if he had believed his eyes.

Then another man, Johann Neufeld, heard a thump on his door. He lit a lamp, and stood silently in the middle of the room, waiting. Another thump, and he called out, not too loudly, Who's there? Another thump, then a faint voice, a woman's voice. He fumbles with the bolt, almost drops the lamp in his haste to open the door. He holds the lamp to the face, or all he can see of the face, two eyes peering through a slot in the scarf wrapped around her head. He takes her arm and pulls her across the threshold, and now he sees the large child wrapped on her back, clinging to her neck, half frozen. She declines the chair he offers, and refuses to be relieved of the burden on her back. She offers no explanations, but demands directions. Johann Neufeld draws on his felt boots, wraps himself in his coat, and escorts her to our house.

'I am Mary Gordon,' she said.

My mother let out a yelp and embraced her. Then she and my Oma Enns began unwinding the layers of ragged blankets that encased you, like unwinding a shrunken mummy, and there you were, standing before us, dressed like a miniature adult in a blue wool suit that had already become too small for you. They began rubbing your frozen toes and fingers, and Mary Gordon's instinctive gesture was to pat your hair down and put a neat part in the middle.

I watched, then I stepped forward and formally introduced myself, 'Peter Enns,' and offered my hand. You took my hand, tipped your head, and introduced yourself with equal formality. 'Antonii,' you said.

Mary Gordon stayed in our house three days and four nights. People would slink in to get a look at her and you, and hear the gruesome details of her story. For three days she held court in our kitchen, wrapped in shawls and bolstered by cushions, 'Like some oriental potentate,' said my Taunte Liese. She spoke rapidly, sometimes in Russian, more often in German, proper High German like she and your mother spoke, punctuated with Scottish curses. Sometimes she had to be cautioned to keep her voice down, sometimes she would speak in a rasping whisper.

Och, sic a time, sic a time, she said. Twelve years now. She and your mother, and that useless lout, Sergei Ivanovich, fleeing to Odessa. Like the *barin* had ordered. The civil war still raging, Whites against Reds. Then the train stops, the tracks blown up, put on a wagon with no springs, *och,* only a tattered tarp for protection against the weather. Sergei Ivanovich becoming surly, no patience for the complaints of a woman in your mother's condition. She goes into labour, they find a filthy inn but no midwife, only Mary Gordon herself to deliver the child. Then put on a coach, crammed full of filthy people, sick, some with typhus, and at last they come to the big house in Odessa, the *barin's* niece, the one who married a Jew. Not welcome. The house already full with more Jews who had fled from their villages, she said, so they put all three of you in a small airless room, in the servants' quarters.

When we couldn't follow the garbled details of her story, Mary Gordon became indignant at our stupidity and had to be prodded to go on. The whole city in turmoil, she said, thousands, tens of thousands swarming the port. Russians, Turks, Greeks, all looking for a ship to take them away. Constantinople, Alexandria, anywhere. And soldiers. Reds, Whites, Peter Wrangel's men scrambling to get out, shooting people. Then the Jew finds a ship, packs up his family and flees, but not you, not your mother and the baby. Abandoned. 'Scum,' she said, '*Bundists,* those Jews, full of big talk about revolution, till they start shooting Jews too.

Then it's sell up an' ship out. Jews know how to get out,' she said, 'they've got connections.'

But your mother, she too had connections – all her old friends, all those who had once been guests in her own house?

'Puh!' said Mary Gordon, 'Communist swine, all of them. Big men in the Party now, or the army. None want to know her. *Nyemtzy*, they say, spy, traitor.' Then your mother found one she knew, one of her old 'friends,' who promised to help. Meet him at the port, he would provide papers and exit visas. So you went, said Mary Gordon, all three of you, with your luggage, but no friend, no papers. Instead, policemen, who arrest your mother, demand to know where her husband is, the *barin*. A terrorist, they say, with a troop of renegade Whites hiding in the mountains, who massacre cadres of Party workers, cut off their heads and stick them on pikes along the road. They interrogate her, beat her, then they take her away, nobody knows where.

Now more people move into the big house, she said, rude, pushy people, filth and quarrelling day and night, she and little Antonii fighting for a place on the floor to sleep. Winter, then summer, then winter again. No food, and little Antonii sick. She leaves you with an old Moldavian woman while she goes looking for food, and for news of your mother. Every day more shouting, more shooting, and the Moldavian woman becomes nasty, demands money. Then coming back, back to the house, *och*, so tired, so hungry. Smoke, fire, the big houses, burning. Running now, she said, through crowds running the other way and drunken soldiers grabbing at her. And there it is – there it was – the old Jew's house. Burned to the ground, still smouldering, *och, och*. She scrambles over charred timbers, shouting, screaming, Antonii! Antonii!

Then a little voice, 'Merry Mary.'

'He always called me Merry Mary,' she said.

'Antonii!' she called. And again, a little louder now, 'Merry Mary.'

Then she saw you, she said, crawling out of an underground fruit cellar, next to the summer kitchen. 'It was like the bonny bairn was risin' from the grave,' she said.

Now where, now what? Sleeping where you could, begging food, no money, nothing. You end up with the low-lifes, she said. Gypsies, Romanians, Cossacks, Greeks, Turkmen, everything. Thieves and murderers mostly. They taught you filthy words in all their filthy languages, how to do tricks with cards, and one taught you how to pick pockets, 'A filthy scoundrel, with only one arm. Who smelled of piss.' So Mary Gordon soon put an end to that. But there was one who was good, she said. A gypsy, but he was clean. Had good manners. He'd been in a circus before the Revolution. He taught you how to throw knives, she said.

Throw knives?

Yes, that she had allowed. Why not? She said the man was like a father to you, the only father you ever knew. Without him you would all have starved. She said he had an 'act,' and people would pay. He had cut an old wooden door in half, and put hinges where he'd made the cut, so he could prop it up. On one half he had painted a man – arms, legs, a big head. Eyes, a nose, a mouth, and a big black moustache. Like Stalin's. And on his chest he had painted a heart, a black heart. He would cover it with a sack, she said, and all three of you would go to the old market where people were trying to sell what they had left, or what they had stolen. The gypsy wore a puffy, blousy shirt with red and white stripes, a flat-topped little hat, like a fez, with a tassel hanging from it. He would take off the sack and prop up the door so people could see. They would come close, look, and start whispering to each other. Then the gypsy would step back ten paces and throw his knives at it. He carried them in a leather pouch, beautiful knives, she said, six of them. She said her job was to watch for policemen, or anyone who might cause trouble.

The gypsy would throw the first knife into Stalin's forehead. Then the eyes, the nose, the throat. Then he would hold the last knife, high above his head. 'One knife left. Where should I put it?' he would call out. And someone in the crowd would shout. 'In his heart! In his black heart!' and the gypsy would raise his left arm and take aim at the black heart. Then he stopped. He would turn to the crowd and say, 'Maybe one of you would like to finish him off,' and he would offer the last knife to some in the crowd. But they would shrink back. 'Cowards, all of them,' said Mary Gordon. Then little Antonii, 'Let me do it, let me do it,' and the gypsy would say, 'shut up, kid.' The crowd would laugh. And little Antonii, 'Let me do it, let me do it.' So the gypsy would turn to the crowd, 'should I give him the knife?' And the crowd would shout, 'Yes, yes. Give him the knife.' And you would step back four paces, she said, and you would do like the gypsy did. You would raise your left arm, take aim, and throw the last knife into Stalin's black heart. You never missed. The crowd would cheer, then you would go around with your cap and people would put money in it, or sometimes just an egg or a lump of sugar. 'Och, the little bairn. So polite, Spasibo, spasibo.' And each time, she said, you made a little bow.

'Shameless, to use the boy like that,' said Groote Graeta.

'Better we should both starve? I did what had to be done,' said Mary Gordon, 'To the very end.' Then she wrapped her blankets tightly around her and clammed up.

'What end? What happened in the end?' someone said, but Mary Gordon dismissed the question with a wave of her hand and sulked.

She studied the faces of the women grouped around her as though she were trying to decide if it were worth the trouble to shock them. Then she and Groote Graeta locked eyes. Two strong women. 'There was a big Uzbek,' said Mary Gordon. She spoke slowly, deliberately, daring Groote Graeta to disapprove. He was drunk, a madman, she said, wore a uniform like some sort of policeman. She hadn't noticed him, hidden in the crowd. When little Antonii had thrown the last knife into Stalin's black heart, he fired his pistol in the air. 'Profiteers! Saboteurs!' he shouted, and all the people ran away. She said he snatched the cap out of your hands, took the few kopeks people had put in it, then he threw it on the ground and stomped on it. Then he took aim at the gypsy, holding the pistol in front of him with both hands, though he was too drunk to hold it steady. 'You!' he shouted at the gypsy. 'Where you want it? In your heart or between the eyes?'

Mary Gordon closed her eyes for a moment and fell silent. Then she looked across the room at you, Antoine, sitting hunched up in the deep sill of the kitchen window, staring through the frosty panes, your angular profile in the shadow of the pale wintry light. You didn't move a muscle, gave no sign. She said the Uzbek had his back to you, his eyes fixed on the gypsy, so he didn't see you snatch the knife out of Stalin's heart, whirl around and throw it at his back. Hit him just below the collar of his jacket, but not hard enough to stick in his flesh. 'The wee bairn didn't have the strength,' she said. But the impact had startled the Uzbek and he fell forward on his face. He lay there a moment, stunned, and in that moment Mary Gordon was on him, both her knees on his back. She grabbed the knife and drove it into his neck just below the skull. 'All the way to the hilt,' she said.

The gypsy picked up the Uzbek's pistol, gathered his knives and you all ran away. The gypsy kept running, east, to the 'stans, but she and you had to find a place to hide in Odessa, in case your mother came back. Before he left, the gypsy made you a present of the knives and the leather pouch, something to remember him by, he said, for saving his life. 'Here, I'll show you,' said Mary Gordon, and she reached down and pulled the pouch out from under the clothes in her bag. 'Only five knives now,' she said. 'We left one in the Uzbek's neck.'

After Groote Graeta and the others had left, Mary Gordon remained seated on her cushions, staring at nothing. No one spoke. I got up from my stool and approached you. 'Were you trying to kill him – that Uzbek?' I said.

'I didn't want him to kill the gypsy.'

'But . . . but you would have killed him, if you could?'

'Maybe,' you said.

She had to get out of Russia, said Mary Gordon. It wasn't just the dead Uzbek. There had been other things too. She said she'd been writing letters, many letters, to your mother's father in Germany, and to Scotland. She'd given them to a man at the Turkish Consul in Odessa. Didn't know if he mailed them or used them to wipe his ass, but then a letter came back, with money and instructions how to escape over the Caucasus mountains. There were tribesmen, said the letter, who took people through Karabakh and into Turkey. There would be money waiting to pay them when she reached Yerevan.

'Lunacy,' said my Oma Enns, and Uncle Knalz shook his head.

'Worse lunacy to take the boy,' said Mary Gordon. She would have to leave you with us, and if she got out she would find a way of getting you out too, and your mother, if she were still alive. There were organisations in Germany and England who helped people, using paid agents or diplomats from different countries.

The next morning you were again sitting at the window looking out. When my mother kept urging you to try her freshly baked cinnamon rolls you politely nibbled at them but you wouldn't speak. And you remained passive and silent while Mary Gordon put on her coat and embraced my mother. Even when she embraced you and tried to tell you to be brave but choked on her own words, you did not cry out. Not till she was about to hoist herself onto the wagon waiting to take her on the first leg of her journey, only then did you run to her, wrap your arms around her, seize the folds of her coat in your tight fists and press your face against her stomach. Three people, Uncle Knalz, my mother and Mary Gordon herself tried to pry off your fists, but each time you wriggled out of their clutches and found a new grip. And still you did not cry out. Only the muffled sounds of your gasps for air. When they finally subdued you and the coachman pulled away, it was not you but Mary Gordon, standing in the wagon looking back, who let out a desolate wail, a wail so loud, so long, so forlorn it crumpled my mother to the ground as though she had been struck.

You brought gloom to our house, those first few weeks. You remained sullen and withdrawn, and our clumsy attempts to divert you only deepened the gloom. Until one night, before bedtime. My mother read to us from one of the few books left in our house, a selection of funny folk tales, one about a mischievous little imp with an unruly head of hair. You were sitting quietly on the edge of your cot, hanging your head. Then you raised your head, smiled, pointed at my hair, and said, 'Struvelpeter.' We all laughed, and everyone took an affectionate tug at my bushy hair. And slowly you began to ease your way into our family.

Struvel. It became everyone's pet name for me throughout my childhood and early manhood, then I was Struvel again in Berlin among you and your mates. In Paraguay I remained Struvel to Groote Graeta, Taunte Liese, and Uncle Knalz, but in Canada I reverted to Peter, though among a few close friends I remained Struvel, even when my bald head made a travesty of the name. It was your mark on me, Antoine, that I've carried throughout my life, though I might have wished for a more dignified moniker. And after all these years in Canada, I still retain scraps of the Scottish accent I picked up from you, that you had picked up from Mary Gordon, that had become your 'secret language' during the years you scraped and scrounged in the streets of Odessa, when you did not want your conversation to be understood by others. Now it became *our* secret language, yours and mine, sometimes amusing, sometimes exasperating our elders.

When you arrived, that January night, 1931, we were already into the second year of the first Five Year Plan, a time so momentous, so calamitous, that some historians now call it the Second Bolshevik Revolution.

For you and Mary Gordon, among the throngs crowding the port of Odessa, the Five Year Plan would hardly have compelled your notice, but for us, and throughout rural Ukraine, 'the breadbasket of Europe,' it was momentous. In 1929 Stalin had decreed that the *kulaks* would be 'liquidated as a class.' He meant us. Our once prosperous colonies were a prime target. Hordes of Party 'agronomists' appeared to make Collectivization a reality, supported by propagandists and GPU brigades, and so-called 'workers' from the cities, the embittered underclass of petty criminals, always a ready resource to do the dirty work of tyrants.

After the Civil War my mother and Oma Enns had little left to collectivize. They owned a good sized vegetable plot, two cows, one pig and two dozen hens. Also a small field for hay and corn, and they had to count on my mother's nephews and the loan of Uncle Knalz's horses to work the field. After Collectivization there was no need for such family arrangements. We were all 'equal' – i.e., the State determined who worked our fields. But above all, Collectivization was supposed to industrialize agriculture, large, professionally managed enterprises instead of inefficient peasant plots. Which meant that inefficiencies were now also on an industrial scale.

What difference could any of this make to you, Antoine? Our world, to which Mary Gordon had entrusted you, would have been strange enough without Collectivization. For the first decade of your life you and Mary Gordon had lived by your wits. I remember you telling me how you had to scrounge, pilfer and scavenge in Odessa to stay alive and keep a roof over your heads, through bad times and worse times and occasionally good times, attaching yourselves to little underground groups of petty criminals and hustlers, keeping a step ahead of the local police who openly demanded bribes for their complicity.

Then you came to us. Collectivization made us utterly servile. Or so it must have seemed to you. In cities there were still opportunities for petty crime but not in our villages. If an old cart appeared on our street with two new wheels it would be noticed, and the owner could be called upon to provide a 'paper trail,' to show the wheels were acquired from a 'legal' source, not some clandestine 'business.'

I can understand now, Antoine, how our regulated lives must have grated on you, even though the regulations were a sham. In our villages there were no colourful gypsies gathering a crowd to watch them throw knives at an image of Stalin. Our people still had to live by their wits, but for them, living by their wits meant grovelling for small preferences, like a job in the dairy or the poultry operation where there were opportunities for a few 'extras.' Or a job in the Maintenance Brigade, where someone in desperate need of repairs to his leaky roof could have his name moved to the top of the list in exchange for certain favours.

Some people didn't grovel, Antoine. Like my mother, Groote Graeta, Taunte Liese. Uncle Knalz didn't have to. The new troop of commissars had identified him as a man of some status and influence in our villages, who could be useful to them. And should he prove not to be he could easily be disposed of. His known connection to my father would have been sufficient. By the spring of 1931 Collectivization was a *fait accompli*, and that year, recalled Uncle Knalz, spring dragged. The days had begun to lengthen toward summer but the temperatures still lagged behind the season, as though the sun no longer saw any point in warming the earth. He said it used to be an easy task to bring in the village dairy herd from their common pasture, for evening milking. The laziest lout in the village, with his pet dog, could bring in the whole herd while he daydreamed about the pretty girl he was sweet on. The cows knew the routine. They would sashay up the poplar-lined road, then along the broad street of our village, and without any signal from the drover or his dog, each cow would peel off from the herd and turn in at the familiar gate of her own *Wirtschaft,* saunter into the familiar stable, slot herself into her accustomed place, and begin munching the sugar-sweetened silage waiting for her.

But not now, said Uncle Knalz, now that a modern concrete stable had been built at the north end of the village where there had once been a cherry orchard. Now it was a struggle to get the cows into their new modern stable. Now all was chaos, a cacophony of shouting and braying and barking. Now every one of Uncle Knalz's herdsmen, and Uncle Knalz himself, were called upon to bring the herd home, assisted, or hampered, by every dog and schoolboy in the village. The stubborn, reactionary creatures were determined to peel off from the herd at the gate of their own *Wirtschaft* as they had always done, and Uncle Knalz and his herdsmen had to be quick to head them off. With their willow switches they beat the cows mercilessly across their noses and kicked their flanks to turn them back into the street, while dogs nipped at their heels and got a mouthful of bloody teeth for their trouble.

Inside the new stable, more chaos. The cows had no clue where to slot themselves. None had her accustomed place, none knew she was supposed to stick her head through one of those modern steel stanchions and be locked in place. The cows herded themselves into a corner, then panicked and tried to turn, rearing up on each other and gashing each other with their horns, braying in confusion and terror.

But the cows did eventually learn the new routine and submit to it. Cows submit more quickly than people do, said Uncle Knalz. And when the day's milking was done, the milk buckets rinsed and stacked and all the women had gone home, Uncle Knalz would stay awhile among the cows in the rustling gloom of the stable. He would nudge their rumps a little to the left or right so he could squeeze between them with his assortment of oils and ointments, for raw teats that needed to be salved or infected eyes to be bathed. He said he sometimes found the company of cows a relief from human company.

Then as the last light of day ducked through the door at the far end of the stable, Uncle Knalz had sensed a sudden darkening. The figure of a man blocked the light. Kaethler. He stood peering into of the stable, then stumbled forward as though the light behind him had given him a push. When his eyes adjusted to the gloom, he patrolled the length of the stable between the two rows of cows, his hands behind his back, fidgeting with a willow switch he had found lying on the ground. Uncle Knalz continued to apply his oils and ointments.

'So you told them not to sign,' said Kaethler.

'Nobody had to tell them,' said Uncle Knalz. *Undisputed confiscation,* that was the legal term for 'agreeing' to sign your property over to the State.

Kaethler began to pace again. 'Didn't do 'em any good, did it,' he said. 'Just made more trouble for themselves. And for me.' He wheeled around and glowered at Uncle Knalz, and slashed a jagged Z in the air with his switch. 'Do they think they can get rid of me? Huh? Huh?' Then he lowered his voice. 'I was in Krivoy Rog yesterday,' he said, 'Guess what I heard? Twenty-two people arrested – important people, commissars, and even GPU people – all Ukrainians. Half of them banished, the other half nobody knows. Or nobody says. So who replaced them, huh? Polacks and

Jews, that's who!' The Ukrainians had turned out to be 'unreliable,' Kaethler explained. Too soft on their own people. They let some of them keep a cow and a small plot of land. Not a mistake the Jews and Polacks would make, he said.

It was no secret, said Uncle Knalz, that Kaethler and his Ukrainian colleagues distrusted each other. To them, he was a personal affront. They assumed their Russian superiors had promoted Kaethler to his current position to spite them. Or spy on them. 'A *Nyemetz* in charge of *Nyemtzy* colonists. Imagine!' they said.

'I thought you were an intelligent man,' said Kaethler. 'Thought I could count on you – to explain things to your people. Make 'em see reason. You tryin' to make me look like a fool?'

Uncle Knalz examined the eyes of the cow on his left, then his right, then the ears. Kaethler lost patience. He leapt across the gutter and wriggled his torso between the rumps of two cows, as though he wanted to get Uncle Knalz within range of his switch. The rumps parted, then squeezed together again, pinning Kaethler's torso between them. He was panting and wheezing now through a froth of spittle, said Uncle Knalz. 'If it wasn't me, here,' he said, 'who do your people think they'd get instead? Huh? Huh? A Polack or a Jew, *that's* who. Because Polacks and Jews hate your *Nyemtzy* guts!' The cows shifted their weight and swayed, and Kaethler swayed between them. 'And in the Polish towns? Who gets the top jobs? Huh? Jews and Ukrainians. Because they hate Polacks. That's how it works,' he said. 'You get the picture? Tell *that* to your people.'

Uncle Knalz told us he did get the picture. Abroad, whether in France, Germany or America, the Soviet Comintern loudly decried all forms of racism. But at home, in the Soviet Republics, the Party counted on it. It fed and exploited longstanding racial tensions. Russians were the dominant 'nationality' in the Soviet Union, but there were regions where Poles, Ukrainians, Germans, Jews or Turkmen had been dominant for centuries, and it was often the vindictiveness of 'foreign' regional officials that determined who would be banished or shot, and how many.

And then came the Famine. What can one say about a famine, Antoine? Famines are boring. Earthquakes, floods, volcanic eruptions, they provide a spectacle, rearrange the landscape, make noise. But famines provide no spectacle. They grind. Later there will be stories of self-sacrifice, a stranger who gave his last crust to a starving child, or villains who guarded their hoard while they watched others die. But compare the story of the painter who puts the last touches on his masterpiece just as the molten lava descends upon the city and entombs it, intact. Or the shipping tycoon, about to sign a big contract. He takes his gold-plated fountain pen from his vest pocket, a gift from grateful shareholders, then he hears a rumble and the floor falls out beneath him. Three days later they dig him out of the rubble, still clutching his gold-plated pen. Or a village wedding, everyone dressed in their finery, making merry, and just as the groom pronounces his vows, 'till death do us part,' the dam breaks. Houses, barns, human bodies and livestock, petticoats and children's toys, all swirling in the deluge that comes rushing down the valley. But stories of famines rarely evoke such picturesque ironies.

Enough said? No, there is more to be said. As you know, Antoine, there was no 'famine' – though between four and seven million people starved to death. 'Famine' implies a scarcity of food, a disastrous crop failure, but there was no crop failure, no scarcity of food. We just weren't allowed to eat any of it. If not a famine then what? Perhaps 'siege' is a better term. And now a Ukrainian writer has come up with the word 'Holodomor,' and the term seems to have stuck. The implicit analogy to the Holocaust is obvious, and some have alleged the term is mischievous on that account, and perhaps it is. Unlike the purges of the *kulaks* that counted on local vindictiveness, the Famine was more rigorously administered. The border between the Ukraine and the neighbouring Soviet republics was sealed, with police patrols and hastily erected watchtowers to make sure no one smuggled any of the food that had been taken out back in. To quash Ukrainian nationalism, to quash opposition to Collectivization, those are the commonly alleged motives.

Women were thought to be more resourceful than men at finding ways to keep their families alive, but my mother was not resourceful. It was my grandmother, my Oma Enns, who had sensed what was afoot and had begun to hide small caches of food throughout the house, and even in the outdoor privy – flour, sugar, lard. She squirreled these away without telling anyone, and rationed them to us as the siege wore on. I remember a cold morning when we sat at our kitchen table and stared at our last five crusts. Then Oma Enns rose from her chair and shuffled to the shelf above the washbasin where my father's shaving mug still waited for his unlikely return. She placed it in the middle of the table and removed the lid. It was half full of bacon fat. It had stood there in full view but none of the Requisition Brigades had thought to sniff the contents.

The Brigades were often led by zealous students and *komsomols*, supported by irregular militia units, mostly older men who obediently did what the students told them. They ordered our people to bring in the harvest as they had always done, but now they weighed and recorded every grain and tuber to be loaded into waiting trains. They poked long steel probes into haystacks, manure piles, bedding, cedar chests, looking for evidence of 'hoarding.' 'Thieves! Saboteurs!'

Some of the girls among the students would take a few children aside, speak kindly to them, and offer them candy if they would tell who they had seen 'stealing' food. Taunte Liese was among a group of women harvesting potatoes when she saw her chance, took a small potato and quickly tucked it under her shirt, then another. But a vigilant child cried, 'Thief! Thief!' and pointed at Taunte Liese's bosom. A student and three militia converged on her, while the child pointed and cried, 'There! There! She put it there!' I remember it all, Antoine. I was standing only a few feet from her, and I heard my mother gasp.

The student, a tall, slender youth, no more than twenty years old, peered at Taunte Liese through his thick horn-rimmed glasses. 'Give me your knife,' he said, to one of the militia men. He grabbed the front of Taunte Liese's shirt and slit it open, exposing the theft. Two small potatoes dropped to the ground. The student stomped on them, mashed them into the ground. Then without taking his eyes off Taunte Liese, he slowly unbuttoned his fly, pulled out his cock and peed on the mashed potatoes, to make doubly sure no one would try to eat them. He stepped up close to her, the two of them staring into each other's eyes. We all waited to see what her punishment would be but he was content to give her a good slap across her face. Then he turned on his heel and left. Taunte Liese continued to stare at the student's back, and I saw her lips begin to quiver. 'Shut up, Liese, get back to work,' hissed Groote Graeta.

The child who had betrayed the theft burst into hysterical crying. We knew that little girl, knew her whole family. She was no better or worse than most of us. She was hungry.

You would remember the story of the nationally honoured 'child martyr.' His 'bravery' was already news in 1932, the first year of the famine. It happened in a village called Gerasimovka, somewhere north of us, and was reported in heart-wrenching detail in the newspapers posted on the wall of our commissary – how this brave Young Pioneer, only fourteen years old but racked by shame and guilt, had informed the police that his parents had hidden a cache of the People's grain. He took them to the exact spot and showed them, all twenty kilos of it. The parents were duly arrested for hoarding and profiteering, and banished to Siberia. The savage villagers hung back and waited for their chance. Then they took the boy from the protective care of his Young Pioneer leader, marched him to the edge of the village, and stoned him to death.

Many of the villagers were shot, the rest banished. The propaganda commissars put on a bigger show than usual to commemorate the brave child-martyr. An agent came all the way from Moscow to dignify the proceedings, and erect a statue in his honour. Here is his picture, glowed our teacher, right here in our textbook, a new edition issued in memory of the child martyr.

None of us would have thought anyone in our village would be inspired to emulate his deed, least of all Katya's Pavelche. No one seemed more indifferent to praise or blame, neither craving acceptance nor fearing rejection. He too had lost his father, one of Kaethler's lackeys who was arrested and disappeared shortly after my own father disappeared. Perhaps for that reason, or in spite of it, my mother had instructed us to be nice to Pavelche and try to protect him from bullies, but it was not easy. He was a pouty, sullen boy. When we would dutifully invite him to join in our games he would glumly set aside whatever he was doing and toddle after us, as though it were *he* who was doing *us* a favour.

Scrawny, witch-like Katya had married the *Russe benjal* who had once been her father's stable boy, when she was already well into her pregnancy. If the term 'white trash' had been familiar to us, there were many in our village who would have applied it to them. She doted on her dear Pavelche as only a mother could. When the two of them were alone together, or thought they were alone, we saw a different Katya from the sour, abrasive vixen we were accustomed to. She performed for him, she laughed and made funny faces to amuse him, and sometimes Pavelche would reward her efforts with a sheepish smile.

After Katya's husband disappeared, she and Pavelche withdrew into a

closed world of their own, with their own quaint courtesies. Katya was
susceptible to allergies, which caused her to sneeze uncontrollably and
very loudly for such a small body. And if she were working somewhere in
a far field raking new-mown hay into swaths, she would call out to her
son in a piercing, lilting voice to inform him that she had sneezed so that
he could shout the appropriate reply. '*Paaaavelche*,' tolled her voice, '*Mama
daed pruuuuuhste.*' Then little Pavelche, wherever he was, would turn in
the direction of the voice and shout back, '*Gesundtheit, Mama.*'

'*Dankschön, Pavelche*,' she tolled, and all was well.

Perhaps it shouldn't have seemed so comical. Merely a way for Katya
to check on her son, to make sure he had not wandered off somewhere,
and they both seemed oblivious to our amusement. And yet it was he who
walked eight *versts* to the nearest GPU office to inform them where a
certain person had buried a few jars of preserves, and where another kept
a few chickens hidden in crates among the bulrushes by the river.
Pavelche was praised for his brave action, given a slice of bread with
butter and marmalade, then he was driven home, in a motor car. The car
attracted a small crowd of the curious, and then, so all could hear, the
GPU officer praised Katya for raising a model Soviet child, in spite of her
criminal husband. All the people Pavelche had fingered were soon
arrested and banished.

No, we did not stone Katya's Pavelche. Katya packed a small suitcase,
took him by the hand and began walking, all the way to Lichtenau where
they boarded a train, but after that no one knew where they had gone.
Weeks later, when she reappeared in our village it was without her
Pavelche. No one ever saw Katya cry but no one doubted the depth of her
grief. Even before the famine there were stories of mothers who had
'given up' their children to be raised by others, mothers who, after their
husbands were banished, tried to make arrangements for the care of their
children before they too might be banished. Usually they would place
their children with a relative in a nearby village but that was not an
option for Katya.

My mother and Groote Graeta spent hours trying to persuade Katya
to go and bring her son back, assured her that no harm would come to
him, but Katya had scoffed at their assurances.

In the early days of the 'famine' I remember being angry – not at
Stalin, not at his local agents, but at my mother, and Oma Enns. Food was

never plentiful, but there had always been some. Why now nothing? Yes, I could see they too had nothing to eat, but not until other children, children I knew, began to appear at our door, crying, begging for something to put in their mouths, and were turned away, the door shut in their faces, only then did I begin to understand. Decades later Hannah Arendt wrote that the famine in the Ukraine illustrates what she calls an *atomized* society. Everybody withdrew, villages withdrew from each other, people in the villages withdrew, crept into their houses and locked the doors. Only immediate family allowed inside. Everyone else was an enemy.

We learned that lesson, you and I, Antoine. We were scavenging at the far end of that field where Taunte Liese had tried to steal two small potatoes but we had little hope of finding anything that might have been overlooked. Then we came to a shallow creek where we had once seen a colony of little burrowing owls poking their heads through holes in the muddy bank. We found the holes, still there, and maybe a few owls might still be burrowed in there too. We went back at dusk, when they would come out if any were there, and you brought one of your knives to throw at them or spear them. We flattened our bodies against the bank next to three holes close together in a row, and waited. Then yes, a brown head with white speckles appeared. You reached back and pressed your hand on my shoulder so I wouldn't move. We held our breaths and waited, only a few seconds but it seemed an eternity. Then the whole bird wriggled out of the hole, turned and blinked. You lunged and speared it with your knife. You pinned it to the ground until it stopped moving, then grabbed it and broke its neck.

It was pitifully small, probably weighed less than half a kilo. There might be more but we had no chance to find out. We heard footsteps, then panting and snatches of hushed voices. We peered over the weedy bank of the creek and saw four boys running toward us. Older boys, one of them my cousin. He was your age but bigger than you, and he had a stick. We scrambled up the bank. 'Here, take it,' you said, and handed me the owl. 'Now run!'

I ran a few paces along the bank, stopped and turned. You blocked their way, held them at bay, pointing your knife at one, then another. They tried to circle around you, then my cousin attacked on your left. You spun around, ducked, and speared his forearm as he swung his stick at your head. Blood oozed through his shirt. I came running but what could

I do. They backed off, my cousin clutching his arm, then slunk away, hissing curses at us over their shoulders. I hissed back. Those were the only words that passed between us.

When we got home, Oma Enns made owl soup for us all, thickened with a few roots and crushed apricot pits. We had stomach cramps that night, but none of us threw up.

Somebody told my sister that the wound you had given my cousin had become infected, had turned an ugly green and pus oozed out of it. When my mother found out that you had stabbed my cousin she was more heartbroken than angry. 'What is happening to us,' she cried. I protested that my cousin and his friends would have done worse to us. 'They had big sticks,' I said, though I remember only my cousin carrying a stick. 'Yes, I know, I know,' she said. 'All of us, we gladly ate that owl soup. But we must go now and ask his forgiveness, the three of us.'

I protested, but we went. My aunt answered the door. She didn't ask why we had come, she stepped aside to let us pass, and called to her son. My mother waited outside. My cousin took his time to appear, his arm covered in oozing bandages. He hardly took any notice of me. He stood glaring at you and said nothing. I stepped forward, lowered my head and asked him to forgive 'us.' You said nothing. You and he continued to glare at each other. His mother said, 'Say you forgive them,' but he didn't. Then we left. I felt we had done our duty, and I was glad my cousin hadn't forgiven us. Let *him* feel guilty.

We trudged home in silence. Then I broke the silence. '*He* should have asked *us* to forgive him,' I said. You smiled, and gave me an approving nudge with your elbow. My mother said nothing.

In the months that followed, quiet settled upon the Ukrainian countryside, a deathly quiet. No dogs barked, no roosters crowed, no cows mooed, no sound of children playing. The few birds that had not been caught and eaten still chirped but stayed out of range of our slingshots. There were no baby birds because we had pillaged every nest and eaten the eggs.

'Yeah, go for it, papa. Stick it to the commies. That'll make even the Nazis look good. Is that your game, papa? Does that soothe your conscience about joining the Nazis?' No, Margaret didn't say that, not in so many words, not even at the peak of her radical period when I was still a respectable teacher. But I knew that accusation wasn't far from her thoughts, and I couldn't honestly deny there might be some truth in her accusation.

And yet, on no other subject does the perfidy of the Western press seem more shameful to me. The biggest and most disgusting liar was that celebrated, much honoured, Pulitzer Prize winning British journalist, Walter Duranty. It was in his report on the 'alleged' famine in the *New York Times* that he coined the infamous phrase, *'You can't make an omelette without breaking a few eggs.'* But there were scores of other famous 'fellow travellers.' George Bernhard Shaw, H. G. Wells, Sydney and Beatrice Webb, they had all been given a privileged 'tour' of the Soviet Union. How could there be a famine, they wrote, when the Soviet Union had just exported 1.8 million tons of grain to western Europe, enough to feed five million people for a whole year? Malcolm Muggeridge was one of very few whose ideological zeal was chastened by the evidence of his eyes and the stench in his nostrils. There was also Gareth Jones, a Welsh journalist, and that incorrigible truth-teller, George Orwell. Aside from these three, I can't come up with another name.

I have no memory of how the Famine ended. I don't remember that anyone declared an end to it, but food began to trickle into our villages again, then a few chickens, cows, then a wagon load of seed grain and slowly we began to fall into our 'normal' routines.

School again. We had to brace ourselves for it. Our day began at dawn, an unhurried breakfast, warm milk and a slice of dark bread, and later a little lard or honey, and as the morning light began to cast shadows we would linger a while around the table, you, me, my sister Sarah, my mother and my Oma Enns. Our conversation would be cheerful enough, though a little forced, until our half hour together drew to a close. My mother did not flaunt her piety but she was meticulously observant, and we were all required to bow our heads in silent prayer for a minute or two, until she said, 'Amen.' Then we put on our coats and scarves and some sort of footwear, slung our homemade satchels over our shoulders and filed past my mother and Oma Enns to receive a hug and a kiss from each. 'God be with you,' Oma Enns would say. 'Remember who you are,' said my mother. Those would be her last words to us, the alpha and omega of her moral instruction. No do's and don't's – just 'Remember who you are.'

Let me try to retrace our steps, Antoine, along the broad avenue of our village, now littered with rusty farm machinery, mowers and binders and wagons with missing wheels, past remnants of a crumbling brick fence with its ornate gateposts now reduced to weed-covered stumps – to our schoolhouse, a solitary two-room structure squatting on the landscape halfway between our village and the next, as decrepit as the rest, a patchwork of raw wood and corrugated tin, distinguished only by the hammer-and-sickle flying above it. 'A shabby outpost of communist right-thinking,' you said, and spat on the ground. Before you came to us you had probably never spent a full year at school, only scattered weeks here and there. You had been home schooled by Mary Gordon, though you never had much of a home, only a series of temporary squats. Sitting in a classroom now, for tedious hours, did not come easy to you.

I was eight years old then. My Oma Enns had sternly cautioned us to say nothing about what we had seen or heard at home, and when we crossed the threshold of the school we switched from normal speech to Soviet-speak. My mother told us to listen to our conscience, our teachers told us that conscience was a ploy concocted by priests to make us submissive to them, the product of hundreds of years of bourgeois brainwashing. It must be purged and replaced by *Soznatel'nost*, the new Higher Consciousness.

At first our teachers were old men, *unse,* reinstalled in their position after the civil war. Some were stubborn and were soon banished, the rest so cowed by the threat of banishment that they dutifully repeated the Soviet-speak in a dull, mechanical monotone. The Russian teachers who later replaced them were no better. The education ministry was not about to waste good teachers on us *Nyemtzy.* Then a stroke of luck. A new teacher, Comrade Harder, one of *unse,* from the Old Colony, who had been a student in Petrograd when the Revolution began. A zealous young communist now, a 'true believer,' much more enthusiastic, and more intelligent, than our former teachers. The older generation he had written off as a lost cause, but us, the children, he tried to save. He coaxed and cajoled, with wit and theatrical exuberance.

You would remember his verbal tick, Antoine, ending every statement with an interrogative 'Hmmm?' But that only made him more entertaining. 'Here's what it says in your bibles,' he shouted, and held the book above his head, opened at the passage he had selected, the story of Balaam's talking ass, one of the many comic farces in the Old Testament, but Comrade Harder debunked it as a literal chronicle. He climbed up on his desk and struck a bow-legged pose as though he were riding a donkey, and he brandished a long stick in his hand to serve as a whip. *Now Balaam was riding on his ass and his two servants were with him,* he read. 'Two servants, hmmmm? So this Balaam was obviously a rich bourgeois.' *And the ass turned aside out of the road into a field, and Balaam struck the ass, to turn her into the road. And the ass pushed against a wall and pressed Balaam's foot against the wall; so he struck her again.* And now Comrade Harder made a face like an enraged lunatic and with his stick flailed at the imaginary ass between his legs, two mighty strokes on the ass's rump behind him, one more on the head in front of him. How could we not laugh, Antoine, and applaud his performance? *Then the Lord opened the mouth of the ass and she said to Balaam, 'What have I done to you that you have struck me these three times? Am I not your ass upon which you have ridden all your life long to this day?'* Then Comrade Harder slammed the book shut. 'Your elders tell you every word in the bible is true. Do you believe it, hmmmm? Do you believe donkeys can talk? Hmmmm? Or is it your elders who are the talking donkeys?'

That got another laugh. 'Don't laugh!' said Comrade Harder, with mock severity. 'How would you like it if *you* were Balaam's ass, hmmmm? What would *you* tell him?' Uncertain laughter now. We weren't quite sure where this was going. 'Don't be shy,' he said. 'Tell me what *you* would tell Balaam. *You* can talk. Hmmmm?' We looked around to see who would rise to the challenge but there were no takers. 'You'd say, Get your fuckin' ass off my aching back, you fat bourgeois pig!' he shouted. Loud guffaws now, especially from the bigger boys. I laughed too, couldn't help myself.

You were Comrade Harder's pet project, Antoine, the lost sheep he was determined to save. He cajoled, he argued, he gave you books to read, including some old classics, like Turgenev and Gogol. You brought them home and devoured them. Then you and he would argue about them for hours, even in class, while the rest of us fidgeted and pelted each other with pieces of chalk.

At the end of the school term he took you to Kiev to hear the approved Soviet writers read from their work. My mother was worried about letting you go, and she had gone to see Comrade Harder to assure herself that you would be in safe hands. He told her the trip would take four days, an overnight train, two days at the congress, then an overnight train back. The travel permits were all arranged, everything had been approved. Nothing to worry about.

I was more excited than you were. An overnight train ride was exciting in itself, and when you came back I was eager for a report of all you had seen and heard. You shrugged. 'They're like little children who have just found a box of new toys,' you said.

A few weeks later, Comrade Harder proposed another trip. A shorter trip, just two days, to Krivoy Rog. Again my mother was wary, but again she was swayed by Comrade Harder's obvious affection for you. 'Look,' he told my mother, 'As the son of a criminal he has no future.' The director of the Technical Institute was his personal friend, he said, and he would introduce you to him, and show him what an exceptional student you were. 'It's his only chance,' he explained, 'or he'll be wasted here, doing menial work on the *kolkhoz*.' My Oma Enns got busy sewing you a new outfit for the occasion, and off you went.

When you came back Comrade Harder put on a brave face and reported to my mother it had all gone very well, that you had indeed impressed the director with your knowledge and your probing questions. But as soon as he was gone we got a different story from you. Yes, Comrade Harder and the director did seem to be old friends, you said. They had joked around and talked about old times in Petrograd. You said it was embarrassing watching Comrade Harder kowtow to the director. 'He wanted to show me off. Wanted me to perform for that pompous ass – so he could show the director what a brilliant teacher he was. Too brilliant to be wasted here, in the boondocks. That was the real point of the trip – to grovel for a job at the Institute.' You said you probably hadn't been of much help to him.

You seemed vindictive now, telling us your story, pleased to have sabotaged Comrade Harder's designs. When the next school term began, he was not promoted but arrested for spreading subversive counter-revolutionary ideas. And maybe you had failed to meet Comrade Harder's expectations in ways I was deemed too young to be told.

His successor was a middle-aged matron from the Volga region, who seemed to regard her posting to our school as a punishment. One of those teachers who instinctively regards bright students as a nuisance. You were no longer the teacher's pet, you were the fox in her henhouse. Her Soviet moralizing became duller and drearier – stories of yet another heroic Stakhanovite who had tripled his production quota, or another brilliant engineer who had squeezed ten more kilowatts out of a dynamo. Then you would hold up your hand. 'Can we move on to something more exciting? Like conjugating irregular verbs?' And you got away with it. She seemed intimidated by you. Had it been me or anyone else we would have been slapped in the face and sent home, and then our parents would have been summoned to explain our bad attitude. I was awed by the pure passion of your loathing, though sometimes you alarmed me.

It did please my mother to see how attached we were to each other, though it worried her a little that I had few friends among boys my own age. She encouraged me to join them in their games, and sometimes I did. I was as good at football as any but the best of them, and I could wrestle and roughhouse with as much vigour, but even as I strained and grunted I would be rehearsing in my mind how I would mimic their silly swaggering for your amusement.

At home our mood was usually more relaxed, almost dreamy. There was rarely any tension among us, and when there was it was sparked by sibling rivalry between my sister Sarah and me. In our house the Bible was important, and as far back as I can remember, Sunday School was a weekly ritual for my sister and me. In the industrial cities, 'rest days' were staggered for different groups of workers in six-day intervals, but in rural areas rest days depended mainly on the season and the weather. You dutifully joined us in these lessons, though when you first became part of our household we were surprised that you were biblically illiterate. Mary Gordon had taught you much but apparently she didn't think 'bible stories' were necessary for your survival.

For me the stories in the Bible were much more enthralling than the routine Marxist-Leninist dogma drilled into us at school, and the stories became even more enthralling when I was old enough to read the forbidden book myself – stories about flesh-and-blood figures like Joseph sold into slavery by his treacherous brothers, young David summoned to play his harp to soothe King Saul's tormented soul, the voluptuous

Delilah who seduced mighty Samson then betrayed him to the Philistines. That a mysterious God brooded over these stories did not make them less enchanting. I gobbled them up – so unlike the smug gloating stories in our Social History text at school. You too spent hours reading the forbidden book, but seemed wary of falling under the spell of those stories. We were told by my mother and Oma Enns that we should have faith in God, and always try to follow Jesus, and that seemed natural to me, if I wanted to be good. (I don't remember much about hell-fire torments. Maybe you have to feel very comfortable in *this* life to find stories of torments in the afterlife entertaining.)

Our German Lutheran Bible had escaped confiscation by the GPU when they took my father's books, but my mother was worried it too might be confiscated. Or we too could be banished, and then all that would remain of His Word were the passages we had committed to memory. So we memorized, and I had an actor's talent for memorizing long passages.

> As the hart pants for flowing streams
> so pants my soul for thee, O God.
> My soul thirsts for God, for the living God.
> My tears have been my meat day and night,
> and all day long mine enemies say to me,
> 'Where is thy God?'
>
> Deep calleth to deep at the noise of thy cataracts,
> thy waves and thy billows roll over me.
> And I say to God, my rock:
> 'Why hast thou forgotten me?'
> As with a sword in my bones mine enemies,
> reproach me, and daily they say unto me,
> 'Where is thy God?'

Verse after verse, the stirring lines of the Psalmist. It has been decades since I last cracked the spine of that Book, yet they remain imprinted upon my memory. When I casually quoted a few lines of scripture to my daughter because they seemed ironically appropriate to the subject we were discussing, she smirked. 'I see you've been reading your bible,' she said. I hadn't, but I didn't bother denying it. She seemed to think I was one of those oldsters whose brain turns to mush in his declining years and tries to make an eleventh hour dash for the throne of grace.

Hard to imagine now, all that fuss about God, both for and against. Our generation seems to have been the last to find the death of God unsettling. For Margaret's generation it provokes little more than a shrug. But for us in Russia, God was not easy to shrug off. Even as a small child I could sense that God had become a thorn to some of our own people, that in certain homes God himself had been banished, all talk of Him suppressed, especially in front of children. Safety, and perhaps a few coveted 'privileges,' lay in submission to our Bolshevik masters, and a careless word or two of God-speak could needlessly provoke suspicion. But for others only faith in God could sustain resistance, could forge a solidarity among us, and the natural language of resistance was biblical – God-speak, not Rights-and-Freedom-speak. A free press, a free market, civil rights, these would inspire some of the later Soviet dissidents, but not *unse*, not our people. Against the monstrous maw of Stalinist terror we needed more vivid language, and if at times God seemed remote and deaf to our cries, Rights-and-Freedom-speak would have seemed utterly absurd – like a gazelle in the mouth of a lion pleading the virtues of a vegetarian diet.

October 30, 1991

'So, what's a Mennonite?' asked Seymour, when we no longer needed to be quite so guarded, could tease one another, ask indelicate questions. But how was he to know his question would unsettle me. Don't ask a renegade to be a spokesman for a people, I could have told him. There were now few Mennonites who would want to count me among their number, and if ever I were tempted to nudge my way back into their communion, layers of sackcloth and ashes would not be enough.

It should not have been so difficult. Seymour's question had been tossed at me often enough by colleagues and others, and I had handled it with ease. The question usually presumes that five minutes of polite attention should be ample, so it's best to milk the subject for a cheap laugh about silly prohibitions against booze and dancing, and pass on. But now I choked. Had I caught an inflection in Seymour's voice that hinted at a hook embedded in the question? 'What is it about Mennonites that made them eager accomplices of the Nazis?' Was that his real question?

I cleared my throat and peddled a safe response, the kind that usually puts a quick end to the discussion. 'Mennonites are a branch of the Anabaptists of the early 16th century,' I said, 'persecuted for their beliefs, in Switzerland, Alsace, and Holland, burned at the stake by both Catholics and Lutherans, united on this issue as on few others. The survivors got the message and fled, I said, some (the Swiss) to Pennsylvania, others (the Dutch) to Prussia, then fled again to the Ukraine and southern Russia.'

'Enough already with the persecution *shtick*. Why the funny bonnets? Why horses and buggies? There's a devil, maybe, in an internal combustion engine?'

'Why streimel and yarmulkes? It is written Yahweh is not fond of baseball caps?'

'*Oy*, he's a touchy one. My apologies already.'

So it *had* been a frivolous question. I was relieved. It's usually religious illiterates who assume there must be a quirky scriptural sanction for bonnets and buggies.

I had already been through this with my daughter. It's not silly obedience to some biblical injunction, I told her, it's a gesture of solidarity, against the silliness and falseness of mainstream society. Just like it is for your hippies, I said. There's an obscure passage in *Das Kapital* maybe, that prescribes blue jeans and long hair as marks of proletarian virtue?

I could take Seymour to a Mennonite church, to let him see Mennonites in modern dress, but it would not be instructive. No, *pace* Antoine, I have not become a churchgoer, except when I have no choice – when my wife and I spend a weekend with my old friend, Brumtup. Abram J. Janzen, proud partner with his son in A&T Janzen Construction, but Brumtup to his friends, a pet name my Taunte Liese gave him in Russia because he always seemed grumpy, though there is often more laughter in his company than among those who cultivate a sunnier disposition. He is now a big, burly man with a thick mane of white hair, a face furrowed like a peach pit, etched by sun and wind, the strength that comes from a lifetime of tossing heavy timbers about and the stubbornness that comes from regretting his lack of formal education. He had to work much harder than I did, had no Doktor Vik to smooth the way for him. But while I have estranged myself from Mennonites, Brumtup has become a pillar of the community, the *Väasettenda* of the *Gemeinde*, (now reduced to Chairperson), and on Sunday morning, in Brumtup's house, you go to church. You have breakfast, sing a hymn, then take a leisurely coffee outside on the deck if the weather is pleasant, in his den if it's not. Then you go to church – if you're a *Paraguaya*. If you're an *Englända* you can express a preference.

And so it happened that on a particular Sunday we witnessed the 'installation' of a new pastor in Brumtup's church. The old pastor, still called an *Ältester*, had been pushed into retirement somewhat earlier than he had intended, and much earlier than Brumtup had wished, and the congregation had voted the beaming, rosy-cheeked fellow now seated beside Brumtup to be their new pastor. He had not been Brumtup's first choice, in fact, not his choice at all, but he was determined to support the congregation's decision as best he could. There remained only the formal ritual of 'installation.' The appropriate hymns were sung, the appropriate words were spoken, the prayers offered, one more hymn, and it was done.

But not without a hitch. It was Brumtup's task to formally welcome the new pastor, to deliver a brief résumé of his credentials and achievements, then extend to him the right hand of brotherhood. He rose, approached the pulpit, placed his reading glasses on the tip of his ruddy nose, and began to read from his notes. 'Although Andrew Schowalter is only a young man he has already distinguished himself in several roles as a church leader. Since his graduation from Seminary with a Master of Divinity degree, Pastor Schowalter has ably served...'

But here Brumtup was interrupted. Schowalter bounced up from his chair, approached the pulpit and intruded his head between Brumtup and the microphone. 'Just call me Andy,' he said, beaming even more broadly than usual. Then he stepped aside and raised his arms as though he were acknowledging the congregation's applause.

Brumtup stared at Schowalter over the top of his reading glasses, and waited for him to finish taking his bows. Then Schowalter turned to Brumtup, gave him a little wink, and his own special smile. 'It's OK, carry on, carry on,' he whispered, to assure Brumtup this was all perfectly appropriate in an 'installation' ritual.

So Brumtup reshuffled his notes and began again. 'Pastor Andrew Schowalter has also . . .' he said, a little more emphatically than necessary, and rushed through the rest of his CV in a dull monotone. Then he stepped over to Schowalter and extended to him the right hand of brotherhood, but nothing doing. Call-me-Andy wanted a bear hug. Again he bounced to his feet and wrapped his arms around Brumtup, who endured the embrace with his arms by his side, then sat down. 'Hymn number four hundred and twenty.'

The programmed cheerfulness of the Call-Me-Andys depresses me more than the dour rectitude of my ancestors. What kinship could I find with Call-Me-Andy and his teddy-bear God? And what kinship can Call-Me-Andy claim with those quarrelsome 16th century Bible-delvers, so enraged by the corruptions of state- and priestcraft that a heap of burning fagots could not silence them? Ecstatic, some of them, singing their praises to the Lord even as their flesh singed. Yet them too I would interrogate. Died, to protest the corruption of their faith? Or a blasphemous parody of their Lord's agony? I see them now, those old Dutch Anabaptists, sturdy, practical burghers and boers with burning eyes, arguing through clenched teeth whether water daubed on the head of an infant is sacrament or sacrilege, whether bread and wine are true body and true blood. I see them, in groups of three or four, huddled around their sacred book in a damp, cold room in Amsterdam, heated by a frugal fire. I see their lips move, their tongues silently shaping the words as they follow a calloused finger along each line of Holy Writ, page after page of dense gothic script – while altogether elsewhere, far to the south in sun-drenched Italy, in a city they reviled, another lay on his back with burning eyes, high on a scaffold in a papal chapel, who now applied the last brush strokes to a finger whose tip carried a vital charge.

And yet will I, nill I, those sunless northern people are my people. Must I say it? My *Volk*. They have marked me.

Seymour is still waiting for his answer, so how should I chronicle this *Volk* that never had kings, prophets or god-appointed judges to give its matter epic weight? A wandering *Volk*, I could tell him, a mere footnote in the annals of more favoured peoples, whose modest aspiration was to live unmolested in some obscure hinterland while others were busy making history. Until Great Catherine, Empress of all the Russias, offered them a tract of land conveniently cleansed of Tatars and roving bands of Cossacks. Then some of *unse* began to think they had found their Canaan, their land of milk and honey. Came so close they could taste it.

I could have gone on, and on, oblivious to Seymour's impatience. I smarted under the tacit condescension of his question, felt goaded into bartering with Seymour prophet for prophet. In those days when there was still a Tsar in Russia, I might have told him, some of our people could no longer abide to paddle their lives in village shallows, and these became mill owners in the cities, or *khutors*, masters of vast estates, and still others, though these were few, became traders and merchants. And one such was Ohm Isaac's father who sent his eldest son to be his agent in Odessa and his youngest, Ohm Isaac, to the city of Astrakhan on the Old Silk Road. And business came easy to Ohm Isaac, I could have told Seymour, he travelled far and became a wealthy man, and then his travels took him to the remote hill country of the Terek, where, among Cossacks and turbaned Turkmen, sheep herders and camel drivers, he came upon a rude colony of Mennonite settlers newly installed on their lands, and took to himself a wife from among them. He brought her to the city of Astrakhan and settled her there, ordered a spacious house with a cool garden to be built for his young wife, provided attentive servants for her convenience and for her amusement engaged a local man who knew the arts of dancing and music, who taught her the graceful turns and fish-like movements of the *horon*.

But more and more Ohm's travels took him to the famous centres of learning, to Bukhara and Tashkent, and soon instead of business it was ancient learning that enchanted him. Here he found venerable rabbis and mullahs who led him through the mazes of their holy books, and hirsute monks from as far as Optina Pustyn, and still others schooled in Maimonides or Spinoza. But his wife pined for the familiar comforts of her own people, felt imprisoned by her husband's riches, isolated by a language she spoke poorly, by customs that made her awkward and food that made her mouth burn. All this she might have endured, and did endure, for years, but then her husband brought with him into the marriage house his mistress, not an earthly woman but Holy Wisdom, and though he told his wife he loved her none the less he devoted more and more of his nights to the pleasures of his mistress.

I see you smile, Antoine, but how else should I invoke a figure of legend among our people? No, not how you would remember him – in rags, blind and half mad, rocking back and forth on a crude bench behind the peeling white-washed cottage where he and his equally demented daughter had been secluded, set apart from the village where his rants could be ignored by our Bolshevik *apparatchiks*. We knew only fragments of his past, eavesdropping on our elders, a tale we were deemed too young to be told in its troubled complexity. Among our people there seemed to be something ill-omened about his story, like a village secret we were all sworn to. If someone dropped a careless phrase that recalled an incident of his former life, an awkward hush would fall upon the room. At other times the ghosts of his past refused to be banished from our minds. Wisps of his story seemed to curl around the eaves of our houses like a morning mist, slither through a gap under the door and demand recognition of their presence.

Ohm Isaac, our own blind prophet and seer, both prophet and proof of God's judgment upon our hubris, or so I might have told Seymour had I presumed upon his patience.

They had to be kept alive, Ohm and his daughter, and since Ohm was distant kin on my mother's side, the task fell mainly to her. Ohm's daughter could boil an egg or a potato but not much more, so three or four times each week my mother, sometimes Groote Graeta or Taunte Liese, would prepare a noonday meal for them, and I would be summoned to deliver it and serve it to them. When food was scarce it might be only a slice of *Schwarzbrot* with a tablespoon of lard, in better times there would be cabbage rolls and a loaf of fresh bread, or a steaming pot of borscht, with two bowls and two spoons packed in a wicker basket.

On good days I might find Ohm seated on his bench in the noonday sun, listening to the calls of birds and imitating their songs. And when he heard me at his gate he would call out, 'Good morning, my boy, and what have you brought us today? Ah, Groote Graeta's red-leaf beet borsht. I can smell it.' When the weather was pleasant I would make a picnic of it, I would ladle the soup into the bowls, hand one to his daughter, then I would guide Ohm's hand to his bowl and put a spoon in his other hand. He was a remarkably clean eater for a blind man. He ate slowly, savouring each spoonful, and when he was done he would lean his back against the wall of his cottage, sigh and smile. 'Listen,' he would say, 'that was a thrush,' and he would repeat its song with amazing fidelity. 'Ch-ch zreew zi-zi-zreew.'

Other days I would find him sitting on his bench murmuring to himself, wrapped in his own world. He would be oblivious to me while I ladled out his soup, he would let me guide his hand to the bowl and put a spoon in his other hand, but he wouldn't eat. I would coax and cajole and in frustration start shouting at him, while his daughter giggled at us. I would have to dunk his finger in the hot soup to get his attention. And then the bad days. Before I was clear of the village I would hear him declaiming in a high-pitched voice as though he were pleading his case before an unruly mob. I would find him at his picket fence, moving his hands from picket to picket as he groped his way along, 'In those days, when there was still a Tsar in Russia,' he wailed, 'a certain Levite sojourned in the hill country of or the Terek where, among Cossacks and Uzbeks, he took to him a wife from among them, a young girl with spirit, with dancing eyes and a languid, sensual manner that belied the rough homespun of her dress. And he brought her to the city of Astrakhan, where he settled her in luxury and honour.'

His wailing made me angry because it would now take forever to make him eat, but it did not frighten me. Ohm and his daughter had been fixtures in my village landscape since I was born, they were too familiar to marvel at. It was said among *unse* that in Ohm Isaac's troubled mind, the events of his own life had begun to blur with the stories of tormented figures in his holy book, among whom, more than among the living, he now found fit company. And those who later told and retold his story, though they were in full possession of their wits, for them too the stories had begun to blur. In those days, they said, when there was still a Tsar in Russia, Ohm had made his house a *caravanserai* for holy men and scholars to be his guests, but the more there were of these the more his wife felt the pain of her exile. And then there were two monks among her husband's guests, ancient, according to the length of their beards, whose spirits had been ripened in a desert hermitage but now like school boys they would peek at her over their shoulders, then whisper and giggle to each other. And one morning while she was bathing in the marble pool at the secluded end of the garden that Ohm Isaac had made to please her she saw them again, these ancients, peeking through the shrubbery, groaning and clutching their groins. '*And his concubine became angry with him*,' Ohm wailed. She scolded his indifference to her humiliation, then she took their youngest daughter, Ohm's favourite, whom he had instructed in the ancient scripts where nimble letters dance across the page from right to left, and she returned to her father's house in the hill country of the Terek. '*Then her husband arose and went after her, to speak kindly unto her and bring her back*,' Ohm wailed, while he tugged at the pickets of his fence as though they were bars of a prison cell. '*And when his wife's father saw him, he rejoiced to meet him, and for four days they let their hearts be merry. But he would not stay. On the fifth day he rose up, and they departed*.'

It was said that when Ohm Isaac returned to his city, the men of Astrakhan had built a great bonfire in the square that lay close by his house. And there were two men, one a rabbi, the other a venerable abbot, and the men of Astrakhan were spitting on them and beating them. So Ohm elbowed his way through the crowd and took the two men into his own house. Then the men of Astrakhan heaped more fagots on the fire and more vodka on their brains. *Bring forth the men that came into thine house*, they cried, *that we may know them*, and they began to beat upon his door.

And now Ohm cried out, '*Behold, here are my daughters and my concubine. Ravish them and do to them what seemeth good to you, but unto these men who have come under the shelter of my roof do not do so vile a thing. So they took his daughters and his concubine and abused them all night till morning came and it was light*.'

But there is never only one version of a legend. Some people said Ohm did not need to send his eldest daughter to the men of Astrakhan for their pleasure, she went of her own accord because she was of their party, because she had no love for her father or for his learning. But then the men of Astrakhan called out to him, 'Send out your youngest, the virgin, that we may use her also. Or are fresh, tender morsels only to be savoured by *Nyemtzy* gentry?' And when they broke down his door and fell upon them, Ohm wrenched his daughter's hand from his hand, and fled from his house. Others told a different tale – that when the mob fell upon them, Ohm wrenched his daughter's hand from his hand that he might with both hands fend off her attackers. And they would have killed him too, they say, had not his eldest said to them, 'Let him live. And let the horror of this day gnaw at his heart like a rabid weasel till he dies.'

In the last hours of the night Ohm Isaac had wandered the streets of the city calling his daughter's name, until his eldest found him. To mock him she took him to a stable and showed him where his youngest lay in a heap, whimpering. Ohm wrapped her as best he could in her own torn rags, and while his eldest jeered at him, his youngest, between gasps of pain, scolded, 'Bad papa. Bad papa.'

'Here's your daughter, your favourite,' said his eldest, 'You wished she would remain a child always, and now you have your wish.' Then she left father and sister and went her own way, whored and schemed her way up the ranks of the Party, they say, till she too was banished, survived her term in Kolyma, then settled in one of the nameless satellite towns that sprang up on the fringes of the camps, and here she spent the last days of her life mated to a *zek* who beat her, and died drinking antifreeze siphoned from the radiator of a tractor.

Ohm carried his youngest back to the smouldering ruins of his house and found his wife on the stone slab of his doorstep. He took what he could carry on his back and they began their journey, till they came to our village. Ohm's wife never again uttered a word to her husband, nor would she take food in the same room with him, and she died two years later, an easy victim of the typhus, while Ohm lay on a concrete floor in the Lubyanka awaiting the next round of his interrogation, when they put out his eyes.

What does it matter now, how the tale is told? What mattered is that the peacock glory of his wealth and learning had failed to protect them. Better had he remained a rustic villager, said some of our people, better, said others, had he filled his house with armed thugs instead of doddering monks and scholars, and made his house and garden a grim garrison where day and night the clack of hobnailed boots echoed along stone corridors, and not a bowered pavilion where slippered feet swished across a marble terrace.

You rarely accompanied me, Antoine, but when you did you would taunt Ohm as though he were a disgraced oracle. I remember only one time, remember it too well. One of Ohm's bad days. You waited till I had packed up the bowls and spoons, then you stepped forward and planted yourself squarely in front of him. You began tormenting him with questions, spitting names at him, his wife's name, her father's name, the names of his daughters. You were cruel, Antoine. You were like a young hooligan jabbing at a caged bear with a long stick. With each name you spat at him, Ohm would jerk his head from side to side as though you had poked one of his sightless sockets. 'You were blind before they put out your eyes,' you sneered, 'Couldn't see past the end of your nose. Couldn't see the God you had cobbled together out of old books had been usurped, by drooling dogs who preyed on his sheep, and peed on his altars.'

I cried 'Stop! Stop!' but you wouldn't stop.

'You and your doddering monks and rabbis!' you hissed. 'You made a net out of old books to enmesh your God. You put him in a gilded cage, like an exotic bird. Domesticated him, and taught him to parrot your own words back to you. Then the Communists came, bursting through your door. Save us, you cried, Lest we all perish! But what could he do, your gilded God? He cowered in his cage and covered his eyes with his clipped wings.'

I tried not to listen, tried not to watch. I began to cry. I gathered the empty bowls and spoons, put them in the wicker basket, and ran home. I avoided you the rest of that day and went to bed early. You probably avoided me too. When you came home to bed and blew out the lamp, you said, 'I'm sorry. It was stupid, and cruel, what I did.'

I started to cry again. 'I don't understand why,' I said.

I had heard you before, venting your contempt for the solemn pieties of some of our elders, or the obliging smugness of grovellers. But this was different. You had seemed as mad as Ohm himself. 'Because they – that whole generation, all of them – have made a mess of the world,' you said, 'and now we have to live in it.'

· · ·

But how to explain all this to Seymour while our dogs played and chased squirrels. Mennonites are like little-league Jews, I told him. He had waited long enough for an answer. We are Jews on a smaller scale, I said. We go back only four hundred years instead of your four thousand. Like you we have our diaspora, a quarter million of us scattered throughout Canada and the United States, mainly in the west, a few thousand in Europe, more thousands in South America and Mexico. Even a couple of dozen in Montreal. Like you, we have our Moses and Joshua who led us out of the land of bondage, though it took only half as long as it took your people, just over twenty years. Like you, we are a wandering *Volk*, with our own food that really *schmecks,* our own improvisations on the cuisine of all the nations who have hosted us, and like your Yiddish, we have our Low German. Like your Ashkenazim and Sephardim, we've got our Swiss and Dutch Mennonites. Our ultra-Orthodox are those horse-and-buggy Mennonites in Waterloo and Pennsylvania, with black hats and bonnets. Our *shtetls* are those villages in Russia, the *Englända* are our *goyim.* Whatever you're drivin', we got the economy model, I said. And like you, within two generations of our emancipation we're in the *Engländas'* face. We've got doctors and lawyers, politicians and musicians. One of the best sopranos in the world is one of *unse,* and we've got a *Helden* tenor who can sing the socks off Pavarotti. Of course, we don't have fiddlers and pianists yet that can stand up to your boys, but we've got some comers.

'*Kuk im on*! You think you got the market covered, then some *schmuck* opens a corner store.'

That's progress, I tell him.

'Don't do it,' he says, 'Take it from an old Jew. Don't touch the culture thing. Look what happened to us, when they let us out of the *shtetls. – Feh.* Look at you! they said, Poor, funny clothes, and look at what you eat! Gefilte fish, kishke, blintzes, and pickles. Pickles with everything. Makes you smell bad. OK, we say. Please, no offence, *ayn klaynigkeit.* We get rich, learn to cook like the French, dress like an English gentleman. No, no, they tell us. Now you're just *nouveau riche. Arrivistes.* No class. No culture. Rich is not enough. You gotta have culture. *Gott im Himmel,* now you're talkin', we say. What we don't know about culture! Polish, Russian, Persian, even Irish. You name it, we've got a piece of it. More German than the Germans, more French than the French. No, no, no! We mean High Culture, they say. *Kultur.* That's not something you pick up just like that, they say. Takes generations, of breeding and refinement. It's gotta be in your blood, they say.

'*Mishegoyim!*' said Seymour, 'Blood we got. Hearts an' brains too, if we need 'em.'

Seymour leapt to his feet and began pacing in front of me, gesticulating. 'But we're determined to please, we Jews,' he said. '*Oy, gevald.* We swoon over their classics, Shakespeare, Leopardi, Cervantes. You wanna know about classics? Our boys are the experts. More *kultur* in our little finger than any Franz-Josef with a six-hundred-year-old name. In two generations our boys are playing Beethoven and Schubert like they never heard. At the Wiener Konzerthaus the tears are flowing. No gentile can break their hearts on a fiddle like our Jascha, or run his fingers up and down a keyboard like our Rubinstein.

'So now do they love us? *Kush mir in toches.* It's like Cultura was their beautiful young wife, and we had cuckolded them. While they were sipping sherry at the Club, or hunting foxes, we scaled the wall of their private estate, climbed through the window and found their beautiful Cultura languishing, alone, on the big bed, bored and neglected, then slipped between the sheets and gave her pleasure. *Schmutz!* they cried, when they came home and found us together, familiar now in their kitchen, making jokes, our hair still tousled from our recent exertions.'

A very stern nanny had been keeping a cautious eye on us. Four little tots in her care, two in a carriage, two tethered to her with a piece of multi-coloured rope. She scowled as she passed near our bench, the toddlers, each with a thumb in his mouth, clinging to her skirt. Seymour and I seemed to notice her at the same time and tipped our hats in unison. Perhaps a little too grandly. She mumbled something to her brood, sniffed at the air, and pushed on.

Seymour sat down again. 'Take a lesson from an old Jew,' he said. 'Forget the culture thing. We Jews, we should've stuck to business. Booze, scrap metal, *shmatte.* The *goyim* would have despised us but they wouldn't have tried to kill us. So don't do it, don't touch their Cultura. Better you let her grow old and brittle in their antiseptic museums.' He turned to watch our dogs run circles and tumble over each other. 'For us Jews it's too late,' he said. 'We fell in love with the bitch.'

November 6, 1991

The call from Doktor Vik came the day the story appeared in the Winnipeg papers, naming three alleged Nazi war criminals, including me. 'You'll need a good lawyer,' he said. 'Don't say anything till you've seen a lawyer. I'll make some inquiries.'

I had already begun to prepare myself for what awaited me. I have a shoebox of papers all carefully preserved – the letters and visas we had been issued in Asunción, the stubs of four airline tickets, my Canadian citizenship certificate and card, issued in 1963 – and the little stone flask that Alvaro, my Guarani friend, had given me when we left Paraguay, that contained the three shrivelled berries, or whatever they were. I remembered how careful he had been not to touch them with his bare hands. '*Schlaechte mensche, em vieht vaech laund,*' he had warned me. '*Miena diena met yaeve.*' One does not need to be stupidly credulous to believe that the Guarani knew how to avail themselves of hallucinogens or poisons, but Alvaro hadn't been clear about their purpose. I spread newspapers on my desk and carefully worked the stopper out of the flask. Three shrivelled berries rolled out. I allowed myself a wry smile that here was my organic cyanide pill if I ever needed it. I rolled them back into the flask, and replaced the stopper.

'Best to leave the Mennonites out of it,' said my lawyer on the morning of my first interrogation by the RCMP, 'And don't go on too long about the Stalinist terror stuff. They've heard it all before. To them it sounds like a confession of guilt.'

'What about my mother?'

'Everybody had a mother. They won't deport you because you abandoned your mother.'

Should I have told him about you, Antoine? The poor man would have groaned at the thought, averted his face and with both hands waved off any such notion. My 'case,' as he sees it, is the too typical story of an ignorant youth in the Soviet hinterland, the victim of one totalitarian regime then another, sucked into a whirlwind of horrors where he has no control over his own fate, his own thoughts or his own actions. But I was not a mindless product of my time and place. I made choices.

In Canada our students are taught that under a totalitarian regime everything is controlled, that the Party organs have a tight hold on everything that happens. A system running like clockwork. Diabolical clock-work, perhaps, but clockwork nonetheless.

That is not how it seemed to us at the time. In my memory, and my lore, almost always things were out of control in the Soviet Union, but certain times were more out of control than others, seemed to be wilfully out of control. During the *Yezhovshchina,* the Great Terror, arrests and executions happened daily, and informing became an epidemic. Day and night furtive figures skulked into local NKVD offices to inform against three or four others lurking in the shadows, waiting their turn. It seemed then as though the fever had to peak before normal, methodical terror could be restored. People now remember only the famous 'Show Trials,' but at the height of the terror, 1937-38, there were 681,692 executions, roughly 1,000 per day, and our villages were awash with rumours. Wher-ever two or three people were seen together they seemed to talk in hushed tones, and when people passed on the street they would turn aside without a greeting.

You were now in your mid-teens, Antoine, almost a young man, and tall enough for my mother and Oma Enns to alter some of my father's clothes to fit you, the wool trousers and puffy pleated shirts he wore when he came back from Germany. The alterations were made on the precious Singer sewing machine my Oma had salvaged from pre-revolu-tionary times, but they could not be made without shedding tears. The alterations were an admission my father would never return. And the clothes that you had outgrown were then altered to fit me.

And soon my sister Sarah began to tease you about the fuzzy dark shadows on your cheeks and above your lip, so on a rainy day in early spring when we had time to ourselves, my mother, with ostentatious ceremony, soaked a cloth in hot water and sat you down at the kitchen table. She told you to hold the hot cloth to your face for five minutes. Then she fetched my father's ceramic shaving mug from the shelf where it still awaited his return, also his shaving brush and razor. She cut a few shavings off a bar of soap into it, poured a little hot water on top, and swished it around until it became foamy. She placed herself behind you while I stood in front of you holding a mirror so you could see exactly what she was doing. She lathered your cheeks and throat, and swished the brush across your mouth, just for fun, to make you splutter. She showed you how to hold the razor, and with her other hand she stretched the skin on your cheek between her thumb and index finger. 'Scrape the razor in the direction the hair is growing,' she said, and demonstrated. I watched, envious and enraptured. 'There, now you're a man, ready to go looking for a bride,' she said when she was done, and we all laughed. Though we knew becoming a man was not a laughing matter.

I was only ten, but I could sense that something bad was happening to us. Women would come to our house, fall into my mother's arms and burst into tears. My mother would set them down beside her on the bed that during the day served as a sofa. They would rock back and forth and weep – while I squirmed in a far corner of the room and tried not to watch. Can I remember now exactly how I felt? I must have felt pity. How could I not? I also felt fear, and anger. These weeping adults were supposed to protect me, feed me, clothe me, give me room to play and grow. When a child is crying you know it will pass. A few kind words, a sweet treat, and the child will soon be laughing again. But when adults cry, publicly, shamelessly, you know the world has spun out of their control. I felt embarrassed to witness their humiliation, and I was relieved when my practical Oma Enns would draw the curtains, set a plate of fresh *tvebak* in front of them and urge them to eat. That made sense to me. I knew from my own experience that you can't eat and cry at the same time.

My Oma understood my need to escape and sent me on an errand – handed me the tall jug and sent me to the dairy to fetch our daily quota of milk and butter. I bolted out the door.

I was in no hurry to get back. I took a roundabout route behind the village, toting my litre of milk and 140 grams of butter. I rounded a corner and came upon a shed for repairing farm machinery. Here I found a group of three men leaning on the fenders of a broken down truck, their heads together, talking in muffled grunts and growls. The front end of the truck was jacked up high but they seemed in no hurry to make repairs. I heard one of them say, in a louder voice, *De varht uk boult uht sien latste loch peepe.*

What? He too will soon be whistling through his last hole? It was said in a tone of grim foreboding but sounded more like gloating over someone's imminent misfortune. I had no idea what it meant, and when they saw me they fell silent and turned their backs.

When I got home I didn't ask my Oma Enns or my mother to explain

it. I went looking for you. I knew where to find you, knew where you
went to distance yourself from the weeping in our house. There was a
haystack that had been fenced off against stray cattle and here you had
made yourself a secluded nest, where you could read the books Comrade
Harder had left you without being distracted. While the whole village
quaked in fear, you seemed fenced off in your own darkness.

'It's just a silly saying, like an old wives' tale,' you said. 'When somebody gets shot, his heart stops, his brain shuts down – but the food in his
stomach keeps on digesting. So his last goodbye to the world is a long,
muffled fart.'

'That's . . . disgusting,' I said.

You laughed. 'Maybe that's the sound of the soul leaving the body,
when it flies up to heaven.' I knew you were teasing me, but I also knew I
had overheard something alarming. *Who* will soon be whistling through
his last hole? Why that guilty silence as soon as they saw me?

'They probably know nothing,' you said. 'Just shooting off their
mouths.'

But then Uncle Knalz and his wife appeared at our house, right at
supper time, and when they declined the offer to join us we knew something was wrong. 'Liese's husband has been taken,' said Uncle Knalz.
'They're holding him in a transit prison in Lindenau.'

'Why? Why him of all people?' gasped my mother. He, a big, gentle,
soft-spoken man, the least likely, one would have thought, to incur
anyone's petty malice.

'Why *not* him,' said Uncle Knalz. As head of the dairy operation, he
could account for every drop of milk from every cow in the stable, but he
knew the director of the *kolkhoz* routinely added water to the milk and
sold the 'surplus' on the *deficit* market. It was no secret, all four workers in
the dairy knew it, said Uncle Knalz, but the director had made them
complicit in his crime by giving them each an extra litre of milk every
week. 'Take it,' he said, 'You all have young children, they need milk.'
When inspectors paid a surprise visit to test the milk for fat content,
someone had to be the scapegoat. The inspectors weren't surprised to
discover Taunte Liese's husband was the son of a criminal, banished in
'29. 'But maybe revenge also had something to do with it,' said Uncle
Knalz.

Revenge? Neither my mother nor my Oma asked him to explain. They closed their eyes and nodded. Not the kind of thing a mother can explain to a child, but my sister Sarah could. She said years ago, before she was married, Taunte Liese also had a nice cushy job in the dairy, and when the director had summoned her to his office and made amorous advances she had slapped his face and bolted from the office. She was then transferred to hard drudgery in the field brigade.

To everyone's surprise, Taunte Liese had become a devoted wife and mother when she married – and he so different from his spritely wife, whom he adored, whose quips and pranks he treasured as though he had known his time was short. And now she went almost every day to the Lindenau transit prison with a small package of food for him – some bread, a slice of ham, and his favourite pepper nuts dipped in egg white and sugar. She waited in line at the prison gate with the other women, all of them anxious for news of their husbands or sons. She said a surly, stone-faced guard at the gate had taken the food, then waved her away. But she had stood her ground, she said. 'It's for my husband. See here, I've written his name. He's a tall man, with a scar under his eye.'

'Yes, yes,' he had said, her husband would get it. 'Yes, all of it. Next!'

Day after day she went, not knowing if her husband was getting the food, or if he was still there in that prison, still alive. Then there was a message from her husband, delivered by the same surly guard. 'He wants a change of clothes – shirt, trousers, underwear.'

Ach, why hadn't she thought of that? She brought the clothes, neatly wrapped up, and more food. The guard took the package and told her to wait.

Wait? She turned to the woman behind her, almost threw her arms around her and kissed her. 'He told me to wait!' she said. The woman nodded. Then a prisoner appeared, apparently one who had privileges. He carried a bundle wrapped in the shirt her husband had worn when they took him. He called out her name and tossed the bundle over the fence. She snatched the bundle, but again stood her ground. She peered left, right, over his shoulders. 'Where is my husband?' she cried.

'Back there,' he growled, 'in a cell, with thirty others. Now shove off.'

She tore open the bundle. Yes, his trousers, his socks, his underwear. Still warm, from the heat of his body. When she got back to our village she came running to our house, to show the clothes to my mother and my Oma Enns. I watched, bewildered, as she held up each item for them to

see, 'See, see? These are his. They're all his. He's still alive.' My mother and
Oma Enns reached out and stroked each item with their own hands,
couldn't help themselves. Taunte Liese pressed handful after handful of
dirty clothes to her face. Yes, yes, her husband's smell.

A week passed and again she took a bundle of clean laundry and
waited to receive the bundle of dirty laundry. Another week, then there
were no more bundles. She came, empty handed, to tell my mother and
Oma Enns. 'He's gone. They won't say where,' she wailed. I cried too,
when I saw the others cry. Taunte Liese had to wait twenty years, till the
Khrushchev Thaw, for the news that her husband had died less than two
years after his arrest. None of us then knew that from Leningrad to
Voronezh, tens of thousands of women like Taunte Liese lined up daily in
front of prison gates begging for news of their husbands or sons, the
famous poet, Anna Akhmatova, among them.

Schoolboys have an uncanny knack for reading the times, however little
they understand them. The poison trickled down and we weren't
immune. Among our older schoolmates there was now something furtive
in their manner instead of their usual sultry bravado. More 're-settlers' in
our villages now, some of them from other Soviet republics, whether
victims or beneficiaries of the 'mixing of nationalities' policy, a policy to
impose a 'unifying' class identity upon 'divisive' ethnic, religious, or
national identities. But imposing a privileged minority upon us was not
unifying. In the schoolyard and on the street there were now fights that
ended in loose teeth and bloody noses. We called them *Russe*, or *Kapusta*,
cabbage eaters, and they called us *kulaks*, but mainly we were just
Germans – Fritz, or *Nyemtzy*. That is how the Great Terror began to
manifest itself among us. We outnumbered the *Russe* but we knew that if
we were drawn into a fight we, and maybe our whole families, would be
punished. The *Russe* knew they wouldn't be. They knew that pranks that
might formerly have earned a stern rebuke were now dismissed with a
wry chuckle.

You didn't fit in, Antoine. You were not a *Nyemetz* like us, nor one of
the *Russe* re-settlers. You remained aloof, you had an aura. You were
resented, but were it not for me they would have kept a wary distance
from you, as though some unspoken taboo shielded you. Me, I didn't have

an aura. I had a big mouth, and I was picked on. Then you would have to come to my aid, wade into the fray, curse them and push them aside. One of them might summon the courage to nip at your heels, then quickly dart back to the safety of the group. 'Oh, you're such a brave little fighter,' said Sarah, 'when you know Antonii will protect you.' Didn't she know I was often picked on *because* I was your friend – that some of the blows I proudly suffered were meant for you?

Grisha was our biggest tormentor, the son of a construction foreman, a born bully and cruel prankster, a tall, fair-haired, foul-mouthed lad with an habitual smirk on his face. He affected a loose-jointed shuffling swagger and spoke in a slow drawl that made everything he said sound like a threat. A big-city boy, from an industrial town just west of the Urals, who used his big-city glamour to collect a gang of rustic disciples around him, sadistic little elves who competed to earn his condescending praise.

The tension on the streets mounted, and whether consciously or not we were all shuffling toward a crisis, as though we were following a script. Grisha and his gang had already heard the story of how you had killed an Uzbek policeman. The story was embellished in each retelling till it became an accepted fact that it was you, not Mary Gordon, who had killed him. I heard Peepche tell his spellbound audience that when the Uzbek fell on his face with your knife in his neck, blood had gushed from his wound, and he lay there with his legs twitching, his mouth open in a silent scream. The eyes of the *Russe benjals* were as big as saucers as they tried to imagine it. Oh yes, Peepche assured them, that Uzbek was already dead when Mary Gordon put another knife in him. This, more than anything else, enhanced your aura. You had actually done it – killed somebody. The rest of us could only fantasize what that must feel like.

You had stayed in practice. You would hide the leather pouch of knives under your jacket and we two would go to the musty old granary beyond the village, long fallen into disuse. We squeezed through the sliding door and waited for our eyes to adjust to the gloom, and for the mice to stop scurrying. I was the only one allowed to watch you. You had found two small cans of paint, one black, one white, and painted an image of Stalin on the planks of one of the massive grain bins – eyes, nose, a black heart, black hair and a big black moustache, just like the gypsy had done, and you threw your knives at him like the gypsy had done. And I would bring playing cards and tack them on the bin, five of them in a row, then you stepped back, exactly seven paces, and skewered each card. You hardly ever missed.

I was keen to show you off to my schoolmates, who would have to be sworn to secrecy, and at last you gave in. 'But no more than four of them,' you said. One of the four was Peepche Panah but he should never have been allowed. He lived in the house next to us, and he and I shared the same desk at school. He wanted to be my friend and sometimes I grudgingly tolerated his company. He was an edgy, fidgety fellow, quite clever but with an insatiable need to ingratiate himself with everyone, with his teacher, with parents, our schoolmates – including the *Russe* – which made him a font of juicy gossip, half of it wildly embellished. We scoffed but couldn't help listening. He had a high squeaky voice, little more than a rasping whisper, which had earned him his nickname, and big pendulous ears pressed against his close-cropped skull. He envied my close friendship with you, and in a generous mood I might let him have snippets of your witty opinions on certain subjects. When he got wind that something was up I tried to put him off, though maybe I was just toying with him. I made him swear, three times, that he would tell absolutely no one what he was about to witness in that granary.

When the first knife stuck in Stalin's forehead, all four of them gasped and were ready to bolt out the door, terrified to witness this ritual enactment of the most dazzling crime they could imagine. Then the eyes, the nose, and his black heart. There was nervous shuffling while I nonchalantly collected the knives and handed them to you. Then I tacked the five playing cards onto a crossbeam, evenly spaced, at eye level. You skewered the first card and startled a mouse out of its lair. It scampered along the beam above the line of cards. Your next knife flew into a plank in front of the mouse's nose. The mouse turned and scampered in the opposite direction. The next knife, and the mouse turned and fled the other way. Again, then again. A brilliant performance, Antoine, better than I could have hoped for.

Three solemn oaths couldn't keep Peepche Panah's mouth shut. Grisha's elves soon heard about your performance in the granary. I heard him describe the mouse trick to those who had missed the first telling, and he exaggerated as usual. He said you had thrown your knives from a distance of ten long paces, maybe more (he demonstrated how long they were), and the last knife had hit the mouse right in the head. Not true, the mouse had escaped through a knothole, but I let Peepche have his moment.

Big-City Grisha, not to be outdone, now regaled his rustic elves with stories of how he and his friends used to deal with certain scum 'back in the city.' One of his favourites was a gay-bashing story, about an effeminate attendant at their athletic club, a former monk who used to swish his mop around their feet when they were taking showers, the better to gawk at their privates. Disgusting, said Grisha. So they lay in wait for him at the little chapel where the monk went secretly to pray every day. They tied ropes around his wrists and ankles and hung him against the door of the chapel, his arms extended, like a crucifix, and then they pelted him with fresh buns of horse shit. They embedded stones in the horse buns, and when they ran out of horse buns they made do with just stones. Until the monk was covered in blood and shit. They left him hanging there, 'like crow bait,' he said. Then, according to Peepche, one of Grisha's elves had said, only half jokingly, 'Maybe we should teach one of our *Nyemtzy* brats a lesson he won't soon forget.'

They were waiting for us, Peepche and me, on our way home after feeding the pigs. It was one of those hot, dog-day August afternoons that seem to cast a spell upon the landscape, seem to smoulder with tension, inching toward a cathartic release. We had to cross a narrow footbridge over a newly dug canal to drain spring runoff to the river, dry at this time of year except for a few pools of greenish slime with flies buzzing around them. No other sign of anything stirring in this heat, not in the village, nor in the fields. They were loitering at the foot of the bridge, in the hot sun, some of them sitting on the railing, some languidly stretching their backs. They pretended not to see us but we could hear their mirthless snickering. 'Here come the *Nyemtzy* pig sloppers.'

They were all bare foot, as were Peepche and I, and because of the heat they had rolled up their baggy trousers to their knees and unbuttoned their shirts. They still wore their caps, tilted back on their heads at a jaunty angle. How can you look menacing in bare feet, with your pants rolled up? There are ways. The way you shuffle your feet, lock your fingers together and bend them back till the joints crack, a furtive side-ways glance. Peepche and I tried to step around them but they blocked

our way. They began jeering and jabbing at our chests. '*Nyemtzy* pig sloppers!' 'Goody goody God-believers!'

'I don't believe in God,' mumbled Peepche.

'I do,' I said. I don't know what I believed, but Peepche's cowardly
denial disgusted me.

'Then you better start praying,' laughed Grisha.

His elves chimed in. 'Yeah, let's hear you pray! In your stupid *Nyemtzy*
language.'

They weren't interested in Peepche. They let him run away. They
formed a circle around me, one of them gave me a push and I staggered
into the arms of another, who pushed me into the arms of a third. All
around the circle. Laughing. Pray! Pray! Then someone tripped me and
put his foot on my back while another kicked dirt in my face. 'You
praying yet? You little *Nyemtzy* shit!'

I did not curse and scream. I kicked and flailed and struggled to my
feet. They knocked me down again, kicked at my legs and arms. Then
they dragged me behind an abandoned dilapidated horse stable. Grisha
himself had stood back and let his elves have their way with me, but now
he took charge. While his elves held me propped against the wall of the
stable, he bound my feet with lengths of frayed harness, then bound each
of my wrists and fed the leather straps through rusty hooks that had been
screwed into the wall to hang bridles and horse collars. I continued to
kick and flail but by now it was only a token struggle. They pulled tight
on the straps until I was a crucified Y, though my feet could still touch the
ground.

The back of the stable was hidden from the village, but news must
have spread among the other *Russe* that something was afoot. They poked
their heads around the corner, then crept closer. A few of them were girls.
Horse buns littered the ground, none of them very fresh but good for
throwing, and there were also pebbles that could be embedded in them.
Grisha threw the first horse bun. It splattered on my chest. Then the elves
threw their first volley. Now I did scream and curse. Cowards! Cocksuck-
ers! Stinking *kapusta*!

'Hold it, boys,' shouted Grisha to his elves, 'Let me shut this *Nyemtzy*
prick's big mouth.' He approached me with a fresh horse bun in his hand.
He put his other hand under my jaw and tried to pry my mouth open.

Then, 'Stop!' Your voice, Antoine. Peepche had run to fetch you, and now you elbowed your way through the line of elves, with your quiver of knives slung over your shoulder, poised to throw the first knife. You sighted along your raised left arm, your right arm, holding the knife, cocked behind your ear.

Grisha turned and instinctively ducked when he saw the knife. Then he put a twitchy sneer on his face. 'Your little friend here is too mouthy for his own good,' he said. He watched you for a moment. You lowered your arm. He turned back to me and tried again to pry my mouth open.

Then thunk. The knife stuck in the boards just above Grisha's head, and close enough to my head that I could hear it hum like a tuning fork.

'You gone crazy?' shouted Grisha, and made a dash along the wall. Thunk. The second knife just in front of his nose. He turned and darted back, to use me for a shield. Thunk. Then he turned to face you, his back to the wall. He pressed his hands against the wall to steady himself, spread his fingers wide as though grasping for an opening he could squeeze through.

You lowered your arm, shuffled your feet and took a deep breath. Again you took aim, sighting along the length of your left arm. And then a dark stain crept down Grisha's trouser leg. 'Oh look, look,' gasped one of the girls, 'he's peeing his pants.'

Grisha slowly slumped to the ground and lay in a foetal position, clutching his groin and whimpering. You cut me down where I hung on the wall and gave Grisha a kick on the sole of his foot. 'Beat it,' you said. He scrambled to his feet and ran. Then you collected your knives.

My eyes were fixed on you but you said nothing. You jerked your knives out of the boards and slotted them back into the pouch. You seemed disgusted by this squalid village spectacle, and disgusted that you had been drawn into it. Angry at me too, for my part in it. Had I failed to play the role demanded of me? After you cut me down, should I have yanked a knife out of the boards and plunged it into Grisha's neck, as Mary Gordon had done to that drunk Uzbek?

Grisha's elves had all run away but a few others now cautiously drew closer. 'Go home,' you said, and they turned and slunk away, looking over their shoulders. Except Sarah. I hadn't seen her till then. Perhaps she had arrived only in time to see the end. You were about to retrieve your last knife when she ducked in front of you and flattened her back against the wall, and with her eyes fixed on you she pressed her cheek against the knife embedded in the wood. 'Can you save me?' she said. 'From what?' you said. 'From . . . from all this,' she said, and flung her arm at the whole scene before her. You yanked the knife out of the wood, slotted it into the pouch, then turned and walked away, across the footbridge and up the track toward the sunflower field, the stalks now bare and brown, the flowers all gone to seed. I waited for a signal that I should follow you, but none came. You shouldn't have abandoned me there, Antoine.

Sarah said, 'We better go home and get you out of those shitty clothes.' She nudged me along in front of her, with her fingertips on my back just below my neck. I don't know if she was worried I would suddenly bolt or if she thought I would find the pressure of her fingertips reassuring. We skirted the village through the fields, avoiding the street. She took me behind our house and told me to take off my shirt. My mother wasn't home, only Oma Enns. She poked her head around the corner, wiping her hands on her apron. 'What happened?' she said.

'He fell into the pig sty,' said Sarah, then she went into the house. Oma followed. 'Did somebody push him?' Sarah mumbled a reply but I couldn't hear what it was. I took off my shirt and threw it aside. I felt faint. I tottered, fell to my knees, lurched forward on all fours, and puked. Sarah returned with a basin of water, some soap, an old wash rag and a clean shirt. 'O my God,' she said, when she saw me heaving over a small puddle of vomit. 'Get up,' she said. 'Clean yourself up, then put on this shirt.' She turned and left. I don't know where.

I washed the slime off myself and put on the shirt Sarah had brought me, then I slunk away, to the granary where you had practised your knife throwing. I don't know if I hoped to find you there or hoped not to. For all I knew, you were already on the run, making your escape. I squeezed through the door. You weren't there, only that cartoonish figure of Stalin painted on the grain bin. Because of the many knives you had thrown into his eyes one of them seemed shut, as though he were winking. I looked for something to throw at him. Found a length of rusty chain and threw it. Picked it up and whipped it across his face, then slumped down on the floor and sat there shaking.

My mother was setting the table and Oma Enns was fussing over a kettle when I came home. Sarah was sitting on her cot, sewing a button on a blouse. She was often sullen and withdrawn so her mood had not alarmed my mother. My mood did. 'What's wrong?' she said. I looked at

Sarah. She didn't look up. 'Nothing,' I said. Then you came home. We all watched you. You went to your usual place by the window, picked up a book and pretended to read. 'When you three are ready to tell me, I'll listen,' said my mother.

We ate supper in silence, and after supper my mother and Oma Enns rose from the table and began clearing the dishes. Then I blurted it out, in fits and starts. My mother stared at you as though she were afraid of you, Antoine. She staggered back until she bumped into the table. She groped for the edge of the table to steady herself. She shook her head and her mouth began to move but no words came out. She inched her way toward Sarah, who was helping Oma Enns wash the dishes. 'Why didn't you stop him,' she hissed. 'I'm not their mother,' said Sarah, and my mother slapped her. The only time she slapped either of us. I ran and placed myself between them. 'It's not our fault,' I said, 'The *Russe* wanted to kill me.'

My mother embraced us. Sarah submitted to the embrace, I returned it. My mother would have embraced you too, Antoine, if you hadn't quietly slipped outside.

Your days among us were now numbered, though they had probably been numbered anyway. You were almost a young man, fifteen years old, too old to be let off with a scolding for your 'bad attitude.' After the sun went down Uncle Knalz appeared at our door with his grain wagon, with its high racks so people couldn't see what was inside it. 'Lads his age have been banished for less,' he said. 'He's old enough to wield a pick and shovel.' He said either Kaethler or a gang of *Russe* toughs would soon be coming for you, so for now you should be hidden in a secluded cottage across the river, where one of his old herdsmen now lived. You should stay there till he found someone in another *volost* who would take you in. You stuffed some clothes and a book into your backpack, then scrambled over the high racks of the wagon and lay flat on your back.

Kommissar Kaethler and the two goons he kept for his private use appeared early the next morning. Kaethler was unarmed, but the two goons had pistols stuffed under their belts. They stood a few paces back, their arms akimbo. My mother went out to them and closed the door behind her, and though they spoke in even, measured tones, we could hear them.

'You can't have him. He's not here,' she said.

Kaethler tried to speak softly, averted his eyes, looked down at the ground. He tried to play good cop while the goons behind him played bad cop. 'If I don't take him the *Russe* will take him,' he said, 'Then you'll find him lying face down in a ditch somewhere.'

My mother said nothing. 'I could arrest you too,' he said, 'for harbouring a criminal.'

'But you won't.'

'Why wouldn't I?'

'Why haven't you?'

There was a pause. 'You better watch yourself,' he said, in a louder, angry voice. 'You, you and . . . you're pushin' your luck.' We heard footsteps, retreating. My mother came in, quickly closed the door and staggered to a chair. She covered her face and gasped for breath.

Mary Gordon saved you. For almost five years there had been no word from her, now here she was, come to take you 'home' to Germany. She arrived in a black official motor car, accompanied by a paunchy GPU agent, her personal escort, to clear away any obstacles a local official might throw her way. She treated him with needless rudeness, we thought. When he presumed to follow her into our house she ordered him back. Told him to wait in the car.

Her appearance was hardly less dramatic than when she had first appeared out of a blinding blizzard. She wore an elegant tweed jacket, a matching skirt, and a huge hat on her head with feathers and foliage, the height of fashion in the West, we assumed. She stepped through the door and scanned the room. 'Where is Antonii?' she said.

'*Och,* my poor baby,' she cried, when my mother and Oma Enns explained what had happened, and why you were in hiding. She raged not only against the whole tribe of filthy Russian savages but also against my mother for failing in her duty. I was sent to tell Uncle Knalz to hitch up his cart and fetch you, from the cottage where you had been hiding for two weeks.

I couldn't bear to go back home to wait with the others, in the same room with Mary Gordon, so I waited at the edge of the village. When the horse and cart finally came into view I ran to meet you. You sat dangling your legs over the back of the cart and I clambered up beside you. 'It's Mary Gordon! Mary Gordon! She's here,' I whispered. But you knew that already. You smiled, and put your arm around my shoulder. 'She said she'd come back for me. And now she has,' you said. I wanted to say, 'Please don't let her take you away,' but I didn't.

You stepped through the door and stopped. No one spoke while you and Mary Gordon took in the sight of each other. She held out her arms and began to sway and moan. You took a few tentative steps toward her, then you fell into each other's arms.

I averted my eyes. All of us in that room averted our eyes.

When she was done blubbering and marvelling at how much you had grown, she pulled a sheaf of official papers out of her bag and waved them triumphantly in your face. 'Here, look,' she cried, 'Proof that you're a German citizen. And here, train tickets, all the way home, to Dresden. 'All arranged. Diplomatic channels, with a little grease from your grandfather's *Reichsmark*. Everything on the up an' up.'

Yes, your mother was alive, in Dresden, in her father's home, waiting. But she couldn't come herself. Not well. Not quite right in the head, after all that had happened.

What *had* happened?

Och, terrible, terrible. Only in rare lucid moments could your mother tell the horrors she had endured. Interrogated, tortured, stuffed into a little cell with twenty other people, just one tin bucket to pee and shit in. Taken from one prison to another, then released when they saw she'd lost her mind. That was in '31 or '32. She had wandered around the port of Odessa, sleeping in doorways. Did what women have to do to stay alive. Till she was rescued.

How? By whom? we wanted to know.

By a German ship, the *Wallenstein*. She had learned the details after she returned to Germany and was shown the captain's report. There were always ships in the harbour, all kinds, from many countries, she said. The wharves clogged with people trying to get out, and soldiers beating them back behind a wire mesh fence. Inside the fence a group of sailors and Russian soldiers were laughing and talking, doing business. The sailors have schnapps and tobacco to trade, Swiss watches and fancy leather gloves. The soldiers have brass samovars they stole from rich people, and those little *matryoshka* dolls – you know, one doll inside the other, the kind sailors like to take home for their *Fräuleins*. And one Russian soldier has a flute he wants to trade. He offers it to a sailor. The sailor puts it to his mouth and plays a few trills. He plays German songs – folksongs and *Liebeslieder*. The sailors clap their hands and sing along, the Russians laugh and stomp their feet. More people now, outside the high wire fence, mostly women, said Mary Gordon, who also want to make business. Then your mother gets some people to help her climb over the fence and onto the flat roof of a small guard house on the inside. She starts singing, whatever song the sailor is playing. *O du lieber Augustin,* or something. She had a good strong voice, said Mary Gordon, she took lessons when she was at school.

For a moment the soldiers are stunned. Then they come running, shouting and pointing their guns up at her. She rips open her blouse and dares them to shoot, but it's bad luck to shoot a mad woman. She throws herself down on the muzzles of their guns, or would have done if they hadn't caught her in their arms. Now the sailor plays a merry tune on his flute and she grabs a soldier and starts to dance. She wraps her arms around him, leers up at him and licks the barrel of his gun. People on both sides of the fence are watching, laughing and clapping their hands. She grabs a German sailor, puts his cap on her own head and waltzes him around. Then another. And then there's a German officer, who's been watching from the ship. Who heard her sing. He comes down the gangplank, takes her arm and twirls her around, looks over his shoulder at the Red Army soldiers and winks, then waltzes her up the gangplank into the ship. The soldiers let her go. She's just a whore. When he's done with her he'll throw her back.

I risked a furtive glance at you, Antoine. This is not the kind of story one wants to hear about one's mother. My mother, Oma Enns and Uncle Knalz stared at the floor. We were embarrassed that you had to hear Mary Gordon's lurid account. She might have spared you that, but you gave no sign that you were shocked. Perhaps you saw what we didn't – that your mad mother had been brave.

Then there's a blast on the ship's horn, said Mary Gordon, and the sailors scramble up the gang plank with their Russian dolls and samovars. The ship slips her moorings and churns out of the harbour, with your mother still aboard. They took her to Constantinople and handed her over to a refugee organization, along with the Captain's report. Who? Moravians or something. When your mother became lucid enough to tell them she had family in Dresden, they sent a letter to her father. He came and took her home, then he wrote to Mary Gordon, still in Scotland, to come and take care of his daughter. 'Och, to see her now! You'd never know her,' she said. 'But the child belongs home, with his mother.'

'He has a mother here too,' said Groote Graeta. 'Let the lad choose.'

So you chose, and who could begrudge your choice. You escaped, while I languished in Russia. You packed your belongings into a small schoolbag, and then there were tears and hugs. My mother gave you my father's shaving kit, 'Something to remember us by,' she said. I can't remember if I cried when you and Mary Gordon got into the back of the black motorcar or if I did all my crying after you had left. All I remember is that you gave me a hug and said, 'Maybe we'll see each other again, someday.' I nodded, but I had little hope of that. Who could imagine, then, that only five years later the Germans would invade, two more years and we would all be fleeing out of Russia, and that I would find you again among the ruins of Berlin, living with assorted riff-raff in a musty, windowless basement under the mess hall of McNair Barracks. And who could have guessed it would then be me, a foundling dropped on your doorstep.

LIBERATED

November 11, 1991

On this day Canadians observe Remembrance Day, to honour those who died in both World Wars. They wear red poppies pinned to their lapels, and observe two minutes of silence at 11:00 AM. I would gladly do the same, but my townsmen would now find it offensive to see someone under investigation for war crimes wearing a poppy.

When the German *Wehrmacht* invaded the Soviet Union on June 22, 1941, I was fifteen years old and I thrilled to the news. For me they came in the nick of time. I had reached the age when I could see too clearly the bleak future that stretched before me. Yes, there had been half a dozen lads in our villages who grovelled and pandered to be admitted to the Technical Institute in Krivoy Rog, but how could I grovel, shamed by your image peering over my shoulder whenever I looked in the mirror? So I smouldered in silent rage. While my teachers groomed a chosen few of my classmates for brilliant careers I, the son of a criminal, was destined for a life of drudgery on the *kolkhoz,* or worse. The invasion put an end to two decades of communism. Who could doubt it, in 1941?

Now that Seymour and I must avoid each other I come to the park when my dog Butzie and I can expect to be alone. I come even in inclement weather when sensible people have found shelter indoors, and

I have only the trees for company. They are not offended by my presence among them, take no notice of me, rustling their leaves in hushed confab with one another. Toward the river stands a grove of tall cottonwoods, nearer, along the path, a row of ancient oaks planted long ago by homesick settlers from Ontario. As the day wanes, dark clouds gather above the trees but in the west the setting sun breaks through a narrow slit above the horizon. The low, slanting rays catch the undersides of the cottonwoods and set the shimmering leaves ablaze, a million little flames bobbing every which way in the breeze. The oaks hardly move at all. Their boughs slowly rise and fall, their leaves, some big as a man's hand, keep their orientation to the sky, their deeper green in contrast to the pale metallic sheen of the cottonwoods. To look at the old oaks you'd think there was no wind at all, the boughs simply nodding of their own accord, aloof, composed. The cottonwoods spread rumours of a coming storm, the oaks remain unmoved. They are older, wiser, but the cottonwoods are taller, and can see further. One counsels calm repose, the other trembling urgency.

But what do I know of trees, me, an ignorant native of the treeless steppe, a novice necromancer conjuring with tree leaves and finding there, predictably, an echo of my own mood. Change the mood and you change the message. Perhaps the leaves of the cottonwoods are not trembling but dancing. Ecstatic heralds of change proclaiming a plunge in the barometer, the thrill of an electric summer storm after a long dusty drought. 'Come, come quick,' they urge, 'there are changes in the air. Get up, get up! Preparations must be made, new positions taken. From our topmost branches we can see new worlds trembling to be born, new tablets waiting to be written.'

'Stay calm,' growl the ancient oaks. 'A minor disturbance in the lower stratosphere, to swirl the dust around and tickle the nose. A few clowns and tumblers to work the crowd before the main event, the usual carnival barkers gulling the local rubes to get in on the next big thing. Not yet, the deluge. When the great winds come, when the continents of electric air roll over us, there'll be no asking the lightning's pardon or the wood's permission. You will hear us crack, cry havoc, hear the roar of giant limbs torn from our trunks, see our trunks wrenched from the soil, see us throw our roots in the air, leaving behind us holes huge as bomb craters, and in the sky a gaping void where once was sheltering shade.'

But in the summer of 1941 there were no wise oaks to caution me, and I was deaf to other voices.

Imagine then, Antoine, a glorious dawn in that first week of September, 1941. An epic dawn ripe with the promise of great deeds, rising out of the fabled East and scattering the indignant night before it. Invincible dawn, in its westward rush across the great continent – a tidal wave of light, cresting above the dark hulk of the Greater Khingan Range then loping across the Mongolian Plateau, over Ulan-Ude then skimming across the ripples of the unfathomable lake. Foiled for a moment by the granite mass of the Tien Shan, a blaze of refracted light leaping from peak to snow-capped peak, then tumbling into the twilit valleys where the shining minarets of Tashkent and Samarkand rise to greet it, *Allahu akbar.* Stirred to life the sooty tractor works of Stalingrad, then sprawled across the flood plains of the Volga, chirped along by choruses of birds, and found us at last in our sleepy villages near the Dnieper. Paused here a moment to tickle us under our chins like a playful courtesan, then waltzed across the Ukrainian steppe and licked an advancing army in the face.

Such a dawn as seldom was before or since, all rosy fingered, a few clouds but just for show, just to bring out the colours, the deep reds and golds. And there we are, Antoine, we three conspirators, three young *Helden,* marching single file on a narrow path across the yawning steppe, breathing hard now because of the unrelenting pace, the warmth of the rising sun on our steaming backs pressing us onward.

Having got an early start and having walked five kilometres along a creek bed to avoid detection, hidden by rushes and overhanging willows, we are now on the open steppe. Me, the oldest and the keenest, now in my fifteenth year and setting a gruelling pace. A knapsack on my back, a long pole in my hand like a shepherd's staff. Our destination is a derelict windmill another five kilometres westward, already dimly visible on a height of land, the skeletons of three of its four vanes drooping sheepishly from their hub. Still an imposing four-storey wooden hulk, at least eight metres wide at its base, almost twenty metres to the tip of its domed crown. One of many such structures whose massive stones once ground the bounty of the Ukrainian steppe, now deemed too primitive to grind modern Soviet wheat.

When we were mere children we had been warned many times by

our mothers against these derelict windmills. Their rotting timbers and rotting floors that once held tons of wheat and barley had been known to fail now under the weight of a heavy rat. The famous story, in fact, was of a two-legged rat, a brigade leader who used his power as purveyor of privileges to entice young women to his high hideaway in the mill's loft (not here but in a neighbouring *volost*), that he had furnished with a feather bed under a canopy of silk curtains like an Arab chieftain's tent, and stocked with Georgian wines and Turkish delicacies. Here he entertained certain ladies from the *kolkhoz* while naughty children hid in the nearby shrubbery to mimic their moans of pleasure. And one hot, humid afternoon the brigade leader's lovemaking had become so ardent, his piston thrusts so vigorous, that the rotten floor joists could not hold the lovers and they came crashing down, down through three floors of cascading planks and timbers, engulfed in a cloud of dust. The children in the shrubbery scattered in all directions and returned with mothers and fathers to behold the scene, saw feathers still fluttering in the air, saw the red and turquoise silks caught on rusty nails as though pleading to be released from their embarrassment, and saw the lovers, still entwined where they had fallen, skewered on the truncated shaft of the main mill stone, 'like a pair of Easter lambs,' said Uncle Knalz.

But what use are mothers' warnings to three young *Helden* determined to save their village from destruction? What alarm can rotten joists inspire when every day, day after day, for two months now, our ears had burned with tales of the advance of the mighty German *Wehrmacht*? June 29, the fortress of Brest-Litovsk fallen, bombed to skeletal ruins. June 30, Lvov captured, but not before the NKVD units burned down the Brygidki prison and killed 4,000 Ukrainian nationalists and intellectuals. Closer and closer. Smolensk, August 5. Coming our way, Army Group South, funnelled between the Pripet Marshes to the north and the Carpathian Mountains to the south. By August 18 the Germans had reached Chortiza where we had aunts and uncles and cousins, another week and they had crossed the Dnieper, their panzer units fanning to the south and east.

And day by day the Soviet evacuations grew more frantic. East, move everything east. Men, cattle, official records, heavy cast-iron safes, east across the Dnieper, then across the Volga, where they would be safe from the invading Germans. Wagon loads of personal files and dossiers in sealed boxes, then the artillery, tanks and half-tracks, and long columns of Red Army infantry, all moving east, to safety.

The last to go were the cattle and horses. A great cattle drive, hundreds of them, beef and dairy cattle, rounded up from every pasture in the *volost,* to be driven east, to stockyards where some would be slaughtered and the rest loaded onto trains to take them beyond the reach of the invading Germans. I remember men on horseback shouting and cursing, boys with switches running after strays, a wild braying, and tractors pulling wagon loads of feed, wheezing and backfiring because of the low-grade fuel. Uncle Knalz seemed overwhelmed by his duties as leader of the livestock brigade, gathering the herds and cramming them into holding pens that kept breaking down. He himself did not look like much of a horseman, his loose-limbed torso sloshing around in the saddle, and the gang of young ruffians in his charge had even less control of their skittish mounts. These youths were the *lumpen* of the *kolkhoz,* the good-for-nothings, spurned and ridiculed by the other brigade leaders and therefore devoted to Uncle Knalz who had taken them on and treated them as though they were his proud Cossack tribesmen. In the middle of the night, in a brutal winter blizzard, they would saddle up at his urging to go in search of a stray calf, but now they seemed to gallop in all directions at once, scattering more cows into the ravines and marshes than they gathered, while Uncle Knalz, in frustration, bellowed contradictory commands at them.

Onward then, we three conspirators, westward, our backs steaming with sweat in the cool morning air, me in the lead, behind me my new friend Franz Willms, the fittest and most athletic among us, always eager for an adventure, and bringing up the rear is Brumtup – still my loyal friend here in Canada – complaining about the exhausting pace and the blister on his heel, but only because he knew his complaining would amuse us.

After Mary Gordon took you away I was left behind to stumble into adolescence and manhood without you. Those were heady times – the German invasion and the occupation of our villages – and it took a long time for me to make new friends. I disdained the company of lads my age, and when Franz began to take an interest in me I rudely rebuffed him, as I had others, but he was too unaccustomed to rebuff to feel the sting. It only made me the more interesting to him, an odd duck. He was an affable lad, good at sports and always up for a dare. He seemed content to regard himself as a big dumbo, and stood in awe of people who were 'smart.' And then Brumtup began to take an interest in me too, though it did not at first seem like a friendly interest. While Franz was delighted by my displays of cleverness, Brumtup grudgingly endured them, took every opportunity to deflate my pretensions, but he would have been disappointed if I had not provided so many opportunities.

'What will happen when the Germans come,' I had asked Uncle Knalz. 'Who knows?' he said, 'It's war. Anything could happen.'

Yes, but what? My Uncle Knalz, who normally needed no coaxing to sift through an endless array of possibilities seemed strangely unforthcoming. From others we had heard about the fate of a Ukrainian town east of the Old Colony, where the Soviet garrison had packed up and fled across the river, leaving the defence of the town to a dozen frightened local militia who had fired a few rounds at the first sign of German panzers, then threw their rifles down a well and hid in the cellars. So the Germans had turned their artillery on the town and blasted the walls out from under the sagging roofs, then the infantry picked off the survivors running through the fields. In another village people had drawn the shutters and locked themselves tight in their houses while the panzers stood ready in the street, and soldiers went door to door shouting '*Raus! Raus! Hände hoch!*' 'Fools,' said my Uncle Knalz, breaking his silence. 'They should have lined up along the street in full view, not cowered in their houses. It would have been another *Blumenkrieg,* like in the Sudetenland.'

And so night after night we had slipped out of our beds as soon as everyone was asleep, tiptoed out of the house on bare feet, to meet in that abandoned granary where you had practised throwing your knives, Antoine, and here we stitched and hammered by candle light and laid in whatever supplies we thought we would need.

The windmill once had a loading stage skirting its base but it had long rotted away or been dismantled for firewood, and now a dense tangle of hawthorn shrubs and brambles had grown up around the mill, to a height of six or eight feet. Franz was the first to scramble up and stick his head inside the mill, Brumtup and I followed. The main floor was littered with old machinery and storage bins. 'Check if anyone's hiding in there,' whispered Brumtup. 'Hallo!' bellowed Franz. Brumtup winced. The idea, he grumped, was not to declare *our* presence but to discover *theirs*. Too late now.

I pointed up to the third storey of the mill, formerly the sack loft, 'That's where we have to be,' I said. Inside the mill a fixed ladder went straight up, and from our perspective it looked dauntingly high. More-over, some of the rungs were missing, and others were loose. Brumtup said we could see well enough from the main floor, no need to climb up there. Yes there is, I said. Not only did we need to see, we needed to *be* seen. Franz started up the ladder, then he stopped and looked at the palm of his hand. Bird shit. We looked up and saw where swallows had made their nests high in the rafters. So? A little shit won't hurt us, I said. We know shit. We have to clean out cow shit and pig shit every day, I said.

'Bird shit's worse,' said Franz.

'Shit is shit,' I said, 'keep going.' Franz gripped the next rung where the shit was at least dry and hard. 'Franz is right,' said Brumtup, 'Bird shit is worse. It's because they don't pee. It all comes out the same hole, shit an' pee mixed together. It's like acid. It can etch a pane of glass, burn a hole right through your skin.' Franz looked at his hand and stepped down. 'You first,' he said.

When I got to the top, I threw down the rope and pulled up our gear. Franz and Brumtup followed without undue grumbling. From the loft a double door opened onto a narrow platform, like a balcony but without a rail, and above it a wooden boom projected over the edge, a rusty pulley still dangling from the end of it. The platform was supported by massive struts from below and it seemed rigid enough to hold the weight of three boys.

The view to the northwest was perfect. The road, little more than two wagon tracks, stretched to the northwest for three or four kilometres before it disappeared behind a ridge. We found some loose planks inside the mill and placed them over the gaps in the platform, and unpacked our gear to be handy when we needed it. Quite pleased with ourselves, we sat down on the platform to have our snack, leaning our backs against the wall of the mill, except for Franz who dangled his legs over the edge.

We tried to guess how many there would be when they came. Surely at least thirty or forty tanks, then a long column of foot soldiers, I thought. But Franz thought there wouldn't be any foot soldiers at all, they'd all come in troop carriers. The Germans had a modern army, he said, not a ragtag outfit like the Soviets. Then we saw a German Stuka circling in the sky, and for a few moments we were afraid it might drop bombs on our villages. But it flew away again. Just a reconnaissance plane, we knowingly surmised, but another sure sign that the *Wehrmacht* couldn't be far behind.

For the first time I asked Franz what time it was. Quarter past eight. We knew the Germans had already crossed the Dnieper at Zaporozhye, and by now they could have covered at least a hundred kilometres. 'What time is it now?' I asked. Quarter to nine. Franz had his father's pocket watch, bequeathed to him, the oldest son, on the night they came to take his father, slipped down the back of his shirt under cover of a hug. 'Soon you'll be the head of the family,' he had whispered. 'Take good care of them.' Franz could draw the watch from his pocket by hooking his thumb under the chain, then run the chain between thumb and index finger, palm the watch and flick open the cover, all in one easy motion. Then he would tilt his head to one side to study the hands for a moment before he snapped the cover shut again.

We waited. Though the sun was higher in the sky, the platform was still in the shade and we were getting cold, because of our sweat-soaked shirts. It must have been about then that I felt the first sickening doubt. What if the Germans don't come. What if they circle to the south and advance toward Berdyansk on the Black Sea? What if they have changed their minds again and turned north toward Moscow? Uncle Knalz and his cronies had pored over old maps going back to Napoleon's day and concluded that this is where the Germans would come. The *Führer* was too clever to repeat Napoleon's mistake, they said. But what if they were wrong? What if we were found by an NKVD patrol? Two young militiamen from Perchib had been caught deserting to the Germans and were promptly shot.

Then Franz said he was going inside, out of the wind. Brumtup stayed with me for a while but then he too got cold and went inside. Now I was left alone with my doubts. An image flashed through my mind of us returning to our village after holding out here for two or three days, hungry, dirty and defeated, and called upon to explain our absence. How ridiculous we would look. Worse than being apprehended by local militia.

I stared hard at the horizon, willing the Germans to appear. There *had* been signs, clear signs that they were near. Some of them alarmingly clear. August 29. A detachment of Red Army soldiers had rumbled into our village. They ordered all the men to assemble and told them they had an hour to pack a small kit and say their farewells. What? Where? Why? For how long? *'Smert nyemetskim okkupantam!'* they snarled. Death to all German collaborators. They took all the men between 16 and 60, to join the train loads of *Volksdeutche* already on their way to Siberia, before they had a chance to collaborate. Only a few brigade leaders and other 'necessary personnel' were spared. Like Uncle Knalz and a few of his 'Cossacks,' still busy herding cattle.

Other signs. The raid on the commissary. Groote Graeta could be dramatic but she was not, normally, foolhardy. Later, sitting at our kitchen table, still panting, sipping the tea my mother had made to calm her down, she said she didn't know what had come over her, what had pushed her 'over the edge,' *aeva yeschnapt.* And all because of a wagonload of pots and pans. But such things happen in moments of uncertainty.

The commissary was a squat concrete structure with two small barred windows and a pair of heavy steel doors, with a padlock the size of a thick social-realist novel. Inside was a wagonload of the People's pots and pans. High quality pots and pans. Soviet manufacture could not make a pen nib that did not splatter ink, or a watch that did not gain or lose half an hour a day, but somewhere near the Urals there was a factory that produced some of the finest enamel cookware in the world, comparable to the best of France and Germany. Normally they were 'sold' at absurdly low prices, though only to deserving comrades. But of late Kommissar Kaethler had been hoarding them, secretly, though the secret was well known. They had been packed and crated, ready to accompany the Kaethlers on their flight east.

Ridiculous? In the frantic scramble to move everything east, documents, livestock, people, is it conceivable that the Kaethlers would fret about pots and pans falling into German hands? Yes, it is. Uncle Knalz had it figured out in a minute. In the coming chaos it would be every man for himself. In 1941 few people had any doubt that the German invasion would put an end to communism, put an end to the Soviet Union, and woe to all who had not been clever enough to make preparations. This hoard of pots and pans, said Uncle Knalz, would be Kaethler's 'capital,' to launch his new career as a businessman.

'Outrageous! Over my dead body!' cried Groote Graeta – as though there had not been worse outrages. She marched to the machine shop at the far end of the village and returned carrying a heavy crowbar. And now some of our women fell in behind her. By the time she reached the commissary there were at least thirty women in her wake. Frau Kommissar Kaethler ran to the commissary and placed herself in front of the steel doors to bar their way. She scowled and shouted threats but when thirty angry faces drew nearer she fell silent. She pressed her back against the steel doors and peered up at Groote Graeta, not scowling now but pleading. Eyes that had always darted pure hate at Groote Graeta now lolled in their sockets, 'like amoebas in a Petri dish,' she said. 'It made you want to grab her face in your fist and pull it off.' She elbowed Frau Kommissar aside and smashed the padlock.

'Come, comrades, come! Pots for everybody!' she cried, while she attacked the crates of cookware with her crowbar. She put a big red pot on her head, its lacquered handle sticking straight out from her forehead, ('Like a big red-headed woodpecker,' recalled Taunte Liese). She began thrusting armfuls of pots into the arms of the laughing women. 'Ooooeee,' she yelped, 'Feel the heft of these pots, comrades. That's quality! Real Soviet quality! Imagine, comrades, your watered-down beet borsht simmering in luxury in these beautiful pots.'

Had Uncle Knalz been there he might have tried to prevent the foolhardy action of these women, but neither he nor his 'Cossacks' had been seen for days. Still driving the People's cows eastward to the stockyards. Kommissar Kaethler was also nowhere to be seen. Neither were his two goons. They had already deserted him. There were still four or five local militia in the village, with guns, and they could have fired on the women, killed some and dispersed the rest. Instead, they elbowed their way through the melee and helped themselves to as many pots and pans as their arms could hold.

Before noon the next day the Kaethlers left the village, without their 'capital,' yet with as much dignity as they could muster, riding in a droshke like gentry, their lackey stiffly perched on the high seat in front of them and their two children clinging to them on either side. Going east. People lined the street to see them off, first in stony silence, then jeering, louder and louder. The driver held the horses to a stately walk, then broke into a trot, then he whipped them into a gallop. My mother too was there, not jeering but silent, standing with her fists clenched by her sides like a soldier standing at attention, looking straight ahead and breathing rapidly through clenched teeth, and as the droshke passed she reached down, grabbed a handful of dirt and flung it at the Kaethlers. A vain gesture. The wind swirled the dirt away and Kaethler probably hadn't even noticed.

That was the last of the communist administration in our villages, we thought. Only us left now, women and children and a few old men. But it was not the last. Another Red Army detachment, a dozen soldiers, in battle gear, under the command of a big mangy sergeant with ammunition belts and grenades hanging all over him like diseased fruit, which clattered and rattled with his every move. They came at a gallop, firing their guns in the air. 'One hour!' they shouted, one hour to pack a small kit of provisions. What kind of provisions? 'Don't matter. Where you're going none of your stuff's any use. Ha, ha.'

They had already taken most of the men, aged 16 to 60, and now the rest of us were to be 'evacuated.' Whole colonies of ethnic Germans west of us, *Volksdeutsche,* had already been loaded into trains and shipped east to Siberia, but time was running out. We had hoped we might be spared. Must I tell you, Antoine, that the same thing was happening even in my beloved Canada at about this time? It happened with less cruelty, but also with less reason – thousands of Japanese farmers and fishermen on our west coast 'evacuated' and resettled in the remote interior of British Columbia. Why not? Canada, like Russia, has vast, cold, empty spaces – always a convenient solution when dealing with 'troublesome nationalities.'

So once more to the Lichtenau train station, but it took much longer than an hour to assemble us, over two hundred of us, old women, mothers carrying their babies, and no horses and wagons left in our villages. It was near midnight before we left, near dawn before we got to the Lichtenau station, and as the sun rose it was a strange sight that greeted us. A small cluster of people huddled on the station platform, about fifty of them, some still wrapped in blankets, others stretching their legs after a difficult night, many of them people we knew. They told us there had been no room for them on the train that had left the day before, a long train, already crammed with about a thousand people. They told us the names of the villages of the people on that train. We knew those villages. My mother's sister and her children were on that train. They were never heard from again.

The train that now stood waiting to take us somewhere in Siberia was a short little train, the locomotive hissing and wheezing impatiently, and a grimy brakeman ducked in and out between the cars with his hammer and his grease gun. The sergeant and his men got busy dividing us into four columns, ready for boarding, but then the station master himself appeared on the platform, looking very officious. He looked us over, studied his clipboard, cursed and scowled. He was an older man, only recently appointed to his job, but some of our people said they knew him. A Hero of the Revolution. A big red star pinned to his uniform. He affected an aloof, officious manner, in contrast to the swaggering sergeant.

How many of us were there exactly, he now demanded of the sergeant.

'Didn't count 'em,' said the sergeant. 'This is all there was, the whole village.'

'Have to report how many,' said the station master. 'Need an exact count.'

Blyads. Count 'em when they get to Siberia.' He kept an eye on the western horizon, checking for evidence of Germans.

Nyet. Gotta count 'em. Somebody might take a bribe and let some escape.'

More *blyads* from the sergeant. A quick wipe of his nose. He takes offence at this insult to his men's honesty. But a Hero of the Revolution is not a man to be trifled with. And he, the stationmaster, will not be bullied by this swaggering, farcical warrior. So they count.

After half an hour, there's an argument.

'This group's been counted.'

'No it hasn't.'

'Has so.'

'Hasn't.'

Blyads. They have to start over again.

All counted, finally. 286 of us, including the children. 'Too many. Not enough cars,' said the stationmaster.

'How not enough? There are six cars. That's enough.'

'No, there are only four.'

'*Blyads.* How, four? There are six! Look! One. Two. Three. Four. Five. Six. Six cars!'

'Two are reserved for military personnel.'

'*What* military personnel?' The sergeant gestured in all directions so that the stationmaster could see for himself. 'Look. All gone. Us is all that's left. Load 'em in!' he ordered.

His men start waving their guns at us and shouting.

'Then you'll have to leave the horses,' said the station master.

In addition to their own mounts, there were four horses loaded with heavy packs. Some of the loot was in bottles. You could hear clinking when a horse shifted its weight.

'The horses go with us,' snarled the sergeant.

'Anyway, it don't matter. We got no engineer,' said the stationmaster.

'How, no engineer! Look, the locomotive's running. Ready to go.'

'The fireman got it running. The engineer's drunk. Somebody gave him four bottles of vodka for a comrade at the front. Drank it all himself. He's in the baggage room, sprawled on the floor like a wet mop.'

'*Blyads.* So let the fireman drive the bloody train!'

'Doesn't know how. Not qualified.'

'Just pull back on the fuckin' lever. Full steam ahead.'

'Which lever? There are four.'

'The big one.'

'That's the brake.'

The sergeant spat.

We had watched this exchange in bewilderment, shifting our eyes from one face to the other. Children were crying, old women keening. 'Shut up!' shouted the sergeant. 'Start loading!' he ordered his men.

'Better load the horses first,' said the station master.

That made sense. The sergeant looked around and spotted a group of us older boys, standing and gawking. 'Move that cattle chute up here,' he ordered. We dragged a chute over to the first box car. In spite of our best efforts we damaged it. The repairs took time because we didn't have the right tools. Then the horses, with their packs, couldn't get up the chute. '*Blyads.* Unload the packs.'

A crate fell to the ground and smashed. '*Blyads!*'

All loaded, at last, both the packs and the horses. '*Khorosho*! Now put that water on board,' ordered the sergeant. He pointed to a row of casks.

'Empty,' said the station master, 'Used it all for the boiler.'

'So where do we get water?'

The station master shrugged.

'We gotta have water,' said the sergeant.

'They got no water either,' said the station master, pointing at us.

'That scum don't matter. But horses need water.'

The telephone rang. The stationmaster made a dash for it. *'Da . . . Da . . . Nyet . . . Otyebis!'*

'What now?'

'German panzers. Moving south from Zaporozhye.'

'Blyads!' The sergeant charged at the row of casks, kicked them and shook them, to confirm there was indeed no water in them.

The stationmaster calmly lit his pipe. He beckoned to a young lad and told him to spread the word that we should all move back at least thirty metres from the tracks and the station. Why? Never mind why. If only Uncle Knalz were here, but he and his cowboys were still driving cattle across the steppe. Groote Graeta said we should do as we were told.

We weren't bored while we waited. In the western sky, a dog fight between Soviet and German fighter planes. Maybe a kilometre away, but close enough for us to hear the roaring of the engines and the gun fire. We saw them pitch and dive and circle, and watched some of them spiral down to earth and explode.

Then the telephone rang. We could hear the station master through the open door. *'Da . . . Da . . . Da.'* Slam. He burst from his office, on the run. 'Forget about this scum,' he shouted to the sergeant, 'This train's been reassigned. Military transport.' He unlocked the luggage room and ordered the engineer to get the train going. He shuffled obediently to the front of the train and climbed into the locomotive, with a little help from the brakeman. Within a minute the train began to move. The sergeant glanced once more toward the west, one last swipe of his nose, and fired a volley over our heads into the western sky. Satisfied now that he had done his duty, he ran and scrambled aboard the train, and his men after him. The stationmaster and the brakeman placed the explosives, then they too ran and jumped onto the back of the train. The tracks blew up, the station caught fire, and we stood gaping at the flames, the twisted rails, and the train retreating in the distance.

God bless you, brave stationmaster, more than worthy of your red star.

I poked my head through the doorway of the windmill and looked at my sleeping companions curled up on the floor. They had found some dusty old burlap sacks and made themselves a bed. I wanted to apologize for something but I wasn't sure what, so I returned to my solitary watch on the platform. No Germans. Only endless fields of brown stubble and burnt grass. A rusty old thrashing machine lay abandoned in a creek bed. No sound but the buzzing of flies and now and then the stupid chirp of a bird. Tears welled up in my eyes.

A pair of swallows had been swooping in and out through the doorway all morning. I had hardly noticed them, but now they infuriated me, with their smug twittering. One perched on the rusty pulley above the door and defecated. I jumped to my feet, grabbed my long staff and swatted at him. Missed. Then he and his mate flew back into the mill loft, almost grazing the top of my head, and I charged in after them, batting at them like a mad dervish, cursing and flailing while they swooped and dodged. I found their nest and smashed it to pieces, a heap of ash-gray clay and egg shells. I charged after the birds again, 'Hroot! Hroot!' I yelled. Franz and Brumtup were sitting up now, holding their arms up to shield their heads, ducking and bobbing to avoid the panic flight of the swallows and my flailing pole. I flailed and whirled, and at last drove the swallows out the door. Then quickly, quickly I heaved the double doors shut, propped my staff against them, and slumped to the floor panting and tried not to sob. 'Have you gone crazy?' said Brumtup. 'Shut up,' I said. 'What's going on?' said Franz, not to me but to Brumtup. 'He's gone nuts,' he said. 'He's like that Don Quixote guy, fighting windmills.' They turned their backs to me and lay down again. I was still breathing hard but three sleepless nights demanded their due and soon I too fell asleep.

When the rumble of engines and tank treads woke us they were almost upon us. We burst through the double doors shouting 'Hurrah, Deutschland! Sieg Heil!' – me waving my staff with the homemade swastika attached to it, Brumtup and Franz unfurling their bed sheet with 'Wilkommen in Russland' stitched onto it in red lettering. I vaguely remember a convoy of about ten tanks, then a line of troop carriers, perhaps six or seven, then half a dozen motorcycles, one or two with side-cars, then an open car with four men in it, the sun glinting off the visors of their caps, and then a closed car. They all stopped at once and I remember the gun turrets of all the tanks in unison swinging round on us and men pouring out of the troop carriers, falling to one knee and aiming their rifles. I remember the buzz and crackle of wood chips flying around us, and then there was a roar and we fell.

The first volley from the guns of the infantrymen took out the rotten struts supporting the platform and spilled us over the edge into the hawthorn shrubs below. I remember a sensation like slipping on ice, then I remember nothing until I looked out through the tangled growth and saw beady eyes squinting at me along the sights of guns. I struggled to disentangle myself and get my feet under me while people were shouting something in barely intelligible Russian, as though from a great distance, though their mouths were only a few feet from me. I crawled out and looked up at a semicircle of muzzles pointing at my head. Franz was already sitting on the ground to my right, at the centre of another semi-circle of muzzles, his hands up in surrender, a little sheepish grin on his face. He was covered in blood, his shirt torn to tatters by the hawthorns. I heard a high pitched scream of pain, and saw two soldiers dragging Brumtup out of the shrubbery. They placed him at the centre of a third semicircle of muzzles, and he glowered up at them with a Churchillian scowl. He too was covered in blood. Only now did I begin to notice my own blood and my own pain. In a hoarse whisper I said, 'Wilkommen in Russland,' but no one paid attention. Men were coming out of the mill and one of them went to a soldier wearing a particularly tall cap, who was not carrying a gun, and reported, 'Nobody in there. Just these three.'

The one in the tall cap approached me and demanded, in mangled Russian, 'Who sent you here? Where are the others?'

'There's only us,' I replied in German, and tried again, 'Wilkommen in Russland.'

'Sprichts du Deutsch?'

'Natürlich.' I became indignant now. Not fair, that they should treat us like this, we who were Germans just like them, and had no thought but to welcome them, our liberators. No need for all this shouting and shooting.

'You're Germans? All three of you?' said Tall Cap.

'Do we sound like Chinese?' said Brumtup.

We explained who we were and what we had been about, presenting as evidence our swastika and the tattered banner we had stitched together, and explained there were only women left in the village, and a few old men, and everyone waiting for the Germans to come and save them from the Bolsheviks. We described in detail how all the Russian troops and officials had fled the village days ago. We hammered it up, exaggerating their panic for the amusement of these German soldiers.

Tall Cap shook his head and chuckled, as though there were no end to the absurd twists in this war. Then he said we were *'wirklich drei brave Buben.'* Had we not intercepted them they would most certainly have shelled our village, expecting it to be desperately defended. Yes, we were brave lads indeed.

Brumtup's injuries were the worst, an ugly gash in his thigh and some broken ribs. Franz also had a broken rib and a few bruises, and I had a broken wrist. Now Tall Cap politely introduced himself, 'Captain von Niessen,' followed by a bunch of numbers and mumbo jumbo identifying his company and regiment. Then one after another we told him our names, and Franz had the presence of mind to salute the Captain. I was embarrassed that I had not done so too.

Nun, what to do with us? They could leave us here and carry on and then send some of our own people from the village to fetch us. Or they could take us with them. 'Yes, yes,' we argued, 'Take us with you,' but the Captain demurred and muttered something about a Geneva convention which forbade the use of civilian shields. He bent down and tried to examine Brumtup's injuries. 'Can you walk?' he asked.

'Of course I can walk,' said Brumtup, 'I walked all the way from the village.' The Captain paused, tried to rephrase the question, then threw his head back and laughed.

Authority came easily to the Captain. Had he given us his name in full aristocratic regalia it would have been Friedrich Parcival Alexander von Niessen. He was a poster-boy Nazi, in his late twenties, pure Saxon from an old military family, tall, blond and blue eyed. His orders were given casually, almost musingly, but obeyed with alacrity. He was a little astigmatic, his one flaw, and therefore he kept a pair of granny glasses in a leather pouch clipped to his belt, which he used for rhetorical effect, to add either gravity or levity. With a sheaf of papers in one hand he could so nuance his fumbling as he mounted the glasses on the tip of his nose that his men knew what followed would be either serious business or, more often, mere *quatch* that he was duty-bound to bore them with.

When he was handed a sheaf of morale-boosting press reports from Berlin he let the glasses rest a little lower on his nose, shuffled through the papers at arm's length, and sighed. '*Nun, was erzählt uns der Onkel Adolf heute?*' Then he would quote a few sonorous phrases, and hand the papers back to his lieutenant, while he looked the other way.

His lieutenant bore more resemblance to Hollywood Nazis in the 1950s. He was a short-legged, stocky man, his shoulders hunched up and his chin tucked in, and because of his short legs he always seemed to be in a hurry, and always quick to click his heels and *Sieg-Heil*. He had an unfortunate tick that made him look as though he were smacking his lips, out of distaste, not relish. He seemed aware that his manner amused the Captain but he neither resented this nor pandered to it, content to allow officers from the privileged classes their eccentricities, knowing that an officer of his own class had to set a better example.

Nor did he now sulk noticeably when Captain von Niessen ordered him to ride in the second car to make room for Brumtup and me in the open car. Because of our injuries, the Captain explained. Franz decided he wanted to ride in the sidecar of one of the motorcycles, a BMW R-75 (when I play bridge I can't remember what's trump, but I can remember that). The Captain tried to dissuade him, it would be very bumpy, he said, 'With your broken rib you won't be happy there.' But Franz was determined. They put Brumtup on the back seat of the open car, between the Captain and the medic, and I quickly climbed up behind Brumtup and sat on the folds of the canvas top, my legs straddling Brumtup's shoulders. The Captain declared he had swallowed enough of the dust raised by the tanks and troop carriers and ordered his driver to lead the way, followed by Franz and his driver. And so it was that we rode into our village in triumph, at the head of the most powerful army in the world.

We entered the village from the south. The street was deserted, but in front of every house huddled a small cluster of women and children, all of them quiet and motionless. Were they now prisoners of the Germans, or would they be told they were now free, under the protection of the *Reich*? Then we could see the women crane their necks, begin to whisper to each other, and point. We held off, gave no sign, stared straight ahead. But at last we couldn't contain ourselves. We waved.

When we reached the abandoned Soviet offices in the centre of the village we were mobbed. Even my sister came through. She pushed her way through the crowd and shouted 'Bravo Struvel,' then gave me a hug.

The next day the medic came to each of our houses to check on our injuries. He was accompanied by the Captain, who corroborated our stories and congratulated our mothers for bringing such brave *Helden* into the world. He told our story much as we had told it ourselves, but when he described how we had burst onto the platform waving our swastika and Welcome banner, he said, 'They looked like those little figures that pop out of Bavarian cuckoo clocks.' We could have done without that.

The Captain charmed everyone. The women told him their many woes, and he assured them that just as soon as this Russian campaign was over they would search the furthest reaches of Siberia and all their menfolk would be returned to them, if they were still alive. We of course spoke High German to him, not our slangy Low German which he wouldn't understand. He marvelled how, way out here on the Russian steppe, we had managed to keep our German customs and language intact, and declared our German was far more *echt* than the mongrel dialects one heard nowadays in the Rhineland, for example, and even in his own Saxony. A polite lie, certainly, since even our High German was peppered with Russian and Ukrainian phrases, and a few remnants of Dutch. And since we had rarely heard or spoken High German except when we read the Bible, High German being our equivalent of Church Latin, our High German had a rather orotund cadence, like someone today speaking King James English on the street. But we allowed ourselves to be flattered.

Then a sudden alarm. A cloud of dust – on the eastern horizon, beyond a low ridge. The kind of cloud that might be raised by a large troop movement. The Captain scanned the horizon through his field glasses. 'What's happened to our air support?' he snarled. He gave orders that sent men scrambling and within seconds there was the roar of engines as tanks and artillery moved into a defensive position. He ordered his men to prepare to evacuate the village, then dispatched two motorcyclists to have a look.

'Cattle,' they reported, when they returned. 'Just cattle. A whole bunch of cattle.'

A thin dark line appeared along the crest of the ridge and got wider and wider. Then we saw the horsemen on the flanks of the herd, and a single horseman in front. Franz snatched the field classes that the Captain had set down and climbed onto the cab of one of the troop carriers. It seemed to take forever to get the focus right. 'It's Uncle Knalz!' he shouted, 'and Sasha . . . and Vitya . . . and the other Sasha . . . and . . .' And then he was drowned out by cheers and excited babble. The Captain remained alert, but then our relief and merriment overcame his suspicions. He issued more orders and then tanks and trucks again revved their engines and began to move about as though they had been choreographed, until they were all lined up facing each other across the wide street. And in front of each column stood a row of infantrymen, ordered by a burly moustachioed sergeant to 'Present arms.' The Captain, with his lieutenant by his side, took his position at the end of the column, in the middle of the street in front of his 'command post,' Kaethler's former office.

As the herd approached the outriders got busy. A sharp whistle here, the crack of a whip there, and two hundred head of cattle obediently formed a narrow column and funnelled down the street between the rows of tanks and infantrymen, Uncle Knalz at their head. He lolled rhythmically in the saddle while our people cheered and waved, all of which he disdained to acknowledge. When he came to within a few feet of the Captain he held up his hand and the whole procession came to a halt. He straightened in the saddle, briskly saluted the Captain, and introduced himself: 'Cornelius K. Reimer, sir, at your command.' Then in a slightly lower voice, 'K for Klaassen on the *mutta kaunt*.'

The Captain slapped his heels together and returned the salute. His lieutenant watched him out of the corner of his eye, his lips twitching, then he snapped his head around, eyes front, jerked his right arm into the air and shouted, 'Heil Hitler!'

Uncle Knalz squinted at him, blinked, then turned in his saddle to look over his shoulder as though he half expected to see the *Führer* himself standing behind him. It was the first time any of us had seen the Hitler salute. It looked a bit odd, but we young lads soon got the hang of it.

For us, this first wave of the Occupation in our villages quickly became the new normal. Except for one intrusion of the old normal. Two foot-weary figures appeared on the road from the east, stooped under the weight of luggage, and followed by two smaller figures. People stopped what they were doing and came to get a better look. Uncle Knalz ordered one of his Cossacks to hitch up a cart and go fetch them. Somebody informed the Captain and he too came to have a look, but he shrugged his shoulders and returned to his quarters.

Yes, them. Kommissar Kaethler and his family. Some of us had heard of Hitler's *Kommissar Erlass* ordering the execution of all 'political commissars,' and yet here were the Kaethlers, wilfully putting themselves into the hands of the Germans. Perhaps no one denounced them because we were struck dumb by their presumption. Now was the moment when we could have raised our fists and screamed for their blood. But the moment was lost. Perhaps we assumed the Captain would take the required action without any of us getting Kaethler's blood on our hands. Perhaps we were embarrassed to act like a lynch mob in front of these *korrekt* German officers.

Before the cart had stopped Frau Kommissar began to wail how much they had suffered since their escape from the Russians.

From the Russians? Of course. Their driver, clever scoundrel, tried to hold them hostage, she said. Took them to the home of his brother-in-law, and held them there in a filthy basement, stinking of rotten cabbage and dirty diapers. He demanded their money, threatened to turn them over to the NKVD. Robbed them blind, then threw them out with nothing but the clothes on their backs. Walking, two days and two nights. And now, praise God, they were safely in the capable hands of our German liberators.

They were anxious to make their report to the *Herr Kommandant* himself. A young corporal in the Signal Corp had been present, and we later heard him mimicking Frau Kommissar's performance to amuse his comrades. *Ach,* how they had struggled, all those years, to protect us Germans from the worst cruelties of the Bolsheviks. *Ach,* you know, how it was with us here, *Herr Kapitan.* Had it not been for her clever husband, God only knows what we Germans here would have suffered. Hundreds of lives he saved. *Ach,* the sleepless nights, in constant fear of informers – about the dangerous game they were playing.

Such is the power of the imagination in times of crisis that when the Kaethlers had finished their story they probably believed it themselves. How much of it did the Captain believe? At the end of their audience with him, he asked them which was their house. They proudly pointed across the street, to the biggest house in the village, and then, a little too late, tried to restrain their pride. Regrettably, said the Captain, that house would be requisitioned for the Major General and his staff who would be arriving. They would have to find accommodation elsewhere. 'I'm sure you understand,' he said.

'But of course, *Herr Kapitan*, we understand perfectly. We are honoured to be of service to the *Reich*. Just give us an hour or two to get the house cleaned up and comfortable for the *Herr General*.' Permission granted, they hurried to their house to give it a quick 'cleaning.' Out went the posters of heroic workers and other Party paraphernalia. Down came the portraits with the big moustache, up went a portrait with the little moustache. And behind the house rose a small column of smoke, solemn evidence of their purifying zeal.

They were survivors, the Kaethlers, always a positive attitude. Soon sentiment in the village turned from gloating horror at their imminent execution to anger at the Captain's apparent indifference. '*Guten Morgen, Herr Kapitan*,' trilled Frau Kommissar, when she brought him his lunch, a steaming pot of real German Schweinshaxe and sauerkraut. Kommissar Kaethler himself rarely set foot outside his little cottage.

November 18, 1991

For us young lads the movement of troops through our villages provided an exciting spectacle, a mixture of roaring engines, barking orders, and awesome efficiency. More tanks, more artillery, and the *Luftwaffe* zigzagging across the sky overhead. Some of the officers were quartered in our village, some in neighbouring villages, and nearby a large tent encampment was constructed with amazing speed, all the tents in neat rows, mess halls at one end, latrines at the other. We were the regimental pets, Franz, Brumtup and I. We picked up the soldiers' slang and peppered our speech with it, and when our elders had no idea what we were talking about we rolled our eyes at each other, astounded at their ignorance. I remember waking to the hubbub of the camp, the young privates and corporals perched on camp stools in front of their tents, shaving, a hundred little round mirrors glinting in the morning sun, the men shirtless in spite of the chill in the air. Brumtup, Franz and I exploited our privileged status as we strolled among these confident, athletic young corporals, chatting with them as though we were now on equal terms. Some of them even let us hold their rifles in our own hands, and we assured them they were far superior to the rifles used by the Red Army. And back in the village, during the slow winding down of the evening, some of the officers would stroll along the wide street, making polite conversation with the women, and one of them would put his big cap on the head of a six-year old child and laugh when all you could see was a little chin protruding under the visor. It was so cute.

After three weeks Army Group South, under the command of *Generalfeldmarschall* Gerd von Rundstedt, broke camp and moved on. Three million men, 600,000 vehicles, 7,184 guns and 3,580 tanks, onward, toward greater victories. Who could have doubted it?

On that last day, when the last of Captain von Niessen's company were leaving our village, a day of shouting and dust and roaring engines, I lurked in front of his command post, hoping to catch his attention. I saw him come out of his office and hand a packet to a soldier on a motorcycle. Then he returned to his office. I moved into the centre of the street, and hesitated. Again the door opened and he came out. He hailed another soldier, gave an order. Still the same, casual efficiency, in spite of all the shouting and excitement. Then he saw me, smiled and waved me into his office. He put his arm around my shoulder and told me he was glad I had dropped by to say good-bye. He recalled our windmill adventure, shook his head at how narrowly we had escaped, and again repeated that it was a brave thing we had done. But I hadn't come to get a pat on the back for my bravery. He still had some unfinished business here, I said.

And what was that?

The Kaethlers. Surely he had not believed their preposterous story.

The Captain slumped into his chair and began rubbing his eyes. He believed them, he said, and would continue to believe them until someone denounced them. Then he would have them shot. 'Are you here to make a denunciation?'

I fumbled for words.

Then the Captain unsnapped the pouch at his belt, took out his granny glasses, and with a sweep of his arm landed them on the tip of his nose. He snapped open his briefcase, and when he found the official form he was looking for, he slapped it down in front of me. 'Here. Sit down. Write out your denunciation in your own words, and sign it.'

I sat down. Why was he angry at *me*? 'If I denounce them they will be shot?'

'Those are the *Führer's* orders. I'll have your denunciation signed by two witnesses, then they'll be shot.'

A fierce German eagle was engraved at the top of the form, then a paragraph of military mumbo jumbo. I picked up the pen and printed my name in the first blank space. I looked at it, it stared back. It was my name, yet something alien and grizzly about it now. I looked up and glared at the Captain. I began printing Kaethler's name in the next blank space, but I couldn't go on. My hand hovered over the form, but it wouldn't write. I started up from my chair and threw the pen down on his desk, splattering ink all over the official form. Then I bolted for the door.

'Sit down!' barked the Captain.

I approached his desk but I didn't sit down. I stood with fists clenched at my side. The Captain took off his granny glasses and leaned across the desk on his elbows. Again he rubbed his eyes with both hands. He said, 'You're not the first, to demand Kaethler be shot.' He said he knew Kaethler was a Party thug, and yes, if he had followed the *Führer's* orders to the letter he would have ordered both Kaethler and his wife to be shot, and their two children deported to Germany to work in a munitions factory. But Kaethler was now a defanged, cowering dog, in fear for his own life. And he'd be damned, he said, if he'd give that *Schwein* the power to rob him of even five minutes of sleep, by shooting him. But I needn't worry that Kaethler would get off scot-free, he said. After his company had moved out, the Occupation forces would move in, including the *SS* units. 'They don't worry about losing sleep.'

He said I did right to refuse to sign. 'Before this war is over we will all have to do things that disgust us. What you learned here today,' he said, 'will give you courage later – when somebody orders you to do something dishonourable.' Then he held out his hand. I hesitated, but I shook it. I thought that would be the last time I would ever see him.

While Army Group South continued its relentless push east and north toward disaster in Stalingrad, we were invaded by a smaller army of *SS* and Nazi civilian administrators whose duty was to get our villages back on a 'solid economic footing,' i.e., to supply the German troops.

So did we collaborate? Hell yes, we collaborated. Even the livestock collaborated. Skinny old cows capered like calves in the meadows, then clenched their teeth and squeezed out one more litre of milk for the *Reich*. Horses neighed their happiness into the cool, crisp morning then stepped nimbly into their traces like schoolgirls into a new frock. Roosters, who only yesterday had scorned their dowdy coop of Collective hens, now crowed approval to their blushing harem, and even the surly sheep took care to lose not a wisp of wool on a bramble bush.

While the *SS Sonderkommandos* got busy in the rear, ferreting out old commissars and Party *apparatchiks,* and installing their own administrations, we in our Molotchna villages were kept busy with practical matters, like repairing the machinery needed to bring in what was left of the harvest. The Germans also sent us *agronoms* and *Gebiets Landschaftführer* to bring us up to date with modern agricultural practices, and they sent us grave old school inspectors to get our schools up and running, provided new textbooks to replace our old Soviet textbooks. And they began taking inventories of the assets of the *kolkhoz* so they could, in good time, be returned to private hands in an equitable manner. The commander of the unit in our village was now *Sturmbannführer* Rösler, a capable administrator but with none of Captain von Niessen's glamour. Franz, Brumtup and I were no longer the regimental pets, we were annoying pests. Our fun now was to mimic Rösler and flaunt our disdain for his pompous officiousness. Not a real soldier, this Rösler, just an official in uniform. What insufferable show-offs we were.

Then Doktor Karl Stumpp arrived, with his troop of young bespectacled research assistants. Doktor Stumpp, the world famous professor of ethnography, *the* expert on the history of *Volksdeutsche* in Russia and the Ukraine. For twenty-four years he and his assistants had been excluded from the Soviet republics, but now at last they could resume their research, and document the survival of German culture and language among us, in spite of decades of repression. His knowledge of the other 'nationalities' in the region – Jews, for example – was also invaluable to the Ministry for Occupied Eastern Territories.

One of Doktor Stumpp's first projects was to set up a *Sonderkommission* to compile the *Einbürgerungslisten,* to officially register us as bona fide Germans. He had prepared a long, detailed questionnaire, and while the siege of Leningrad was nearing its hundredth day and masses of tanks and artillery were gathering near Stalingrad, Doktor Stumpp's young assistants went from family to family to help us fill out the long form correctly, tracing our lineage through five or six generations to an ancestor in the *Reich.* The young student who came to our house did not take his job very seriously, but my Oma Enns was keen to demonstrate she was indeed *echt deutsch.* In fact, until the Bolsheviks had put an end to letter writing, she had corresponded regularly with a cousin in Hanover, she said. Or was it Hamburg? No, Hanover. Definitely Hanover. And there was also another cousin, a Heinrichs daughter. And a niece, Louise, married to a Stolzfuss. Good family. Merchants. Living in Frankfurt now. Ach, what street was it? Bahnhof Strasse, or something.

'Which Frankfurt? – *am Main* or *an der Oder?*'

There are two? Oh yes, she remembers. Frankfurt am Main. Wasn't far from Berlin.

'Then it must be Frankfurt an der Oder.'

Ach, schon gut! Put down *an der Oder!*

Which was done. Niece: Stolzfuss, Louise. Bahnhof Strasse, Frankfurt an der Oder.

'That Doktor Stumpp, he's an enthusiast,' said Uncle Knalz, 'Always on the go, always smiling, going from *volost* to *volost* with his little troop of assistants.' He disappointed me, Uncle Knalz did. He didn't seem to have caught the Herr Doktor's enthusiasm.

At the rallies in our *volost* – and in the neighbouring *volosts* where there were large German settlements – Doktor Stumpp played a prominent role. These were usually open-air events, on a sports field or football pitch, and when we heard there would be a rally near Ohrlof, I knew we had to be there – my two chums and I, Franz and Brumtup. I pretended to be disdainful, as I imagined you would have been, Antoine, but I was giddy with excitement. Franz needed no persuading, Brumtup only a little. I explained that as the duly acclaimed heroes of the windmill action we were obliged to make an appearance. We got an early start on foot, then hitched rides from others going to the rally.

There were hundreds of us crowded in front of a hastily constructed stage, about fifteen metres wide, festooned with flags and banners. A dozen dignitaries sat on the stage on either side of the podium, all of them in uniforms of one sort or another, and behind them stood a school choir, sixty or seventy voices strong, most of them our age or a little younger. About a hundred troops marched onto the sports field from a nearby camp, preceded by a colour guard and a twelve-piece brass band. An officer barked loud commands, 'Eyes left!' 'Eyes right!' 'Halt!' 'Present arms!' etc., and then the choir burst into the *Deutschlandlied*. *'Deutschland, Deutschland, über alles.'* When they got to the third stanza, the conductor turned to the crowd, a signal for us to sing along. Some people sang, a few didn't. I sang. With gusto. Franz sang with even more gusto. Brumtup barely moved his lips. He turned left and right to search the faces of others standing near him, as though he were puzzled by this outburst of *Vaterland* fervour from the mouths of people normally averse to such displays. Franz was being Franz, Brumtup was Brumtup, but you were there too, Antoine, in my mind's eye. Over and over I had imagined the delirious passion that must have seized you, wherever you were, when you woke up to the news that June morning, the glorious news that Germany had invaded the Soviet Union. It would be the one event that might shatter your ironic detachment. And yet, I couldn't imagine you singing along beside me. Couldn't imagine you even silently moving your lips. You might have smiled at my boyish enthusiasm, and allowed yourself a moment to gloat that communism had now been routed, but you would have remained aloof from this shoddy spectacle.

Yes, I knew that. But it made me sing with all the more fervour. I looked around (out of the corner of my eye) to see who else was or wasn't there, and saw others doing the same – a trick honed by twenty years of Soviet watchfulness. Since all the men 16 to 60 had been schlepped to Siberia, they were mostly women and older men, and youngsters like us. Groote Graeta and Taunte Liese weren't there, neither was my mother. She had disapproved of my going but what could she say? Remember who you are? That no longer carried much weight. I still wanted to be good but my former notions of good now seemed childish – mere wallowing in filial piety. Being good should have an edge to it, should challenge approval, should fearlessly fly its colours. And being aloof had never come naturally to me. I wanted to be in the thick of it. I wanted to 'make a difference,' as parents in Canada now encourage their teenage children to do.

Uncle Knalz wasn't at the rally either, though he'd been personally invited by *Sturmbannführer* Rösler a week before notices of the rally were posted. I overheard him tell my mother how Rösler had put a confiding arm on his shoulder and said he understood how important it was for a man of his standing in the community to set an example. He had even hinted Uncle Knalz might be offered a chair on the stage among the other dignitaries. But Uncle Knalz had politely declined the offer. He had explained that these *Volksdeutche* Mennonites were deeply grateful to the Germans, but many were avowed pacifists who might look askance at a man in his position participating in a military spectacle.

He had expected Rösler to curse him, and remind him there were people in Germany who had been imprisoned for the crime of pacifism. But Rösler seemed stunned. Then he tried to be understanding – as though Uncle Knalz had confessed an embarrassing medical condition to him, a prostate or bladder problem, that required quick access to an outhouse to avoid peeing his pants. They both laughed, he and my mother, but I didn't see the humour.

After the *Deutschlandlied* came a formal, unctuous welcome from Rösler, followed by the 'Horst Wessel' song. Then Doktor Stumpp stepped to the podium. He said he didn't need to tell us that Europe's intellectuals and politicians had woefully misled their own people, had made them blind or indifferent to our suffering under the communist yoke. Those bourgeois democracies – England, France – now stood revealed in their true colours, allied against us. 'Not enemies of Soviet communism, but bedfellows!' he thundered. One country, one alone, had routed the communists from its own lands. One country, only one, possessed the military might and the moral resolve to come to our aid. This we all knew, he said. 'Wolves in sheep's clothing, those bourgeois liberals. That is how they emasculate a whole people. Drug them with material goods and sham freedoms, lure them into debt, then into servitude.'

'*Ja, ja, so ist das,*' he sighed, 'Bourgeois individualism, that leering, seductive enemy of the *Volk*, the virus that gnaws at our heroic traditions, at the grandeur of our arts and culture, that threatens to reduce the *Volk* to bovine passivity. These masticating, self-made, self-proclaimed, self-deluded liberal individualists – for whom mounting their females and stuffing their stomachs is an acceptable destiny. What can they do but look to their left and their right, then return to their grazing, smug in the conviction they have made a *free choice*.'

He paused a moment to let us absorb the scandal. 'Oh no,' he said, '*so geht das nicht, meine Lieben*. Only with the strong hind legs of the *Volk* can one leap to greatness.'

But *Lebensraum*, that's what the *Reich* required, and these vast steppes of Russia and the Ukraine would provide *Lebensraum* for a thousand years. He had been present himself, said Doktor Stumpp, standing right next to the *Führer* when he revealed his plan for the future of these Eastern Territories. It was a moving moment, he said. Tears, *ja, ja, tatsächlich*, tears had come to the *Führer's* eyes. 'Eastward. Eastward in Russia lie the fertile plains which shall nourish the sturdy sons and daughters of the *Reich*,' he had said. 'The steppe will become one of the loveliest gardens in the world, where twenty million Germans will till the rich fields and reap the bountiful harvests.' And when the *Führer* had finished there wasn't a dry eye in the hall.

The dignitaries on the stage leapt to their feet and Heil-Hitlered but Doktor Stumpp wasn't finished. He said the *Führer's* plan had already been brilliantly set out by *Obergruppenführer* Richard Walther Darré, *Reichsminister für Ernährung und Landwirtschaft*. You would know him, Antoine – an expat Argentinean German, like you – a man with a vision, who had once stared long and sorrowfully at the virgin *pampas* and the indolent *mestizos* scratching a living upon them, mere savages who passively endured their allotted time on earth before their bodies were again returned to it, both they and the *pampas* little changed since the retreat of the ice age. *Ach*, if only one could install free, industrious German *Bauern* on those *pampas!* Alas, not possible, not for generations. But on the Russian steppe, yes! In his mind's eye the future *Reichsminister* saw our Russian steppe teeming with proud Nordic yeomen, a sturdy *Bauernstand*, 'the life source of the Nordic race.'

'It is all written right here,' cried our Doktor Stumpp, holding a copy of the *Völkischer Beobachter* high above his head, spread between his hands for all of us to see. Then he read:

Out of this Nordic yeomanry grew that moral standard which measures the deeds of free men according to their faithfulness to the land, not to standards of individual self-interest. These are the true bearers of a healthy Völkisch legacy, the fountain of youth from which again and again a whole People draws its vitality. Throughout the ages in the lands conquered by these Nordic yeomen, through their ur-alt traditions and land laws, they have upheld the values of Blut und Boden, a free yeomanry against the unhealthy predominance of the cities.

The good Doktor could have stopped here. Our own imaginations supplied the rest – thousands of little Hänzchen and Heidies in *Lederhosen* and blond braids, gambolling in the fields, and our more bashful Paetjes and Tientjes among them, the golden stalks of whiskered wheat as tall as themselves. And in the afterglow of a lingering sunset the *Bauer* and his *Hausfrau*, resting on their stoop, would feel, hear, smell the long-suffering steppe stir to renewed life, and feel the same vital stirrings in themselves. And as night settles on weary limbs made light by fruitful work, the distant sound of laughter and singing wafts up from the river where young lads and lasses make exquisite their aching desires.

Oh yes, yes. Here, from our little corner of the endless steppe we would feed the whole *Reich*, the whole world, bounty beyond bounds. That is how it would be. No, no. Not just how it *would* be, how it once *had* been and would be again. We were *it*. *We* were this free, vital yeomanry, and had been for generations before the Bolsheviks all but destroyed us. We were *here* already, the living embodiment of the *Führer's* great vision. This was no pie-in-the-sky fantasy, this was graspable reality. Out of this rich black soil of the steppe and the *Führer's* bountiful vision would spring a brave new world and we were right here, ready to make it happen.

'So you believed that fascist crap. Like a bunch of dumb peasants,' sneered Margaret.

You didn't have to be a dumb peasant to believe, I said. Martin Heidegger, I reminded her, still hailed today in France and America as the most brilliant philosopher of the century, the sage of Freiburg, did he not suck on the same teat? And he never bothered to wipe his lips. Unrepentant till the day he died. 'And you?' I said. 'Have you forgotten how you used to dog me around the house, spitting quotes from Chairman Mao's *Little Red Book* in my face? Did you have to be a peasant to believe? Had you, you and your 'radical' friends, never heard of Mao's Great Leap Forward? Between 30 and 40 million dead? Or the Cultural Revolution that piled another 20 million corpses at his feet? How deep in the sand did *you* have to bury your head?

Did we know? Did we know, did we know, did we know. I had often imagined that question lurking in the eyes of my colleagues and townsmen. If they could put the question to a doddering oldster in a remote village of Bavaria they might have to believe him if he told them he didn't know. Not probable, but possible. Relatively few of the Jews murdered by the Nazis were German Jews, fewer than 3%, by some counts. The Ukraine, Belarus, Poland, Latvia, these were the killing grounds where millions were murdered. And they were not 'professionally' dispatched in remote installations like Auschwitz, deep in the Polish bush. They were shot near towns and cities and buried in nearby pits. How could we not know?

'They were murdering Jews right under your nose, papa. Millions of them,' she said.

'No, we didn't know about the millions,' I said, though I confessed that we'd heard disturbing reports, not all of which could be dismissed as anti-German propaganda. We heard Jews had been massacred in Zaporozhye, near Chortiza. And that thugs with Mennonite names had participated in the massacre.

'Mennonite names? Why Mennonite *names?*'

Because they were not Mennonites, I said, their crimes incriminate only themselves. Throughout the Bolshevik decades there were some in our villages who had loudly disavowed their Mennonite faith and become zealous communists, then with equal alacrity became eager recruits for the Nazi *Einsatzgruppen*. 'Like our own Kommissar Kaethler,' I said. He had terrorized us for twenty years, then without batting an eye he became a zealous Nazi. Yes, he knew about Hitler's *Kommissar Erlass,* ordering all 'political commissars' to be shot – but he also knew the Nazis could use him. I told Margaret how we had stood stunned as we watched him and his family piling their belongings into a shiny black motorcar, under the patient supervision of an *SS* officer. And as they drove off, Frau Kommissar, smiling from ear to ear, waved to us through the back window of the car.

And not long after there was another late-night gathering around our kitchen table – Uncle Knalz and his wife, and five or six others. But the mood was different now, no fear of informers, no tightly drawn circle of faces around a single candle flickering low. A bright kerosene lamp stood boldly in the middle of the table, and Uncle Knalz did not lean across the table on his elbows so that he need not raise his voice to be heard. He slumped back in his chair, and while he spoke he stared at the steady flame of the lamp. He said Kaethler had sent him 'dispatches,' from a town called Neshin, not far from Kiev, where he'd been 'posted.' He wanted to gloat. Not only had he survived, he was thriving. 'In big' with the Nazis. He wrote that during his interrogation by the *SS*, he had dropped a few hints that he could be useful to the *Reich.* And it wasn't long before he was summoned to the office of the *Kommandant* himself, one who understood the 'challenges' the Nazis faced in their conquered Eastern Territories. 'Not to boast,' Kaethler had told the *Kommandant,* 'but I know what's what and who's who.' Give him just two weeks and he'd put together a *Sonderkommando* of local recruits who would clean out all these undesirables in a jiffy. Like the Jews.

The people around our kitchen table had listened to Uncle Knalz in bowed silence. Then my mother spread a clean white cloth on the table, and they did what they had come to do. They celebrated Holy Communion. For twenty years under the Soviets this is how it had to be done – furtively, late at night, in different houses, sometimes no more than nine or ten people present, sometimes in a barn loft with twenty or thirty present, under the pretence that it was a birthday party. When you were still with us, Antoine, you once watched one of these 'strange' kitchen Communions at our house. It puzzled you, and it was the only time I remember you asking my mother to explain our rituals. Yes, she said, it was a sacrament, like a wedding or baptism, but no, priests and robes weren't necessary, nor a silver chalice. 'In times like these,' she said, 'your best everyday cup and a clean white cloth on the table suffice.' In better times, of course, it was celebrated in a church, with a revered elder to break the bread and repeat the words Jesus had spoken to his disciples, but that wasn't necessary either. All that was necessary, she said, was that you felt a need for His presence, and the presence of the others. And for once, Antoine, you had no witty reply to that.

Furtive kitchen Communions were no longer necessary during the Nazi occupation, yet those people gathered around our table seemed to know that once again they had to brace themselves to resist evil times. Did I understand that then? No.

'But *they*, at least, *did* know,' said Margaret.

There were others too, I said. Ohm Isaac knew. His raving was a worry to us, and we tried to keep him and his daughter out of sight in their cowherd cottage at the edge of our village. But there was no telling when a fit would come upon him. Like the night when a late-summer electric storm shattered the night sky above us. Sensible people were huddled inside their homes but half-mad Ohm Isaac was not sensible. The pellets of rain battering my window pane could not drown out his wailing. *'Behold, a people has come among you from the west,'* he cried, *'and their voice roareth like the sea. Our eyes failed, ever watching vainly for help, for help from a nation that could not save. Behold and see our disgrace.'* Another of his raves from the Book of Jeremiah, a book he knew by heart.

He was my responsibility. I leapt from my bed, pulled on a pair of trousers, threw a coat over my shoulders and ran out to find him. And did find him, lit up by bolts of lightning, bareheaded and barefoot in his nightshirt, shuffling sideways along the picket fence that ran from his cottage to the village, hand over hand from picket to picket, to guide him. I tried to calm him, tried to pry his hands off the pickets and lead him home, but he hung on tight. *'The Lord hath made them known to me, and made known their evil deeds, but you are like lambs led to the slaughter,'* he cried.

The German sentries turned a searchlight on him, and me, and I tried to duck out of the beam. *'Because you trusted in lies you will be scattered like chaff in the wind,* saith the Lord. Then you will tear your clothes and lament your abomination. *Cursed be the day I was born,* you will cry, *Wherefore came I forth from the womb that my days should be cloaked in shame?*

While Ohm wailed, two armed German guards approached us. *Because of the greatness of your iniquity, saith the Lord, your skirts shall be lifted up and you shall suffer violence. And I myself will hold your skirts over your face that your shame will be known.'*

The rain pelted his scraggly skull, and in the glare of the searchlight his thin wet nightgown, clinging to his skin, seemed to render him naked. I tried to assure the guards these were the ravings of a harmless madman. 'Take him away!' they said. Uncle Knalz came, put a cloak around his nakedness, and led him to his own house.

So did we know? Did we know, a mere twenty years ago before the feminist movement drove the indisputable knowledge into our heads, that we men had oppressed women, even those we loved and pampered with courtesies? How could we not have known? Albert Einstein once said, 'We can observe only what our theories permit us to observe.' He was talking about physics, but perhaps a similar rule applies to our moral perceptions. We can know only what our image of ourselves permits us to know. 'Cognitive dissonance' is Doktor Vik's term, which conveniently reduces a moral failing to something clinical.

Victor Klemperer, son of a rabbi, scholar, professor of romance languages, cousin of Otto the great conductor, how could he not know? Yet in his diary in 1933 he wrote, 'We, we Germans are better than other nations, freer in thought, purer in feeling, juster in action. We are a truly chosen people.' But two years later, 1935, the cracks began to appear. 'I am fighting the hardest battle for my Germanness now. I must hold on to this: I am German, the others [i.e. Nazis] are un-German.'

When did the cracks appear in *my* self-image? At what point did *I* know? It was not a gradual process. It was a sudden sickening blow. Even after I had seen Warsaw reduced to a blackened, corpse-strewn ruin I didn't know. After I had come to know comrades who relished the spectacle of cruelty, shared sleeping quarters with them and ate at the same table, even then I persuaded myself these were the thugs who always appear in times of crisis. Not till the end of the war, when a combination of fate and folly had brought me once again into the company of Captain von Niessen, when all that remained of his former glow was a grim resolve, only then, when I saw *he* knew, did *I* know.

THE TREK

January 8, 1992

Two years, September 5, 1941 to September 19, 1943. That was the length of the German occupation in our villages. The dreaded rumours began soon after the German defeat at Stalingrad. Then came Kursk, then Kharkov. A chill ran through our bodies with each report. 'Traitors.' 'Collaborators.' Words we had banished from our minds now demanded their due. We knew, and the Germans knew, that the Red Army's cruellest vengeance would be exacted upon collaborators, upon us. That's how it always is in war. So we abandoned our village to the dogs, chickens and looters and began our trek. Whereto nobody knew. All we knew was that we were scrambling west to escape the vengeance of the advancing Red Army.

The Germans could have abandoned us, that would have been normal. German Divisions were in desperate retreat, ill-equipped and poorly supplied, trainloads of dying and wounded, the rest freezing and hungry. Yet they spared precious manpower, both military and civilian, to 'evacuate' tens of thousands of *Volksdeutsche*, we Mennonites among them. For some there were trains, thousands crammed into boxcars, the rest of us plodded along in farm wagons and two-wheeled carts hitched to a pair of old nags, a skinny foot-sore cow tied behind, pulling in the opposite direction. About 35,000 of us when we started. In our group alone there were 47 carts and wagons, 116 horses and 30 cows, among 56 families. Our dream of escaping communist Russia had become real, but a bitter reality because of those we were leaving behind. Their absence howled at our backs.

The grim hope of our people was to find refuge in some obscure hinterland where they could once again rebuild their lives in defiance of the big world around them. It was not my hope. My hope was to find you, Antoine, in Germany, or wherever you might be.

The Germans set up a *Betreuungs Kommando*, with *Obersturmführers*, civilian officials and *Hilfswillige* ('volunteers', most of them captured Red Army soldiers), and enough military support to coerce the burghers and villagers along the way to lodge and provision us, and to protect us from increasingly bold partisans. Also some Red Cross nurses to take care of the sick. Yes, we were primitively equipped, we suffered cold, hunger, terror and exhaustion, and some died, but a million German soldiers suffered worse.

'So the Nazis looked after their own. That was big of them,' said Seymour, when I explained how we had got out of Russia.

We should have demanded to be saved by people with cleaner hands? The Americans? The British? They had never shown much inclination to save us, not during the Ukrainian 'famine', not during the purge of the *kulaks*, or during the *Yezhovshchina*, the Great Terror. And now they were openly Stalin's allies. 'If it hadn't been for the Nazis, the Communists might have killed us all,' I said.

'If it hadn't been for the Communists, the Nazis might have killed us all,' said Seymour.

I quote from Uncle Knalz's journal of our trek, three thin notebooks crammed with his small script and tied up with a yellow ribbon – bequeathed to me, by his request, after he had died, and sent to me from Paraguay by his son:

October 28, 1943
   Near Novy-Bug. They put a new man in charge. Wendorf. Asked him where we'll spend the next night – shakes his head, can't say, security

reasons. Probably doesn't know. On good days we make 40km, bad days less than 10. Hard to plan. But he seems like a good man. Very *korrekt*. Official forms for everything. My horse needs shoeing, so I get a requisition form. Signed and stamped. Watched the blacksmith hammer nails into the hooves – big surly fellow, hard hammer blows – probably imagined the hoof was my skull. We are not loved by these people. Not surprising.

November 3, 1943

Sutiski. More rain. More mud. Made only 8 kilometres. The courage of these women who have lost their men humbles me. Have to care for both aging parents and young children, have to barter for food, for themselves, hay and oats for the horses. Children crying and complaining, because they're cold, or dreadfully bored. The mothers try to keep them entertained. Sometimes there is even laughter and singing. Amazing. But also spats of anger and frustration. Always it's the same families who break down. In one wagon, it's a young mother and three old women – and a child running a fever – pitiful. But a week ago they had a chance, their wagon wobbling like a fat duck, should have traded their fancy samovar for a new wheel. Much grumbling but we can't abandon them. And yesterday the Waldorfer group overtook us – 120 families, 80 wagons – cleaned out the whole village where we spent the night, nothing left for us, no clean straw, no oats, no firewood. Today the same thing. Had to struggle on roads chewed to ribbons by the Waldorfer wagons. Damn them.

November 10, 1943

Near Kamenetz-Podolskjy. Still more rain. Wendorf says the *Mittelstelle* gets our supplies by train from Germany. Admitted a lot doesn't get through. Ends up on the black market. Or partisans blow up the railway lines. Talked to his assistant, Herr Buss, a crude fellow, had to butter him up a little – You Germans are so efficient, shortages everywhere yet the supplies for our trek get through. Through? He laughed. Most is 'requisitioned' from the local people, he says – but not without some persuasion at gunpoint, you might say. They're sneaky devils, he says. Soon as they hear the trek is coming through their town they hide everything – potatoes, oats, coal, flour – everything. He said in Novy-Bug they found 40 kg of potatoes hidden in a coffin – buried in the graveyard. People dying like flies – fresh graves all over the place – who's got time to dig up all the caskets and look inside? But this time they made a mistake – put an old tombstone at the head of a fresh grave. Stupid peasants.

If the Germans ever abandon us, the local people will take no small satisfaction watching us starve and freeze to death.

November 19, 1943

Varnovitza. Today the Germans put some of us in houses, the rest in barns and stables – after two nights in the rain. They put Sonya and her family – Struvel, Sarah and old Oma Enns – in a farmhouse near the village. Sonya says the *Hausfrau* broke down and cried. Said she couldn't take it any more – more and more filthy refugees, no end – you get a few supplies laid in then they clean you out again. Said the refugees treat them like servants – take the best bed, tell the *Hausfrau* and her husband to go sleep in the stable, some even stole their shoes. Sonya said she couldn't believe that, the *Hausfrau* said she could believe what she wanted. Sonya told her she and her family would sleep in the stable. They let old Oma Enns sleep on a cot in their kitchen.

December 4, 1943

Podolien. Snow then rain then more snow. They have assigned more *Hiwis* to the trek, mainly Latvians and Russians, also more regular soldiers – because of the partisans. The Poles resent us no less than the Ukrainians. The more surprising when one of them doesn't. Like the one today. Remarkable woman. Cheerful, kind – though we're her third group in two weeks. She tears up an old pillow case to bind our Oma's feet. Bosses and scolds her husband – let the boy play with your chess men, he won't eat them. Spends hours staring at that stupid chess board, she says – here, go fetch some water. He rolls his eyes at me but does as he's told. After supper I let him beat me at chess.

Because the main roads had to be kept open for military transports, our trek had been confined to narrow back roads, sometimes little more than trails for local farm vehicles. My mother, old Oma Enns and my sister Sarah rode together in a covered wagon, with all our possessions, and I followed with Ohm Isaac in a two-wheeled cart, just the two of us. Ohm's daughter rode with Uncle Knalz's family. On rainy nights when the *Mittelstelle* couldn't find lodging for us in the towns and villages, all five of us would cram into my mother's wagon.

Ohm had become more tractable on the trek, but I was becoming a quarrelsome teenager, and he alone seemed to endure my company without complaint. I did take good care of him – bedding him down each night, fetching water for him to wash, and leading him to a private place where he could relieve himself, waiting till he was done – though sometimes I became impatient. He had more cause to become impatient with me. Sometimes for hours and hours he had to listen to me spout scandalous opinions. 'How can you believe in a just or merciful God after all that has happened, after all you yourself have suffered?' I said. 'This God of yours, if he exists, should be cursed, not worshipped.' I thought I was giving vent to profound, bitter disillusion but I was merely prancing on my hind legs.

Ohm let me sulk a while, then he said, 'Could the world have been created better? Have not poets and romancers tried to imagine a better world, a world with no injustice, no suffering, endless pleasure? And yet,' he said, 'except for the silly ones among them, they soon wearied of their utopian dreams. Would you rather God had created a world that is beyond our power, and beyond our will, to make either better or worse?'

I managed a hollow harrumph in answer to his question.

When we heard that Katya's cart had broken down near Kamenetz-Podolskjy, and several wagons had passed her in silence, my mother made us go back for her. Katya had loaded what she could onto her horse, and the rest onto her own back, and was walking through ankle-deep mud pulling the horse behind her. We loaded her gear into my mother's wagon and tied her spavined old mare behind it. Oma Enns grumbled, but Katya said, 'I work like a horse and eat like a bird.'

From then, except for a brief time in Poland, Katya was inseparable from my mother. She thought my mother was too meek and passive to survive, so she took charge. She said a woman of my mother's 'class' never had to learn how to scratch and claw. Katya had, so she scratched and clawed for both of them. I was supposedly the male head of the family, but Katya didn't think my scratching and clawing talents amounted to much.

. . .

October had been hard slogging through the mud of the Ukrainian steppe, everybody out to lighten the load, the girls at the front pulling on the halters, women and boys at the back pushing, but our panic had abated as we began to trust Germany's resolve to rescue us. October became November and then our trek entered a spruce forest, a novelty to us steppe mice. A world of mists and craggy rocks, the roads narrow and stony and laced with roots, but better than mud. The forest seemed to invigorate us, especially we young folk impatient for a change of scene and mood. Against the west wind we pressed eager faces through odours we had never smelled before, heard night-sounds never heard on the steppe, and when the sun did break through the mists, instead of warming us it teased us by bouncing along the tops of trees. Only 160 kilometres to the Polish frontier, we were told, then we'd be beyond the reach of the Soviet Union. Already my lungs seemed to sense a change in the air, and my breath came in quickening gulps.

When we reached the east bank of the Bug we were deflected northwards, toward the town of Nemirov, all traffic funnelled toward a high-level trestle bridge that spanned a deep gorge at a bend in the river, and here we camped under the stars and waited till there would be a lull and we too could cross. Trains, trucks, wagons, half-tracks, every possible means of conveyance carried men and supplies east to the front, and wounded soldiers west, back to hospitals in Germany. A section of the bridge had been dynamited, either by Soviet guerrilla units active behind the German lines or Polish partisans, but in less than two weeks the damage had been repaired by German engineers. Some said it was neither Soviets nor partisans, just local saboteurs, who had bungled the job.

Across the Bug, on the west bank, scattered groups of houses nestled among trees and fields, whose lights twinkled in the dark, so near yet so far because of the river that ran between us. Some of our people looked longingly at those faint lights, telling of warmth within in spite of their faintness, casting an illusion of peace and permanence. Those were homes and we had none. Soon the front would roll over those villages and crush them but it made the illusion no less dear. And they, the people in those homes, they too would have listened for more nights than we had listened to the rumble of traffic on the bridge, searching each other's faces, feeling the need of a decision pressing upon them. And yet the near certainty of destruction was not enough, not yet, to make them pack up and flee, so strong a hold had that plot of land on them, that little plot among all the real estate in the world. We could understand that, but it would make no sense to people of my grandchild's generation – who see no necessity to any plot of land, whose needs can be indifferently served whether they live in Vancouver or New York, London or Shanghai.

'Teach me about cities,' I said to Ohm Isaac as we lay in our open cart, tucked into our bedrolls, and listened to the ebb and flow of traffic rumbling across the bridge. I gazed up at a starlit sky and let my mind conjure visions of shimmering electric cities, the great cities of Europe that might now lie within my grasp after decades of Soviet captivity.

'Cities glitter in the sunlight and glow at night,' said Ohm. 'They lure us. And like all things of the earth, they grow, they flower, then they fade and die. Some are forgotten, and some become fabled cities. What more is there to say?'

There had been spats during the long weeks of drudgery, but Ohm Isaac and I had now come to feel at ease in each other's company. I lent him the benefit of my eyes with a running commentary on the passing scene while he recalled scenes from his former life when he still had the use of his own eyes. Our conversation could better be called an exchange of monologues, with long gaps of silence, each of us talking as much to himself as to the other, but neither of us seemed to mind. 'Say why some cities enchant us and others not,' I said, 'say why the mere name of some is sufficient to cast a spell.'

'There are cities with a thousand faces to charm the traveller,' he said. 'Others have but one face, like a monolith. These lay claim to a big dot on a map because a single vein of ore runs under them, or a towering smoke-stack looms over them. They are like a tedious companion who can talk on only one subject.'

Though Russia had cities with a thousand years of history, I had never seen one. The windswept Eurasian steppe had been a land of villages, pockets of kinship where people were known not only by their names and by their fathers' names, but by the plot of dirt that bore them – their *zemlya*, both ground and distillation of all other kinships, whether tribe, clan, or nation – many now buried under modern Soviet habitats of humanity that fit no known designation, neither village, town nor city. Urban clusters created by ministerial edict, abstractions made material, a grid thrown across the land, then tons of steel and concrete heaped upon it. And off to one side, blocks of stacked compartments, six or eight storeys high, like mausoleums to house the living dead. But I had never seen a real city.

'A city should have gates,' said Ohm, 'and the purpose of gates and walls is not to keep some people out and others in, but to serve notice to the traveller that once inside the gates things are of a different scale. Here ambition is greater, dreams more splendid, tastes more exacting, and here,' he said, 'failure is greater.'

I knew something about the ancient antagonism between the village and the city and I had made my choice. Once out of Russia I would find you, Antoine, whether in Dresden where I knew Mary Gordon had taken you, or in some other fabled city. And you would be my guide, you would initiate me into the pleasures of cities – the two of us strutting along the broad, electric avenues, looking left and right, picking among the plenty on offer.

Vain fantasies. None of us knew then that the cities I dreamed of would soon be reduced to rubble, that the carpet bombing of Europe's great cities had begun.

'In cities there are restless souls who strive to do great deeds,' said Ohm, 'and others, *flaneurs* and *boulevardiers,* who have perfected the art of idleness. But a city must have a heart, a centre,' he said, 'an esteemed monument where people gather at uncommon times. Where women can swirl their scarves like banners and men throw their caps in the air. Or stomp on them in protest.'

As we lay in our cart, visions of the cities Ohm had know in his youth passed in bright procession before his inner eye. 'Cities breed excess,' he said, 'in cities there are pockets of squalor that offend the eye, and public squares where the eye is trained to feast upon beauty, where the gold-capped domes of churches vie with colonnaded mosques, and these with the glittering mosaics of synagogues – as though each would entice their God to abide with them a while instead of with the other fellows. And why not. We do as much for lesser guests. Even in market squares fruit vendors have a sculptor's or a painter's eye,' he said, 'and display their wares to model a geography of plenty. Mountains of bright apples rise in receding layers to a ruddy peak, flanked on either side by lesser peaks, the foothills of golden pears and peaches. Then the rolling plains of plums and apricots, and finally the cool pools of berries. And above them all, from a lattice roof, hang purple clouds of grapes.'

We lay on the ground lulled by the sounds of our own encampment, the murmur of young mothers cooing to their children, the restive snuffling of our horses. Then we heard a loud crash and the screeching of wheels on steel rails, men shouting and horses shrieking, then the splash of heavy things hitting the water. No one knew how much weight the bridge could bear till it had borne too much, but we knew that if the bridge were now impassable we would be pinned here, on the bank of the Bug, at the mercy of the avenging Red Army.

More confused shouting, more battering and banging, followed by a brief respite. Then the roar of engines began again, the screech of wheels on steel rails began again, and our normal breathing began again.

Across the river, from a deeper distance beyond the village, we now heard the muffled, melancholy tolling of a church bell, as though the ritual occasions of grief and celebration still waited upon its ratification. 'Time too is different in the city,' said Ohm. 'It is fickle, it flits here and there, and must be seized before it ducks around a corner. In the village, time is like the slow spinning of a web, with births, deaths and marriages at the nodes, but in the city time moves in convulsive heaves, one age layered upon another, gilded baroque upon carved granite, polished marble upon rough flagstones. Yet here and there soaring spires and arches bear witness of a former time that stands in judgment upon our time.'

While I gazed up at the stars and conjured images of the shimmering world that lay in my future, Ohm's reveries had turned sombre. 'Even the cemeteries are layered,' he said, 'the dead layered on other dead, and the living hardly aware the ground beneath them is honeycombed with tombs. The more recent dead lie in groomed cemeteries, where sculpted figures rise above more modest tombs to defy oblivion. But in obscure corners beyond the cemetery walls,' he said, 'you find graves marked only by small limestone slabs, all much the same, and bearing a similar laconic record of a failed life – a name and two dates joined by a hyphen.'

And when I enquired of Ohm whose graves these might be he said they were the graves of suicides, men and women now lying in close community, who had lived and died in utter solitude, or so they thought.

'Because their lives became unbearable,' I said.

'No, their lot was not harder than the lot of others. Their lives were not unbearable, only their desires.'

I felt a chill run down my spine. 'And yet there are cities that are loved,' I said.

'Those we love are where sad women remember us fondly.'

'Must they be sad? Is it written?'

'Have not the poets always told us? Is there not always a great sadness in the music we hold most dear? Is not that song sweetest that has passed through a constricted throat? Such things would be, had it never been written.'

On the far bank of the Bug I could now see flames, and I could hear the thin cries of women and children across the water. Behind me I heard angry grumbling among our people. 'Tell me what you see,' said Ohm.

'They are burning the villages on the other side,' I said, and then we fell silent.

We did cross that river and as we approached the Polish border the towns and villages became more sparse, some little more than logging camps. More rain, but day by day a balmy west wind drew us on.

Through the wilds of Galicia and across the Polish frontier, through Kielce, and at last we were camped near Litzmannstadt, as we called it then, assured by our *Obersturmführer* Heinrich Wendorf that the Red Army would never be allowed to set foot in the *Reich*. Here we rested for almost a month, and here we were herded in groups of fifty into communal showers, real showers, with water. While we showered, our clothes were boiled, dried, then returned to us, and on the back of our right hand we were duly stamped, *Entlaust*. No lice allowed in the *Reich*!

Less haste, less urgency now. A reprieve, and time to grieve for those who had not been sufficiently wept, who had died en route, or were left behind in the Soviet gulag.

We continued a few kilometres further west and camped at the bend of another river while we waited for the *Mittelstelle* to organize the last leg of our trek into the Warthegau. Early spring, 1944, and the warmer weather began to lift our spirits.

'Tell me what you see,' said Ohm, and I told him we were once again on a rolling plain. I said there was a rocky beach at the bend of the river, and above it an outcrop of grey limestone. I said some of *unse* were lodged in a nearby village, and the rest of us had drawn our wagons together here in a semi-circle. The wagons were unhitched, the horses hobbled and left to graze on the new grass above the bank. I said beyond the village there were fields, just bare ploughed ground at this time of year, and beyond the fields the land rose gently to a line of trees. It all looked very peaceful, I said.

Many of the women, both those in the camp and those lodged in the village, were doing laundry in the pools among the rocks, and though the water was icy cold some of the young ones had waded in up to their knees, the better to rinse the soap out of the clothes. I said a colourful patchwork of clothes was already spread on the rocks to dry, and some hung on lines drawn between the wagons. I said the old *Omas* were sitting on boxes and benches around fires, wrapped in blankets while their clothes were washed and dried, and Ohm Isaac said he could hear the flapping of the clothes in the breeze.

'Take me to a high place where I can sit,' said Ohm, so I led him onto a limestone outcrop where centuries of wind and rain had scooped out a ledge like a stone bench. Ohm lifted his face to the sun and began to hum a hymn. 'Struvel,' he said, 'gather the people. I want to preach.'

I tried to dissuade him, told him the people were busy and would not be in the mood for a sermon just now. 'If you tell them they will come,' he said, so I went among the people and told them Ohm Isaac wanted to preach. They were indeed not in the mood. My news was received with dismissive grunts. But now Ohm had begun to sing, in his somewhat rasping voice but with a robust rhythm. Being blind he had no use for a hymn book and he didn't need one. He knew the hymns by heart.

Mennonites can resist a sermon but they cannot long resist the sound of someone singing hymns. The people began to hum, and then to sing along, scrubbing their clothes on the rocks to the rhythm of the music. And soon they began to gather around him, sopranos to the left, altos to the right, and behind them tenors and basses. Ohm would call out the numbers of the hymns as though he were still in a church in Russia, 'Number three hundred and ten.' Then he would begin, '*Wer nun den lieben Gott lässt walten,*' and the rest would join in. If it were a less familiar hymn Ohm would chant two lines in a monotone, then the people would repeat them in four-part harmony.

They sang the old chorales, and it being the Lenten season they sang, *O Haupt voll Blut und Wunden / voll Schmerz und voller Hohn.* The words of these hymns offer no easy solace, they are graphic and often grim, the stark images of sin and suffering, but the music is surefooted, stately, clear-eyed. These are not hymns to make you sway and swoon and fall to the ground, they are hymns to help you stand. They are not hymns to incite belief but to forge solidarity, not to overwhelm emotions but to clarify emotions. They do not cajole or coddle, neither do they whine and plead. They assert.

Then Ohm Isaac began. He preached like the old preachers, with their rapid impulsive rhythms. 'It is written that on the fifth day God created the fish of the sea and the birds of the air,' he said, 'and on the sixth day he created all the creatures that roam the dry land. *And God saw that it was good.* And so it was,' said Ohm. 'It gave Him pleasure to see his creatures soar in the air and gambol in the meadows, to hear their chirping, mooing and cooing. But God became bored with only chirping, mooing and cooing for company. And so he created man, *in his own image, male and female created he them,* endowed with reason and imagination, with whom alone among all his creatures, he could have a conversation. And again *God saw everything that he had made, and behold, it was very good.*'

'But no,' said Ohm, 'it was *not* good, my brothers and sisters. For it is written that even in the days of Noah when the world was still young, *God saw that the wickedness of man was great, and that every thought of his heart inclined to evil.* And it is written that *God repented that he had made man on the earth, and it grieved him to his heart.* And God said, *I will blot out man, whom I have created, from the face of the earth.*

'You know the story,' said Ohm. 'A remnant of creation saved in the ark. And after the waters had abated God said, *I will never again curse the ground because the imagination of man's heart is evil,* and He placed a rainbow among the clouds, his covenant *with every living creature upon the earth, for all future generations.* But how, how can God now be held to his promise?' said Ohm. 'Those who had provoked God's wrath in the days of Noah were mere novices in the arts of evil and carnage, compared to our own time. If ever God had good cause to look again upon his creation with loathing it is surely now,' said Ohm. 'But where, you cry, where then was the ark that might have saved us, God's faithful, when the first droplets of Stalin's terror began to rain down on us? Did we dream that our Molotchna colony would become our ark? A floating island upon the deluge? A foolish dream. Not forty days and forty nights but twenty years of death and terror rained on our heads.

'And when the Nazis came, did we dream that *they* were our ark? A sign of God's mercy upon us?' cried Ohm. 'And when that dream failed, did we think they would part the Red Soviet Sea and lead us dry-shod to a new Canaan? Another foolish dream,' said Ohm, 'and may God forgive us. Have we forgotten the lessons learned by our ancestors? Have we now put our faith not in God and the love that binds us, but in the woolly visions of presidents and *Führers*, who promise a new reign of liberty and justice, as *they*, in their vanity, see fit?'

'Oh, I have heard you curse God's Holy Name, my brothers and sisters,' said Ohm, 'if only under your breath. I will not presume to scold you, for these have been my own quarrels with the Almighty. Yes, we have suffered, and whatever our sins, they are not equal to our suffering. But if God's wisdom, God's love, God's justice has become bitter to us, we have endured enough of man's wisdom, love, justice to know it is not less frightening.

'Now hear my confession,' said Ohm. 'I have not loved you as I should, I have mocked your homespun theology, your quaint moralizing. I loved first the ancient sages, Augustin of Hippo, Meister Eckhart and Judah ha-Levi. With these I sought communion, these had all my love, but that love blinded me while yet my eyes could see to the love of living creatures, frail, imperfect, but could love me back – you, my brothers and sisters. Now I too would accounted be of your fraternity, I am that prodigal son returned, my brothers and sisters. Embrace me.'

'You go now to a land where I cannot follow,' he said, 'wherever that land may be. Know that when this is past there will be other perils to endure, more loss to grieve. The earth provides an infinite supply of spines, and of polished boots to crush them. But do not curse God, nor the earth, nor the flesh that bore you. A vain curse, my brothers and sisters. Even as our mouths speak our final malediction upon God's earth, our ears begin to hear a low, distant chord, octaves below our normal range of hearing, a dark, swelling, churning chord, and then over it, and around it, we hear the wavering melody of a single violin, *I will not let thee go unless thou bless me.* So go now, my brothers and sisters, be of good

courage and love one another. Amen. Number three hundred and
seventy-six, verses one to five.'

We crossed that river too, but it would be Ohm's last. The days grew
longer and warmer but they did not invigorate Ohm Isaac.

He became frail and gaunt. He ate very little and his skin hung on his
bones in loose folds. When I bathed him I had to lift the folds on his
buttocks and stomach with my free hand so I could get into the creases
with my wash cloth. He no longer spent most of the day seated beside me
on our cart but lay on the bed I had made for him of straw and blankets,
and he would fall into a deep sleep there in spite of the jolting of the cart
and the rhythmic creak of the wheels.

Our wagon train came to a halt along the shore of a long narrow lake
so we could water our horses and prepare our noonday meal. I unhitched
our old nag and the two horses from my mother's wagon and took them
down to the lake. When I returned, Ohm still seemed to be asleep on his
straw mat. I shook him, and found his body had grown cold.

The funeral service was brief. We buried him on a knoll near the lake,
but for a long time we lingered there, loathe to abandon Ohm, indifferent
to the shouts of our German marshals ordering us to move on. I collected
large stones and built a cairn. I made a wooden cross using the floor
boards of our cart and engraved his name and dates on it with my pocket
knife, and a line from Psalm 51: *Lord, let the bones you have crushed rejoice.*
Then we left him.

March 1, 1992

I grieved Ohm's death bitterly, Antoine. More than I had thought I would. We had often quarrelled, and I had often become impatient, tending daily to his bodily needs but I see now that caring for him had held me in orbit as I became more and more unmoored. Now I felt adrift. I no longer had any interest in the hopes and anxieties of our people, the endless meetings and briefings about what the *Mittelstelle* now had planned for us. The grim reality that confronted me when we crossed into the *Reich* was nothing like the fabled West I had dreamed of all those years since you left us. No glittering cities and treed boulevards, only thousands of ragged refugees just like us, herded from one makeshift shelter to another. I would brood for hours then lash out in anger and frustration. There was no longer any trace of that bushy-tailed little lad who greeted you when Mary Gordon brought you to our house.

Then a fifth *Hiwi* was assigned to our group. The others had been assigned to us shortly after we crossed the border into Poland. *Hilf-swillige* was their official designation – Red Army soldiers who had been captured early in the war (or deserted), then 'volunteered' their services to the *Reich* to escape the horrors of a POW camp. Their job was to assist the civilian German officials in charge of the trek, and the few soldiers the *Wehrmacht* could spare. They had a dubious para-military status. Their main job was to scavenge for us – commandeer the local villagers and farmers to supply water and hay for our horses, 'requisition' fresh horses and new wagon wheels when ours wore out, and if necessary fend off small gangs of self-styled Polish partisans. They were each issued a uniform of sorts, a good horse, and a service-able rifle of World War I vintage. They were a dishevelled bunch who regarded us as a troublesome nuisance and generally kept aloof – except for the women they took for company. We refugees regarded them with equal contempt. Filthy, illiterate savages, we said, and complained about them to the Germans. 'Keep your filthy paws off their women,' they warned the *Hiwis*, but the warning rang hollow when some of them laid their own filthy paws on our women. And a few, exhausted by trudging through mud behind a wobbly cart, bent and aching from schlepping water for themselves and their horses, were ready to strike a bargain. Most weren't. 'That woman needs help,' said

Uncle Knalz to a *Hiwi* half asleep in his saddle, and pointed at a woman sitting in the mud, leaning against the hub of a broken wheel, and sobbing. 'Yesterday she said she didn't need a man,' growled the *Hiwi*, 'Tell her to make up her mind.'

But Yuri was different. He was magnificent, mounted on his white Andalusian stallion, his Cossack sabre strapped to his side, a bright red sash around his otherwise drab tunic. He moved among us with the feline grace of an athlete, both affable and arrogant, laughing and singing Cossack songs in his lush baritone voice. He buoyed up our spirits, sometimes with an amusing prank, sometimes with a timely kindness to an exhausted old woman. He was ungrudgingly helpful without being ordered by the Germans, or badgered by us. At the end of the day he would patrol our camp with his bucket of grease, inspecting our wagons for squeaky wheels, inspecting the hooves of our horses, and repairing frayed harnesses.

He buoyed up my spirits too. I turned to him for relief from our bossy Mennonite women and anxious elders, from tedious, dutiful routines, from hours of futile arguments and speculations about what the Germans now had in mind for us. I began dogging him around the camp, helping him with some of his tasks, and pestering him with indiscreet questions. No, Antoine, this won't surprise you. I have always been inclined to attach myself to someone who seemed glamorous, exotic. But he was not like you. He would have found us quaint, a little odd, but he was not aloof. Did not keep a measured distance from us.

He was thirty-six years old, almost old enough to be my father, but treated me like a young comrade. He had spent a carefree childhood on the steppe, most of it on horseback, had learned to ride before he could walk, or so he claimed. When the civil war broke out he had joined the *Makhnovtze*, and after the war he had been in and out of different uniforms – Petlyura's nationalists, Budyonny's Red Cavalry, then captured by the Germans.

Did he not, as a *Hiwi*, feel like a traitor to his own people, I asked him. There must have been many times when he could hardly resist slapping the presumption off my face.

'Let me tell you something,' he said. 'There are Cossacks in the Royal Yugoslav Army, Cossacks fighting alongside the Italians, Cossacks with the Banderovtsy, shooting at Cossacks in the Red Army. So? What army should I join to make sure I never fire upon my own kinsmen? In this war, you don't fight *for* anything. It's just to kill people.'

Sometimes he ignored my impertinent questions, seemed absorbed in the task of mending a bridle or oiling his gun, and when I'd quite forgotten the question he'd come back to it. 'Listen. When the Germans capture English soldiers it's all very *korrekt*. Geneva conventions. They get food, beds, almost like a country club. But Russian POWs? Hah! They put us in a barbwire compound an' forget about us. Let us starve to death in our own filth. *Blyads.* To get out of there I told them I'd fight with Vlasov's Company. Of course, we didn't fight much. Not Aryan enough. Just good for propaganda. Vlasov, making big speeches, about our sacred duty to liberate Mother Russia from the Bolsheviks. I'd had enough of sacred duties. I buttered up a fat lieutenant, persuaded him I knew horses, so he let me be a *Hiwi.*'

'Some people here say you rode with the *Makhnovtze* when they terrorized our villages. Some even say they recognized you,' I said.

'There was a civil war. What's a young Cossack supposed to do? Stay home and plant cabbage? Milk the goats?'

But why Makhno? Why not the Whites?

'Makhno was like us, a peasant, not a big General with a fancy uniform. *Batko*, we called him. He was like a father.'

That made you feel safe?

'Puh. Whenever did young men follow a man who promised safety?'

So what did he promise?

'Women and vodka and good company, what else?'

Rape and murder?

Yuri didn't answer right away. He kept applying grease to the hub of a wagon wheel. Then he said, 'Some raped, and killed, some watched. And some went behind the stable and puked.' He kicked the newly greased wheel back onto its axle with enough force to break a spoke. *Blyads!*

'You need the bad ones,' he said. 'The cruel ones. They make sure you're hated. Make sure you can't go home when you're sick of it. Every gang of village toughs would hear about it – Yeah, one of Makhno's men is back. A chance to avenge somebody's sister, and brag about it. They get you when they know you'll be alone, when you're coming out of the outhouse, still buttoning your fly.'

He wasn't always in an ebullient mood. There were times when the whining and complaining of our women, or the officiousness of the Germans, would put him into a snarling funk and he would condemn us all to the devil. He would sulk for a day or two, then take matters into his own hands. Not long after he joined us, our trek came to a halt. Partisans, we were told. We would have to wait till the area had been 'pacified' before we could proceed. Three days, four days, still waiting, and we were running out of food. Our people began to whisper, then began to wail. Having led us this far, were the Germans now abandoning us? When Yuri had heard enough of this wailing, he packed his bed roll, leapt onto his white Andalusian, and with a wild Cossack cry turned a neat pirouette and charged through the camp, scattering children, mothers and grandmothers before him. Near the edge of the camp, still at a full gallop, he took his sabre from its sheath and in a breathtaking display of horsemanship, leaned far out of his saddle and skewered the last potato roasting on Willy Penner's campfire.

Poor Willy. He raised both arms to heaven on high. 'It was almost cooked!' he cried.

Late the next day Yuri returned, perched on a wagon pulled by two fresh horses, the wagon loaded with sacks of potatoes and flour. His Andalusian stallion plodded sheepishly behind him. When he was pressed to account for his loot he mumbled something about a dumb peasant who had left the wagon unattended while he stepped into a *Gasthaus* to have some fun with the barmaid. Stupid peasant. Thieving partisans would have stolen the horses and wagon in a minute. Thick as steppe mice in that area. Yuri said he had shot a few holes into the stucco walls of the *Gasthaus,* so the peasant could tell people he'd been attacked by a whole troop of partisans.

He hardly concealed his contempt for the Germans, mocked their pretence of legality when they 'requisitioned' supplies for us, but he had made himself too useful to them, and to us, to fear any rebuke. I envied his casual disdain of petty scruples while some of our people agonized about the morality of trekking on Sundays, the Lord's day. I scandalized my elders by my shameless attempts to emulate him, and at one point I even tried to persuade Yuri to let me join him on his next forage.

'Hey, *tovarish*, what are yuh talkin? Listen. There are three things you never have to teach a Cossack – how to ride, how to dance, and how to steal. None of that comes natural to you Mennonites.'

I noticed that my camaraderie with Yuri had earned the envy of some of the other young lads in our group, and I had also become more interesting to the girls. But I knew that there was another reason he sought out my company. I was a convenient pretext to manoeuvre himself into the company of my aunt, my Taunte Liese, with whom he had fallen in love.

His courtship of Taunte Liese did not begin well. When her cart became stuck in the mud, and no amount of clucking at her horse or flailing with the reins could get the horse to move, she had climbed down, struggled through the mud to the front of the horse, grabbed the bridle and pulled. The horse lurched forward, but now Taunte Liese's feet were stuck in the mud. 'Whoa!' she shouted, but the horse kept coming, and she fell flat on her back, under the horse. The horse did stop then, straddling her between its legs.

The screams of Taunte Liese's two children brought Yuri to the scene. By then she had rolled over, caked in mud, and had raised herself on all fours under the belly of the horse. Yuri dismounted, squatted down beside the horse, and grinned at her. 'What did you lose down there? Your false teeth?'

Taunte Liese glared at him, wiped the mud from her face and bared her teeth, to show she still had all the molars God gave her. Yuri laughed, then he offered his hand to help her out from under the horse. She grabbed the hand and bit his finger, hard.

For another week or two Yuri and Taunte Liese tried to maintain a show of mutual aversion. The pretence soon became transparent, but instead of provoking a scandal Yuri's courtship was so proper that Taunte Liese could be teased about it. Until it got beyond teasing.

We arrived in Posen on March 18, 1944, the end of our trek. Here, in this prosperous province in the northwest corner of Poland, we would be resettled. We were now in the benign care of *Obergruppenführer* Arthur Greiser, the *Gauleiter* of the *Reichsgau Wartheland.* We were provided with medical care, warm clothes, coal, flour, welfare for the old, schools for the young. Some of us would be settled in towns and given work in factories, paid work, not slave work, and others would be settled on little farms recently 'vacated.' First the Jews and then masses of Poles had been driven from their homes to make room for 300,000 *Volksdeutsche* refugees. Those from East Prussia and the Baltic countries had already been settled here and now it was our turn. Many of our people were relieved when they were issued documents entitling them to confiscated homes and farms, but Uncle Knalz had some misgivings about their value. 'We might have to burn these papers when this war is over,' he said. No, it was not our finest moment, but do not judge us too harshly, Antoine. You once tried to save someone who had done worse, under less duress.

There was still, at this late date in the war, a remarkable attempt at order and efficiency among German officials but there were signs of the end. More criminal gangs now, some calling themselves partisans, others not bothering with the pretence, and Yuri was the only one of our *Hiwis* who had not deserted. They had taken the best horses, some supplies, and disappeared. 'Shameful,' said our Herr Wendorf. They would be hunted down and punished, he said, and maybe they were. Yuri's comrades knew, as he knew, that once we refugees were settled, they had served their purpose. They would be sent to the front to die fighting against their own people, or meet a worse end if they were captured. Yuri's fate was now precarious. He was no *Volksdeutscher*. The *Reich* owed no obligation to the likes of Yuri. I had seen Taunte Liese tearfully pleading with my mother, and with Uncle Knalz. 'We have to save him. We *must!*' she cried.

Our *Obersturmführer* Wendorf also seemed to have become somewhat attached to us. He took pride that under his guidance we had been safely delivered to the *Reich,* and now the German *Mittelstelle* had to get thousands of us settled. Not an easy task in peacetime, an enormous task in a country at war, a losing war – and Wendorf seemed a little overtaxed by his duties. So while we waited to be sorted out, Uncle Knalz and Yuri saddled their horses, packed a bedroll and some food, and went to have a look around, 'to get a feel for the place.' When they returned a few days later Uncle Knalz reported what they had seen. They had come upon an estate in a village called Dunstdorf, one of those picture-perfect estates in the Warthegau, a half-timbered manor house with a dozen cottages clustered around it, three workshops, including a saddlery, and the courtyard shaded by sprawling chestnut trees. *Edeltum.* It all looked so peaceful, he said, hard to believe that only four hundred kilometres to the east the *Wehrmacht* was launching a desperate counter attack against the advancing Red Army. But when they got closer the estate did not look so picture perfect. There was a half-ploughed field with the plough still standing where it had been abandoned in the fall, a tractor with its hood removed amid a litter of greasy disembowelled parts, cows and chickens roaming at will in the courtyard. Nearby stood a box wagon half-loaded with seed potatoes, tipped over at an angle because one wheel had collapsed. A team of Belgian draught horses stood idly by while two women in long skirts, one middle-aged, the other old, shovelled seed potatoes out of the wagon into a wheelbarrow. When they had filled the wheelbarrow they shouted and gesticulated to a group of four men and three women at the edge of the courtyard, lounging under a chestnut tree. The men snickered and shouted something back. It sounded like Ukrainian, said Uncle Knalz.

'Ostarbeiter!' explained the middle-aged woman. 'Lazy good-for-nothings,' she said. 'And they steal, steal everything. Even our underwear, right off the clothesline. Unbelievable!' Uncle Knalz believed it, though he didn't say so. Why wouldn't they steal when they'd been sent here in cattle cars with nothing but the clothes on their backs. She said her husband, the *Graf*, had died fighting for the *Vaterland* at Smolensk, her oldest son missing since Stalingrad, the other captured only a few weeks ago in Italy. All the men in the village had been conscripted by the *Wehrmacht*, the women working in hospitals or munitions factories. So only she, the *Gräfin*, was left, she and her mother-in-law, to try to keep the estate running. She said she had filed petitions with the *Arbeitsdienst*, pleading for help, and these shiftless Ukrainians is what they had sent her.

By the time she had finished her litany of grievances, Yuri had jacked up the wagon, repaired the wheel, and hitched up the Belgians. That was when Uncle Knalz had begun to conceive a plan how his family and a few others might hold out until the end of the war, on land that had not been 'vacated.' He had told the *Gräfin*'s sad story to *Obersturmführer* Wendorf, with whom he'd become quite chummy, and when he was done, he said, Wendorf sadly shook his head and raised his arms in despair at this sorry state of affairs. Uncle Knalz confessed he might have added a little colour to the story when he told Wendorf how shocked he had been to see these two gentlewomen struggling with a wheelbarrow, in their billowing long skirts and dainty footwear, while the estate fell into ruin around them. Take the dairy herd, for example. Nothing but skin and bones. 'It pains me to say it,' he had told Herr Wendorf, 'I mean no disrespect to German cattle breeding, but I've seen bigger udders on Mongolian yaks.'

Herr Wendorf had sighed. *'Ja, ja,* this is what it's come to,' he said. In fact he had personally paid a visit to that estate. A real Lady, that *Gräfin.* Broke his heart to see her struggling like that, and he had tried to assure her every effort would be made to find the 'resources' to get the estate up and running again. But where in these times can you find the personnel, he said. And Uncle Knalz had said that surely among all these recent 're-settlers' from the east, these *Volksdeutsche Umsiedler,* there must be some with experience in managing a large agricultural enterprise, who could keep the machinery running, and knew how to get an honest day's work out of a pack of lazy Slavs.

'Among these ragtag refugees? *Nicht möglich!'* scoffed Herr Wendorf.

'Warum den nicht?' Uncle Knalz protested. Why, he himself, for example, had been on the management team of a 2,000 hectare *kolkhoz.* They had even managed to turn a modest profit, in spite of the meddling of know-it-all commissars from Moscow.

'Nah, tatsächlich?'

'Tatsächlich.' Well, not quite the truth of course, but at times like this Uncle Knalz thought the truth could be stretched a little.

Wendorf's eyes lit up. Well then, would Uncle Knalz himself be willing to take on the task? Give him just two or three days, he said, to send in the forms and make it all official.

Uncle Knalz said he had tried not to seem too eager. He told Wendorf he'd had his heart set on one of the little farms they had been promised, but . . . he was willing to do his part. 'Until this war is over we all have to make sacrifices, *nicht wahr?'*

And so Herr Wendorf had clasped Uncle Knalz's hand in both his hands and thanked him sincerely, on behalf of the *Vaterland.*

Of course he would need more personnel, reliable German personnel, whom he knew to be good workers, said Uncle Knalz.

'But of course, of course, Herr Reimer, *selbstverständlich.'*

And of course, said Uncle Knalz, it would all be quite impossible without his man Yuri, to keep those lazy thieving Slavs in line.

This gave Herr Wendorf pause. That would not be so easy, but be assured, he said, he would do everything humanly possible to find a loophole in the regulations.

It did take a little longer than Wendorf had promised, but then he summoned Uncle Knalz to his office – all smiles. *'Gemacht!'* he said. Done.

Uncle Knalz could have whatever personnel he needed, including his Cossack *Hiwi*, who had been reassigned to a civilian department.

They took Yuri's rifle and his uniform, but they let him keep his sabre and his Andalusian stallion. The *Mittelstelle* had distributed bundles of clothes to us, donated by the local German people, and among the bundles was a well-worn but serviceable blue business suit. Taunte Liese said she could alter it so that it would be more practical for work on an estate than behind a desk in an office, and when she was done the fit was perfect. 'My, my, what a proper German gentleman,' she teased.

Yuri grinned, like a schoolboy fitted out in his first Sunday suit. It fit him like a yoke, I thought. Yuri, now reduced to a tractable farmhand. Did I begrudge him this slim chance of surviving? Would I rather he had joined the other *Hiwis* and deserted, to make their way, by hook or by crook, to Spain then to North Africa or wherever? For a career as mercenaries during the last decades of European colonialism, as many demobbed soldiers would do? Yuri would have been their natural leader. Would I have begged him to let me join them?

I now understand, Antoine, that while I was training my instincts to be more like a Cossack, Yuri, for the love of my Taunte Liese, was training his to be more like a Mennonite.

During the trek his courtship of Taunte Liese had been so proper, so discreet, that people could kid her about it, but by the end of the trek it got beyond kidding. Years later, in hindsight, Uncle Knalz said he had done wrong, he should have tried to keep Yuri and Taunte Liese apart instead of throwing them together, but it seemed cruel to stand in their way. Only a matter of weeks or months at most, before they would all be scattered helter skelter. If then, in the time remaining to them, a man and a woman should try to make their lives more bearable by sharing a little human warmth, so be it. So he had thought then, he said.

Uncle Knalz would have known that Taunte Liese could fend off cruel gossip but not grief. She would not have been able to suppress the memory of her husband, perhaps still alive in Siberia, and she was too honest to pretend, as some pretended, that she had become a 'kept woman' out of desperation 'for the children's sake.' I remember lying awake at night overhearing the stifled murmur of Taunte Liese making her confession to my mother, how in the long hours between sleeping and waking she would see one man's image through her pinched eyes, then the other, then the first again. She would try to suppress one image, then the other, but the images would not obey her will, and she would spend tearful nights pleading for their forgiveness.

Our family – my mother, my Oma Enns, Sarah and I – were not among those who moved into the cottages on the *Gräfin's* estate. Since we were a family with fully grown children, one of us a healthy young male, we were among those entitled to our 'own' farm. We were all given a wagon and a team of horses and led in procession to the farms we had been assigned. Leading the procession on his motorcycle was *Bauer-führer* Schwandt, a low-level civilian official, a paunchy little chinless fellow who always seemed to be looking down his nose with half-closed eyes. He had a clipboard with a detailed map, and at each farm one of the wagons would pull over, *Bauerführer* Schwandt would select the appropriate keys, peer along his nose, and present the keys to the grateful new 'owners.' When we saw the farm that had been assigned to us, we gasped. It was one of the prettiest. A small farm, only twenty hectares, of which one hectare was still a woodlot, a two-storey house with hooded dormers, a little orchard, freshly painted barns, even a dovecote.

My sister and grandmother soon took on proprietorial airs as they explored the nooks and crannies of the house. My mother sat at the kitchen table and stared at her folded hands. I explored the barn and stables, but with less enthusiasm. I did not want to become a farmer.

On our third day in our new home, toward dusk, we noticed a dark figure lurking at the edge of the woodlot that lay across an open field. After several minutes he turned and disappeared among the trees. No sign of him for the next two days, then he was there again. My mother took off her apron, handed it to my sister, tucked a few vagrant strands of hair under her kerchief and strode across the field.

'*Sonya! Vaut velst du! Bliev hiah!*' scolded my grandmother, but my mother kept striding across the field toward the dark figure at the edge of the woodlot. I ran to catch up to her. No telling how many men might be hiding among the trees, or what their purpose was.

When we approached, he disappeared into the underbrush. 'Don't go,' shouted my mother. We stopped at the edge of the wood and waited, and after a few minutes he re-appeared. My mother said 'Please tell us what you want.'

The man spat on the ground.

'That was rude,' said my mother in an even tone, without taking her eyes off him.

He stared back, then he jerked his head toward the house and the barns. 'That's my farm,' he said, 'I should be more polite?'

'I'm sorry,' said my mother, 'I know it must be hard. To see it – like this.'

'You're sorry? That makes it right?' he sneered. They stared at each other. I thought he would spit again but he shook his head and rubbed his sleeve across his nose.

'If not us, the Germans would give your farm to somebody else,' I said. My mother dropped her gaze to the ground, and I felt ashamed.

'If there's something in the house or the barns that you want, please take it,' she said.

He laughed. A mirthless laugh. 'What would I do with it? Everything we own now is wrapped in two bundles, at the foot of our bunks. In barracks, with thirty other families.'

'Do you know what will happen to you?' She reached out and touched his arm with the tips of her fingers. He glanced down at her hand but didn't move his arm.

'They'll deport us. To their munitions factories in the Ruhr. Slave work.'

'Maybe, after the war, they'll let you come back. And give you your farm back.'

'Not too likely,' he sneered. Then he asked my mother, 'How many of you are there?'

'Just four. My mother-in-law, my son here, and my daughter.'

'Only four? The farm will make a good living for you then,' he said. 'Does he know anything about farming?' He looked me over from head to toe.

'A little. In Russia we lived on a big collective farm.'

He looked at his fields and barns, taking in every detail, as though he were seeing it for the last time. 'No point in planting any corn on that hill,' he said. 'Every year it dries out. Good only for grazing.'

'Thank you for telling us,' said my mother.

'The young cow, the Jersey,' he said, 'after two litres she hunches up her back and stops her milk. No point to keep trying. Wait a minute, and stroke her a bit. Let her relax. Then she'll give you another eight or nine litres.'

'Why don't you take her. Please, take the cow,' said my mother.

'Huh! They'd say we stole her. Just waiting for an excuse to hang some of us, an example to the others.'

They were both silent, and now they both looked back over the field at the house and barns, a picture-book scene of rural tranquillity, except for my grandmother and my sister still standing in the yard peering toward us, now barely visible in the gathering dark. Every few minutes my grandmother energetically waved her shawl, to beckon us back.

'We just butchered a pig,' he said, 'There are two hams hanging in the smoke house.'

'Yes, yes,' said my mother, 'We saw them. My son will fetch them.'

'Thank you,' he said.

'And tomorrow morning we'll bring some milk too, and some eggs. There'll be something here every morning for you. Till you have to leave.'

'Thank you.'

I did go, every morning as soon as I was done milking. I put a can of milk in a wheelbarrow, also some eggs, cheese, some sausage, all securely packed in a stone crock. In the evening I went back to fetch the empty can and crock. Then one evening the can was still full, the eggs and cheese were untouched, and we knew the Poles had been deported.

All the while my sister had grumbled and my grandmother scolded. She said if the Germans discovered what we were up to they would probably take away our farm, and then what? My mother said we'd soon find out. She had already told the Germans we didn't want the farm. They would be moving us somewhere else in a day or two.

We had not been consulted, and my grandmother and my sister now began to rail at my mother in earnest. 'Why do we always have to be better than everybody else,' said my sister. 'It's war. We've suffered too. These people, they had it good – while we starved, there, in Russia. You lost a son and a husband. Remember? *I* remember. I lost a brother and a father. Look at this place, for God's sake. It's a little Garden of Eden.'

'In this garden, we're the snake,' said my mother.

A wagon came with a team of two horses to move us out of our Eden.

Bauerführer Schwandt, and sitting beside him his helper, a big burly
fellow. Schwandt was not amused. My mother's refusal of the farm did
not make us popular, not among the petty German officials nor among
our own people. There were a few others who refused but not many.

Bauerführer Schwandt and his helper were silent while they threw our
few possessions into the wagon. When we were underway he could no
longer restrain himself. Had we entirely lost our senses? Did we understand nothing? What did we hope to accomplish with this *Scheisserei*?
With this holier-than-thou attitude. *Wahnsinn! Lauter wahnsinn!* Well,
since we loved this Polish trash so much, we would have a chance to
observe them up close. In a detention camp where a new batch of Poles
were awaiting deportation.

The enclosed camp consisted of three squat barracks, guarded by four
reservists. A crowd of curious Poles clustered around the gate to gawk at
us. The appropriate papers were signed and stamped. The gate opened,
we went in, the gate closed. *Bauerführer* Schwandt got back on his wagon,
tipped up his nose, half-closed his eyes, and left us to our fate.

We were grilled by the Poles and tried to explain how we came to be
there. My Oma Enns now vigorously denounced the Germans for
installing refugees on farms 'stolen' from the Poles, and a few of the
women mumbled that this showed we were not bad people. They were
shouted down. A feisty middle-aged matron approached my grandmother
and began fingering her shawl, a Kazakhstan shawl made of fine wool
that she had managed to hang on to since pre-Revolutionary times. The
matron tipped her head and smiled up at my grandmother. 'Oo-la-la, so
soft,' she said, then in an instant she tore the shawl off my grandmother's
shoulders and wrapped it around her own shoulders. She folded her arms
and stared into my grandmother's face, daring her to protest.

A big rangy Pole leaned against the frame of an open door, cleaning
his finger nails with a long knife that he held by the tip. He mumbled
something we couldn't understand but one of the women, who seemed to
have *kapo* status in the camp, translated. 'You sleep on the floor, at the
back. No beds. All taken. Come with me.'

My dog was still with us then. When we left our villages we'd been
told dogs weren't allowed on the trek, so I had given my dog to a
Ukrainian boy who had promised to take good care of her. But on the
fourth day of the trek, about forty kilometres from our village, my dog

was spotted by Brumtup, a few wagons behind us. She was trotting along beside the road, shy of getting too close to the wagons, her tongue hanging out, exhausted and famished. When I heard Brumtup shouting I jumped from the wagon, ran, and embraced my dog. She was still dragging what was left of rope she had chewed through, tied around her neck. There were a few complaints about us keeping her but they soon relented. On nights when we all had to sleep in our wagons, the dog lay between my sister and me and helped keep us warm. But when the dog now tried to follow me inside, the man with the knife gave her a kick that sent her sprawling. All I could do was scowl at him. 'No four-legged dogs allowed inside,' said somebody. 'Only two-legged.' And everybody laughed. I took my bedroll and camped outside with my dog.

After my mother, Sarah, and Oma Enns had been settled, they came out and joined me and my dog near the gate. Soon children gathered around us. They made a game to see which of them was the bravest. One by one they pranced in front of us, as close as they dared, and with their index finger made the universal throat-slitting sign. Stuck out their tongues and popped their eyeballs, then ran giggling to the safety of the group.

In the morning a farmer came with two big cans of milk, and I lined up with the others. I was pushed to the back of the line, and long before it was my turn the milk ran out. Then a van came with loaves of dark rye bread and this time it was my sister who lined up, and again the bread ran out before it was her turn. Later my grandmother found an old woman who seemed to take some pity on us, and she traded one of her elegant ebony combs for half a loaf. Then the woman took me aside and said there was a path through the trees behind the compound that led to another farm, and maybe that farmer would let me have some milk. 'There's a hole. You can get under the fence. But watch out for *Gestapo* patrols,' she said. 'Sometimes they shoot people.' Was this kindness, or was I being lured into a trap?

My grandmother gave me her other ebony comb to trade, and off I went. Since there might be cause for stealth I did not want to take my dog, so I tied a rope around her neck and told my sister to take her to the front of the compound where she couldn't see me leave. I didn't want the dog to make a big fuss when I left, or try to follow me.

I found the farm, traded the comb for half a bucket of milk, and saw

no sign of a *Gestapo* patrol. I was almost back when I heard my dog
barking and yelping, and my sister shrieking. Then the yelping and the
shrieking stopped. I dropped the bucket and ran but I was too late. The
dog lay dead, her throat slit, and the big Pole stood leaning against the
door, with his knife, cleaning his fingernails. My mother and sister and a
couple of young Polish men restrained me, wrestled me to the ground, or
I might have died there too, trying to avenge my dog. Then we gathered
our belongings and pleaded with the four German guards to please let us
out. They had witnessed the scene, but they pretended to ignore us. Then
one of them went to the gate, fumbled with the lock, and they all turned
their backs. The gate swung open a few inches and we squeezed through.
We walked toward the town. We were silent except for my old grandmother who could not resist reminding my mother that she had warned
her what would come of this stupid high-mindedness.

There seemed to be excitement in the town. People had lined the main
street to wave at a shiny Mercedes slowly making its way through the
throng. I asked a young girl who this was, and she could hardly contain
her excitement. 'The *Gauleiter,* the *Gauleiter* himself,' she said, '*Gauleiter*
Greiser.' On a tour of his *Gebiet.* And who were these people waving?
Germans, she said, most of them from the eastern parts of the *Reich.*

The *Gauleiter* sat in the back of the Mercedes, looking left and right
with evident satisfaction, nodding to the waving groups of refugees in
recognition of their gratitude. Then he saw us, a sorry looking troupe
trudging into town with our clattering gear hanging on our backs. The
car stopped and he glared at us through the window. He said something
to his driver. The driver rolled down his window to ask who we were,
and what we were doing here. He addressed us in Polish, and my mother
replied in German. She said we were refugees. We had been lodged in a
compound for Polish people but it was too dangerous for us there. 'They
killed my dog,' I said.

The driver reported what we had told him to the *Gauleiter.* He rolled
down his own window, to address us. '*Deutsch?*' he demanded.

Ja, we said.

He rolled up his window and said something to his driver. The driver
shrugged, shook his head. The *Gauleiter* seemed angry. He rolled down his
window again and beckoned to my mother. Who had done this, he
demanded, who had lodged us in that Polish camp?

Bauerführer Schwandt, we said.

The *Gauleiter* wrote something on a piece of paper and handed it to my mother, and told us to be in his office in an hour.

We waited huddled in a corner of a large room, while clerks and typists rushed back and forth between their desks and a wall of filing cabinets. Some SS men were shouting orders to the typists and to each other, and one was shouting into a telephone while he held a second phone in his other hand. Then the *Gauleiter* arrived and everyone stood to *Heil Hitler* him. He acknowledged the salute, barked a few orders and cracked a few jokes, then turned his attention to us. He barked another order over his shoulder and someone scurried to fetch that Schwandt fellow, that *Dummkopf.*

Bauerführer Schwandt presented himself and barely got out his *Heil Hitler* before the *Gauleiter* walloped him across the face. Then followed a thorough dressing down, the *Gauleiter's* face getting redder and redder, *Bauerführer* Schwandt's face whiter and whiter. What in the name of God was he thinking, demanded the *Gauleiter,* to lodge Germans with Polish trash? *Bist dann ganz verrückt?* Had he lost all his senses? 'A disgrace, a disgusting disgrace!' he shouted.

The *Gauleiter* assigned a more competent official to look after us, who took us to a bigger town and installed us in a comfortable apartment. My mother was given a job altering officers' uniforms, but my sister was the lucky one. She was taken to the town hall and given a job in the *Bürgermeister's* office. She proved so proficient at the work that she was soon promoted to an administrative position in the *Arbeitsdienst,* the municipal department in charge of rationing scarce manpower to the surrounding estates and factories – including slave labour. She too had become aloof and withdrawn, and had as little to do with our people as possible. Only to my grandmother Enns could she still be civil.

So who was this *Gauleiter,* Antoine, this wonderful benefactor of all us *Volksdeutsche?* Two years later in Berlin he was in the news again, when reports of captured and arrested war criminals dominated the front pages of both the German and American papers. I remember showing you his picture. You grimaced and turned aside. Arthur Greiser, a man of many titles, *Obergruppenführer,* also *Reichsstatthalter* and *Gauleiter* of *Reichsgau Wartheland,* from 1939 to 1945. One of the most brutal of all high-ranking Nazi goons. By 1942 he had practically cleansed the Warthegau of Jews.

Under his direction, *Obergruppenführer* Wilhelm Koppe and *Sturmbahn-führer* Herbert Lange had established the first extermination camp at a country estate near Chelmno, to kill the Jews from the Lodz ghetto. Then he had turned to the task of cleansing the Warthegau of Poles, so that this province of the *Reich* could be pure German. His zeal and efficiency had been the envy of all the other *Gauleiters*. After the war he was put on trial by the Supreme National Tribunal of the newly established Polish government, convicted and sentenced to death. He alone was accorded a special distinction. He was put in a cage and paraded through the streets of Poznan, and hanged on June 20, 1946, the last public hanging in Poland.

What purifying rites are there, Antoine, for those who have accepted the kindness of monsters?

My mother and my sister now seemed well-positioned to wait out the war. Or so I told myself. What were my options? I had two – 'volunteer' to join the *Wehrmacht* or wait till I was conscripted. Because I looked younger than my nineteen years I had evaded the notice of recruiting officers, until my mother was handed a letter instructing me to report to the recruitment centre in a nearby town. She had torn it up and burned it, hoping to stall the process a few more weeks until the war might be over. But I knew they would come for me. They had already recruited Franz, my old friend and comrade in the windmill caper. He among others were now waiting to be sent south for training. I thought I would find him grimly resigned to his fate, but he wasn't. 'No, I want to go,' he said.

Maybe they'll put you in the signal corps, I said.

Franz made a face. 'Dit dit dit, dot, dot dit.' Then he laughed. 'No. I want to fight. I want to kill as many communists as I can. We've taken enough shit from those bastards.'

I was taken aback. I had always thought Franz was a bit, well, shallow. Always good company, always game for any prank or harmless mischief, but I had not thought he was capable of such profound hate. He shamed me. My clever displays of rebellion now looked cheap, mere loud-mouthed posturing.

I waited a day before I told my mother I had enlisted. 'No,' she yelped, and covered her face with her hands. I tried to explain that it was a rational decision – that if I enlisted before I was forcibly conscripted I might be given options about which branch of the military I would join, or where I would 'serve.' But we all knew that was unlikely. The Germans did not send our young men to the western front to fight the Americans or the British. They knew most of us would surrender or desert at the first opportunity. They sent us to the eastern front to fight against our own countrymen. Because they knew we would fight to the death rather than risk capture by the Russians, and a cruel death when they discovered we were traitors.

My mother knew my arguments were a sham. She grabbed my shoulders and squeezed till it hurt. Why, in the last days of this war, she said, would I volunteer to add my body to the senseless pile of corpses? And finally, when all else failed, she argued Mennonite pacifism. I scoffed at the argument. 'Haven't you heard the prayers of our elders?' I sneered, 'Thanking God for his mercy when they hear reports that the Germans have driven back the Russians? We want Germans to kill the Communists but want to keep our own hands clean? That's sheer hypocrisy.'

And moreover, we had heard the macabre stories about the savagery of Russian soldiers when they occupied a town or city. 'When those savages come to our house, raping and murdering, I'm not about to cower in a corner,' I said, 'fold my hands and pray God will work a miracle to protect you.'

'Do you think you can save us by shooting a few soldiers when you're miles away at the front? Or when you're dead? But the reason for pacifism,' she said, 'is not to make us martyrs. It's to hold out some hope that our young men will never ever be among those doing the raping and murdering.'

'*That* is what you're afraid of?' I said. 'Me, your own son?'

She closed her eyes and pinched her mouth shut. Then she said, 'How many young men have there been, in all of history, Struvel, decent, upright young men, who, when war began, could imagine they would become rapists and murderers?' Then the anger drained out of her, she held me tight in her arms and moaned, 'No, no, I didn't mean that.'

Then Uncle Knalz came to talk sense to me. He said people were doing things no people has ever done before. Horrible things. 'We, our people, are only bit players in this chaos,' he said. 'But if we survive without doing something terrible it won't be small.' And when it's all over my family will need me more than ever, he said. And not only my family but all of *unse* – all our people will need young men like me. Clever, educated young men, who can speak different languages, who can speak for our people under whatever government we might find ourselves. 'That's how it's always been done,' he said.

What? Me, a spokesman for our people? Me, sitting there in some stuffy bureaucrat's office, rolling the brim of my hat in my sweaty palms, waiting my turn to plead for certain rights and privileges for these quaint Mennonites? No thanks. I laughed in his face.

They did not understand. None of them. I felt my life slipping away from me. We had made it. We had escaped Stalin's Russia, what only a few years ago had seemed unbelievable. And for what? To be tethered to the fate of these Mennonites? Wherever I turned, they were there, jostling and shoving, scrambling for the real or imagined preferences they now thought they were entitled to. When we were fleeing Russia under threat from the avenging Red Army they showed courage, had worked together, but in the relative calm of arrival they now had occasion to vent their petty rivalries. I was sick of the hypocrisy, and sick of overhearing snide comments about my sister Sarah's morning sickness.

I imagined myself above their squalid little quarrels but I was wallowing in my own squalor. I didn't like the person I had become – embittered, snarling like a cornered dog. I had to do something rash, perverse, to stop being that person. As you had done, Antoine, that hot August day when you came armed with your knives to save me from Grisha and his sadistic elves. A desperate, reckless act in defiance of the shabby life on offer to you. A desperate leap out of the shifting shadows into the glare of the flood lights. You needed only to appear, and Grisha's fustian swagger would have shrivelled to a sheepish smirk. But no, you brought your knives.

How else could I understand it? So bring it on, bring on the worst. I cast my frustration in heroic terms. I wanted to be tested, I told myself, with no one but myself to fall back on. I wanted to see what stuff I was made of, I wanted to hold my soul to the fire to see if it would glow or shrivel. I will not claim my decision was rational, only that it was irrevocable the moment I made it. I craved decisive action, as an antidote, any antidote, to passive endurance, a craving to make that irrevocable vault in despair of leaden scruples, to leap upon the back of that raging, red-eyed beast-of-the-world, and ride! Ride that beast through fire and flood. Not to subdue it. All that mattered was to stay mounted on that beast to the end.

I tore myself from my mother's embrace and shouldered my pack. 'Remember who you are,' were her last words. But I did not want to remember. It was a hollow gesture. I would have been conscripted anyway. But it wasn't innocent.

I had two months of training, near Munich, then five months in the *Waffen SS*. I had expected to join the *Wehrmacht*, but after a brief interview the recruiting officer had me signed up for the *Waffen SS*. I had little notion of the difference. I was assigned to an intelligence unit as an interpreter, then I made a rash request to be transferred to the front.

I saw only four weeks of combat but that was enough to give me a lasting impression of the slaughter. The Red Army had taken a town southwest of Königsberg, and we were ordered to counterattack. The attack failed, and I and my comrades were caught in a no-man's land between German and Soviet artillery, between our own *Panzers* and the Soviet T34s converging upon us. The earth convulsed, rose up before us like a tidal wave of wind and steel, of trees, dirt and body parts. When the air cleared a little I took a few futile shots at the Soviet tanks, then ran until I tumbled into a crater where two others had tumbled in before me. I could see tanks engulfed in smoke with flames shooting through open hatches, like an absurdly huge cigarette lighter that a giant's thumb had flicked open, and little black men stuck their torsos out of the hatch like burning wicks. And then, as though the lighter were running out of fluid, the flames died down and licked lazily around the shell till it became a blackened hulk.

The firing moved down the line and we scrambled out of the crater and ran, over dismembered bodies and corpses. I stumbled over one who whimpered, '*Kamerad, hilf mir,*' and for a moment I hesitated. Then I crawled over to him, or to that part of him that had a head on it, and cradled the head in my lap. '*Ja, ja, ich bin hier,*' I said. '*Kamerad, ich sterbe,*' he said. '*Wir sterben alle,*' I said, then I wiped his brow and kissed it. I hummed a lullaby while I rocked his head in my arms, till someone kicked my shoulder and shouted, 'Leave him. He's dead!' I took off my coat, covered him, and ran.

What remained of our regiment was then given a brief respite from the front. We were assigned the task of guarding a trainload of Jewish prisoners until our depleted ranks could be reinforced. The Jews were stranded at a railway station where their train had broken down and it was supposed to take only a few days till it was operational again.

My dear Sara came from Winnipeg as soon as she heard my wife and I were under siege by journalists and neighbourhood voyeurs. She came roaring down our street, honking her horn, scattering journalists and television crews behind their vans for safety. She wheeled into our driveway, jumped out of her car and shouted obscenities at them. She picked up a lens that a cameraman had lost when he fled and threw it at one of the vans. I ran down and tried to calm her. 'Let's get out of here,' she said. 'Get in the car.'

We sped down the main street, a sharp left onto the bridge across the river, and soon we were out in the open country. She drove randomly, zigzagging across the grid of prairie roads, cursing through tears of anger. I couldn't restrain my own tears, for her, for the pain and shame she felt because of me. We came to a bend in the road at the edge of a deep, wide coulee where there is a small parking lot for those who wish to stop and take in the view. We got out of the car and leaned against the wooden rail placed there for our safety. It had turned wet and windy. We turned up our collars and folded our arms on our chests for warmth. 'Those damn Jews,' she said, 'they've really fucked up your life.'

I slapped her hard, she slapped back. I slapped her again, then we embraced and sobbed into each other's shoulder. But who was I slapping? My slaps were a confession that I was struggling to suppress the same shameful resentments.

PEACE AMONG THE RUINS

May 5, 1992

Seeding time on the Canadian prairie. Two weeks later than normal because of a wet spring. The land has to dry out before it can bear the weight of monstrous tractors and thirty-foot seeders. For the last few days the telephone lines across the province would have been buzzing – farmers consulting each other, debating, getting anxious. Now? Or better wait another day? As though the earth were teasing them. Then two monster tractors are spotted on the land, and the next day there are hundreds. Everywhere you look.

For thirty-two years I have witnessed this spring ritual, but this may be my last. You don't have to be a farmer to feel your pulse quicken. Battalions of heavy machinery – trucks, tractors, rakes and seeders – mobilized with an efficiency that would make any military commander envious if its purpose were to kill people. There is no order from the Department of Agriculture, no troops of officials and soldiers to make sure it's all done to regulation, there is only the pooled wisdom of farmers to determine what to seed and when.

Peace on the Canadian prairie, noisy, exuberant, confident. Not what peace felt like in central Europe when the war ended on this date, May 5, 1945. 60,000,000 people had died in our war, and 12,000,000 refugees were swarming into Germany from Latvia, the Ukraine, and the eastern provinces of the former *Reich*. Those are the figures historians have now settled on. Can you get a grip on all those zeroes, Antoine? – four times the number of deaths in World War I, sixteen times the number in the Napoleonic Wars, and the number of refugees matches the whole population of Canada at that time.

In France, England, Holland, and throughout Canada, jubilant throngs cheered the end of the war. You were in Paris on August 26, 1944, you would have seen the American tanks parading down the Champs-Élysées, and those pretty French girls scrambling onto them to hang garlands around the necks of their liberators. There was little cheering east of the Oder-Neisse Line. People fled from their Soviet liberators. Millions of them. You and I were still alive but neither of us was cheering, neither you in Paris nor I in Poland. My chances of surviving the peace weren't much better than my chances of surviving the war had been.

I wanted to confide in you when we were together again in Berlin but you seemed wary of undue soul-baring. 'We all had to make difficult choices during the war,' you said. I didn't want to whine and grovel, so I told you only the bare facts, that I had deserted and spent the last two months of the war wandering aimlessly around western Poland as the front rolled through, dodging *Gestapo* patrols looking for deserters then Red Army patrols looking for traitors, either one of whom would be quick to hang me or shoot me.

During the last months of the war, after I deserted, I was not that limp lump of flesh you saw when you first laid eyes on me in Berlin. I was angry, vengeful. I felt I had been cruelly betrayed. I had put my hopes in the Nazis, to save me from the wretched life that awaited me under Stalinist communism, then found myself complicit in worse squalor. I was wary of everyone I met. Everyone was a real or potential enemy, and I was determined to go down fighting if I had to. I still had my P08 Luger and a full box of bullets. If I were apprehended by either the *Gestapo* or the Red Army, I was determined to shoot as many of them as I could before they killed me.

Germans to the west of me, the Red Army to the east, so I turned north toward the Baltic coast, hoping to find a 'neutral' ship that would take me to Sweden or Denmark. I came upon a field of mud where there had recently been a battle. I saw an old man sitting in the mud, his back against a shattered tree. He wore a long gray coat of World War I vintage, with medals and gold braid adorning it, and he was clutching his abdomen. He also had a gash on his cheek but no other obvious injury. 'Those were my men,' he said, gesturing toward the field of mud. '*Volkssturm*. Most of them local lads, some only fifteen years old. They were brave, but they didn't stand a chance.'

A thin crust of frost had formed on the mud, and splinters of ice covered pools of murky water, and I could see now that the angular stalks protruding through the debris were legs and arms. There were half a dozen old women wading among them, perhaps not so old. Perhaps they looked old because all their movements were laboured, staggering through the mud. Bent black hulks, combing through the corpses like ghastly gleaners. They were not gentle, these women. Sometimes they would fall upon a twisted shape, would grab an arm or a leg and pull, staggering with the effort, would wrestle the body out of the mud as though they would dispute earth's right to claim her own. Then they would turn the body onto its back and scrape a gob of mud from the face. Sometimes they grabbed the back of a collar and pulled, or they would grab a handful of hair, jerk the head back and peer into the face, then let the face plop back into the mud – mothers, looking for the one face that would buckle their knees, the face they could press against their own warm cheek and begin to grieve.

I too had a mother somewhere who would be scanning every face she met. I turned again and walked south. I approached a range of low mountains covered in dense forest and I could see, or imagined I could, human figures entering the forest ahead of me, or they would come out to the edge of the forest, take their bearings, and then disappear into it again. I could hide there from both Soviet and *Gestapo* units, and take my chances with those forest renegades. I did not expect to find love.

Do you want to hear about Eva? I couldn't tell you back then, in Berlin, not without pleading for your pity, but maybe now, after so many years, you will indulge my neediness.

Tramping through the forest. On rare sunny days it got surprisingly warm but the nights were still cold, and often sleet was mixed in with the rain. I knew nothing of forest lore, and it came as a surprise that a labyrinth of footpaths penetrated the otherwise impenetrable forest. The snow had withdrawn into soggy depressions, coarse and dirty, and even at midday there was only a dank gloom. Every sound, the snap of a twig or the raucous cry of a crow, made me whirl around and reach for my Luger. Then the path I'd been following suddenly opened onto a clearing, like a notch cut out of the steep slope. It was almost bare of snow, with a glint of new green grass. A stony brook gurgled along the lower side of the clearing, then tumbled over some boulders into the forest below. To my left, on the upper side, rose a steep cliff with strange yellowish rock formations, and huddled near the cliff stood a haystack sheltered from the wind. A secluded pastoral interlude among craggy rocks and trees.

The haystack promised warmth and shelter from the rain. I dug in with my hands and pulled out small clumps of hay until my fingers began to bleed. The hay had been skilfully stacked to resist the wind and confound unwelcome foragers. I could make no progress. I walked around the back, hoping to find a spot where the hay was more loosely stacked, and suddenly there was a place. I pulled out a whole armful of hay, and then another and another. A tunnel. I clawed my way in until my hand touched something covered in coarse cloth. Round lumps under the cloth. A sack of potatoes? I pulled out my pocket knife and cut it open, and began eating potatoes as though they were apples. After the first two I took the time to peel them. Then I noticed there was room to straighten up on my knees. I reached up and felt rafters and boards. This was no haystack. This was a small sturdy hut hidden under the hay, to conceal a cache of food. It would be dangerous to stay here but it was warm and dry.

There were other bags. Different sizes. One of them smelled like onions. When I had gorged myself I made a bed to lie on. I lay down and fell asleep – till I heard someone grunting, crawling toward me. I groped for my Luger. I saw only a black shade etched against the pale light of dawn behind her. It is not easy for a girl to crawl through a low tunnel when she's wearing a long coat and a skirt, and pushing a tin bucket in front of her. She kept stepping on her coat with her knees. 'Anngh, anngh.' My eyes were accustomed to the dark but hers weren't, and when she reached out and groped for a sack of potatoes she found my knee instead. She explored a little further up my leg. 'That's my leg,' I whispered. She gasped and jerked her hand back.

'What's your leg doing here?' she whispered.

'Keeping the other leg company. I have two of them.'

She scrambled backwards out of the haystack and ran, and I ran after her, shouting 'Stop! Stop! Please stop. I won't hurt you. Please don't tell anyone. I'll go away.'

When she reached the brook at the bottom of the clearing she stepped nimbly across it, from stone to stone. I was not so nimble. I slipped and fell. I hit my head on a rock and badly twisted my ankle. I must have lost consciousness for a few moments. The first sensation I remember was water lapping at the edge of my mouth and I turned my head so I wouldn't choke on it. I lay with my eyes closed for I don't know how long. Then with a start I remembered what had happened, and opened my eyes. I saw Eva's face above me and looked into Eva's eyes. She stood a few feet back, balancing on stones at the edge of the brook, and craned her neck forward, the better to see me. It was almost morning now, enough light to see everything but I saw only her. Not the trees behind her, or the sky above her, only her, suspended above me.

'Are you still alive?' she said.

'I don't know,' I said. 'Are you an angel? Or just a girl?'

'Just a girl,' she said. And she smiled. I wasn't trying to be funny. I was dazzled. I had forgotten that a human face could be beautiful. She had black hair, cut short, framing her pale face as she leaned over me. She spoke German, with a Polish accent. 'You're bleeding,' she said. 'The water around your head is all red.'

I tried to get up but yelped and lay back when a stab of pain shot through my ankle. Tried again, and managed to get up on one leg, tottered, and almost fell among the rocks again. She moved closer and held out her arm to steady me. 'Did you break your leg too?'

'No. Maybe my ankle.' She helped me hobble out of the brook. 'Careful,' she said. 'Big step. It's deep here.'

She eased me down on the bank and watched while I took inventory of my injuries. 'You've got a bad cut behind your ear,' she said. 'You should bandage it. Do you have a scarf, or something?' I shook my head and closed my eyes again. I didn't have the will or the energy to think about bandages. She took a handkerchief out of her pocket, dipped it in a pool of clear water, and washed some of the blood off my head. 'It's bleeding bad. It needs a bandage.' I looked around as though I expected a bandage might miraculously appear from somewhere. 'Do you have a knife?' she said. 'I can cut a sleeve off your shirt.'

My knife was in my pocket. She helped me sit up, then knelt beside my shoulder and made a cut at the top of the sleeve wide enough to get her fingers through it and rip the fabric. But she couldn't rip the seam under my armpit. She bent her head down so she could see what she was doing and began sawing at the seam. She was trying to hurry, because of the bleeding. Without thinking, without knowing what I was doing, I reached out and stroked her hair. She jerked back and jumped to her feet. 'I'm sorry,' I said, 'I didn't mean anything. It's just . . . just . . . you have beautiful hair. I won't touch you again.'

She knelt down again and attacked the seam of my sleeve, slipped it off my arm, and tied it around my head. 'There's a lot of blood,' she said, 'I'll have to cut off the other sleeve too.' When she was done I forced myself onto my feet but I could only hop on my good leg, so she held my arm and helped me hobble back to the haystack. She sat me down beside the tunnel and crawled in to fetch my coat. 'You should get out of those wet clothes or you'll freeze. Do you have matches to build a fire?' I said I did. She went back into the hut to fetch her bucket of potatoes. I reached for her hand and this time she didn't pull back. 'I can't walk. I'll have to stay another day,' I said. 'Please don't tell anyone I'm here.'

She dropped her eyes to the ground, then lifted them to meet mine. 'I won't,' she said.

She came back the next morning, alone. I had crawled out of the haystack and dragged myself about twenty metres up the slope into the trees. I wanted to trust her, but I couldn't be sure so I hid and watched through the underbrush. She approached slowly, looking left and right, then came around to my side of the haystack where the tunnel was. She crouched down and called softly. 'German man?' Then louder, 'German man?'

'I'm over here, Polish girl.' Which startled her, then she laughed and I told her my name and she told me hers. She had brought clean bandages, and a clean flannel shirt with two sleeves. Her father's, she said, but it was old. He wouldn't miss it. We hobbled down to the brook and Eva sat me down on the bank, removed the old bandage from my head, rinsed it in the brook and began washing the dried blood off my forehead and cheeks. And when she was done with the bandaging we talked. She said the front had moved through the region at the end of January, and that it had been terrible, especially for the German women down in the town.

They raped Polish women too, but usually only the young ones, and then they let them go. There were some Ukrainian girls too. The Germans had brought them to work in the factories in Łódź. The Russians said they were all whores and collaborators. So they raped them too. It had not been so bad up here, in the hills, she said. Theirs was just a little village. A few Russian soldiers came through one day but they hardly stopped.

She said up here in the hills it was the partisans who were now in control. In the beginning there had been all kinds, even Jewish partisans, but now they all called themselves communists. And tried to cosy up to the Russians. Most were just looters. She said there had been a Jewish family that survived the war by hiding in a cave. Not far away. And some people had helped them, brought them food. They knew the Jews still had some money.

But some of them are real partisans, she said, and she herself was betrothed to the leader of one of those partisan bands. A long story – not pretty – but never mind. Down on the plain, to the north, most of the towns were German, German names, everything German, been like that forever, she said, but they had treated Polish people badly so now they wanted revenge. She mentioned Breslau and Nemmersdorf. She said she too had hated all German people. So it wasn't safe for me here. The partisans would kill me.

I said both the Germans and the Russians would kill me just as quickly. I said somehow I had to get through the lines to the Americans, or to the British, but I would have to stay hidden here until my ankle healed. She said she was the only one who came here to fetch food when they needed it. Her mother was old and had bad knees, and her father and her little brother were busy running errands for the partisans. She said her father had made the cache so the Germans wouldn't steal their winter supplies, then so the Russians wouldn't steal them. Yes, maybe some of the neighbours knew about the cache, but they were too afraid of her betrothed to steal any of it. She said that if I looked under the sacks of potatoes and turnips I would find two stone crocks with smoked ham and sausage, and some jars of preserved chicken.

The sun was already over the tops of the trees when she left, so I stretched on my back and let the rays warm my face. Then I dragged myself into the trees behind the haystack, found a stout crooked stick and started whittling at it to make a crutch.

She did not come the third morning, but she came again on the fourth, before dawn. This time she brought soap and an old towel. After she had filled her bucket with potatoes she said, 'I'll help you get down to the brook, if you want. To get washed.' It had been months since I'd had soap for a bath. She led me over some slippery rocks into a pool that was about knee deep, then she went back and sat down on a fallen tree with her back to the brook. 'It's OK,' she said, 'I won't look,' so I took off my clothes and began lathering my body. The icy cold water took my breath away, but I kept lathering. 'Don't slip and fall,' she said, and then I slipped and fell. I let out a yelp, and she came splashing through the water to lift me back on my feet, and lead me back to the bank. Then I kissed her. She drew back. 'You fell on purpose,' she said. I fiercely denied it, but maybe I did. She picked up my coat and draped it around my naked body. Then we kissed again. She didn't pull back.

We hobbled back to the hut and stood next to the entrance of the tunnel that led inside. Neither of us could think of anything to say, so she crawled into the tunnel and I followed her. And there, in the musty warmth of that bunker, on a knobbly bed of potato sacks, among odours of smoked ham and Polish sausage, we made love.

All the clichés about first love are true, Antoine. The stars and the moon are bigger and brighter, the air you breathe has flavour, birds sing with more fervour. Together life quickens, apart time drags. It is all true. She was more frank and more adventurous in the arts of love than I was, and in the dark of that musty bunker, where we could hardly see the whites of each other's eyes, my flesh tingled as her hands and lips explored my body, and it seemed to me that under her touch I was not only restored but re-created – every part of me made new.

Two more days, then she came again. She brought her father's straight razor and again we hobbled down to the brook and she gave me my first shave in months. She sat me down on the fallen tree and began shaving the bristles off my cheeks, then my chin, then I closed my eyes and tipped my head back while she scraped the razor along my throat. And like all barbers, while she shaved she talked. She talked about the subject that more and more had begun to trouble me. Her betrothed. A brute, she said, and the betrothal had become a sick joke. She said when the Germans first invaded he had indeed been a hero, the leader of a band of real partisans who did kill some German soldiers. But he was a braggart even then, she said, especially after he lost his eye. He had placed a bomb in a tavern where the *Gestapo* went to drink, and it had gone off before he could get out. Now he wore a patch over his left eye like a medal of bravery.

She said after the Germans retreated there were more and more gangs of 'partisans.' If you didn't have one to protect you the others would rob you blind. She said when her father noticed that Patch Eye had become 'interested' in her, he had fawned over him, treated him like a big Polish patriot, began strutting around the village with his arm around his shoulder and called him 'my son.' He told her she should be 'nice' to him, and her mother began doing his laundry and mending his shirts. At first her younger brother hated him, and hated her for being 'nice,' until Patch Eye gave him a gun and told him he was now one of 'The Men.'

Yes, she had been flattered, at first, to be courted by a big patriot, a local hero. Patch Eye brought gifts, and they all sat at the kitchen table, Patch Eye and her father drinking, the others just listening while he told them how he and his gang had broken into a German collaborator's house further down the valley, and thrown all his belongings onto the street for the poor people to divide it up among themselves. Then they burned down the house. Then he told how they found a whole family of rich German swine, in the winter when it was very cold, trying to escape down a forest road with all their family heirlooms piled on a child's sleigh, paintings of their ancestors and expensive clothes. They burned the paintings and clothes, then told them to take off the clothes they were wearing and burned those too. They took them, naked, to a village where German *Gestapo* had killed all the men, and left them in front of the church, at the mercy of the widows and mothers.

The change had come suddenly, she said. Suddenly everything about Patch Eye had sickened her. Even the littlest things, the hair on his nose, the way he yawned, such a self-satisfied yawn, the way he rolled his shoulders when he walked. All his swaggering and boasting began to nauseate her. And the more he sickened her the more he wanted her to do disgusting things. To show she really loved him. Her whole family now sickened her, and she sickened herself. They soon dropped all pretence, she said. When Patch Eye arrived at the house, there was the same hearty welcome, ho ho ho, but now he just grabbed her wrist and led her into the bedroom. Her father made a few hollow guffaws, then they left the house. So the young couple could be alone. It was all so sick, she said.

When we returned to the hut Eva said, 'I shouldn't have told you all that. You'll think I'm just a whore.' I said I knew what women had to do in a war, and then I told her I had real crimes to confess. I told her some of what I had seen and done, including what had happened at a train station where we were guarding Jews. I ended with a litany of should-haves – I should have done this, shouldn't have done that. 'Shush, shush,' she said, 'all that matters is that we know it was all wrong.' Then we crawled into the hut and made love again.

The easy absolution of a young girl lying naked beside you, smothering you with kisses, is not to be scorned, Antoine. No, it is not enough, but at that moment it was much.

On the sixth day, and the seventh, she didn't come. I waited and imagined every terrible plot to explain why she hadn't come. I spent most of the day hidden just inside the forest, beyond the upper edge of the meadow, lying flat on a mossy rock where I could keep an eye on the spot beyond the brook where Eva's path came out. I jumped to my feet a dozen times when I thought I saw her, saw something move among the trees. Once I was sure it must be her. Something blue moved among the trees, but she was not there.

She came again on the eighth day. At midday, tearful and angry. She said her betrothed and his men had all gathered in the village to make a big celebration, together with another band of partisans. At least twenty of them. They showed off their new guns, captured from the Germans, and they all got drunk. It had been a terrible day and a more terrible night.

We had to leave right away, she said, the next morning at the latest. We? Yes, we. Both of us. She said her family had begun to look at her strangely. First her mother, but now also her little brother and her father. Maybe it was just her imagination, but maybe not.

I wanted to embrace her but I held back. It would be lunacy, I said. If they already suspected, her absence would confirm their suspicions. They would call her a Nazi whore, and every partisan gang in the region would hunt us down and kill us. I said I must leave immediately, alone.

'Listen,' she said, 'let me tell you how we live.' Patch Eye had begun to sicken her whole family, she said, and they all lived in fear of him now. Patch Eye knew – and he made sure they all knew – that they needed his protection more than ever, that all the people who hated him now hated them too. So he began to toy with them. She said he showed up one day with a little velvet sack full of jewels, expensive jewels, and he spread them on the kitchen table for them to see. There were a pair of earrings with little red stones in them, she said, and he told her mother to put them on. She tried to refuse, she pretended she was too modest, but he said, 'Don't be afraid, *pane,* try them on,' and so she did, and he oohed and ahhed how beautiful she looked. Then he tapped the side of his nose with his finger and winked. He said he had just made 'a very profitable trade.' There was this Jewish family he had been hiding and 'protecting' since the beginning of the war, and this family had indeed made some generous 'donations' to the Resistance, wink, wink. But the donations were drying up, and then one of his informers had told him about a Jewish family up in the hills, very poor, apparently, but he'd heard these Jews had hidden money and jewels under the seat of their outdoor privy. Maybe just a rumour, maybe not.

The trouble was, Patch Eye explained, this family belonged to a rival gang of partisans. 'So I talked to this Tadeusz. Tadeusz, I says, I'll trade you my Jews for your Jews.' (That's how he always talked, said Eva – 'Tadoooz, I says' – enough to make you puke.) Then Patch Eye told them how he had duped Tadeusz. He had cleverly admitted – right off the top – that he had pretty well bled his Jews dry. But they had two gorgeous daughters. 'A bit young yet,' he had told Tadeusz, 'but they'll be a good investment when they mature.' Eva said Patch Eye thought it was very funny when a communist like himself talked like a capitalist.

So they had traded Jews, he and Tadeusz, and then Patch Eye and his comrades had paid a visit to their new 'property.' He said there was a teenaged son who became argumentative, and one of his men had to put an end to the argument. After that, no trouble persuading Mama Jew to show them where the jewels were hidden. Then Patch Eye rolled around on his chair and grinned at Eva's mother, 'So how do you like your new earrings, *pane?*' Eva said her mother had snatched at them and tried to tear them off her ears until her father bellowed, 'Leave them on!' Patch Eye thought it was all very funny. 'Don't worry, *pane,*' he said, 'they look much better on you than on that Jewish cow.'

Eva said she did try to defy her father, and he had beaten her, but after he had beaten her he broke down and cried. He said he had wanted what was best for his family. Now there was nothing he could do. Now the safety of the whole family depended on her, he said.

'Monstrous!' I cried. 'Coward! He has no right to demand such a thing!'

Yes, she said, it was cowardly. But it was also true. She knew it before he said it.

She was shaking, her breath came in quick gasps. 'So I have to leave. With or without you,' she said. She could no longer live in that house. If she had to go to him again she would hide a knife under the pillow and kill him in his sleep.

'No,' I said. I pulled my Luger out of my belt and brandished it above my head. 'If he must be killed I will kill him.'

She said we would not have to kill him if we left the next day, very early. She said Patch Eye and his men, and Tadeusz and all his men, had gone to Bielewa, a big town a hundred kilometres away. The Russians had called together all the partisan bands to negotiate the terms of a new Polish government. Patch Eye had said the partisan bands must now let bygones be bygones, forget their old rivalries and present a 'united front' to the Russians. She said they had all been very excited, Tadeusz and Patch Eye and all their men, drinking toasts and singing patriotic songs, and then they all left together, some on horseback, some in wagons, a few even on bicycles. She said her father didn't want to go but Patch Eye had shamed him into it. She said she had dreaded that Patch Eye would force a 'quickie' on her before he left, but he had given her only a wink and a little peck on the cheek. She said if we left tomorrow before dawn we would be long gone before Patch Eye got back.

I stopped her. I held my hand in front of her mouth, then I took a step back while the elements of her story came together in my mind. Then I grabbed her shoulders and gave them a happy shake. This was good news, I said, very good news. I said she had seen the last of Patch Eye. I explained what would happen when that motley assemblage of partisans in Bielewa confronted the Soviets. It was a trap, I said. I knew how Russians 'negotiate.' They wouldn't much care whether or not the partisans presented a united front. The partisans had served their purpose, and now they were a meddlesome inconvenience to the Russians. They would deal with Patch Eye and his negotiators as they dealt with all negotiators. Before Patch Eye and his merry men could clink their glasses and drink a toast to Stalin they would be on a Soviet train to Siberia. I was certain of this, but to allay Eva's fears I tried to appear even more confident than I was. Eva jumped up and down and clapped her hands like a little girl, and she kissed and kissed me, as though it were my own cleverness that had so handily dispatched her tormentor.

Oh, we made plans, Antoine, a breathless jumble of plans. She would bring the earrings Patch Eye had given her mother. We could sell them. Surely the Jewish lady herself would approve if she knew her earrings had helped two young lovers escape the clutches of the man who had murdered her son. We would use the money to buy train tickets. Some of them were running again. And she had papers, she said, the Germans had given everyone papers, no good then, but maybe of some use now. We would go to Sweden, or maybe Australia.

'Let's dance,' said Eva. 'I can't dance,' I said, 'but I can sing.' So I clapped my hands and sang a merry tune while Eva danced on the green meadow. Two star-crossed lovers.

That last night in the hut I filled the sack Eva had given me with sausages, potatoes and preserved chicken, tied it shut and tested the weight. Then I lay down and waited. I got up, untied the sack, took out the heavy jars of chicken preserves and replaced them with more sausages. I lay down again, got up, and stuffed the chicken preserves back in. Long before dawn I sat staring down at the trees where Eva would appear.

The sky began to gray but no Eva. Then it was daylight. The sun began to pierce the mist enough to cast shadows. I took my sack and retreated to the mossy rock hidden among the trees, lay there and waited. Please, please come, come soon. Then I saw something move but it was not Eva. It was a man with a patch over his eye. Then two more men, one an old man, the other a young kid, who wore a blue jacket. Patch Eye and the kid had rifles, the old man didn't. He and Patch Eye approached the haystack, circling along the edge of the forest while the kid hung back to cover them. Patch Eye was pushing the old man ahead of him, jamming the barrel of his rifle into the old man's back. When they got closer he shouted something at the haystack. They came around to my side and Patch Eye pointed his rifle at the opening of the tunnel, which I had not bothered to camouflage. He shouted again. Then he set fire to the haystack.

I levelled my Luger at Patch Eye, but he was too far away. I slid off my rock while they watched the haystack burn. It began to burn slowly, then burned fiercely. The kid was there too now. The heat of the fire exploded the jars of chicken preserves and sent more sparks into the air. It sounded like gunshots, so they fired their rifles into the burning haystack. I moved closer. I went down on one knee behind some brush and I shouted, 'What have you done to Eva.' Patch Eye and the kid whirled around and fired into the trees. 'We took care of the whore!' shouted Patch Eye. He scanned the trees at the edge of the meadow, his rifle raised to his good eye, but he couldn't find me. 'She won't be fucking any more Nazi swine!' The old man fell to his knees and started praying, 'Dear God, forgive me, please forgive me.' Patch Eye swore at him over his shoulder, and continued to peer into the trees. The old man scrambled to his feet and charged at his back, yelling, so Patch Eye wheeled around and shot him in the chest. The kid ran to his father and knelt over him. Before he could get to his feet again Patch Eye shot him too. I had stepped out of the trees and was hobbling toward Patch Eye with my Luger levelled at him. We shot at the same time. He missed, I didn't.

I left them there, all three of them, while the haystack burned. I ran across the meadow, splashed through the brook and stumbled down the path. The path forked, and crossed another path. I tried one, then the other. I heard shooting in the distance, with big guns, and ran as fast as I could. Then the path was flooded by spring run-off and I had to make a detour through the underbrush, then I couldn't find the path again. I saw smoke rise above the trees and scrambled toward the smoke. When I finally reached the village there was no sign of soldiers, only frantic people with water buckets, trying to put out smouldering embers. Women shouted, children cried. The village had only one street, and at the near end stood what remained of a small stone church, smoke rising from the smouldering roof that had collapsed inside it, and next to the church stood the crumbling wall of the cemetery. On a crude stone bench near the cemetery gate sat three old crones, wailing and rocking their bodies back and forth. One was fat and two were thin. 'What happened?' I said.

The fat one did all the talking. 'What happened! Russians. That's what happened. Two trucks, with soldiers, and big guns. Everything smashed, burned. There, look. And there. Children in there, burned alive!' She pointed at two smouldering houses where people were now trying to get in through the smoke. 'Hie-ya. Murderers! Murderers!'

'Why?' I said.

'Why! Because of the partisans! Stupid partisans. One gang wanted the Russians to kill the other gang. The Russians wanted them both dead. Hand over your partisans, they shouted. They said we were hiding them. They're all gone, we said. So they burned the village.'

'Do you know Eva?'

'Hie-ya!' she wailed, 'Eva! Eva!' She turned her face aside, as though she were fending off a blow. Her companions shook their heads. 'Everybody knew Eva,' she said.

'Where is she?'

'There.' She pointed to a mound outside the cemetery wall. The other two did the same.

'Where?'

'There. Look. That's her grave.'

'No,' I said. 'No. No. She left the village early. Before dawn.'

'It's her,' she said.

I stumbled toward the mound of dirt. Someone had driven a crude wooden cross into the ground at the head of the grave, and carved her name and two dates in the wood, August 14, 1924 - April 29, 1945. I knelt down and touched the mound and felt nothing but cold, damp earth. I began clawing at the mound with my bare hands. I must hold her one more time in my arms, if it were truly her. 'Wasn't the Russians did it,' said the fat one. She had come up behind me while I clawed at the earth. 'Partisans. The one with a patch on his eye. Waited till the others had left then shot her.' Then she came up close behind me, the better to drive home the message. 'Shot her because she was screwing a German. Are you the one? Why didn't they shoot you?'

'They tried.'

I flung my body onto Eva's grave. I pressed my face into the shallow hole I had clawed with my hands, where her head would be, and I called and called to her.

'Bunglers, all of them,' she said, 'A big talker, the one with the patch. Wanted to be the Big Man here all by himself. Tried to trick the other one – Tadeusz. But this time Tadeusz tricked him. Now look. Everything burned down. Murderers!'

I lay across Eva's grave for I don't know how long, till a group of women and a few old men arrived and shouted at me to leave the village. One of them had a rifle, some of the others had axes and pitch forks. I leapt up and waved my Luger at them. They shrank back. Then I turned my back to them and walked to where the path came out of the forest. I stopped there, to give them a last chance to shoot me in the back, but they didn't.

Is it impossible for two people to fall so deeply in love in so short a time, Antoine? Yes. It was impossible not to. We flung ourselves at each other. I know now that we were both sickened by what we had become, and we each hung our hopes on the other to help us recover a shred of the innocence we had lost. For many years I couldn't tell anyone about Eva, not till I told my dear little Sara. I told her as a warning that it was dangerous to love me too much.

I couldn't tell you about Eva so I told you only how I had ended up in Berlin. I even tried to be funny. I remember telling you how I discovered the war was over, how I found myself in a town whose name I've forgotten if I ever knew it, and saw a throng of people crowded onto a railway platform. I expected to see soldiers herding them onto the train that had pulled into the station, but there were none. These people seemed desperate to board the train of their own free will. I tugged on someone's sleeve to get his attention. 'Why are there no soldiers?' I said. 'The war is over,' he said, but he didn't sound too pleased about it. Some of the people scrambling to board the train were quite respectably dressed, and a few, like me, were in tattered rags. Most were women and older men. Some of them waved their hands in the air, holding little stubs of paper. 'Tickets, tickets! We've got tickets!' they shouted, but no one paid them any attention. I remember telling you it would have been smarter to shout, 'Typhus, typhus! Highly contagious!' It would have made the crowd shrink back and allowed the ticket holders to duck through the throng. That got a wry chuckle from you.

I let myself be pushed and jostled till I was on the train too, and the doors closed behind me. The train began to move, and those who had been left behind ran alongside the cars, screaming and pounding on the doors with their fists, till they got to the end of the platform. And now I felt a little ashamed of myself, I told you. All those people desperate to board the train, and there I was, chugging along, with no idea where the train was going and I couldn't have cared less. I might have felt a little guilty about that, if I'd been more lucid.

The train stopped at other towns and the scene was repeated, people fighting to get on, others pushing and kicking them back. At one stop I saw an arm protruding through a tangle of legs and torsos, so I instinctively held out my hand. The arm grabbed my hand and pulled, and sure enough a man's body emerged out of the tangle of limbs. He thanked me, then elbowed his way to the other end of the car. Then the train slowed to a crawl as we passed through what seemed an endless landscape of bombed out ruins. Finally it came to a stop and officials on the platform shouted *Endstation! Alle 'raus!* So I let myself get jostled and pushed off the train. I asked someone where we were, and he said Berlin. He too seemed annoyed by my question. I had no idea then why all these people wanted to be in Berlin, but now I assume they were the people who had fled the city for the countryside, to escape the bombing and the fighting in the streets. When they heard the war was over they were anxious to get back, to see what was left of their homes before the looters cleaned them out.

I remember vividly now my first impression of the city, a mass of impenetrable rubble. Then I noticed it was not impenetrable. It was full of holes. Little holes, with rats brazenly sticking their heads out of them, bigger holes with children crawling in and out of them, and still others where shrivelled old women would stick their torsos out of the rubble as though it were Judgment Day, would look around, see they'd made a mistake and disappear again. Under the rubble were holes I couldn't see, the grottos where the remnants of families had burrowed. Thin wisps of smoke rose through holes that now served as chimneys. A few stooped figures crawled around on the rubble rearranging some stones and bricks. They paid no attention to me, or I to them. I don't remember hearing any of them speak or gesticulate to each other, but maybe I had become deaf to human voices. Numbed myself. Except for the stench. Excrement. Three million Berliners and refugees still had to shit, it seems, even if they didn't eat. *Durchfall,* diarrhoea, little patties of it everywhere, covered by a swarm of fat flies. The occasional whiff of wet plaster and charred wood came as relief.

Above the piles of rubble gaped other holes, in walls where windows and doors used to be, or bigger holes at the ends of rooms where a wall used to be, and holes gaping upward where roofs used to be, vertical shafts three or four storeys high. The skeletal walls seemed to totter precariously as though any gust of wind could bring them down. A drooping stone cornice or lintel seemed to defy gravity, then I would hear a crash behind me and duck. I would whirl around, expecting the walls to come down like dominoes but there was only a small puff of dust. The walls still stood, silent and composed, as though it would be bad manners to acknowledge the commotion. Like a dignified oldster down on his luck, pretending it wasn't he who farted.

I spent months begging and scavenging for food by day, then finding a secluded place to spend the night. I don't recall telling you any of this back then. Nobody in Berlin would have found it remarkable in the fall of 1945 – September or October, or whenever it was. I told you only the little I remembered about the night I was 'arrested' and beaten bloody by a patrol of Ami MPs – accused of stealing their regimental mascot, a four-hundred pound pig.

There had been a mad search for that pig after it disappeared from its pen. For months it had been on public display at the monumental entrance to what was now McNair Barracks, in a niche formerly occupied by a twelve-foot statue of Field Marshal von Moltke, a hero of the Franco-Prussian War. The Amis had toppled the statue from its pedestal and installed their pet pig there instead, 'a gloating elbow in the ribs of starving Berliners,' you said, 'to remind them who had won the war and who had lost.'

That night I was wet and cold and knew I would only get colder. I was nowhere near the base, didn't know where I was, and as night fell, I did as I had done for months, I began looking for a sheltered place to sleep. And suddenly there it was – a pig – luminous in its whiteness against the gathering gloom. It was climbing a pile of rubble on its delicate feet when I attacked. I caught her by her hind leg and she squealed like all the devils of hell. She kicked debris down on my head but I held on. Did I think I could butcher her right there with my pocket knife? Cut out a few choice cutlets before I was overwhelmed by a mob of hungry knife-wielding Berliners? No, fresh meat was the furthest thing from my mind. I hated that smug sow – with a fury like half-mad Ahab unleashed upon the white whale that haunted his feverish mind, the incarnation of inscrutable evil. Ridiculous? Yes, ridiculous. I had never read or even heard of *Moby Dick,* but that is how I see it now.

Then I felt a sharp blow between my shoulders and someone shouted 'Nazi pig fucker!' I was tossed into the back of a jeep, bounced along dark rubble-strewn streets, then blinding flood lights and someone shouted, 'Military Police. Raise the gate.' I was dragged up a flight of stairs and dumped into a tight closet among buckets, brooms and mops. After that my mind goes blank but you later got the story in detail from one of the Ami MPs – that the culprits had not been starving Germans but pranksters from the 3rd Airborne Brigade, determined to avenge their disgrace in a football game on Columbus Day.

I spent the night in that cramped closet, then I remember being dragged into the mess hall through a throng of jeering GIs and strapped into a chair, limp and barely conscious. 'Hang the Nazi bastard!' 'Cut off his balls!' Yes, they were just having fun with me, a stand-in for the real culprits, but I remembered other soldiers having fun with their prisoners. My own comrades. They made their prisoners sing naughty barroom songs while they dug their own graves. And butted their heads with their rifles when they didn't sing with enough gusto. I did not expect these Ami soldiers to be less inventive.

Then a strange figure appeared, dressed in a formal black jacket, a white shirt and a black tie. 'Wait!' he said, and the GIs cleared a path for him so he could approach me. I thought you were a clown, Antoine, part of the entertainment. You began asking me questions – in German, then Low German. And then I recognized you. A miraculous reunion? It certainly seemed so to me, but when millions of refugees are on the move there are thousands of miraculous reunions. It is the most common theme of their oral histories.

You saved me from the clutches of that mob and carried me down to your basement bunker under the mess hall. You laid me on a cot and hung tarps and army blankets around it to make a secluded little cell. You said I could rest there till I regained my strength.

For two weeks I was attended by you and your fellow squatters in that basement, who brought me food from the mess hall and a new shirt and trousers from the PX, probably the only place to buy new clothes in all of Berlin. You said it was against regulations for civilian staff to live on the base, but the Amis seemed to turn a blind eye to it. There were the two Australians, there was a black American, an Egyptian, the big German and the two German girls. A motley troop. 'How did they all end up there? In Berlin, of all places,' asked Sara, no longer a cuddly child huddled on my lap but a young woman now, and still prompting me with questions about my past life. What should I have told her? I said we were like castaways marooned on an island in a sea of rubble, and none of us seemed in a rush to be rescued.

When I got a little stronger you lugged in a pair of wooden crates from the wine cellar of the officers' mess. They were the size of bedside tables when they were turned on end. 'You can keep your stuff in here,' you said. To me they were a token – that I was now a permanent resident. No document, signed and stamped in triplicate, could have been more binding. And slowly I began to explore the layout of that sprawling catacomb under the mess hall of what had once been a Prussian cadet academy. It was a dark low-ceilinged vault supported by a dense grid of concrete pillars, about half the size of a football field as I remember it, but maybe it seemed so because we rarely ventured into the gloom beyond our corner near the entrance. I marked out my own territory among the clutter of tarps and cots and makeshift furnishings and began to carve a niche for myself in the affections of your companions, a gaggle of shiftless riff-raff, as Doktor Vik called them. I soon learned my place in the pecking order and was content with it.

I was still illegal on the base. Then one day you came home early, shook the first snow of the season off your coat and boots, and beckoned me to our cluttered table. 'We have to get you a job here, on the base,' you said. A job? You had persuaded the mess sergeant to give me a job as a janitor. You could still do that, Antoine. No one could refuse your so-reasonable requests without feeling small-minded and petty. That much hadn't changed since Russia. Then you took a sheaf of six pink sheets from your jacket pocket and spread them on the table. 'But first you have to be de-Nazified,' you said, and you began filling out the long *Fragebogen* for me, all 131 questions. You mostly wrote NA, NA, NA, and where necessary frankly lied. You wrote that I had been born in Breslau, Poland, and was recruited by the *Wehrmacht* in November, 1943.

'But that's not true,' I said.

'You can't say you were in the *Waffen SS*. That's a no-no. And you can't say you were born in the Ukraine. The Amis would feel obliged to hand you over to the Russians for repatriation.' So Breslau it was. A new birthplace, a new nationality.

The bigger problem was the medical exam. There was no way to hide the SS blood group tattoo under my left arm, but you said you knew someone who would do the 'examination' and put his signature on the appropriate forms, a doctor who worked for UNRRA, 'that United Nations organization that's supposed to clean up this refugee mess.' You said he often had to fudge medical certificates in his line of work, and he owed you a favour. Then you persuaded our mess sergeant that the UNRRA medical would serve until a proper exam could be scheduled with an Army doctor. 'You just have to sign here,' you said, and I signed.

I had vaulted from destitution to privilege. A million Berliners and millions of refugees would swoon to have what I had now, a real job that paid real money however little, two hot meals a day and access to American cigarettes from the PX (though this required the complicity of a cooperative GI). And within the walls of McNair Barracks I was safe from repatriation to the Soviet Union. I knew I was lucky, but not *how* lucky. 'Repatriation,' that was the dark cloud that terrified millions of Soviet refugees. Not even you were safe, Antoine, though you had changed your name to obscure your origins. Reputable historians now claim that by the end of December, 1946, between three and four million Soviet refugees (including *Ostarbeiter* who had spent the war in Germany as slave labour) had been loaded into box cars and sent to camps in the Soviet Union, in compliance with the Yalta Accord. Only a small fraction escaped the combined British, American and Soviet dragnet. An astounding operational feat. They were scattered across Germany and Austria among eight million more refugees from the eastern provinces of the *Reich*. Roads, trains, communication networks, all were in shambles, acute fuel shortages, and all the other administrative crises after a ruinous war – but they did it. They rooted them out. When, in the annals of the Cold War, is there another such instance of co-operation between the Soviets and the Anglo-Americans?

Mennonites were luckier than most. Fewer than two thirds of us were repatriated – 23,100 out of the 35,000 who had begun the trek in the fall of 1943.

I remember the night you and I went to a seedy tavern in Steglitz. It was the first time I had ventured off the base since my 'arrest' for stealing the pig. Until then we'd had little chance to talk privately down in our basement lair, and it had seemed to me an unendurably long time. I wanted to be regaled with stories of your adventures since Mary Gordon came and plucked you to safety – after your 'knife attacks' on Grisha and my cousin who had tried to steal our burrowing owl during the Famine. We walked north, and here there was again more bomb damage. 'Talk German. Not a word of Russian,' you cautioned as we set out, since Russian was still the language that came most naturally when there were only the two of us. You said even a careless *Khorosho!* might be enough for some busybody to report us to a local policeman who would call us in for questioning.

The *Kneipe* where we ended up was well beyond the ring of bars and brothels around McNair Barracks, on a street of two- or three-storey tenements with shops on the ground floor, and a patchwork of newsprint and rags to cover broken or missing window panes. No sign on the door, only a fluttering gas light above it and a murmur of voices from within. When we entered, the murmuring stopped for a moment. The patrons, about twenty of them seated in small clusters around crude tables, turned and looked at us over their shoulders, then resumed their huddled formations, leaning forward on their elbows. They were middle-aged or older, and there were three or four matronly women among them.

I had seen you and the publican exchange a token nod when we entered but no other greeting. You approached the bar, ordered two beers and paid for them with American coins which the hawk-faced publican pocketed without so much as a glance at them.

We sat near the bar, on a short bench with our backs to the wall, an upturned beer keg for a table. The murmur of the patrons seemed casual enough, though sometimes it lurched into grunts and growls, then one of them would slap the palm of his hand on the table and declare, *'Ja, ja, so geht es nun,'* that's how things are now, and someone would glance at us over his shoulder. 'What are they talking about?' I said.

You cast a cold appraising eye around the room. 'Probably the Nuremberg trials.'

'Are they against them, the trials?'

'They'll be complaining that Churchill and Bomber Harris should be on trial too, for war crimes. But some of them pretend to be more outraged than they are. They're hoping the trials will mean *Schluss* – an end to the witchhunt for little Nazis. For once, they say, it's the big boys getting the noose, not the little people *forced* to do their bidding.'

You had let your gaze settle on one cluster of patrons, then another. Maybe none of them noticed, but it seemed to me they squirmed under your gaze.

When I could still barely speak because of my smashed jaw I had asked you about your mother and Mary Gordon. I assumed you had been in Germany since you left us to be reunited with your mother but you told me you'd spent only a year here before you emigrated to Argentina. You said your mother had lost her mind, didn't even remember she had a son, and when Mary Gordon had presented you to her – 'Look, here is your son, all grown up' – your mother had simply smiled and said, 'That's nice.' Your grandfather had wept and embraced you but his health was failing, and when he died you and your mother were left with a pile of debts. His farm implement factory had gone bankrupt when the German economy collapsed after the Great War, but your mother had a brother, you said, the errant son who had emigrated to Argentina after a bitter quarrel with his father. You said he had become rich there, and before your grandfather died he had written to his errant son and pressed upon him his duty to take care of his enfeebled sister and her poor son.

You said your uncle had always despised your mother, accused her of bringing all her trouble upon herself, first by marrying 'that Russian savage with pretensions to nobility,' then consorting with a pack of dissolute revolutionaries. Nevertheless, he did grudgingly agree to support her and her son, and also her 'companion,' if they moved to Buenos Aires. And from then until your mother died in 1939, you said it was Mary Gordon who had to fight with your uncle for every penny to pay for your mother's doctors and for your education. Including two years at Heidelberg University. 'For them – my mother and Mary Gordon – Buenos Aires was a trial,' you said, 'but for a kid like me it was exciting.' There was a large ex-pat German community with its own weeklies and a literary quarterly, alongside a vibrant colonial Spanish culture. Also a vibrant Italian community. Some of them were communists, most were zealous fascists, you said, 'all of them full of fire and passion, on the cutting edge of the *avant garde.*' You shook your head and chuckled.

You said after your mother died your uncle disowned any further responsibility for you, or for Mary Gordon. 'So I went to Paris and she went back to Scotland. She had no friends in Buenos Aires. My mother and I had been her whole life.'

'Why Paris?'

You dismissed the question with a shrug. You said you wanted to be a writer, 'and every writer wanted to be in Paris, the undisputed capital of Western art and culture. But I arrived too late. The bloom was off.' You grinned. Your ironic signature grin. As though you were done with such childish delusions.

I asked if you were already there when the Germans invaded.

'Yes,' you said, 'And some of the writers I admired thought it was a good thing – that a dose of Nazi fascism would invigorate a decadent French culture.'

'Why did you leave, after the war?'

'Because I was no longer welcome there,' you said. My questions must have annoyed you, Antoine. I knew I was prying, but I didn't understand why I should have to. I waited for you to say more but you didn't. You stared at your glass of beer and ran your finger around the rim.

I watched one of the patrons, a big stout fellow, get up from his stool and swagger to the bar to get more beer. He wore a faded brown jacket with unfaded patches where certain insignia of rank had been removed. He took four cigarettes out of a package and handed them to the publican. The publican tapped each cigarette on the bar, then curled his index finger to indicate he needed more cigarettes. There was a growl of protest from the man, then he tossed two more cigarettes onto the bar. The publican scooped them up and filled his glass.

'Why does he do that, tap the cigarettes on the bar?' I asked, to change the subject.

'Because he knows his business.' You said it was a common scam. People pick the tobacco out of a cigarette with a hooked needle, then repack the empty tube more loosely. And after repacking five cigarettes there's enough tobacco left over for one more. A twenty per cent profit. 'Everybody's trying to make *Geschäft* these days,' you said.

You got up and went to the bar to get us two more beers. I saw you ask the publican a question. He shook his head. You came back with our beer and sat down, lit a cigarette, and took a deep drag. Then you returned to my question. You said you had published a few short stories and articles in a journal that had become too cosy with the German Occupation, so after the war you were a *persona non grata* in France. When a well known writer, Robert Brasillach, was executed for *intellectual crimes*, it seemed best to leave while you still could.

But why come to Berlin? Why not anywhere but here?

You said it was Doktor Vik who arranged it. (I had met him only a few days ago when he appeared in our basement lair looking for you.) You said you had both been 'active' in the *Studentenbund* when you were students at Heidelberg. When the war started you went to Paris and he went to America to continue his medical studies, but he had stayed in touch and he knew you had to leave Paris after the 'liberation.' He had tracked you down when he came back to Germany, and found you working on a farm in the Vosges. To get you out of France he put you in touch with his American friends, whom he'd met through his work with refugees. He knew the American colonel who had been put in charge of dealing with refugees in Berlin, and he told you this colonel was looking for a 'private interpreter,' someone fluent in French, English, German and Russian. So, here you were.

I think even then I found your story a little too pat, as though you had rehearsed it. Years later Doktor Vik added a few details during one of our regular dinners in Winnipeg at his favourite restaurant. I asked him how he had found you on that farm in the Vosges. Yes, you had enemies in Paris, he said, but you still had some 'admirers,' and they had found a safe place for you. 'So there he was, one of the most brilliant minds of his generation, shovelling cow shit and trying to teach a calf to drink milk out of a bucket. It pissed me off, to see he'd just . . . given up.' That was all he said. In Berlin, when he was waiting for you to finish your day at the officers' mess, he would sometimes tease us with tidbits of information about you, wink, wink. But now he has to be prodded to talk about you.

'Doktor Vik told us you were soul mates at Heidelberg,' I said. I tried not to scoff.

'Soul mates?' You said he had been a token communist when he arrived from Canada, but it took only a few weeks for him to switch from token communist to Nazi idealist, 'with all the zeal of a new convert.' You said at student rallies he would mount the podium and harangue his fellow zealots with soaring oratory. He would quote lines from his favourite English poet, '*Oh wild West Wind, from whose unseen presence the leaves dead are driven, like pestilence-stricken multitudes. Destroyer and preserver, hear, oh hear!*' Then he would raise both arms and declaim that only Hitler's National Socialists had grasped the fact that nothing short of a 'cleansing violence' could staunch the rot of our leaderless, moribund civilization. And only they, the Nazis, had the conviction and courage to tough it out. 'Poetry was never his strong suit,' you said.

'Were you an idealist too? Back then?'

You shrugged. You said your support for the Nazis had been more pragmatic than idealistic. 'I wanted revenge on the communists, so the enemy of my enemy was my friend. But the Nazis bungled that too. Soviet communism is now stronger than ever.' You said you had never been zealous enough for Viktor and his crowd. 'He would turn livid if I made even a harmless joke about Hitler's puny little moustache, compared to Stalin's luxurious bush.'

Then I asked, 'Why does Doktor Vik dislike me so much? Because I told him I used to be a Mennonite, like him?'

'That didn't help,' you said, 'but it's mainly because he thinks I'm wasting my time down there, with the likes of you.'

I was still smarting from my first encounter with him. I had heard talk of him among the others, a few sardonic quips, but nothing had prepared me for his grand entrance. He was tall, handsome, fair haired, with quick blue eyes and an actor's resonant voice, equally at ease in German and English. I had seen men like him pictured in the newspapers, confident, distinguished looking men, in gray fedoras and flowing white scarves, gray wool coats with wide lapels, their buckled briefcases bulging with important documents. But I had never seen one up close, never been in the same room with one. He always entered with a flourish, with the theatrical heartiness of a rich uncle from America returning to his village, flush with the latest news from the Big World where he was privy to the confidences of generals and politicians. Everybody tried to match his heartiness, everybody but you. You sat back and let him entertain us with his stories of skulduggery between rival Soviet and American administrations – till he signalled it was time for the two of you to leave and talk 'business.'

I'd been told he was a doctor from Canada working for UNRRA, and you had told me he grew up in a Mennonite community in Canada. 'But he doesn't talk about it much,' you said, and flicked the tip of your nose with your finger. And I laughed. When you introduced me to him as an old friend from Russia, I held out my hand, beaming from ear to ear. 'I'm a Mennonite too, from the Molotchna Colony,' I said, in a rush of ethnic recidivism.

He didn't shake my hand. He turned and sneered at you. 'This your idea of a joke?'

You shrugged and grinned. 'His family took me in, for four years, when I was just a kid.' He looked me up and down out of the corner of his eye. 'So now you've added a pet Mennonite to your collection.'

'Viktor thinks I should be more ambitious,' you explained. You said he was now contemptuous of the Nazi leadership, for bungling their mission to launch a new age of progress and enlightenment, but he was still an idealist. 'He thinks people like us – intellectuals, scientists, visionaries – must seize the moment while the future is still up for grabs. To make sure the bungling mediocrities don't have it all to themselves.' You shrugged. 'But there I am, down there with you riff-raff, lapping up the crumbs of American largesse. It offends him.' I uttered spluttering guffaws to show how absurd I found that, but I will confess to you now, Antoine, what I couldn't confess then – that I too felt disappointed, let down. I wanted the old Antoine back, aloof, disdainful of our schoolmates, our teachers, our elders. I had expected a similar disdain for the riff-raff down there in your musty lair, yet you seemed to have a chastened affection for them. They had no particular virtue to recommend them but you seemed to find their frailties forgivable and were grateful to lose yourself in their company.

'Are you still writing?' I said.

'No. I have no craving for either glory or vilification in Viktor's world.'

The stout patron in the faded *Blockleiter* jacket, with the unfaded patches where his rank insignia had been removed, now sat hunched across the table so that he had to squint at his companions out of the corner of his eye. His every gesture was calculated to let his companions know he'd seen through all the sham spouted by both the Allied adminis-trations and grovelling German politicians. It was all high-minded posturing to cut honest, simple folk like themselves out of the market. He never turned to look at us, but others at the table threw quick glances at us. There was a woman among them, sitting opposite him, who had to crane her neck and bob her head left and right to get a look at us.

I said, 'What is the . . . business . . . that Doktor Vik always wants to discuss with you?'

Business? You said at those high-level meetings, hosted by your colonel friend, your job was 'to keep the tongues of the delegates greased with cognac and vodka,' and keep your ears open. You said there would be heated arguments among the 'allied' administrations about how to deal with the refugee problem, and of course that was useful information to someone working for UNRRA, like Doktor Vik.

I remember watching you stub out your cigarette with more force than necessary.

You paused a moment, uncertain whether to say more. You let your gaze drift around the room, from table to table, and lit another cigarette. 'There's other stuff too, that Viktor wants to know – like the names of prominent Nazis the Amis and the Russians have their eye on. Including some of his professors at Heidelberg – who had offered their expertise in eugenics to the Nazis.' You said he had helped a couple of them escape to Argentina and Paraguay. He had connections to the 'ratlines,' a network of embittered Nazi loyalists who helped people escape, and he also had his own network of petty thugs and blackmailers, 'like the scum at that table over there.' You said there was an 'underground economy' in Berlin, selling information to the Amis and Russians.

'Is it dangerous?'

'It could be. But he thrives on it. The information he gets from his own agents he barters for favours and concessions from the Amis, then repackages it and sells it to the Russians, to make them all look like fools.'

The man in the *Blockleiter* jacket got up from his chair, stuck out his chest and approached us. He glared down at us, shifting his eyes from one to the other. 'What are you doing here?' he demanded. 'Are you Russians? Are you spying on us?' He spat on the floor. Your glass of beer was half full. You threw it in his face.

Before he could wipe the beer out of his eyes the publican was behind him with a two-foot iron bar. He clamped the bar on his throat and dragged him back to his table. It was obviously not the first time he had to settle a scuffle among his patrons. 'Mind your own business,' he said. 'Everybody's money is good here.'

You put on your jacket and dropped a few American coins on the upturned beer keg. Then you slowly walked out the door, me behind you, looking over my shoulder, ready to fend off any attack from the patrons hissing curses at us. When we were back on the street I slapped your back and let out a triumphant whoop. That was the old Antonii I knew in Russia! The arrogant, self-assured Antonii, who could scare Grisha and his spiteful little elves into peeing their pants! I was determined to coax your old self back to life.

The German staff who worked in the kitchen and scullery, about a dozen of them, consisted of middle-aged matrons and two elderly men. We all got along, as I remember, though we had little to do with them in our off hours. They too had been de-Nazified, and a few had indeed opposed the Nazis before the war, and suffered for it.

I tried to fit in. I was even promoted. From janitor to chief dishwasher. It happened after a new woman was hired as a cook. When our mess sergeant introduced her to us, she went from one to the other to shake our hands until she came to the chief dishwasher, who had ruled the roost in the scullery till then. She shrieked, began to shake, and wagged her finger at him. 'That's the man who sent my husband to Dachau!' The mess sergeant quickly stepped between them and pushed them both into his little office. He closed the door but we could hear more shrieking from the woman, and muffled protests from the chief dishwasher. Then he bolted from the office and left without a word of farewell. Later we learned the new woman's husband had been a Confessional Lutheran pastor and was arrested for distributing anti-Nazi propaganda. He was tried and sentenced to ten years at Dachau, where he died. The chief dishwasher was the judge who had sentenced him.

That night, down in our lair, I listened while the others speculated what the judge's fate would be. I said I too had not been truthful on my *Fragebogen* but they laughed it off. 'Most of the German staff had to stretch the truth a bit,' said the tall Australian. 'The Amis know it, but they don't give a pinch o' wombat shit. They wanna catch the big boys – stuff they can feed to the tabloids back home.'

The next morning our mess sergeant beckoned me into his office. I was still nervous. He bid me sit down, then told me I'd been promoted to chief dishwasher, with a fifteen-cent raise in my hourly wage. We sealed the contract with a handshake, and the whole kitchen staff applauded when he made the announcement.

The scullery beside the mess-hall kitchen was state of the art. It glistened and glowed, and I was now in charge of the big industrial-size dishwasher – with buttons and levers and blinking lights, pulleys and rubber hoses tentacling out of it, and a stainless steel hood that flew up on rails when I tripped a lever with a red wooden handle. Once I got the hang of it I performed my duties with a flourish, with panache. I rammed the trays of dirty dishes under the steel hood – swoosh, clatter, bang – and hardly had they come to rest when I yanked the big red handle and down came the hood, boom. With the heel of my other hand I hit the red start button and fourteen hot water jets sprang into action. I set the timer and loaded the next set of trays. I picked up a heavy stack of plates and deftly turned the stack on its side, and in one smooth motion shuffled them into their slots as though they were a deck of cards. Then the cups and bowls and then the timer ding-dinged and I tripped the red lever and flung the cage skyward. Engulfed now in a cloud of steam, I sent the trays of clean dishes careening on rollers into the hot-air dryer and slammed the door shut. Done. Then I got a short break, a chance to swagger around the scullery like a captain doing a tour of the ship, and watched approvingly while lesser minions removed the sparkling clean dishes from the dryer, restacked them on a trolley, and returned them to the mess hall.

Behind the kitchen was our dusty, airless stairwell leading to the storerooms below and here we gathered during our breaks. There was always the smell of sweat and stale cigarette smoke and here we chatted and argued and teased each other, gossiped and bartered with one another for days off. The mood was one of expectant indolence, if there can be such a thing, and I basked in the hum of approval. I stifled my memory of the recent past after I left my family to begin military training. At times my thoughts would leap across that period to an aching memory of my mother and sister, of Uncle Knalz and Taunte Liese, Groote Graeta and the others, but that time now seemed decades ago. I felt like I had been whisked away to a limbo-like netherworld, and had it been within my power, this is where I would have spent eternity. No past, no future. Just this, forever.

Now, from a distance of another continent and half a century, I see us all through a gauzy veil, through lazy strata of cigarette smoke, and our voices seem muffled by a denser medium than air. When my granddaughter Sara was in her early teens she found my stories about us in our basement lair fascinating. 'Were you looking for something to believe in?'

She wanted there to be something noble about us, like monkish anchorites guarding a precious remnant of a lost civilisation. Yes, I see you smile, Antoine, but why should I spoil her fantasy, and since these were not among my painful memories I allowed myself to become whimsical. I tried to pass us off as endearing *roués*, tried to give us a wayward glamour. The two Australians were avowed communists who liberally sprinkled their conversation with revolutionary cant, and I had expected you to set them straight in a hurry. But you indulged them, even egged them on, and they seemed content to provoke our predictable scorn. I told Sara what an odd pair they were, Max who baked bread and pies for the GIs and Luke who fried their eggs and flapjacks, Max tall and lanky with a perpetual frown pasted on his face, Luke short, stocky and pugnacious, always a mischievous grin on his face. Luke's German was basic but Max was quite fluent, and when they finished their day they would go to one of the newly opened *Bier Stübchen* north of the base, dismal beer emporia with long rows of rough hewn tables and backless benches, where a hundred Berliners could drink themselves to tearful oblivion. And when Luke got drunk he would jump up on one of the tables and lead the hall in a lusty sing-along, beginning with popular German songs and ending with Australia's 'unofficial national anthem.' He had done it so often the regulars could join in the chorus, '*Valtzink Mateelda*,' they sang, '*Valtzink Mateelda*' – which made Sara laugh. But often the evening would end in a brawl when Luke would kick somebody's beer stein down the table as though it were a soccer ball. It would bounce off a groggy Berliner's head and knock him off his bench. Then someone would try to pull Luke off the table and Luke would punch him in the nose. Then Max would wade in, wielding a beer stein in each hand. It was often the Ami MPs who brought them home, Max cursing, Luke spitting blood, but still singing.

That happened only twice, as I recall, but for Sara's sake I made it sound like a weekly event. 'Were they crazy? Did they pick fights because they hated the Germans?'

No, not particularly. I said they had languished for a year in England after their basic training, and finally, on D-Day, they were actually going into a combat. They were part of the airborne operation, but they were blown off course and dropped in a swampy area too close to the German lines. They were captured before they'd disentangled themselves from their parachutes. So maybe this was how they compensated for missing all the action.

The Egyptian was the opposite, soft-spoken and impeccably polite. He had been a student in Zurich through most of the war and when his visa expired he had come to Berlin. He couldn't go back to Egypt because he had got mixed up in some political trouble and he was now trying to clear legal hurdles to emigrate to England or America. He was a model of oriental courtesy, so effortless, so natural that we hardly noticed it, courteous even to the loud, rasping whores who promised him free tricks if he would smuggle them past the guards and into the GIs' barracks – but I spared Sara that detail.

The German. We called him Wolfgang. Was that his real name? A big affable lout, well over six feet tall, fair haired, with twinkling blue eyes set deep in his furrowed face. He was the laziest man I have ever met. He spent most of his working day on the stairs behind the kitchen, smoking his Lucky Strikes and leafing through the glossy American magazines the GIs left lying around. We had to do most of his work, and sometimes I did lose my temper. I would slap the magazine out of his hands and order him to help carry the clean dishes back into the mess hall. He would scowl for a moment, more puzzled than angry, then his face would light up. '*Gut. Das mach ich,*' he would say, as though quite out of the blue, I had hit upon a brilliant idea. He entertained us with stories of those heady days of the Weimar Republic before the war, when he and his pals were *Halbstarke,* half-gangsters. When the Nazis came he was arrested and spent almost two years in jail, which made his de-Nazification a cakewalk. He had a vast store of Berlin jokes, most of them quite witless, I told Sara, but it didn't matter because he was the world's worst joke-teller. He would be convulsed in giggles just thinking about his joke, squeak out a few lines, then again dissolve in giggles. We groaned at his jokes but laughed at his struggle to tell them.

The American. A tall handsome Black man from Chicago who played the clarinet well enough to do a few gigs at the jazz club some of the GIs had formed, and little by little he initiated us into some of the mysteries of his music ('yatz,' we called it, until he tactfully corrected us). He had fought with Patton at Metz and the Battle of the Bulge, but after the war he found it difficult to return home and play the role of a 'good Negro.'

'Were there no girlfriends?' asked Sara. A delicate question to ask a grandfather. I couldn't tell her yet that I was still grieving for Eva, so as delicately as I could I told her about Gioconda and Tatiana. 'They were not exactly girlfriends,' I said. 'Not our girlfriends.' They had suffered the most at the end of the war. They had both been raped by the rear guard of the Red Army and now they were on display behind the cafeteria counter. Sara was no prissy little schoolgirl but it would hardly be proper to tell my granddaughter about the overheated sexual atmosphere around the base, the strip bars and brothels, with girls and young widows cruising the perimeter of McNair Barracks, looking for a GI lover. Until they found one, they would sometimes settle for one of us because we worked on the base and could provide at least a few luxuries from the PX – leather gloves, Florida oranges, and cigarettes. Most assignations took place off the base because it was difficult to get the girls past the guards.

I could have used a little help from Seymour to explain it to Sara. 'If you wanna lib'ralise the sekjooal morrays of the masses, all you gotta do is lose a war,' he said. 'Half the young men are killed, an' half of the other half come hobblin' home on crutches. So what are the ladies gonna do? Sit home, prim an' proper, waitin' for their gentleman callers? *Past nit.*'

But Tatiana and Gioconda could not have been more different. Tatiana bunked in our basement only when she was between GI lovers. They found more convenient quarters for her off the base (though there were regulations against that too). She would move only a few of her belongings out of our basement when she found a new lover, as though she were going on a short holiday. She was pretty and flaunted her promiscuity, maybe not only for pleasure, or for the gifts her GI lovers lavished upon her. She was brazen with a vengeance, it seems to me now – to avenge herself upon the generation that had made all Germans objects of loathing, this *Helden Volk* now become a *Ratten Volk* in the eyes of the world. She gloated as she told us how she would walk down the street on the arm of a brilliantly black GI, and when she heard the hiss of '*Ami Hure*' around her she would pull his curly head down and kiss him fiercely while she wriggled her groin against his thigh.

Gioconda was the opposite. Demure, dreamy, and a little on the pudgy side. She had set her hopes on both true love and a ticket to America. She was more like a sister to us, I told Sara, and we had given her that name because it was so inapt. There was nothing enigmatic about Gioconda's smile. It was frank, open, and contagious. She had lost her father and older brother at the front and now had to provide for herself and her traumatized mother. It was she, not Tatiana, who eventually bagged the big prize – a lieutenant from Texas, son of a millionaire oil man, who came back to Germany after he was discharged and proposed marriage.

These were now 'your people,' Antoine, who then became my people for two years, a provisional brotherhood and sisterhood that held no common creed, knew little about each other, demanded little, and made no promises. And I was grateful to be one of them.

We were an argumentative lot. Politics, religion, music. We all had our quirks and hobby horses and we sparred and jousted with one another, but if anyone seemed in danger of being knocked off his horse, one of us would switch sides and rally to his defence. I remember only one occasion when our jousting drew blood, and it was provoked by you, Antoine, though it wasn't your nose that got bloodied. On that night Max and Luke had just returned from one of their sorties to their favourite *Bierstübchen,* where Max had once again harangued a group of beer-sodden Berliners about their naïve hope that the Americans and the British would not abandon them to the vengeance of the Russians. 'What's in it for them? Berlin's just a pile of rubble,' he had told them. 'If the Russians want it, they can have it. *Bitteschön!'* He gave us a detailed account of how he had sparred and paried with those stupid naïve Berliners, and Luke mimed his rhetorical triumphs with quick jabs and uppercuts. Max gloated over the fate of those anxious Berliners, but the rest of us weren't so sanguine about it. Our fate was entwined with theirs, and we launched our own fierce rebuttal of his arguments. I can smile now at our youthful jousting, so easy to forget that there was some urgency then, however we may have misconstrued the issues. Battle lines were being drawn for the Cold War, and the fate of Berlin was still up for grabs. The Berlin Blockade was imminent, the Berlin Wall still fifteen years in the future. None of us suspected that West Berlin was destined to become a showpiece of capitalist nirvana.

Then Doktor Vik arrived and that might have put an end to our arguments, but Max was still flushed with his beer hall triumph and wouldn't shut up. I saw Doktor Vik roll his eyes and grin at you, Antoine. 'May as well let these yokels amuse us for a few minutes,' he seemed to say. He took off his hat and coat and cheered Max on, interjecting a few Marxist slogans of his own against the perfidious lies of capitalism. 'Bigger cages, longer leashes!' His taunts were laced with sarcasm which Max blithely ignored. 'That's it, that's what they want, these dumb Berliners,' he shouted. 'This Master Race! Now grovelling for crumbs tossed through the bars of their cage.'

Luke closed his eyes, stuck out his tongue, and lapped up a few Ami crumbs.

Max got in one last salvo. 'Germans have always been the barbarians at the gate, suckin' on the hind tit of European civilization. An' now they're suckin' on the Ami tit.' And that seemed to be the end of it. Doktor Vik rolled his eyes and reached for his coat and hat, a signal for the two of you to leave and 'talk business' somewhere. But you seemed to have drifted off into your own revery. You had sat quietly in the semigloom at the edge of the circle of light cast by our solitary light bulb. 'Maybe you're right,' you said, and flashed Max a wry grin. 'The Germans arrived late at the banquet of European civilisation.' You said the other guests, the French, Italians, Dutch, even the English, had already sated their appetites, and sat burping with indigestion. 'But Germany still had a ravenous appetite.' For centuries Germans had been Europe's rustic country cousins, you said, their warriors were as brave, their women as beautiful, yet they remained in the shadow of their Latin neighbours. Because they had been denied the advantages of Roman occupation, you said. Rome's legions had marched east to the Bosporus, and north and west, up the Rhone valley, through Gaul and across the Channel, all the way to Hadrian's Wall near the Scottish border. But Germania remained impenetrable to them. To the north, the impenetrable Alps, and when the Roman legions skirted around the Alps into Gaul they faced the equally impenetrable Hercynian forest to the east, home to savages rudely clad in animal skins, and horns stuck on their heads.

'That's all crap,' said Doktor Vik, 'Aryan-the-barbarian crap. It's what they're all saying now. Not what you and your friends in Paris were saying before the war.' He was now impatient to be gone, but you seemed to be toying with him. You said those rude savages never came to know, intimately, either Roman rectitude or Roman decadence. So for centuries they lagged behind their more cultivated neighbours. They had to learn their manners from the French, and their art and architecture, even their music, from the Italians. Compared to the English and the French, their poetry was wooden and formulaic. Then came the nineteenth century.

Now it was their turn, you said, and the rest of the world took note. In Russia, fashionable aristocrats let their French lapse and started learning German. Germany schooled the world in all the agonies of romanticism, and German scholars and scientists made those of France and England look like amateurs. 'But there was always something of the *arriviste* about them,' you said. 'They were pushy. And a little sweaty.'

What sense could I, a rube from the Russian hinterland, make of these musings? I looked at the others, for a sign, but their blank, slack faces told me they understood as little as I did what you were up to. Then came the Great War, you said, and after the war the Treaty of Versailles, and now Roman Europe was determined to teach these German upstarts a lesson – quash their vulgar aspiration to live above their station. They were still allowed within the castle walls, you said, but not as guests. They were told they would have to eat downstairs with the servants. 'That hurt,' you said. 'Not surprising that they should resent their betters.'

There was silence for a few moments, until it was broken by Max. 'So why didn't they toss out their betters,' he said. 'Why didn't they take over the whole stinkin' castle, make a revolution? That was their chance,' he said, 'and they blew it. Instead, they got the bleedin' Weimar Republic, a bunch of thugs in flashy new cars, and artsy ass lickers, pandering to their fetishes. While the working class starved.'

'Compared to what came after,' you said, 'the Weimar Republic was an exotic flower. It bloomed for a season, then withered in the glare of Nazi headlights.' But you weren't looking at Max. You were watching Doktor Vik. 'Then came the German *miracle*,' you said. 'While America and the Western democracies were wallowing in their Depression, and while the Famine in the Soviet Union was killing millions, Germany was booming. The world looked on in wonder. Even starry-eyed youngsters in Canada wanted a piece of the action,' you said, and gave Doktor Vik a sly wink. 'Very funny,' said Doktor Vik, but he wasn't laughing.

Then Wolfgang waded in. He had been watching the simmering tension between you and Doktor Vik. He was probably as perplexed as any of us, but he had experienced the Weimar Republic in the flesh. 'Me, I'm teenager den, in sa Weimar time. I run errants for sa big gangsters. Me and my big brudder.' Wolfgang shook his head and began to giggle. 'Yeah, dat vas fun,' he said, 'Dey pay goot money. My brudder, dey give him a *Motorrad*. Vroom, vroom. But sometimes, how you say? . . . vee get beat up, vee get shit kicked out. From bigger boys who run errants for bigger gangsters. But vaht vee can do? Ven vee git bigger, vee kick out shit too.' Wolfgang found this funny, like one of his interminable jokes, and he started to giggle. I had only a vague idea then of life in Germany before the Nazis came to power. I had heard of the Weimar Republic but attached no images to the term, either positive or negative, and had no idea the subject could generate enough heat to draw blood.

'*Ach, ja,*' sighed Wolfgang, 'My brudder, he big shot too den. Mercedes, fancy girlfriend. Actress. Sometimes singer too. Sometimes she sing better *mit* clos off.' Another fit of giggles, and now he had us laughing along with him. 'Me too, I'm little bit big shot. I have gang, vee steal cars, sell to my brudder. Sometimes udder tings too. Den de Nazis come,' he said, 'but who gives shit? *Macht nits.* Nazi schmatzi. Tomorrow vill be somebody else.' A few more giggles as Wolfgang paused to contemplate his youthful naiveté. 'Come sa Brown Shirts – gangsters mit uniforms. Udder gangsters not so happy. Before, ven gangsters get picture in sa papers, dey very happy. Even my big brudder he get picture in sa paper, *mit* girlfriend. Now? Gangsters don't vant picture in sa paper. Now picture in sa paper means jail. Or means dead. My brudder, he change apartments fife times in two years. Fancy girlfriend, she likes not so much to sing anymore. Vants babies now.' Wolfgang shook his head in disbelief as he recalled this bizarre turn of events. Then one morning, he said, his brother had got up early, shaved and bathed, and was out the door before his girlfriend had finished checking for new wrinkles in the mirror. Mid afternoon he returned, wearing an *SS* uniform. 'And sa girlfriend? She is very happy. She make a Heil Hitler salute.' We had heard stories like this before. We found them grimly amusing, but otherwise unremarkable. When I now strain to get a clearer picture of the Weimar period, Wolfgang's story of his brudder seems like a parody of what happened among those more sophisticated, more culturally savvy Weimar debauchees. They too must have become aware that their glamour was fading, that they had exhausted their repertoire of kinkiness, had run out of ideas how to *épater la bourgeoisie*. For them too the *Gleichschaltung* would have come in the nick o' time, just when their livers had begun to fail, their wit become forced – how else can I picture it, Antoine? Then one day they are rudely awakened, open the shutters and stand squinting into the bright noonday sun. *Holla,* what's this? Excited chatter outside their windows. At this time of the morning? Fleshy matrons returning from market laden with fresh produce, older gents dusting off their war medals, and everywhere bands of radiant youths, fit as a fiddle and newly scrubbed, strutting their stuff. How timely this invigorating blast out of the Wagnerian mists, this surge of Nordic health. The new vogue now called for clear mountain air, sturdy *Lederhosen*, knapsacks and knee socks. Doktor Vik was not amused, but you, Antoine, you sat grinning at Wolfgang, egging him on. You tossed verbal sticks for him to snatch out of the air like a playful puppy, then mimicked the righteous zeal of young Nazi converts. '*Schmutz!*' you cried, shaking your fist in the air. 'No more, dos fancy fops, *mit* grease paint and fezzers in sa hair! No more, dos naughty cabaret ditties, no more Kurt Weil and Lotte Lenya!'

'*Genau so! Genau so!*' cried Wolfgang, convulsed by another fit of helpless giggling. Then he too raised his fist and struck a defiant pose, '*Genug!* Enuf already! Now sa people vant *Heimatlieder*. Gif us *Heimatlieder!* Real *deutsche Heimatlieder,* someting ve all can sing, All togedder now, *Eins, zwei, ompah!*' Then he collapsed into his chair, holding both his sides. He tried to say more but managed only a feeble squeak among a rush of giggles. 'That's the view from the gutter,' snarled Doktor Vik. He'd been there too, at Heidelberg, he reminded us, and from his loftier perch what he saw was German *Ordnung*. Order. Idealism. German science, art, medicine – they were the envy of the world. '*Ja, ja!* Dats how it vas!' yelped Wolfgang. He half rose from his chair and waved his finger in the air as though Doktor Vik had just confirmed everything he had said. '*Genau so!*' And that's when Doktor Vik rushed him, punched him in the face, and knocked him down. Then he lined up to give Wolfgang a kick in his stomach before Luke could jump on his back and put a chokehold on him. It was Wolfgang who suffered Doktor Vik's blows and kicks but they were meant for you, Antoine.

May 8, 1992

And then there was Uschi. She was my 'find.' None of you had met her, and when I described my first encounter with her the next morning, I played up the farcical elements to conceal the giddiness I felt.

It was late at night when I clamoured up the marble stairway with my bucket and mop. I was still a lowly janitor then, not yet promoted to chief dishwasher. The two other janitors and I had finished mopping the mess hall, kitchen and scullery and that left only the more stately upper floors, the officers' mess and meeting rooms. I could have waited till morning but I was putting in time while you 'worked' the Blue Room, another crisis to be resolved by the military brass of the four Allied administrations. We planned to go to another *Kneipe* for a beer or two, one nearer the base where our presence would attract less attention.

I still had only a vague notion then how important your presence was at these late-night meetings, hosted and chaired by your Colonel Simpson. It was you he counted on to douse hot tempers with the finest cognacs, vodkas and liqueurs, or to smooth the ruffled feathers of yet another Congressional delegation from Washington. And I didn't know that while you leaned over their shoulders to fill their glasses, Colonel Simpson also counted on you to eavesdrop on private conversations around the table, whether in French, German or Russian, conversations that could be useful to him – and also to Doktor Vik.

The grand stairway was in the Prussian neoclassical style, frescos depicting heroic Roman figures and their gods and goddesses, and above them plump plaster *putti* leering down from the cornice. The plaster had flaked and chipped but it was still an imposing ascent to the upper floor and the domed central hall with its tall windows overlooking the parade square. To the right, double doors led to the officers' mess, to the left the Blue Room.

When I got to top of the stairway with my bucket and mop, I turned on a light and began mopping, making sure I didn't mop myself into a corner, and I had probably been mopping absent-mindedly for several minutes before I saw her, like a vision, right in front of me. She sat curled up on the deep sill of one of the tall windows, her back propped against the oak-panelled casing, her arms clasped around her knees, head tipped forward. American officers rarely brought their *Fräuleins* onto the base,

unlike many Russian officers who liked to show off their women wherever they went, so her presence here was the more unexpected. I
remember a long black dress and a white ermine jacket carelessly draped
around her. Her amber hair hung down below her shoulders, and when
her head tipped forward, two woven tresses fell on her breast. She called
to mind childhood images of proud queens led in mocking procession
among the spoils of war, or one of those radiant figures in old folk tales
who suddenly appear before an ignorant rustic, a shepherd or a wood
cutter, to request some small service of him that might save her from a
tragic fate.

Then I recovered my senses. Just another overdressed Ami whore. I
mumbled a surly apology, collected my bucket, turned off the light and
started down the stairs. 'Please, finish your job,' she said. 'You don't need
to stop because of me.'

I stood undecided for a moment. 'I'll only be a minute,' I mumbled. I
turned the light on and resumed my mopping. Now I began to see that
my first impression wasn't that far off the mark and I became flustered.
My mop bucket was the latest American model, with a foot-pedal on one
side that activated a pair of rubber wringers. I stepped on the pedal acci-
dentally, stumbled over the wringers, and upset the whole bucket with a
great clatter, and flooded the floor. Uschi instinctively drew in her feet.
'You must be new at this job,' she said. She covered her mouth with her
hand to stifle a laugh.

'Everybody's got a new job now,' I grumbled.

'Yes. Of course. What did you used to do?'

'Before the war I was an eye surgeon.' I tried to salvage a little dignity
by being huffy.

'I'm sure you were very good. You have such steady hands.'

'What were you before the war?' I snapped.

'I was a princess.'

'I never operated on a princess.'

'That's because we have very good eyes,' she said, and in spite of myself
I couldn't help looking at her eyes. In spite of herself, she couldn't help
popping them open a little wider.

Then we laughed. 'You're not from here, are you?' she said. 'I mean, a
Berliner.'

'No. *Volksdeutscher*. From the Ukraine. A small village near the Dnieper River.'

'Do you miss it?'

'No. There's not much left of it.'

We were quiet for a few minutes while I finished cleaning up the mess I had made. She turned and hung her legs over the edge of the sill and leaned forward, her hands clasping the edge of the sill on either side of her. 'Are some of your family still there, alive?' she said.

'My father might still be alive. He was an artist. Might have become a great artist. He sabotaged a propaganda poster, then escaped before the NKVD came for him. But he was never heard from again. They probably caught him and killed him.'

'And the rest of your family?'

'We all fled to Poland – when the *Wehrmacht* began its retreat. A long trek, with horse-drawn carts or on foot. It took eight months, but most of our people made it. During the German occupation we were called collaborators, we *Volksdeutsche*. So if the Germans had abandoned us, the Red Army would have slaughtered us. And you, you're a Berliner?'

'No, I'm from East Prussia. Königsberg,' she said. 'I'm also a refugee.'

'Do you still have family there?'

'No, not close family. My brother was in the navy. He died when his submarine was blown up. My father died when he and I were trying to escape from the Red Army. My mother might still be alive. She disappeared before the war. There were often admirals and generals and big Party people at our house – a lot of toasting and Heil-Hitlering. My father, he tried . . . to adapt. But my mother had a sharp tongue. She often embarrassed him.'

'Did she embarrass you?'

'She frightened me. I knew something bad would happen to her. Especially after she started drinking.'

I finished mopping the floor and began to pack up my gear. 'In a war you have to expect that many young men will die,' she said, 'but not all this . . . chaos. All these refugees. Usually, after a war, people flee *out* of the country that lost, not into it.'

'Your young man, was he killed too?'

'He was also in the navy. A Lieutenant Commander on the same ship as my brother. I had known him since I was a little girl. He was very handsome, very charming. Both our families thought it was a perfect match. But it might not have worked out.' She looked down at her feet. 'He was also embarrassed by my mother,' she said, 'and even before the war we had big arguments. He wanted me to be both his lover and his adoring little sister.'

Within fifteen minutes of first setting eyes on each other we were casually exchanging intimate details about ourselves, and our families. 'It was bad there, at the end, in Königsberg,' I said.

'You were there? Were you in the *Wehrmacht?*'

'I was *Waffen SS.*'

Uschi wrinkled her brow and frowned. 'How did the Amis ever let you anywhere near the base, if you were *SS?*'

'I have a friend here, who has friends who can do favours for him.'

'We all need friends.'

'Is your friend in there?' I pointed my thumb at the tall double doors to the Blue Room.

'Yes.'

I blushed. 'You're lucky – to have such a friend,' I said.

'Luck is fickle. When they start showing you photos of their kids back home you know it's soon time to look for another friend.'

The door opened and a man came out. Cigar smoke billowed through the doors behind him, and through the smoke I could see men stripped to their shirts, getting up to stretch their legs. He too was stripped down to his shirt with the sleeves rolled up, so I couldn't tell he was a General. I resumed my mopping and he ignored me. 'I'm very sorry,' he said, and planted a kiss on her forehead, which she received with closed eyes. 'Looks like this thing's goin' all night,' he said. 'Some dumb Congressman shot off his mouth an' now the Russkies want their pound of flesh.' So she better go home, he explained. He said he had called his driver but he probably wouldn't get here under half an hour. Uschi said, 'That's OK, I understand.'

'Have you got your key?' he asked.

'Yes.'

He cast me a glance, then returned to the meeting. 'He's a nice man,' said Uschi, perhaps a little too distinctly.

'My friend is in there too,' I said.

'Oh?' She raised her eyebrows and smirked, but I didn't catch her meaning.

'He's their waiter,' I explained. 'His job is to douse the tempers of the French and make the Russians blissfully drunk. I'm just putting in time here till he's off work.'

'Was he an eye surgeon too, before the war?' she said, and we laughed.

'He was a writer. In Paris. But I didn't know him then. We were friends before that, back in the Ukraine, when we were just boys. We met again here quite by chance. It's a long story.' She got up and cast a look at the door, behind which we could hear a heated debate. I said, 'I'll walk you to the gate, if you like, to wait for your driver. Then I may as well go home too, if this meeting's going all night.'

'Where's home?' she asked.

I pointed at the floor. 'Down there.' She looked at the floor, looked at me, and I explained that a bunch of us lived down there in the basement. 'Not much light, but it's rat-free.'

She kept asking and I kept explaining. Did all of us work on the base? Was it legal? 'Men only, or women and children too?' she asked. 'Two women, but no children,' I said.

When her driver came she said, 'Maybe we'll see each other again. My ... friend ... got me a job at the PX. I'm not there every day, but it makes me legal on the base. And available.'

On my first free day I went to the PX and hung around near the door until she arrived. We chatted a few minutes while she smoked her cigarette, then she said, 'Wait here.' She went inside to leave a message with the cashier for her General – that she had run into an old family friend and wouldn't be back till after lunch.

Then we went for the first of our many walks. We talked casually about trivial things, scoffed at the uppity French who now claimed equal status with the British and American administrations in Berlin even though they'd contributed little to the defeat of the Nazis. Then we drifted toward more personal things. I told her I had enlisted when every-body knew the war was already lost, that I'd been assigned to an Intelligence unit in the *Waffen SS*, then asked to be transferred to the front, to the company commanded by the very same officer who had invaded our villages in 1941. Captain von Niessen. 'I was just a kid then,' I said. 'I idolized him, a gallant hero come to save us from the Communists.' Then I asked, 'How did *you* survive, after Königsberg?'

She was silent, and I felt ashamed. We had seemed so at ease in each other's company, it hadn't occurred to me how impudent the question was. 'I'm sorry,' I said.

'It's OK. I have to learn how to talk about it. You're not the first to ask.' She said there were only three of them left on the estate at the end – she, her old father, and one of her father's tenants. Werner. A big strong black-smith, the only one who stayed to the very end. By then her father wasn't well, and wasn't thinking clearly. He refused to leave, pretended to run the estate as he always had, even when everyone had fled. And so she and Werner had put him in a wheelbarrow, and heaped a few belongings on top of him – while he cursed them and struggled. 'He did come to his senses,' she said, 'when he saw the hordes of refugees scrambling west-ward as fast as they could.'

They didn't get very far before the Red Army rolled over them. She said the first wave of tanks and trucks passed through, scattering and terrifying the refugees, but it was the second wave that did most of the killing and raping. They shot Werner and her father, she said, and she knew what they would do to her. She saw a big scruffy corporal standing apart from his comrades. Instead of trying to run away she ran *to* him, took his arm and pushed him into a shop that had already been looted, closed the door and offered herself to him. 'For the first minute or two, he just stood there, stunned,' she said. She spent the night with him in that looted shop, and at dawn, when it was quiet, they buried Werner and her father in a garden behind the shop. Then he found a house owned by an old Latvian couple, and ordered them to hide her till he came back. She said he turned out to be the gentlest of all her friends. When his unit moved on he passed her on to a lieutenant, who was not so gentle. He was rough but he protected her from the others, until his unit was also sent somewhere else.

Yes, Antoine, rape has always been one of the spoils of war, and no doubt when you were in Paris you heard reports of French women raped by the Nazis, then the stories of Allied soldiers who raped German and Italian women at the end of the war, but nothing like the frenzy of rape by Red Army soldiers on the eastern front. I saw some of those mutilated bodies, where the Red Army had recently passed through a town or village. 1,400,000 rape victims in East Prussia and Pomerania. That is one of the lower estimates among reputable historians. When killing reaches a certain level of horror we have a word for it – massacre. There should be a comparable word for a raping frenzy. Ten men would rape one woman, one after the other, then go on to the next. Not for pleasure but for revenge, and to humiliate German manhood. That is why old or young didn't matter, fat or skinny, sick or healthy, and that is why gang raping was the norm. It must have enraged those Soviet soldiers to find German women, even in the last months of the war, still living in pretty little towns, well dressed, even *chic* in their eyes. What right had these fascist bitches to any womanly charms? Rape and mutilation was the Soviet version of racial cleansing. Eliminate the breeders. That has become the prevailing theory.

But only 130,000 rape victims in Berlin. Why so few, relatively? Were the women of Berlin not to Ivan's taste? Not plump enough? (It was said that many women in Berlin felt a sensation of sweet revenge when they saw that the well-fed wives and mistresses of Nazi officers were Ivan's first choice.) Most of those women were raped after the fighting was over, after the surrender, and by then many women realized that their best defence was to attach themselves as quickly as possible to the biggest brute or the highest ranking officer they could find and become *his* woman, his personal loot. One way in which a man could still be useful to a woman, to protect her from other men.

The Americans didn't need to rape. Yes, they had 'consumer goods' they could exchange for sexual favours, canned ham and fish, lipstick and cigarettes – but they also felt less hate. Only one of their comrades had died for every 30 Soviet soldiers killed on the eastern front, and not one American had lost his wife, daughter or mother – while almost fourteen million Soviet civilians were killed. Our modern wars have made killing easy, it can be done at a distance, enough distance that you can't hear their cries, see the limbs torn from their torsos, see the face twist in terror. We don't need to lay hands on the people we kill, and feel their desperate will to live. But the technology of rape has not changed since Biblical times. It must still be done at close quarters. So rape now requires more hate than killing.

On our next walk Uschi told me how an English colonel had become her friend. The front moved west, and when she heard the English had

taken a town twenty kilometres to the south, she escaped. The English
colonel could be more generous than the Russians, she said, could give
her fine clothes and a decent place to live. The Russians would slap her
around, sometimes just on principle – to remind themselves not to feel
any affection for a German woman – but the English colonel was cruel in
a different way. He was more 'civilised.' In public, among the other officers, he played the gentleman, discreetly displayed her and flaunted her
'tony Junker background.' Though there were rules against fraternization,
some officers could ignore them. In private he sneered at her 'classy pedigree,' which made her more contemptible in his eyes, more deserving of
her 'fallen' state. He taunted her with stories of what Nazi officers had
demanded of their mistresses.

He took her to a party, at Schloss Hehlen, she said, where she had
often been a guest before the war. The surviving 'owner' of the estate was
Jonny von der Schulenburg, who had opposed the Nazis when they came
to power and fled to England. When he came back after the war he had
generously offered the use of his house to the Allies in gratitude for liber-
ating Germany from the Nazis. The British administration had converted
the second storey to offices and meeting rooms, and during the day it was
a busy place. Jeeps and lorries coming and going. But they let Jonny
pretend he was still the owner of the Schloss and they his guests, though
he now lived in a little room in the servants' quarters. Uschi said the two
families, hers and the Schulenburg's, had once owned seaside houses near
each other, and when they were children she and Loremarie, Jonny's
younger sister, had been good friends.

The party was held in the Knights' Hall, a grand gothic hall with a high
trussed ceiling. The banquet table ran almost the full length of the hall,
and life-sized portraits of the family's ancestors lined the walls. Several
English gentlemen-officers had come for the occasion, and to hunt deer
and wild boar in what had been the family's park. They had brought their
own hounds from England and a chef from France. She said Jonny had
tried his best to play the charming host, though he was already too drunk
to carry it off. Yes, of course Jonny had recognized her. By then, she said,
she was no longer so ashamed to be seen on the arm of an English
colonel, especially not by Jonny. He had always been the errant son of the
family, a denizen of the Berlin cabarets during the last years of the
Weimar period, so he was not the kind to get righteous. Uschi said he

pretended to be shocked when she had introduced her colonel to him, but it was shock with a wink, at her new-found 'respectability.'

The banquet lasted late into the night, said Uschi, there was music and 'entertainment,' and the party became rowdy. Then Jonny found an English motorcycle outside and rode it into the Knights' Hall, rode it round and round the Hall, while he threw empty wine and whiskey bottles at the portraits of his ancestors on the walls. The English gentlemen cheered and kept him supplied with empty bottles. Some of those ancestors, said Uschi, might have opposed Hitler more effectively than Jonny had done, if they'd been alive before the war.

After that party, she left her English colonel. Germany was now divided into 'Zones' and in the British Zone there was less danger of rape. She tried to manage on her own without 'friends,' but she couldn't always count on kind people to feed and house her. She said in a way she was grateful to Jonny and that English colonel. She had been going down the same road as Jonny, but the spectacle of his indulgent self-contempt had disgusted her.

She became more and more curious about the basement lair where we squatted so I brought her down to meet the other riff-raff. Everyone fawned over her. Everyone but you, Antoine. She too seemed to find our lair a refuge. She began to drop in on us more frequently and when she finally broke off with her general she appeared at our door with two small suitcases. We burst into cheers. We sent Max and Luke to scrounge for delicacies on the black market to prepare a feast, and instead of drab brown army blankets Wolfgang brought home more colourful and more feminine drapes to partition her 'apartment.' We found her a good bed, and since she was already legal by virtue of her token job at the PX, she didn't need to be de-Nazified to get a 'real job' in the mess hall, serving meat and potatoes to the GIs.

I wanted so much that you and she would like each other, Antoine, and yes, fall in love with each other. I wanted to make each of you a gift of the other, wanted each of you to save the other. Was I not in love with her myself? Is it possible to love a woman and not wish to possess her? To wish that she should love another? Yes, I loved her, but I never pictured myself as her lover. She was out of my league, too beautiful, too refined. It would be like Caliban lusting for Miranda. I was more like a pet dog that couldn't stop wagging its tail in her presence – but no, it was more than that. There was a bond between us, perhaps more like brother and sister, as though we'd known each other all our lives.

But you didn't wag your tail. You and Uschi circled each other warily, and if you spoke at all you spoke in sharp, edgy quips, circled each other and took care not to touch. You and she might be oblivious, or pretend to be oblivious, to the erotic charge building between you but it was obvious to the rest of us. We knew it couldn't go on, but didn't know how or when it would end. Uschi, languid, sensuous, who could not speak without purring, whose hands always seemed to be reaching for something to caress, whether a human shoulder or just the back of a chair, she could hardly keep her hands off you. And you, the opposite. Always the Antonine reserve, always you kept a small but measured distance between yourself and others, always that *noli me tangere* aura about you, hardly perceptible perhaps, but in Uschi's presence it became palpable, it bristled, became a provocation. Or so it seemed to us. When the two of you passed near each other it was as though the air between you whooshed, as though every electron in your bodies leaned out of its orbit toward the other but could not yet break free of its magnetic field. We waited nervously for it to happen.

Then the American brought home a phonograph and a stack of scratchy vinyl records, seventy-eights, for which he had traded four cartons of cigarettes. The device was familiar to Carver and to you and Uschi, but not to the rest of us. In Russia it was rumoured that Kaethler had such a device in his bedroom on which he would play recordings of Stalin's speeches, but I had never seen or heard one. The records included opera highlights, Beethoven's *Eroica,* and some Schubert *Lieder.* Then Carver picked up a record with a red label. '*Francisco Canaro y su Orquesta,*' he lisped.

'Put that one on,' you said, and you took Uschi's hand and led her out of the clutter of our common area into the nether world among the concrete pillars, and there in the semi-darkness you danced the tango. How could any true son of Argentina, a *porteño* of Buenos Aires, resist those rhythms, rhythms like the slash of a knife across a cheek. We stood in a cluster and watched as the two of you spun around an invisible axis, stopped, slunk deeper into the darkness, spun again, your faces stone still and each pair of eyes trained on the other like magnets. Your bodies were as close as two bodies can be without dissolving into one another, and every step promised, or threatened, a more complete surrender. We had never seen dancing like this before and were struck dumb except for a breathless 'ooh' or 'aah,' and when the music stopped you both stopped but still held each other's eyes. The only sound now was the click-click, click-click, click-click of the phonograph needle. Then you leaned toward each other until your foreheads touched and we whistled our consent to this match made in a musty, cavernous vault under McNair Barracks.

I think you did love each other, but there always remained that tango tension between you. In the months that followed I thought I could see signs of the old confident, arrogant Antonii coming back to life. You laughed more, even swaggered a little, though there were still those moods when you withdrew into a world that remained closed to the rest of us.

June 1, 1992

It wouldn't surprise you to hear that Doktor Vik has had a brilliant career since you last saw him in Berlin. When he and I meet for our regular dinners at the Factor's Table, his favourite restaurant in Winnipeg, I don't have to sing for my supper but I have to listen to him agonize whether, at his age, he really wants to take on another director-ship somewhere, or take a temporary leave from his clinic to 'clean house' at some famous institute that's wallowing in factionalism, between the pill pushers and the knife wielders. When we arrived in Canada he had only recently moved to Winnipeg to become director of a small clinic, 'a mediocre, underfunded operation,' he said, but by god, he had thrown all his energies into that job and turned it into a world-class Institute.

Did he ever tell you about his humble beginnings, Antoine, on a farm in southern Manitoba, not a very successful farm? It was not a subject he was eager to talk about. At one of our dinners I prodded a little and he told me his father was still alive, and he had two older sisters. They still lived on the farm where he had grown up. He said his father was 'a feisty old codger,' who always saw himself as a man under attack, always at odds with his neighbours and the municipality, suing them or threatening to sue, and he had an ongoing feud with the Mennonite community in that area. 'They shunned him, and shunned my mother too, when she married him.' He said he had little memory of his mother, who had died when he was only five. His two sisters had never married, and it was they who now kept the farm going. He said he visited them occasionally, but they rarely came to Winnipeg. In fact they rarely ventured further from the farm than the grain elevators in the next town.

I learned more about his family from the janitor at my school. He and I were the only ethnic Mennonites in our town. Janitor Jake, we called him, and he had been the janitor at our school for eighteen years before I arrived. He was at first wary of me, with my Mennonite name, but when he gleaned that we had both moved to our town to put some distance between ourselves and the Mennonite settlements to the south he became more talkative. He readily confessed that he'd always had a 'battle with the bottle,' as he put it, and after two failed marriages he seemed to have resigned himself to the status of a 'bottom feeder.' He was an amusing raconteur, once he felt assured he would not be urged to 'better himself.'

It turned out that he had grown up on a farm not far from the farm where Doktor Vik had grown up, and they had gone to the same two-room school, though he was two grades behind him. He said his family weren't rich farmers either. 'Darp Menniste,' he said. That's what the more 'worldly' Mennonites called them. 'It means somethin' like hillbillies,' he explained, 'conservative, no organs or pianos allowed, women in little black bonnets.' Their farms were near the American border, where the land gets a bit hilly, full of sloughs and creeks that flood every spring. Like Viktor, he said, he had grown up hearing the deacons and elders mocked and reviled, especially by his mother, who had a sharp tongue. But his family were content to make fun of them in private. Not Viktor's father. He had a vengeful streak, said Jake, 'spoilin' for a fight. Even when he was a young fella, he'd go to church just to make a nuisance of himself. He'd stand up in the middle of the sermon an' start shoutin' at the preacher. Anyways, that's what people say.'

He said Doktor Vik's father was known locally as 'Communist Kroeger,' a card-carrying member of the Communist Party of Canada. 'He'd pull the card out of his wallet an' show it to people waitin' in line at the Wheat Pool, or at the hardware store. Specially at election time. An' then he'd start yakkin' about what a great statesman Stalin was, turned a backward peasant society into a modern industrial country, in just ten years.'

I said, 'That must have pissed some people off.'

'Yeah, s'pose it did,' said Jake, 'But most people just thought he'd gone off his rocker. They'd probably have left him alone,' he said, 'but then he started goin' around with the daughter of a rich Mennonite, a deacon in the church. There were seven boys in the family, and only the one girl. 'They spoiled her, I guess. Give her everything she wanted. And a good looker too, when she growed up, could melt your heart, they say. But she got a bit wild. Nothin' serious, mind you, nothin' you'd call wild nowadays, but the more her family tried to rein her in, the wilder she got. People weren't surprised when she took up with Viktor's father. Weren't much surprised neither when they up an' got married by a Justice of the Peace, over in one of the French towns.' The girl's family went berserk. Hired a lawyer to get the marriage annulled, but no luck. It was in the books. 'Prit near drove her old man crazy. Hard on Viktor's mother too, when they shunned her, cut her off from her own family. But she stood by her man. Loved him, I guess.'

He said the elders gave Viktor's father a rough time, but he could give as good as he got. 'Sunday mornin' he'd get his family all dressed up, then they'd drive to church. But they wouldn't go *in* the church. They'd all stay sittin' there in the parkin' lot. Country music blarin' on the radio. Just sittin' in the car, waitin' for the service to end. When folks started comin' out, he'd give it another minute, then he'd start up the engine, rev' her up real good, an' go chargin' out of the parkin' lot. Spewin' gravel at all the other cars, with their shiny new fenders.'

For him and his chums, said Jake, it was all a lark. As soon as the preacher said Amen they'd rush out of the church to make sure they didn't miss the show. But the older folks didn't think it was so funny, especially those with stone chips in their fenders.

He said Doktor Vik's father was one of the last to get the electric put in, and when he did, he put in only one light. In the whole house, just one bare light bulb, hanging over the kitchen table. It was so Viktor wouldn't hurt his eyes when he did his school work. The rest of the family, if they wanted light, would use kerosene lamps. 'The old man said communists don't believe in all that fancy capitalist stuff. But he was just a skinflint.'

He said his family still had a horse back then that he liked to ride, so he'd sometimes ride out to their farm. Old man Kroeger was always friendly to him, so were the two girls. They were very shy, but they always gave him a piece of pie or cake, and something to drink.

'The old man loved his kids, yuh gotta give him that,' said Jake. 'An' they all stood behind him. He could work like a demon, an' so could the girls, especially the oldest. Could keep up with any man.'

But Viktor himself wasn't much help on the farm. While the others were in the fields, Viktor was at the kitchen table doing his school work. 'An' when they come in from the fields it was all ssssh, ssssh, don't disturb Viktor. They waited on him, hand and foot, so he could do school work. When he was twelve years old, he was already doin' college correspon- dence stuff. That was the old man's plan,' said Jake, 'that's how he'd stick it to the elders, get his revenge. Viktor was gonna be famous some day, famous for bein' smart. Guess it worked,' said Jake, 'He's a big brain doctor now, ain't he?'

Already in Berlin Doktor Vik left us in no doubt that he had lofty ambitions. When you were present his manner towards us was cheerfully obliging, entertaining us with juicy tidbits of the backstabbing and bungling among the four allied military administrations. He could mimic both the lazy southern drawl of the American generals and the surly righteousness of the Russians. He could be very funny then, and charming. But he never let us forget that the two of you went 'way back,' a relationship between equals, not a relationship with riff-raff that happened to be convenient. You and he had a history. He would direct cryptic little asides to you that hinted at a shadowy past, something heavy lurking in the murky depths, while the rest of us flitted lightly enough upon the lily-pond surface. But when you weren't present, when he had only us for an audience while he waited for you to come home, he would converse with us as though we hungered for a glimpse of life on a loftier plane. He would regale us with accounts of the newest psychiatric procedures at some of the leading Institutes in America. Perhaps we had heard of Insulin Shock Therapy? A very promising development for treating schizophrenia. Actually, he had published an article about it in *The Lancet*. 'Usually they bring in the patient strapped down on a gurney. Completely delusional, violent, all the usual symptoms. What happens is we virtually kill him, then we bring him back to life. First we inject a shot of insulin into the muscle. Calms him right down, you might say. Then we keep him under close surveillance. One nurse assigned to monitor him constantly, just him. Pulse, temperature, all that stuff. And everything keeps going down, down, down. Then, 'Doctor! Doctor! I can detect no respiration!'

Doktor Vik had to chuckle at how excited some of these nurses get at this point. 'So you go in, give the patient a few slaps in the face, shout his name into his ear, that sort of thing. Nothing. No breathing, no pulse. Now you have to move fast, to give him the adrenalin injection. And *voilà!* He starts breathing again. In five minutes he's sitting in a chair, looking around like he just woke from a long sleep, and he remembers nothing. Quite amazing, actually. The nurses get quite silly fawning over him, as though they've just seen a miracle. No miracle, of course, just good science.'

But his current interest was something called post-traumatic stress disorder, he told us. That's why he'd signed on with UNRRA. 'It's a whole new area,' he said, and Germany provided a wealth of trauma cases. He already had about twenty file folders crammed with 'case studies,' enough for a monograph on the subject when he got back to America.

Were *we* trauma cases? Were we destined to appear in his monograph as Herr P and Frau S? 'I'm glad we could oblige,' said one of the girls who'd been raped.

Astounding, all this, Doktor Vik charting his career as though the world had already shrugged off its brief flirtation with disaster. Most of us expected that the basement of McNair Barracks was as high as we were likely to rise in the world. We might have felt a little lost on our island amid the rubble but we weren't sure we were ready to be rescued.

After my first year in Berlin, I remember Doktor Vik's visits becoming more frequent, and there seemed to be more urgency to the 'business' he had with you. He was a little less affable, and quickly became annoyed when you didn't come home at your usual time after your shift in the officers' mess. Or didn't come home at all. There were days when you would pack a knapsack of provisions from the PX or from the mess kitchen and disappear. When you returned, after a day or two, you would mumble something about an old friend who needed help, some clothes and food. We assumed it must be a writer you once knew who was now in disfavour among the Allies, and we didn't press you to tell us more.

Then there he was, Doktor Vik. Early in the morning. He had always appeared late at night and waited for you to finish your day. We didn't know what to make of it. It was he who now seemed to have something urgent to tell you, and he had expected to find you still in bed. The two Australians and the three women had already left to serve breakfast to the GIs, so there were only three of us, half awake, finishing our own break-fast. 'So where the hell is he?' he demanded, but all we could tell him was that you hadn't come home last night.

'We were supposed to meet – after Simpson sent the Russians home with something to chew on. I waited half the night,' he said.

We said we had no idea where you went when you didn't come home.

'Did you ask Uschi?'

'No,' said the American, 'she was in a bad mood. She's always in a bad mood when he disappears like this.'

Doktor Vik took off his coat, flung it onto the sofa, and began pacing. I was tickled to hear you had stood him up, Antoine, that you weren't always at his beck and call, but I didn't say a word to him. I sat quietly munching my toast and jam. Suddenly he turned to me and said, yes, if I wanted to know, he had indeed grown up in a Mennonite community. He said it as though I'd been nagging him about the subject ever since we first met.

It was in southern Manitoba, he said. A cesspool of bigotry and superstition, tyrannized by puritanical deacons and elders. But luckily, he said, his father had the good sense to get himself shunned by the community. The pious brethren had taken offense when his mother appeared in public with a fashionable hat on her head instead of a kerchief. So he had grown up in a home where he heard nothing but curses against Mennonites. 'And now, can you believe it? I run into them again, these Mennonites. Right here, among the millions of refugees swarming into Germany. Like a plague of locusts.' And they had confirmed all his aversions to the tribe. 'Actually, there's a whole camp of them in Gronau, near the Dutch border,' he said, housed in an old textile mill or something. About a thousand of them crammed in there, mostly women and children. 'Ugh! The stench of urine and dirty diapers. And old women grabbing your sleeve, demanding food, clothes, official papers. They think they're God's chosen people. And there's a batch of relief workers, Mennonites from the States and Canada, encouraging them in their delusion. Well, they'll get no special treatment from me, I'll tell you.' He said in Lübeck alone UNRRA was processing more than 6,000 refugees a day, 'but no, these Mennonites gotta have their *own* organization, their *own* refugee camps. There's even one right here, in Berlin. About four hundred of 'em. Trapped, in the middle of the Soviet Zone. Shittin' their pants, 'cause they're afraid they'll be sent back to Russia.'

My head was spinning, but Doktor Vik ranted on. The first time I heard the name 'Peter Dyck' it was spat out of Doktor Vik's mouth. 'The American Mennonites have sent this kid out here,' he said, 'a cheeky little Saskatchewan hayseed. He and his buxom wife are pokin' around in the rubble, looking for lost Mennonite sheep. Then they go running to this Colonel Simpson – yeah, the same guy our Antoine's so buddy with. They put on a big show – Please, Colonel Simpson, our people need housing.' He said Simpson had already requisitioned a big old house for these Mennonites, on the Ringstrasse, not far from the base, but there were always more Mennos crawling out of the rubble. 'This cheeky little Menno wants to be their Moses,' said Doktor Vik, 'and the Amis are supposed to pass a miracle – part the Red Sea of the Soviet Zone – so he can lead his people out of bondage. What a farce.'

I sat there staring at him, with my mouth open. He pulled out his watch again and checked the time. 'Where *is* that bastard?' Now I too was on my feet, yanking at his sleeve. What? Was this true? Some of *unse,* Mennonites, right here in Berlin? 'Yeah, there's a whole mess of 'em here, most of 'em still hiding under the rubble around Viktoria Luise Platz. You should check it out.'

I did not drop everything and head for Victoria Luise Platz. The American or one of the Germans would have covered for me, yet I hesitated. Yes, I yearned to know if any of my family were still alive, and yearned to see them, yet I also felt bitter shame at the prospect of showing my face to them. When you came home I told you what Doktor Vik had said. You smiled and gave me a pat on my shoulder. You said refugees rarely stay put long enough for anyone to keep track of them, so finding someone who might have information about my family would be unlikely, but I should try. I waited two more days, till my day off.

A little to the north of the base, a streetcar line had been cleared and repaired, and I rode east toward Tempelhof for about two kilometres, then I walked north. The streets became more and more clogged with rubble. As the morning mist began to lift, flecks of colour poked through the prevailing gray – pyramids of yellow bricks, patches of red roof tiles, even a few incongruous patches of green. I saw grim lines of people passing pieces of rubble hand to hand and piling them on mounds. Like a chain gang, but they weren't prisoners. Most of them were women, *Trümmerfrauen,* clearing rubble piece by piece, trying to reclaim their city.

Viktoria Luise Platz was still a labyrinth of skeletal structures with narrow paths snaking through the streets, with here and there a charred truck or a twisted piece of artillery. When I asked people if there were refugees from the east camped in the rubble I received at best a dismissive shrug. And when a kindly looking older man did stop to listen his face turned angry. '*Puh! Jawohl. Da, guk mahl.* They're everywhere. See the smoke rising from that pile of rubble? They're under there. And there, and there. More refugees than rats here.' I asked others. They shook their heads and scuttled away. Then I heard a strange sound, familiar all my life, but strange in this setting. Low German. Two boys were poking at a hole in the rubble with a long stick, trying to roust a rat out of its lair.

'*Doah es ha! Doah es ha!*' one of them shouted when he spotted a pair of beady eyes in the rubble, and jabbed more vigorously with his stick.

'*Raed ye Plautdietch?*' I said.

They stopped. This man spoke Low German? They looked at me, then at each other. '*Jo,*' they said.

'*Sent hiea wo Menniste?*' I asked them.

A strange man, looking for Mennonites? They dropped their stick and ran away.

I did not run after them. I waited, and soon they returned – with their mother and an older man. They approached warily. Who was I? Who had sent me?

I told them my name, the name of my village, my parents' names, uncles and aunts. It took only a few moments to verify what I had said. Did I know a Jasch Ewert from Pordenau? Yes. Married one of the Koop girls from Kleefeld, I said. They nodded. I said I was hoping to find news about my family and they pointed down a narrow alley. They said there was a family down there from a village near mine. Maybe they could help.

Yes, they knew my family, my mother, my sister Sarah, my grand-mother Enns, and Katya. Then an old woman and a young girl led me to a pile of rubble that had once been a bank. The facade had crumbled but three of the massive walls still stood and supported the concrete floor of the second storey, sagging under the weight of debris that had fallen on it. The old woman pointed down a narrow passage through the rubble where a wooden door leaned against a small opening. 'They're in there,' she said.

I knocked and heard the muffled voices inside fall silent. I pushed the door aside and peered into the gloom. Then we fell into each other's arms. 'You're still alive!' 'Yes, and you're still alive!' Even Katya embraced me.

As we listened to each other's stories, we held each other's hands and stroked each other's cheeks, and I noticed that my hands were now much softer than theirs. It was over a year since I began working as a dish washer. I was also better dressed. My clothes weren't threadbare and randomly patched, and the soles and uppers of my boots weren't held together with twine. I asked about Groote Graeta, Uncle Knalz, Taunte Liese and Yuri. My mother said they had lost contact, they'd had no news of them, didn't know if they were still alive. 'When the others fled, we had to wait,' said my mother, 'Sarah couldn't leave her job in that *Bürgermeis-ter's* office.'

I looked at Sarah. Couldn't or wouldn't? Had she trifled with their safety because she'd become attached to her fancy office job? There had been no hint of accusation in my mother's voice, but she seemed to know what I was thinking. 'It was dangerous for Sarah to leave,' she said. 'She was doing . . . important work. I couldn't leave without her and lose you both.'

Important work? I let that pass. Then I told them you too were in Berlin, and told how we had found each other. Then my other big news. I said I'd met a doctor from Canada, a friend of yours, who had been sent here to process refugees, and he had told me there were thousands of *unse* still alive in Germany, and the Mennonites had a relief agency working here. The MCC. They had bought two big houses, right here in Berlin. I said I would find out where, and then they could move out of this rats' nest – before the weather turned cold.

I was proud that I could finally be of some use to them, save them from their squalor and fear. I spent the next day gathering provisions to take them, and I was touched by the eagerness of the riff-raff to help me find the necessities. Wolfgang brought me a kerosene lamp, the Egyptian brought three blankets and some bed linen, the girls smuggled a whole ham out of the mess kitchen, oranges from Florida and fresh baked bread, Uschi brought a pair of men's boots, socks and underwear from the PX (women's clothing was hard to find). I stuffed everything into two burlap sacks, and early the next morning you and I left together, Antoine, each of us with a burlap sack slung over our shoulder. We looked like a pair of black market hucksters toting our loot on our backs.

We squeezed through the narrow entrance, me first, you behind me, and we felt arms embracing us before our eyes could adjust to the gloom. My mother wrapped you in her arms and wept, Sarah fell on your neck and wouldn't let go. 'Don't smother the poor man,' said my mother. She held her hand on Sarah's shoulder until she let you go.

My mother wanted to know everything. What happened after Mary Gordon took you to Germany? Was your mother there, waiting for you? You added a few details you hadn't told me. You said Mary Gordon was distraught after your mother died, and despaired of staying in Buenos

Aires by herself, begging for money from your miserly uncle. 'My mother
and I had been her whole life.'

My mother took your hands in her hands. 'Mary Gordon was . . . a
very strong woman,' said my mother. 'When she had to leave you with us
she never thought it would be five years till she saw you again. And now
it's she who needs you?'

'Yes,' you said. I didn't understand, then, of what use you could be to
Mary Gordon while you were in Berlin and she in Scotland, but it wasn't
the right time to ask.

I made three more visits to Viktoria Luise Platz before I moved them
to the house on the Ringstrasse that the Mennonites had turned into a
refugee camp. My eighty-year-old Oma Enns could not walk to the
nearest S-Bahn station but you came through again, Antoine. You
persuaded the big affable MP who had arrested me, had smashed my jaw
and broken my ribs, to take us there. And so it happened that my grandmother and I were driven to the S-Bahn station in an open Jeep, by two
helmeted MPs armed to the teeth with bullet belts and billy clubs. At the
station in Zehlendorf, an MCC car was waiting to take us to Ringstrasse
107.

I remember a sprawling suburban mansion clad in gray stucco, not
very elegant but it was undamaged and big. About 100 refugees were
crammed into it. We were welcomed on behalf of the MCC by Elfrieda
Dyck, Peter's wife, who then handed us over to the capable hands of the
Hausmutter. She explained that there were newborn babies and old
people, sick people and well people, and some refugees were suspicious of
everyone, even the MCC, fearful of repatriation. She told us the name of
her village in Russia. She said all the refugees were expected to help
wherever they could, in the kitchen, or moving beds and tables around,
and she looked at Sarah and me. I explained that I myself would not be
moving in since I had been lucky enough to find a job on an American
army base. She said that was lucky indeed, then she ushered my mother,
my Oma, Sarah, and Katya into a small corner office to be registered. She
explained that feeding and sheltering them was now the responsibility of
the MCC and the Mennonite churches in Canada and America. The
international relief agencies, like UNRRA and the IRO, provided aid to
millions of refugees but not all. She said Mennonites fell through the
cracks. The Nazis had saved us from the vengeance of the Russians

because we were deemed to be ethnic Germans, *Volksdeutsche*, but that was no longer a coveted status. We were ineligible for UNRRA aid – as perpetrators of the war, not its victims. We were eligible only for repatriation to a gulag camp in the Soviet Union.

When the *Hausmutter* had taken down all their particulars – date of birth, name of our village, relatives in Canada or America, if any – there remained one last thing. They were each issued an 'official' MCC document, signed and stamped, stating they were neither Soviet citizens nor German citizens, but Mennonites, whose distant ancestors were Dutch. A nebulous claim that neither the Soviets nor the international relief agencies would recognize, but we didn't argue.

It took only a few days to get news of Uncle Knalz and his family, Groote Graeta, Taunte Liese and her two children. They were all still alive too, at the main MCC refugee camp in Gronau near the Dutch border.

The big house at Ringstrasse 107 was already crammed full of refugees so my family and Katya were put in a smaller house nearby. The rooms were partitioned with blankets but it was luxury compared to anything they had seen since they had fled from Poland. A luxury my Oma Enns enjoyed for only a month. When she could no longer take her meals in the common area, it was Sarah who brought bread and soup to her bedside. Then one morning they found her dead. 'She died with hardly a moan,' said my mother. It seemed as though she had reached her goal when she was in the care of the MCC and no longer needed to struggle. She had struggled most of her life, and maybe it was the struggle that had invigorated her.

Sarah was inconsolable, stunned by the sudden loss of her Oma, who had loved her unconditionally. Back in the fall of '41 when Sarah's 'forward' behaviour with the *Wehrmacht* corporals had set pious tongues wagging, and later when she lay in agony after her back-alley abortion in Poland, it was her Oma who had been her fiercest defender. And it was Sarah who, during the last months of the trek, had anticipated Oma's every need, who had propped her up with pillows and blankets to cushion the jolts of the wagon, who emptied and rinsed her chamber pot after each use, and read to her when her eyes had begun to fail.

I thought I had now done all I could for them, till the MCC could get them out of Berlin and settled somewhere else. It was a week till I went back to share in the grief of my family – only to find more grief. Again I found my mother weeping, surrounded by a cluster of women trying to console her. Sarah had not been seen for three days, they said. What happened? Surely *someone* must know *something,* I demanded. Katya said there were three boys who said they had seen her take a bicycle someone had left leaning against a lamp post. She got on and rode. West. During the month of December I went several times to Ringstrasse 107, hoping for news of my sister. A sad Christmas, and after the new year still no news of her.

The locus of my life had now shifted from the basement of McNair Barracks to Ringstrasse 107. Most of my free time, and most of my thoughts, were now focussed on my mother's needs, and little by little I found myself moving toward the margins of the daily routines and enthusiasms in our basement lair. Everyone was kind, but the more solicitous they were the more I felt I was not one of you anymore.

On a cold January day I was again at Ringstrasse 107. The big house was hot and steamy, made so by the hundreds of bodies crammed into it, including those lodged in the smaller house. 'What's happening?' I asked my mother.

'We're all waiting for Peter Dyck to bring us news,' she said.

He arrived, all smiles, waving his hands. Great news, he said. The Americans had promised to provide a train to take them through the Soviet Zone to Bremerhaven, where a Dutch ship is waiting to take them to Paraguay. When? Soon, very soon. Pack your bags, he said, and be ready to go on short notice. His wife Elfrieda said she had already cancelled the next delivery of coal.

For a few the news was a disappointment – they still hoped that Canada would take them, but Canada had closed its doors to all but immediate family – brothers, sisters or children who'd been left stranded in Russia after the Mennonite exodus in the 1920s. So the choice was Paraguay 'the green hell,' or repatriation to the tundra of deepest Siberia.

When I got back to the base I was bursting to tell you the news, Antoine – that the Berlin refugees would be leaving on a train provided by the Amis, and escorted through the Soviet Zone by a detachment of American soldiers. 'That would be quite a coup,' you said. Did you sense that I *wanted* you to be sceptical? No, I did not want to go to Paraguay, with those Mennonites. I wanted to stay in Berlin, with you and the others, but how could I, again, abandon my mother? You listened while I tried to persuade myself that my mother would be well cared for by the MCC, and she would be together again with Groote Graeta, with Uncle Knalz and Taunte Liese. And Katya would be there, who would be of more help to her in Paraguay than I could be – as she had been throughout the trek.

Then Doktor Vik appeared. 'What a load of crap!' he sneered, 'It'll never happen. That Saskatchewan hayseed is leading them into a trap.' He said the Russians had agents all over Germany, poking through the rubble to find every last Soviet refugee. 'And now, glory be, somebody serves up a whole train load of 'em. Pre-packaged, ready for export. Use your head, for god's sake,' he said. 'You think they'll just . . . let 'em go? *Bitte schön? Bon voyage?* Bullshit. The Russians will stop 'em soon as they get into the Soviet Zone – load 'em into one of their own trains an' clickety-clack, off we go to Siberia, thank you very much.' He said it was a trap, and the Amis were playing along. The Russians get their nationals back, 'these traitors and collaborators,' and the Amis get rid of a pack of pain-in-the-ass refugees. 'Without getting any shit on their face,' he said. 'Oh yes, boo-hoo, a great tragedy, they'll tell the press back in America. They'd done all they could to keep these poor people out of Stalin's clutches, but they were determined to make a break for it. My god, it's just classic.'

The next day I hurried back to Ringstrasse 107. The house was hotter, stuffier, more crowded than before, the windows covered in steam emoting from sweaty bodies and hot breath. They were clustered in groups around some grave spokesman on whose opinion they could hang their own hopes and fears, while children ducked and darted among the legs of the adults, indifferent to the worries weighing upon them. My mother and I, and Katya, had found a nook where we could have a little privacy, and these urchins kept tumbling into us. Their mothers would shoo them away but not before they themselves had satisfied their curiosity about me. As a dishwasher on an army base, might I have seen or heard something Peter Dyck didn't know? Then Katya, good old scowling Katya, placed herself squarely in front of us to fend them off, rudely if necessary. She had her back to us but could hear every word I said.

'That Canadian doctor, Antonii's friend, he thinks it's a trap,' I said. 'He says the Russians will never let us out, and the Amis know it. He says they'll be happy to be rid of us. He thinks Peter Dyck is being duped, mama. This doctor has no great love for Mennonites, because they treated his family badly, in Canada, but he's no fool. He knows people, important people, who tell him things other people don't know.'

I waited for a reaction, but my mother did not seem as attentive as I thought she should be. 'Antonii says he doesn't believe the Amis would knowingly betray us,' I said. 'He knows this Colonel Simpson – that Peter Dyck is always talking about. He says Simpson is a good man, but nobody can trust the Russians. Whatever they promise today they'll do the opposite tomorrow. He says there might be another way. He says this Canadian doctor might help us get out of Berlin. Later. In the spring. He's helped other people escape.'

'What else has Antonii told you?' she said. 'Do you know what's tormenting him?'

Hadn't she been listening to me? 'Something is always troubling him. That's just Antonii,' I said. 'He's always been like that, even when we were schoolboys in the Ukraine.'

'He's different now,' she said. 'I am very sorry you will have to choose between us – staying here with him or coming with us, to Paraguay.'

That stung. 'I'll never abandon you,' I said, 'especially now that you have only me.' I caught Katya looking down her nose at me. 'Me and Katya,' I said.

'Antonii is like . . . a brother to you,' she said.

She seemed about to say more, then Peter and Elfrieda Dyck arrived, and the moment was lost. Before they had a chance to take off their coats it was obvious they had bad news. 'Operation Mennonite is off,' said Peter. 'The ship will have to leave Bremerhaven without you.' The Americans had decided that escorting a trainload of Soviet 'nationals' through the Soviet Zone was not worth the risk of an 'incident.' Elfrieda said she would make a phone call to reinstate the order for more coal.

Those people had just been told their doom, Antoine, and what did I feel? Relief?

I did not go back the next day, or the next. I did not want to face the gloom in that house on the Ringstrasse. I began gathering a parcel of treats to take to my mother and her friends, to assuage their disappointment. Then there he was again. Doktor Vik. Early in the morning, triumphant. I was barely dressed and you were still in bed. You quickly got up as soon as you heard him.

He flung his briefcase onto the table, took off his scarf and his hat, and began unbuttoning his coat. He hitched up his trousers and gave you a knowing wink. 'The ship's gone,' he said, 'sailed from Bremerhaven yesterday. Probably in international waters by now. With a few last-minute stragglers aboard (wink, wink).' Then he turned to me. 'And would you believe it,' he said, 'the Russians let the Berlin group through. That cheeky Saskatchewan hayseed did it. They're all gone, the whole lot. My man in Bremerhaven tells me they held the ship till two in the morning, till the train from Berlin arrived.'

He paused to allow himself a wry chuckle at the absurdity of it all. 'That pipsqueak,' he said, 'that cheeky little Peter Dyck. Just marched into Clay's office and told his secretary he wouldn't leave until he'd had a word with the big man himself. General Lucius D. Clay, yes sir, Commander in Chief of U.S. Forces in Europe.' Doktor Vik let that sink in. 'NOBODY,' he said, 'gets into Lucius D. Clay's office. But that pipsqueak did. An' next thing you know there's a big meeting. Highest level. Up there in the Blue Room. Clay and Sokolovsky, head to head. And all their little minions, including our Colonel Simpson. Blah blah blah, then all of a sudden, *Khorosho!* Sokolovsky signs the transit permit – with a flourish. An' passes it to Clay.' Doktor Vik gave you another sly wink. 'But our Antoine already knows that,' he said. 'Somebody must've whispered something in somebody's ear.'

I rushed to Ringstrasse 107, pounded on the door, shouted my name, shouted my mother's name, and finally someone opened the door – the old woman who lived in the attic, now the housekeeper but once the Lady of the house. Yes, yes, it was true, she said, 'They're all gone. Except for two families who refused to go.' She explained they were willing to risk repatriation while they waited for news that their relatives in Canada could get them out.

I felt relief. Relief that my mother was safely out of Germany, and relief that I was still in Berlin where I wanted to be. And I felt shame because I felt relief.

In the weeks and months that followed I went back to the house every few days to get a report. Yes, they had arrived in Buenos Aires. No, they hadn't left yet for Paraguay – they were living in tents in Argentina, waiting for a civil war in Paraguay to end. Three more months, then yes, the civil war was over – just a few thugs shooting at other thugs. Now they were on their way, up the Paraguay River to the Chaco. I kept asking about a letter from my mother, but none came.

There was still an MCC representative at Ringstrasse 107, and that was how I heard there would be another ship, the *Heintzelman*, scheduled to leave for Buenos Aires in a few months. He assumed the news would give me hope, that if I could get through the Soviet Zone to Bremerhaven I would yet be able to join my mother and the others in Paraguay.

When I told you about the *Heintzelman* you said it might be possible for me to get through the Soviet Zone, 'but of course, it's risky.' You said you'd ask Doktor Vik about it.

He didn't appear again in our basement lair until weeks later, and when he did appear he was dripping with solicitude. 'Bloody rotten luck that you weren't there, with the others, when the Amis arrived to take them out,' he said. He shook his head sadly and put his arm around my shoulder. Then you told him that I'd heard a second ship was scheduled to leave Bremerhaven in a few months. His face lit up. 'Is that so?' he said.

Yes, I nodded.

He took a few moments to stroke his chin and stare at the floor. 'Actually,' he said, 'I think I can get you out of Berlin, if that's what you want.' He said he was putting together a plan to get two scruffy characters through the Russian Zone to the Baltic coast. 'You could join them. Just don't ask them too many questions,' he said. 'Might make em nervous.' He explained we'd have to wait till the summer. We would be disguised as itinerant farm labourers, and passed from one 'safe' farmer to another. Quite a complicated little network, but he had used it before. 'Don't worry about the money,' he said. Once I reached Hamburg all I'd need was a carton of Lucky Strikes to get to the Mennonite refugee camp in Gronau.

This scene has haunted me for decades, Antoine. It seemed . . . staged.

'Should I go?' I asked you.

You leaned back in your chair and rubbed your face with your hands. You took a deep breath. 'You should go,' you said.

· · ·

How quickly the memory of physical pain dissolves, Antoine. A month, two months later, it takes an effort to imagine the excruciating sensation. Last summer I went to a *Paraguaya* reunion in Winnipeg. A picnic in a shady park on a hot summer day, where we could gather and get caught up on the news. Who died, who married whom, who had moved to BC. I had not seen Peepche Panah for two or three years, and it turned out we had both recently survived an attack of kidney stones, and had both passed the stones before they had to be surgically removed. We agreed it was the worst pain we could imagine. I told how I, already at the hospital, already in my blue surgical gown and paper slippers, had decided I would give it one last shot and shuffled off to the washroom. The pain was so acute I thought I would faint. Then, *eureka*, I passed it. I looked down and there it was, floating in the toilet bowl, a bristly yellowish brown thing. I snatched it out and went shuffling to the nurses' station as fast as you can go on paper slippers. 'Cancel the operation,' I shouted, 'I passed it.' Peepche's passage had happened while he was still at home. We competed with each other in our descriptions of the pain. I said it was like a chunk of molten metal in my urinary tract, but Peepche trumped me. 'It was like somebody pulling a red-hot barbed wire through my pecker,' he said. And then we all laughed.

But emotional pain remains fresh. Half a century later it's still as raw as an open wound. 'No, don't go. Stay here, with us. Your mother is in good hands, with those Mennonites.' Is that what I expected you to say, when I asked if I should go?

You said, 'You should go back to your own people.' As though you'd told me to go back to my village, where I belonged.

So I went, five months later. There was a festive send off for me the night before I left, Gioconda had baked a cake and you 'borrowed' some wine and cognac from the cellar of the officers' mess. In the morning there were tearful embraces and then I joined Doktor Vik's two scruffy characters and escaped to the British Zone.

June 4, 1992

I won't bore you, Antoine, with the details of my escape through the Soviet Zone. Doktor Vik's 'agents' did what he had paid them to do. We three escapees didn't talk about ourselves, didn't say much at all to each other. One of them had the manner of a military man. I have no idea why he might have been wanted by the Allies. The other had the manner of a more sleazy underground operative. He was more talkative, quick to vent his grievances against both the Allies and the Berlin city officials. We were conducted, by one after another of Doktor Vik's agents, to a prearranged place and told to wait there until we were contacted by the next agent. Then he disappeared. Sometimes we waited two or three hours, which made us nervous. It seemed to us this was an indication that not all the details of our escape were in place. Now I understand the point of it – to make sure that no agent set eyes on any other agent, or knew his name, so if one of them got caught he couldn't betray the whole network, even under torture. I was glad to leave my companions as soon as we got to Hanover, and strike out on my own to the refugee centre in Gronau – on foot, by train, or hitching a ride on the highway. I need only hold a package of American cigarettes in my outstretched hand to induce a truck driver to stop and give me a lift.

I arrived in plenty of time to join 800 more Mennonite refugees on the *Heintzelman*. For sixteen cheerless days I kept to myself on the voyage across the ocean, and across the equator, rarely talking to anyone if I could help it. I spent hours at the rail of the ship, staring down at the water, dreading my exile.

Have I already described my arrival, and my reception in Paraguay? I'll tell you again. As the ship entered the port of Buenos Aires, the imposing skyline of the city rose above wafting palm trees and flowering jacarandas. So this was the city that had once excited you, Antoine, and I tried to identify some of the landmarks you had told me about. I would gladly have explored the city but we were held on the ship for two days after it docked while customs officials inspected and stamped our documents, then herded into a fenced compound, guarded by local militia in case some of us got a notion to escape into the barrios of the city.

Asunción had none of the charm of Buenos Aires. Squat, splotchy baroque facades, a few tattered palms and scraggly jacarandas, no longer in bloom if they ever had been. We were met by friendly, efficient MCC representatives, including four Canadian nurses to tend to the ailing and elderly. Most of our people were gladdened by their reception. I remained indifferent, even contemptuous of this cheery welcome. Then we were loaded onto smaller, rustier steamers to take us further north, upriver, to the barren tracts of land the American Mennonites had purchased from the Paraguayan government. Some people disembarked en route at the struggling Mennonite colonies that had already been established in the 1920s and 30s, the rest of us continued north. At a bend in the river a wharf appeared and we were loaded into waiting farm wagons, for the last leg of our journey. As we jolted along a rutted trail through tangled brush, I became more agitated. I might have burst into tears. A kindly old woman bouncing along next to me assumed my agitation was pure joy. 'Yes, yes,' she said, 'soon we will see our loved ones again.'

Then we were ambushed, by little children, maybe eight to twelve years old. A sudden burst of life. Girls in wide-brimmed straw hats with red ribbons around them, the boys in less flamboyant hats, turned up at the back. They had been waiting for us in the sparse shade of the under-brush and now charged toward us, waving their arms and shouting, in Low German, 'Welcome to Neuland! Welcome to Neuland!' They trotted alongside our wagons, laughing and waving, sometimes getting danger-ously close to the big wagon wheels. One of the little girls couldn't keep up, so I jumped off the back of the wagon, took her in my arms, hoisted her over the tailgate and scrambled up after her. She climbed up beside the driver and waved to her friends below, flaunting her privileged posi-tion. They lifted my spirits, these children, but not for long.

The whole village was there to welcome us, the new arrivals, gathered in front of their squat adobe church. Uncle Knalz and his wife, Groote Graeta, Taunte Liese, they all embraced me when I stepped down from the wagon. Then they stepped back and scanned the faces of the other arrivals. 'Where is your mother?' they demanded.

I could make no sense of that question. 'She's here. With you,' I cried. 'Why didn't she come? Is she not well?'

'Don't talk funny!' said Groote Graeta 'You tell us where she is.' She grabbed my shoulders and shook me. 'Your mother stayed with you, in Berlin. What's happened to her?'

'No, no,' I protested, 'she must be here!' But my howls of protest were met by stone-faced suspicion that I had abandoned my mother. How, now, from this primitive outpost on the opposite side of the globe could I begin to search for her? Or any news of her? I spent sleepless nights with my fists buried in the sockets of my eyes, silently screaming at myself for the horrible mistake I had made when I left Berlin. My grief at not finding my mother would have been painful enough without the added pain of their tacit accusations that I had abandoned her to a cruel fate. For months after I arrived I kept apart from the others, sulking in my little mud hut at the edge of the village. But I had to eat, so little by little I began to lend a hand to Groote Graeta and Taunte Liese, clearing scrub, planting, or repairing a leaky roof – in return for the hot meals they brought me.

The colony struggled, and the disappointments were heartbreaking. Locusts. Drought. No one knew if it was possible to make the Chaco yield even a minimal living. Then came two days of rain. Children frolicked in the downpour, old men and women gathered in the street with their arms outstretched, laughing, their faces turned up toward the sky to let the raindrops pelt their cheeks and foreheads, mouths open, tongues stuck out to catch a few drops and let them trickle down their gullets. Even old *Omas* doffed their black kerchiefs and turned wobbly pirouettes to make sure they got wet on all sides.

But the blessed rain came at a cost. Now the invigorated weeds threatened to overwhelm our fledgling crop of peanut plants. Everyone into the fields then as soon as the ground had dried out a little, and I was shamed into joining them. We all hoed together in one field, then moved to the next until everyone's field was done. Men, women, old and young, sometimes they kept up a lively babble while they hoed, sometimes they sang, and sometimes they fell silent, each one wrapped in his or her own reveries. Even Uncle Knalz might fall silent for an hour or more. That is a boon of brainless, repetitive work, denied to those who work in office cubicles, noisy assembly lines or classrooms.

But for me, hoeing did not free my mind. It tyrannized it. Most of the weeds were tough and deeply rooted, the ground became brick hard, or so it seemed to me. After months of listless sulking my muscles had grown flabby and my hands were as tender as a baby's. Within an hour my palms were blistered, another hour and the blisters broke, the skin peeled back, and blood oozed through raw flesh. My back, legs and arms ached, and salty sweat stung my eyes.

Humiliation was added to my pain. Everybody in the field proceeded down his or her row at about the same pace, even the young teenaged girls, while I lagged behind. They kept up an amiable babble like the honking of migrating geese, and when they reached the end of their rows, they stopped for a drink and a brief rest, then leapfrogged to the next set of rows while I still struggled on my half finished row. As they approached I could hear the girls giggling, and I knew they were vying with each other to see which of them could come up with the most cruelly comic description of my misery.

Sweat blurred my vision, and as often as not it was a young pea plant instead of a weed that fell victim to my hoe. I shortened my grip and bent lower, the better to see, and the better to attack these insolent weeds with vengeful strokes. 'Not like that,' said Uncle Knalz. He had dropped back to help me. 'It's just a stupid weed,' he said. 'You have to stand straight, head back, and look down your nose at the weed. You have to despise it. Just flick the blade of your hoe under it and slice it off. Like this. See? Don't chop. It's a hoe, not a pickaxe.'

He took a roll of gauze out of his pocket and wrapped my hands in it, tucking the end in neatly so it wouldn't unravel, then he and I hoed side by side at our own pace. We hoed in silence for a few minutes, then Uncle Knalz said, 'You've been asking about Yuri.'

I *had* been asking about Yuri, but no one was eager to talk about him. I knew only that he had tried to escape into France to avoid being turned over to the Russians and shot as a traitor. But he didn't make it.

I didn't respond to Uncle Knalz immediately. They had accused me of abandoning my mother, and I was still angry enough to accuse them of abandoning Yuri. 'He risked his life for you, scrounged and stole for you, and probably killed for you,' I said. 'Then you threw him to the Russians like raw meat through the bars of a bear cage – when he had served your purpose.'

Uncle Knalz hoed in silence for a few minutes. 'We did try to save him,' he said, 'He was with us from Dunstdorf to Gronau.' He said they had spent the whole summer working on that *Gräfin's* estate in the Warthegau, he and his family, Yuri and Taunte Liese with her two children, also two other families. When things began to unravel, he and Yuri would ride through the countryside to get a sense of what was happening, and in those towns where there were still Polish people, they noticed they had become busy. Busy buying and repairing wagons, trading horses. And instead of cursing and scowling at them, they began to smirk. 'The Poles knew better than the Germans how close the Russians were, or before the Germans would admit it to themselves,' he said. 'They knew we *Volks-deutsche* would soon be fleeing for our lives. Then they'd be ready, with their new wagons. To get what they could before the Russians got it. Or burned it.'

So Uncle Knalz and Yuri had got their own wagons ready. At first the *Gräfin* went into a rage, accused Yuri and Uncle Knalz of defeatism and threatened to report them to the district *Gauleiter*, but she relented when only a few days later the first refugees begin to trickle in from East Prussia. Then flood in.

They had crossed so many rivers, he said. They had hoped they'd be safe when they crossed the Oder. Now it was the Elbe. Yet every day the front came nearer. 'By day a dark cloud behind us, by night a pillar of fire, driving us out, not leading us on.' But of course Yuri would be safe nowhere under Allied Occupation, whether British, American or Russian. *Unse* tried to stay together, he said, but it was too chaotic. My grandmother, my mother and my sister were with another group, and he never saw them again.

At Gronau they were welcomed with open arms, 'safe at last,' said Uncle Knalz. 'Here we were among people who were glad we had survived.' The MCC had bought a textile mill and turned it into a refugee camp, six big buildings, a big kitchen, a hospital with 56 beds, staffed by Canadian nurses, a distribution centre for food and clothing, and next to it were the offices where all the paperwork for immigration was done. 'But they weren't so glad to welcome a Cossack *Hiwi* like Yuri.'

Of course there had to be screenings, to make sure these refugees were 'fit' for immigration, both medically and politically. 'Word had got out,' said Uncle Knalz, 'There are people called Mennonites who are getting help to emigrate to Canada. And suddenly scoundrels came out of the woodwork who claimed to be Mennonites. Many were rejected, but as you know, some got through who shouldn't have.'

'But not Yuri. Yuri didn't have a Mennonite name,' I said.

'No, he didn't.'

He said when Canada shut its doors to all but close relatives, Paraguay became the only option. 'Paraguay asked no questions,' he said, 'lame, blind, old, young, it didn't matter. *Volksdeutscher, Reichsdeutscher, SS, Gestapo,* it didn't matter.' But the MCC still had questions. Thousands of hard earned dollars had trickled into collection plates across North America to charter a ship, the *Volendam* – to save their Mennonite brethren from the terror of 'repatriation' to the Soviet Union.

'But not Cossack *Hiwis,*' I said.

'No, not Cossack *Hiwis.*'

Uncle Knalz said he found an MCC representative who seemed to be willing to overlook a few technicalities. He asked to speak to him in private and was invited into his office. He closed the door and asked him to take a seat. Then Uncle Knalz told him there was one of his group who had not yet been registered.

'Why not?'

'Because he's not a Mennonite.'

'What is he? Catholic? Lutheran?'

'He's a Cossack. From the Kuban.'

The man blinked, and stared at Uncle Knalz. 'He was a *Hiwi* on the trek,' he tried to explain, 'but he wasn't like the other *Hiwis.'*

'Is there a woman involved?'

'Yes. She has two small children.'

'Ei-yei-yei,' said the man, and ran his hand through his hair. 'She's a widow?'

'That's a difficult question,' said Uncle Knalz.

The man said the MCC had come across such 'difficult questions' before, and the question was difficult enough when it was a Mennonite man and a Mennonite woman, with a 'blended family.' He said the following Sunday there would be a multiple wedding. Eight couples who had been living together. But they could not be married if they had a spouse who might still be alive in Russia. He waited for Uncle Knalz to reply. Then he said, 'I suppose this Cossack behaved admirably on the trek. Except for that . . . that affair with this woman.'

'He behaved admirably even then,' Uncle Knalz blurted out.

'Some of our people might not understand how you can live admirably in sin,' said the man. He said the churches in Canada and America had sent *Praedyas* to Germany, to minister to the spiritual needs of the refugees – for which most of them were deeply grateful. He said most of these *Praedyas* did understand that our people had lived in Soviet terror for two decades. Sheep without a shepherd. Then two years of Nazi occupation, then the trek and the *Zusammenbruch*. Not surprising that some had faltered in their faith.

'It's a miracle,' said Uncle Knalz, 'that so many held to their faith, and could still hear the voice of their conscience.'

'Agreed,' said the man. Agreed but. It takes only a few who doubt the miracle, he said, and one such had published a letter in the Mennonite papers in Canada and America. He wrote that some refugees were living like beasts, men and women living together in sin, their squalid offspring untended, untutored, young men and women as ignorant of Christian teaching as the most primitive African savage. Then the collection plates in Canada and America dried up, he said. So Peter and Elfrieda Dyck went back and preached in more than fifty churches across North America, in just a few months. Then the collection plates begin to fill up again.

'And you listened in silence to this sanctimonious drivel,' I said.

Uncle Knalz said he'd had lots of practice. For twenty years he had to listen in silence to sanctimonious communist drivel, knowing people's lives were at stake.

'Have the woman and her two children been registered?' asked the MCC man.

'Yes, they're here, in the camp, but she won't leave the man she loves.'

The man said he did not want to know this Cossack's name, or where he was now in hiding. 'It could get awkward,' he said. 'We're supposed to report Soviet traitors like your *Hiwi* to the British. Who'll turn him over to the Russians.'

'To be shot,' Uncle Knalz had said.

The MCC man rubbed his face with his hands and took a deep breath. 'There are a few nuns, down in the village east of here. They run a small hospital. I've heard rumours they're hiding some people in what's left of their convent. Maybe you should go to that hospital and ask a few discreet questions. Meanwhile, I'll talk to some of the elders.'

Uncle Knalz said the 'convent' was perched on a hill, enclosed by a high stone wall with a pair of heavy double doors. It had once been a pretty place, two rows of linden trees along the path leading up the hill, but they had been clumsily cut up for firewood, the branches lopped off leaving only the trunks standing. When Uncle Knalz first saw them it was the morning after a big snowfall and the tall stumps were each capped with a dome of snow, like giant mushrooms. There were only eight nuns left now, he said, and they were hiding a Russian POW and two Ukrainian *Ostarbeiter* in their stable. He had pleaded with the nuns to hide Yuri as well, just for a week or two. The nuns knew it would be longer than that, but they consented, and yes, they would let Yuri hide his Andalusian stallion in the stable as well.

Yuri had agreed to move to the convent, Liese fought against it. They and the two children were living in a shabby *Gasthaus*, crammed into a small room. Constant traffic in and around the *Gasthaus*, including local police and British police. It was not safe, but she refused to be separated from Yuri. She said she'd seen notices posted in the town, promising amnesty and free passage to Australia for all Cossacks who had been captured by the Germans, and were afraid to return 'home.' So to hell with these nuns and these Mennonites, she cried. She and Yuri would turn themselves in to the British. Uncle Knalz said he and Yuri had to argue long and hard to disabuse her of the idea. It had become well known that the English had used the same ruse in Austria. They had lured two thousand Cossacks to Lienz and Judenburg, then betrayed them to the Russians.

After a few days the MCC man called Uncle Knalz back into his office. He said he had arranged for Uncle Knalz to plead Yuri's case in front of a tribunal of *Praedyas*, one from Canada and two from America. He had tried to sound encouraging. But there was another *Praedya* from Canada, who got wind of the plan and asked to be present 'as a silent observer.' Uncle Knalz had already run into him. He was hard to avoid. A very pious fellow, and very busy, and Uncle Knalz said he couldn't get the image of a weasel out of his mind. Ingratiating, lots of hand wringing, especially when the sensitivities of the faithful back in Canada might be at issue. Apparently an educated man, always dressed in a neat dark suit.

The meeting began with a prayer that God would grant the tribunal the wisdom and compassion to deal justly with their erring sister and her Cossack companion, to which the weasel pronounced 'Amen' more loudly than the others. Then Uncle Knalz provided a sheaf of statements from various 'witnesses,' testifying how time and again Yuri had saved their lives. And he told the tribunal that both Yuri and Liese had promised not to have any relationship with each other as long as it remained a possibility that Taunte Liese's husband might still be alive.

That had drawn another cry of protest from Taunte Liese. 'Hypocrites! All of you!' Uncle Knalz and Groote Graeta sat her down and argued that it must be so, that she must promise, or Yuri would never get on the ship that was waiting for them in Bremerhaven. 'But when we get to Paraguay we can live in sin again?' she said, and for a moment, Uncle Knalz thought Groote Graeta would slap the sneer off her face, but she restrained herself. She told Liese once they got to Paraguay they must be guided by their conscience.

Uncle Knalz stopped hoeing. He took off his hat and wiped the sweat from his brow. He said he had told Taunte Liese that everyday some woman or other was getting news of her husband in Russia, and sooner or later, she too would get news. 'Stupid, how stupid!' he said. As soon as the words were out of his mouth he had felt a stab in his gut. He had meant to hold out hope, but the hope he held out was that her husband in Russia was dead. He said Liese had let out a terrible cry, then she broke down. 'All I want is to keep the man I love, and they keep taking him away.' She was beaten now. After that she glumly did whatever they told her, though you couldn't be sure what she was thinking.

Uncle Knalz thought the reports of the 'witnesses' might have won over the tribunal, but then the weasel could no longer hold his tongue. 'If I may be allowed? Just a word?'

A word! It was a harangue, said Uncle Knalz. Had they no idea, demanded the weasel, how this would play out among the *Gemeinde* back in Canada and America – when they found out, as they surely would, that the hard earned money they had sent to MCC had gone to save a Cossack savage? Who was rumoured to have run wild in their villages with Makhno? Yes, of course, we are moved to pity by Brother Reimer's story, he said, and maybe this Yuri does sincerely love that woman. Maybe, in this case, it is not just a shameless ploy to save his own skin. But what do we tell the brethren back home when this Yuri, as soon as he's safe in Buenos Aires, jumps ship without so much as a *do svedahnya* to his dear Liese? The MCC's whole relief effort could be jeopardised. 'So let me put a question to you, Brother Reimer,' he said. 'Tell me please, are you prepared to see thousands of your brethren sent to Siberia for the sake of one Cossack?'

'Yes, I am,' said Uncle Knalz. 'If there must be a choice between hope for many and justice for one, then justice must prevail.' Uncle Knalz said he didn't know if it were always true, but he knew that to say anything else would be sinful treachery.

'Well, fortunately, Herr Reimer, you have been spared the choice,' said the weasel, 'The choice has been made for you.' The mandate of the MCC is perfectly clear, he explained. It's to save Mennonites, not thieving Cossack renegades.

And that was when Uncle Knalz had dropped his little bombshell. 'Yuri has asked to be baptised,' he said.

Silence. Then the weasel. 'Puh!' he snorted. 'With what? A bottle of vodka poured over his head?' Then he did regain his theological composure. 'If it is not an impertinent question,' he said, 'who has catechized this Yuri in the articles of Mennonite faith and tradition?'

'I have,' Uncle Knalz had said. 'And *Ältester* Ewert. Also Ohm Isaac who died on the trek. There could be none better.'

Was this true, I asked.

True enough, said Uncle Knalz. Quite often toward the end of the trek, Yuri had ridden up alongside his wagon, thrown the reins over the head of his horse and climbed up on the seat beside him – and began plying him with questions. So Mennonites had no priests? No saints? No icons? Why not? Uncle Knalz said he had done his best to explain, and when he was stumped he had consulted *Ältester* Ewert or Ohm Isaac. And one day, out of the blue, Yuri had asked, 'If I were baptised, would I be a Mennonite?' Uncle Knalz said at the time he didn't know how seriously to take the question. 'Yes, you would,' he had told Yuri, 'if you truly believed and freely chose to live your faith among us.' Uncle Knalz said he had no doubt that by the end of the trek Yuri knew as much about Mennonite beliefs and traditions as most baptismal candidates. And if he had ever come across a baptismal candidate who was moved purely by the promptings of the spirit, his memory failed him.

All very interesting, said the weasel. A Biblical seminary on wheels. But he should like to hear it from Yuri himself. Where is he now, he said, that we might hear a confession of faith out of his own mouth?

'He is in hiding,' said Uncle Knalz.

'Pfffff!' said the weasel. 'Confession by proxy is it? That's not how our ancestors proclaimed their faith, before they were burned at the stake.'

'When I tell it now, it sounds like a stupid farce,' said Uncle Knalz, 'Back then it was deadly serious.' Should he risk smuggling Yuri into the camp to face the tribunal? On the trek, Yuri's questions about Mennonites had been sharp and probing, and his answers to Uncle Knalz's questions had been frank and confident. But in this setting he would sense the suspicion of the tribunal. No telling how he would react. Nevertheless, they had to try, and so they disguised Yuri in women's clothes and brought him to the camp.

Yuri had picked up enough German to answer some of the tribunal's questions directly but he preferred to answer in Russian and let Uncle Knalz translate. He sat stiffly and stone-faced on a chair that had been placed for him at the foot of a long table, Uncle Knalz beside him, the tribunal at the head of the table, the weasel at their side. The room had formerly been used for medical examinations, said Uncle Knalz, and smelled of disinfectant. The walls were bare except for an eye chart.

The *praedya* from America began. Was it true that Yuri had been living in sin with Liese Redekop?

Da, said Yuri, and Uncle Knalz translated. It was as Uncle Knalz had feared. Yuri's answers were curt monosyllables.

Had he and Liese repented of their sin, asked a *praedya.*

Da, said Yuri, and Uncle Knalz translated.

And was it true that he now wished to be baptised, as a Christian and a brother in the Mennonite church?

Da, said Yuri.

Another question from each of the other two, on certain tenets of Christian faith, and then the weasel. Was it not true, he demanded, that all his life Yuri had been a soldier? First with the Makhnovtze, then the Red Army, then the Vlasovites, then the *Wehrmacht?*

Da, said Yuri, and Uncle Knalz translated.

So it wasn't for his country that he had fought and killed, or for his political convictions, or for freedom or anything of that sort. Just a hired killer for any army that would pay him? And on the trek had he not thieved and terrorized the Polish population at gunpoint?

Da, said Yuri. They waited for him to say more. Uncle Knalz tried to prompt him. 'How could he fight for his country when it was enslaved by the communists?' he said, and waited for Yuri to respond. 'And on the trek, he had often defied the Nazis. And what he stole we Mennonites consumed with gratitude. Was this not true?' prompted Uncle Knalz.

Da, said Yuri, and Uncle Knalz translated, both his promptings and Yuri's assent.

'But you have seen the evil of that life, as a bandit and a rogue soldier,' Uncle Knalz continued, 'And you have sincerely prayed that God in his mercy might forgive you.'

Da, said Yuri.

'So now you're a pacifist, like us?' smirked the weasel. 'So let's say you come home from the fields in the evening and you hear screaming. You rush through the door and find a soldier has torn the clothes off your dear Liese and proceeded to rape her. What do you do?'

Yuri rose from his chair. He glared down at the weasel and spoke in a clipped, level voice. 'I take knife and cut off rapist cock. I stick cock in rapist mouth, and jam cock down rapist throat. With heel of boot,' he said. Uncle Knalz didn't have to translate.

Uncle Knalz said all his life Yuri had lived by his instincts, and his instincts had seemed infallible. He might have died a dozen times but each time a quick grasp of his predicament had saved his life, and often the lives of others. But when he tried to become a Mennonite he began to second-guess his instincts. He was like a boy who has lost the use of his right arm and must learn to throw a ball with his left. As a Cossack he had known exactly what to do when men pointed guns at him. Now he seemed defenceless when they pointed Bibles.

The ship that would take the refugees to Paraguay was waiting, as they celebrated their last Christmas in Germany – with a mixture of dread, hope, and gratitude. But Uncle Knalz said his heart had not been full of goodwill toward men. He avoided people, could hardly bear their presence, avoided Taunte Liese, Groote Graeta, his own family, and he would have avoided himself if he could. For two decades under the Bolsheviks he had ducked and dodged and managed to keep himself and his family alive, and maybe a few others. Then the Germans came, and more ducking and dodging. Yet through all that ducking and dodging he still knew who he was. Now he no longer seemed to know. In the dining hall where people lingered in the evening to talk, to console or encourage each other, the lights had been dimmed and the MCC staff had placed a candle on each table, in a nest of spruce boughs. The candles were supposed to cast a warm glow, but to him, he said, they cast only grotesque shadows. They contorted people's faces into ugly masks. He had known some of these people all his life, and now they seemed alien to him. Whether they laughed, prayed or quietly conversed, their faces looked twisted and deformed. Back then, when he wanted to know who he was, he need only look into the faces of those around him to see his reflection there. Now the reflection was abhorrent to him.

He said he tried to remember these people as he once knew them, tried to salvage scraps of their past and connect them to the present. He tried to remind himself that we are all God's children, whatever our failings, but the words rang hollow.

It was their singing, he said, that had slowly begun to draw him out of his dark corner. They stood clustered around tables, shoulder to shoulder, and sang the familiar carols. More facial contortions, mouths wide open – but different now. People are better than themselves when they sing together, he said, something rises within them that is stronger and older than they are. No, it doesn't last long, but for a few minutes it's there. He knew the songs and felt the words constrict his chest, he said, then a few words escaped through his own throat.

His mind reached back to past Christmases, he said, when there was still a Tsar in Russia and he a child on his father's *Wirtschaft*. He remembered how the early dark began to settle on the shortest day of the year, the eve of the celebrated birth, and he remembered how he and his siblings would be shooed from the gloom in their house into the deeper gloom outside and told to play. But they were in no mood to play. They loitered in the yard in front of the house and waited as the winter darkness drew close around them. They pulled their mufflers more tightly around their throats, they kept their cold little fists clenched in their pockets and scraped meaningless hieroglyphics in the snow with the toes of their boots.

Then the door opened and they were called to. They bolted for the door, blocked while they fumbled to remove their boots, then ducked past the legs of their parents into the big room, the *Groote Stov*. Always exactly as they had expected, always the same, yet always more wonderful than they remembered. The *Groote Stov* transformed, fragrant, garlanded and boughed, and in the centre the tree with its tip tickling the ceiling, illuminated by twenty candles attached to the boughs like precocious winter fruit. Had there been two hundred candles they could not have glowed more brightly. And on the table sat a platter, one for every child, heaped high with exotic fruit from the fabled South, grapes, oranges, figs and pomegranates, fruit that no one had ever seen on any tree but somewhere there must be such trees. You hold the grape between your teeth, close your lips over it, slowly bite down on the tart membrane and the sweet, juicy warmth of the South explodes in your mouth. Just like it had always done but who can remember what a grape tasted like a year ago.

Uncle Knalz said there was no doubt in his mind, then, that the fruit had come from that same southern land of the miraculous birth, that the very same fruit had hung in bowers over the infant's crib on that momentous morning near the beginning of time, no doubt that the holy mother, smiling, would have plucked a grape from the vine and popped it into the infant's mouth, and no doubt at all that he had clamped his toothless gums on the tart membrane and felt that same wine-red sweetness explode in his mouth. It was like a first communion, said Uncle Knalz, and no communion after was ever so palpable.

These people were now going to Paraguay, another southern land, and perhaps the cold of the German winter had made it more alluring, though they knew the Chaco was a dry, prickly, cactus land, not a land of juicy fruitfulness. They were trying to be hopeful, and Uncle Knalz said he knew he must not hate them for it. He reminded himself that he had encountered senseless cruelty many times before, and sometimes his faith had been sorely tested. And now the cruelty of a pompous ass with a Mennonite name should defeat his faith? He heard the muffled voices of those on the far side of the room, saw their faces crimped into cautious merriment, enfolded in the familiar glow or brotherhood.

'But Yuri was cut out of the glow,' I said.

Uncle Knalz began hoeing again. He said neither he nor Taunte Liese could risk going to the convent to see Yuri, but they had a go-between, one of the nuns, a Sister Aganetta. Taunte Liese would go down to the hospital where the nuns worked and give Sister Aganetta a letter for Yuri, and receive one from him. Neither would this nun risk coming to the camp, but early one morning she was there. She asked a young lad loitering near the gate if he knew Herr Reimer. He said he did and she said go get him.

'Yuri is gone,' she told him. She said he had been acting strangely of late. Something woke her in the night, and she had gone to her window and saw a faint glow in the small window of the stable. At first she thought the stable was on fire but it was a low, steady glow. She had waited and watched. It was not seemly for a nun to go where Yuri and the *Ostarbeiter* were sleeping, so she woke another Sister and they went. Yuri was grooming his horse. He was not rude, she said, just absorbed in his grooming. One of the *Ostarbeiter* said he'd been at it for hours. Grooming, and singing softly. The next night the same glow but Sister Aganetta had not gone down. Then she heard the sound of hooves on cobblestones. She rushed to the window in time to see Yuri leading his white horse across the dark courtyard. She put something on her feet and ran down but he had already closed the big doors behind him. She ran to the other door, the little door for everyday use, and saw Yuri galloping down the hill. She shouted his name but he would not have heard. She knelt down in the snow and said a prayer for him, then she got dressed and came to tell Uncle Knalz. 'Pray for him, Herr Reimer,' she said, and tears ran down her cheeks.

Yuri had left two letters, one for Uncle Knalz and one for Taunte Liese. To Uncle Knalz he had written that he would try to get to France, then Spain, then maybe a ship to Buenos Aires. He thanked Uncle Knalz, said he loved them all, and charged Uncle Knalz to protect his Liese and the children. What he wrote to Taunte Liese no one knows. She tore the letter in pieces and burned it.

How far did he get?

Not far. Uncle Knalz said there was an Englishman, a civilian, who sometimes came to the camp. He spoke German perfectly and asked a lot of questions. *Unse* were suspicious but Uncle Knalz slowly began to trust him. He said he was a journalist and a poet but now he worked for the British Foreign Office. His job was to go to the libraries in all the towns in the region and advise the librarians which books they should remove from their shelves, and which books that the Nazis had banned they could now bring up from the basement. He said he was collecting material for a book about life in Germany since the surrender.

Uncle Knalz asked him if he had heard reports about a rider on a white horse, and a few days later the Englishman came by the camp again. He said the countryside was a-buzz with reports of sightings. Some children scavenging for firewood swore they had seen a rider on a white horse galloping across a field. The engineer of a train had seen him, caught in the light of the locomotive, galloping toward the train across a trestle bridge. He had pulled on the brake and the steam whistle, and at the last moment the rider had veered down an embankment and disappeared. An old man, wakened by the howling of his dog, had cleared a circle of frost in the window with his breath and swore he had seen him, on a bare hill top, horse and rider silhouetted against a full moon, the horse rearing on its hind legs, forelegs pawing the air. Then a cloud had passed over the moon, and when the moon appeared again horse and rider were gone. The Englishman chuckled. He said the man had read too many Karl May novels. He said at times like this people who normally know better are susceptible to strange visions. They want to believe some avenging spirit is wandering the earth.

Two days later the Englishman came again to the camp, this time with a report that was no fantasy. A rider on a white horse had tried to cross the Rhine at a British checkpoint near the town of Wesel. He said he had seen the report and had talked to the soldier who had been on watch when it happened. It was at night, said the soldier, but the checkpoint is garishly lit with arc lights, mounted on a scaffold-like structure. There is a guardhouse, with two bunks and a stove to make tea, and that night there were six of them on duty, including two Russians. Only one was kept on watch outside because of the cold. They changed the watch hourly. Then the guard on duty thought he heard hoof beats, muffled by his fur-lined hat. In his report he claims he could see only the dim outline of a rider at the foot of the bridge. He shouted Halt! and fired his gun into the air. Then the hoof beats broke into a gallop and the horseman charged into the circle of light, yelling something in some crazy language and wielding a sabre left and right like a madman. Two more guards had come rushing out of the guardhouse, yelling Halt! and one of them narrowly missed being hacked to pieces by the sabre. Horse and rider easily cleared the barrier and charged across the bridge. Now all six were at the barrier, firing at him, but he was crouched low so they hit the horse instead. The horse stumbled and the rider catapulted over its head and lay sprawled on the cobblestones. He struggled to his feet, turned and faced them, his arms stretched out, and yelled something again that nobody could understand. There were two more shots, and unfortunately they had to finish off the horse too.

Uncle Knalz stopped and leaned on his hoe. He cupped his hands over the end of the handle and stared down at the ground. He took off his hat and ran his sleeve across his face, but it was not sweat he was wiping from his eyes. I dropped my hoe and embraced him.

From where I had built my little mud hut on the edge of the village I could see Taunte Liese's house. She was then in her mid-thirties. No longer the high-spirited woman she had once been but there was still a liveliness in her step, her bearing still erect, and still that frank fearlessness in her look that she had when she was younger. She was still the subject of gossip and kept a distance between herself and the others.

There was a man, a Johann Koop, who had come with the first group, on the *Volendam*. He was one of the few eligible bachelors in the colony, a man in his late thirties who had never been married. A tall, muscular man who was not afraid of hard work, or of Chaco heat or Chaco mosquitoes, and he would have noticed that Taunte Liese had weathered the hard times better than most women her age. He would have seen her struggling with a plough and a team of oxen, would have seen how she had to hang her weight on the handles of the plough to hold it down, would have seen the handles lurch when the plough snagged on a root and threw her onto her side, together with the plough, while the oxen kept plodding along. It was so much easier for him, with his greater weight and strength.

She was grateful. She sent her little girl and boy to Johann's house, one carrying a little pot with steam rising from it, the other carrying a broad-brimmed bowl, covered with a white tea towel. The children waited until Johann finished his dinner. He gave the pot and the bowl a quick rinse, then the children came back home. A few days later patches appeared on the elbows of Johann's shirts, but this time the gossips were thwarted. Taunte Liese kept her distance.

There were others in the village, eligible widows with young children, who made sure Johann's shirts and trousers were well patched, and soon there was a wedding. Johann and widow Friesen became man and wife. Their house was diagonally across the street from Taunte Liese's house.

It was laundry day in the village when I visited Taunte Liese, an unusually cool day for Paraguay, and I was sitting at her kitchen table trying to amuse her little girl and boy while I struggled to find the right words to broach the subject of Yuri. The children were excited because that morning they had seen a snake in the cattle trough, as long as their outstretched arms. Taunte Liese feigned disbelief that there had been any snake, accused them of fibbing, which made them protest all the more fervently. They tried to enlist my support in the cause of their truthfulness while their mother, engulfed in steam, scrubbed laundry on the washboard below the kitchen window – laundry for her own family, for her aunt's family, and also for her old mother-in-law. Women's clothes. Dark skirts, aprons, long stockings, women's underwear, and then the more colourful children's clothes.

Through the kitchen window Taunte Liese would have seen the clothes that were flapping on widow Friesen's line. I tried to keep my mind on my games with the children yet I could not help but notice Taunte Liese sometimes looking out the window while she rubbed the clothes up and down on the rough washboard. Then I would see her avert her eyes from the window, see her stop scrubbing, see her pinch her eyes shut as though they were stung by the rising steam, then she would slap a skirt or a blouse onto the washboard with more vigour than necessary.

She would have seen, though she tried not to see, a man's clothes. Plaid shirts and a pair of denim bib coveralls, sent from Canada. She would see them flapping in the wind, see them billow, see how the wind moved the arms of the shirts, how they seemed to reach out in an embrace, would see how the wind filled the legs and the bib chest of the coveralls, and she would see though she tried not to see how the hips were thrust back and forth by the wind.

> *Oh, let there be nothing on earth but laundry,*
> *Nothing but rosy hands in the rising steam*
> *And clear dances done in the sight of heaven.*
> *Bring them down from their ruddy gallows,*
> *Let there be clean linen for the backs of thieves,*
> *Let lovers go fresh and sweet to be undone.*

From Richard Wilbur's poem. Taunte Liese would never know the poem, but if I had known the poem then and had told it to her, something inside her would have ached to hear it.

In 1954 she had got the news that her husband had died in the winter of 1941, less than two years after he was taken, but it wouldn't have mattered then. She had lost too many men. She did not emigrate to Canada, though she had a chance. Both her daughter and her son got married and raised families, but they stayed by her side in Paraguay to the end.

June 18, 1992

In 1975, I returned to Berlin, after an absence of almost thirty years. 'Go,' said my wife. 'Maybe it will give you some peace.' Yes, Antoine, it was the year of the fall of Saigon. I read about it in the Berlin papers, saw the reports on the television in my hotel room. I would never have guessed that you might be there . . . to experience it.

It hadn't been easy to track Uschi down but I found her. She owned a tearoom in Spandau. Uschi had become a business woman! She was in her mid-fifties then, and though her face was more lined, it had acquired an ageless beauty rather than aged. She was still tall and trim, the same soft blue eyes, the same languid manner, the same purr in her voice. Some gray streaks in her auburn hair, cut a bit shorter now. Only her teeth betrayed her a little, no longer quite so white, stained by a lifetime of heavy smoking, and there was no longer that edginess that reminded you she might, at any time, do something reckless.

Spandau is more like a provincial town than the borough of a big city. There was some graffiti, but otherwise little evidence either of Berlin's seedy charm or its frenetic energy. Many of the pre-war buildings had been clumsily repaired, others demolished and hastily replaced with shoddy structures behind glass facades. Uschi's tearoom, and her apartment above it were, by contrast, quite charming, quite genteel.

I had written many letters to you from Paraguay, some in care of the mess sergeant at McNair Barracks, some addressed to General Delivery/Steglitz, the nearest post office, where I thought you might check to see if you had any mail. They all went unanswered, if you ever received any of them. When we got to Canada, I immediately asked Doktor Vik if he knew how I could contact you but he said he had lost touch since he left Germany in 1948, and whenever I brought up the subject he was dismissive, as though that chapter in his life were long closed. Years passed, then one day, without any prodding, he blurted it out. He had just returned from a conference in Germany, and we met for dinner at the Fort Garry hotel. He seemed not quite himself, seemed distracted. I knew his aged father was failing so I assumed that was the reason. Since he didn't have his car, I drove him home. He remained distracted till I turned into his driveway. 'I did look up Uschi once, when I was back in Berlin,' he said.

When? Where? And what about you? Had he seen you too?

As soon as the words left his mouth he seemed to regret having said them. 'It was a few years ago,' he said. He became evasive, and when I pressed he got tangled up in his evasions. He said you and Uschi had moved to an apartment not far from the base, and shortly after that, 1951 or 52, you had 'run out' on her. 'She doesn't have a kind word to say about your friend Antoine,' he said. 'It was quite sad, actually, Uschi living there all by herself in that dumpy apartment, like a wilting old maid.' When I continued to pry he said he couldn't remember the exact address. 'Something like Kufsteiner Strasse. Just a short little street. Her building was brick. All the others were that dreary gray stucco.'

There are in fact four brick apartment blocks on Kufsteiner Strasse, not one. Four identical squat structures with little flower beds and a patch of grass in front of them. At the second block I got lucky. The concierge was an elderly fellow, and after much pleading he agreed to check his records. He took obvious pride in how meticulously he had maintained them, going back decades – records that could be of little interest to anyone, but now someone was interested. A vindication of his archival zeal. He unlocked his cabinet and began leafing through yellowed account books, starting in 1949. And there you were, Antoine, you and Uschi, among the first tenants after the building had been repaired, and yes, Uschi had stayed on in the apartment until she moved out in 1958. But moved where?

About that the concierge had no record.

Might there still be tenants in the building now, seventeen years later, who would have known Uschi? Who might know where she had moved?

That, said the concierge, he was not at liberty to disclose. He could not give private information about his current tenants to just anyone off the street, he said. When I threatened to post myself outside the entrance, for days on end if necessary, and accost everyone who entered or left the building, he did relent. There might be one, he said. A Frau Bender.

She was an old woman, well into her eighties, leaning on a cane, but still energetic, with bright eyes in a smiling face scored by deep wrinkles. The concierge introduced me, told her my business, and then he left us. She looked me up and down, then stepped aside and invited me in. It was an old-woman's apartment, cluttered with knick-knacks, but all carefully placed and recently dusted. There were two upholstered chairs, covered in a faded floral pattern, on either side of a low table. She bade me sit in one and sat herself in the other. I politely asked about her own history and she told it in unadorned detail. She had been one of those thousands deported from the Sudetenland after the war, 'to make it *Deutschfrei*,' she said. A terrible time, but long ago now. Then before I could begin asking *my* questions she began plying me with her own. Where was I from? Canada? Yes, but before that? Russia? Aaah. Now who exactly was this woman I was seeking? What did she look like? Her name again? Hmmm. And she had lived here, in this very building, all alone?

Yes, I said, when she moved out in 1958 she had been living here alone.

Yes but . . . before that? *Ach*, her memory wasn't what it used to be. Hmm. No, there *had* been someone else.

Yes, for a few years a young man had been living there too, I said.

'Aha. I *thought* so!' Her questioning had begun like an interrogation, but now she began to coax and cajole, wheedling information out of me about that young man, with a mischievous twinkle in her eye and quizzical sideways glances. She plied me with coffee and crunchy biscuits, more coffee, then a glass of schnapps. 'And this young man, a Russian? He was her . . .?' And finally I understood. She wanted me to confess that *I* was that young man, Uschi's lover. The famous Russian poet, the one who suddenly had to pack up and flee Germany to escape the KGB – who were out to get him, to punish him for the anti-Soviet poems he had written, whose agents were determined to hunt him down wherever in the world he might be hiding.

Perhaps this is the story Uschi had told her. Or perhaps Frau Bender had embellished the tale to suit her own fancy. But yes, I 'confessed' that I was you, Antoine, that I was that young man for whom the *gnäd'ge Frau* had kept her lonely vigil all those years in that apartment across the hall, waiting, and at last despairing of my return. And now, after so many years, I'd come back.

Frau Bender heaved a sigh, leaned back in her chair, closed her eyes and smiled. A tear trickled down her cheek. Yes, yes, she said, she knew where I could find my *Liebling*.

. . .

Uschi was working behind a pastry counter when I walked through the door of the tearoom, cutting dainty servings of *Torte* and *Strudel* and carefully placing them on paper doilies. I stood at the door, grinning. When she saw me she let out a little cry and quickly covered her mouth with her hand. Then she came running from behind the counter and stopped, the pastry knife still in her hand. She took a few tentative steps toward me and stopped again, shaking her head, an almost pained expression on her face. Then she threw herself into my arms. She said I should wait for her in her office but I said I would have a cup of tea and one of her pastries. She led me to a table set apart in an alcove, took off her little apron and sat down opposite me. The two girls could take care of the customers on their own, she said, and the tearoom would be closing shortly anyway. We stayed and talked after everyone had left. I had more tea and Uschi had the first of the cigarettes she allowed herself each day. I felt her watching me, as though waiting for me to clarify something, and the more I became aware of her watching the more effusively I babbled. After I explained how we had ended up in Canada, thanks to Doktor Vik sponsoring our immigration, she said, 'You and Viktor? You've become . . . friends?'

Well, yes, sort of. I had to laugh at her reaction. Yes, we had aggravated each other back then, whenever he made an appearance in our basement lair at McNair Barracks, but maybe we had both matured, I said. And yes, we had indeed become friends. I told her his help had been invaluable to us, to my whole family, after we got settled in Canada. And he had become like a godfather to my two children. She shook her head and gave me a searching look as though there must be more to the story, but I could only smile and shrug at what must seem to her a strange turn of events.

I was there every afternoon during the week that followed, for tea and pastry and then a long talk with Uschi. The tearoom looks typically tearoom, blue-and-white chequered cloths on the tables, a small vase with a rose or whatever flower is in season, lacquered cane chairs with matching cushions, a well worn wooden floor. Toward closing time, the late-afternoon sun finds a gap between two tall buildings on the opposite side of the street and streams its beams through the lace curtains, and for that brief time the room basks in a gauzy glow. The daytime bustle and chatter dwindles to a rustle as the last patrons gather their bags and parcels, *ciao, ciao,* then one of the girls pulls the shade the full length of the front door and locks it. When the last cups and plates have been washed and stacked, the lights dimmed, and when the two girls have also left and shut the door behind them, the tearoom seems to exhale softly and close in upon itself, seems to withdraw from the street scene and become a private place. As the windows of the other shops on the street become more brightly lit, the windows of the tearoom darken and mirror the street scene back upon itself. Only the two of us then, at our corner table, Uschi and me, the room suffused by the soft glow from the refrigerated pastry counter. The cane chairs with their rounded backs have been tipped forward across the tables, leaning their heads together as though engaged in their own earnest conversations.

I remembered Uschi as she had first appeared to me, seated in that tall window alcove above the parade square, waiting for her General to finish with his meeting and take her home. Little evidence now of her caged edginess. She had withdrawn, content to let the world carry on without her, and a little wary that my intrusion would draw her back.

You were not a subject that was easy to broach, Antoine. I tried to make it easier by recalling some of your idiosyncrasies and quirks, like your refusal to wear anything but your formal waiter's uniform. Even on a hot summer day your only concession to casual dress was to take off your jacket and tie and loosen the top two buttons of your shirt. And I mentioned your perverse refusal to read anything. All of us read whatever we could get our hands on, books, magazines, in English or German, and when we shoved a magazine or a book under your nose, certain you would find it interesting, you would politely decline it.

'He was still like that,' said Uschi, and sometimes it annoyed her, that you, who had once been a writer, now refused to take any interest in what people were writing. As though you wanted to block out the world. She said she had come across an article in one of the new magazines that was trying to be more highbrow. It was about a famous French writer, an 'existentialist,' and she was sure it would fascinate you. Perhaps you had even met this writer when you were in Paris. But no. You turned your head aside. Didn't want to see it. So she began to read the article to you, forcing it on you. She said you hammed it up, you pressed your hands over your ears and contorted your face into an expression of pain. But she kept reading, until you snatched the magazine from her hand, threw it on the floor and stomped on it. Then you grinned. You always did things like that, she said, and she could never tell if you were serious or just teasing.

Do you know why he left, I said. Did he leave a note?

I could feel Uschi tense. 'The note said he wanted to see the East, the Far East, before the Communists and the Americans made a mess of it. He was a little too late for that.' She said you did tell her once that the Americans or the Russians – maybe both – had become suspicious of Viktor and his 'business,' and it was only a matter of time before the Amis would connect you to Viktor. 'If that was why he left, we could have escaped together.' She said she would have followed you anywhere in the world. Anything would have been better than you just sneaking away. Yes, maybe she could forgive you, but only by keeping her hate alive could she keep you near, she said.

She stayed in the Kufsteiner apartment for almost seven years after you left, waiting for your return, or for a letter, but none came. Then Gioconda had returned from America. She had married her lieutenant – the Texan whose papa was a rich oil man – but it hadn't worked out. She tried her best to be a model daughter-in-law but his family let her know that their son had married beneath him, that they still regarded her as a tart, a 'gold digger.' Gioconda said she had tried but the atmosphere was pure poison, and so she had come back to Berlin, with a modest divorce settlement, and she had persuaded Uschi to form a partnership and buy the tearoom. It had belonged to a relative before the war. 'She said she couldn't bear to see me wasting away in that gloomy apartment, like a jilted bride in a cheap novel. That made me angry,' said Uschi. 'Not at her, at myself – for what I'd become.'

Uschi's investment was the 4,000 American dollars you had stuffed into the envelope you left on the kitchen table the day you disappeared. Instead of putting the money in a bank where it would have earned interest she had kept it in a jar all those years. 'Stupid me,' she said, 'but I wanted to keep it handy, to throw in his face if he ever came back.' She and Gioconda had intended to convert the tearoom to a restaurant, but it had done well as a tearoom, especially with that English garrison nearby, so they never bothered. 'Can you imagine me a cook?' said Uschi. 'I hardly knew how to boil an egg until after the war.'

Then Gioconda had married again, to a German this time, from Munich, so she had sold Uschi her share, for the exact amount she had originally invested. A pittance of what it was worth then. Because she felt guilty for 'running out' on her, she had told Uschi. Does Gioconda's loyalty make you wince, Antoine?

I asked her if there had been other men in her life since you left. She said, 'None that amounted to more than a dinner or two at a fancy restaurant.' She tried to laugh but it was a bitter laugh. She said she was now content to be an old maid in her apartment above the tearoom. Then she asked again about my 'friendship' with Doktor Vik and so I babbled away in a mocking manner that I thought might amuse her, about his stellar rise to the top of his profession, or almost the top, about his three wives, and our dinners at the Fort Garry. She was attentive, but not very amused. And then she asked about my mother and I told her. 'She never made it to Paraguay,' I said. 'She wasn't on that ship with the others, and she wasn't on the train from Berlin to Bremerhaven. She disappeared. She and another woman, Katya, who never left her side.' Then I told Uschi the whole story. She covered her face with her hands. 'I'm so sorry, so sorry,' she said, and when she raised her head again her eyes were moist. She reached across the table and grasped my hands. 'Do you know . . . do you know what happened?' she said.

I said I knew very little. I said when I first arrived in Paraguay, the others who had sailed on the *Volendam* a year earlier accused me of abandoning my mother in Berlin. They said a strange man had come to that house on the Ringstrasse only a few hours before the rest of them were loaded into Ami troop carriers and taken to the train station. This man had said I sent him, and that my mother should gather her belongings and follow him to a house where I was waiting for her. So they went, my mother and that Katya woman who refused to leave my mother's side. I told Uschi that for the next eight years, until 1956, I wrote letters, maybe a hundred of them, in three languages, to Germany, America, Russia, to every agency I had heard of. Some were scams but since I had no money I didn't lose any. It was not till I got to Canada that an old friend brought me news of that Katya woman. He had managed to get in contact with his long-lost cousin whose family had been repatriated to Russia, and when he asked his cousin about other people from our village, he wrote back that there was a Katarina Kaminsky, nee Bergen, who now lived in Orsk, Zhukov Street 71.

I said I wrote immediately. Katya's reply was a mere six lines. She wrote that it was true, that she and my mother were taken to a sleazy bar by a man who said I had sent him. Another man, who said he was a policeman, had demanded their papers and told them to wait. Then four Russians came and took them to a prison in the Soviet Sector. They were interrogated and put on a train to Siberia – to Norilsk, a mining camp near the Arctic Circle, where my mother had died, November 14, 1948. I wrote more letters but received only one more reply, little more than a yes or no to my questions. Could she tell me more about the man who said I had sent him? No. Had my mother suffered terribly before she died? Yes.

Again Uschi let out a cry and covered her face.

There remained a few traces of the wariness I had felt at our first meeting, but soon we talked as though it had been thirty days, not thirty years since we had last seen each other. We went on walks, like we used to, and we laughed when we recalled some of the antics of the Australians and the other 'riff-raff' at the base, and at the absurd turns in our own lives. Sometimes she drifted into melancholy but there were many shades of it, sometimes tinged with anger, sometimes wistful, and when we veered too far toward sadness, she would take my arm and squeeze it, and quicken our pace.

When Uschi was busy with her tearoom I would stroll around Spandau by myself, so it wasn't long before I came upon the prison where Rudolf Hess was then the sole inmate – the most bizarre of all the lunatics among Hitler's inner circle, who in 1941 had jumped into a *Messerschmitt* without breathing a word of his plan to his *Führer,* and flown solo across the North Sea to Scotland. He ejected from his plane and let it crash into the heather, and when he was found by the local police, still entangled in his parachute, he presented his credentials and demanded a meeting with members of the British war cabinet – to negotiate a peace treaty. A huge embarrassment to both Hitler and Churchill. When the story came out during his Nuremberg trial we all laughed at the utter silliness of it. 'It sounds like a college fraternity prank,' said the American. Hess was now the last of the six Nuremberg convicts still imprisoned here. It is a large prison compound made of pinkish granite, designed to house 500 prisoners, but since 1966 its solitary inmate had been guarded by British, French, American and Soviet detachments in monthly rotation, a staff of up to thirty men, which made Hess the most expensive prisoner in the world.

I found it unseemly, this brazen memento of the Nazi era in this sleepy borough. While the burghers of Spandau bustled through their daily routines, behind those walls Hitler's Deputy still grumbled about the food and took his twice daily walk in the garden, as he had done for almost thirty years, and would continue to do for another ten until he finally died at the age of ninety-three. I began to play a silly game, would stop passers-by on the street and ask for directions. When I asked a young woman, the response was at first a blank stare. Prison? Do we have a prison here? Then it clicked, and her face lit up. 'Oh, *that* prison. It's not far. Just around that corner. There, see? Big pink building. Looks like a castle. You can't miss it.' As though it were a geological curiosity in the middle of the city.

Uschi said she too tried not to 'see' the prison, especially since one of the former inmates had once been a frequent guest at her family's estate before the war. Erich Raeder. 'They let him out in 1955, because of his failing health they said, but maybe they had second thoughts about whether he was really a war criminal.' She said he was godfather to her oldest brother, and when she was just a little child he had bounced her on his knee and sung nursery rhymes to her. When Hitler made him *Grossadmiral*, head of the whole navy, the family saw less of him, but none of them were surprised when he had to resign in 1943, and Hitler replaced him with Dönitz. Yes, he had publicly supported Hitler, at the beginning, she said. Publicly supported him, privately despised him. Raeder was loyal to the *Vaterland*, but he was fanatically loyal to the navy, and Hitler had promised to rebuild the navy. In 1960, when she read that Raeder had died, she went to his funeral. She said she kept her face covered by a veil, like the other women, and she had talked to no one. She thought she recognized one or two of the mourners, mostly women, and maybe they had recognized her too.

In the days that followed Uschi and I did some of the touristy things, strolled along the glitzy Ku'damm, saw the partially restored *Reichstag*, the Brandenburg Gate and the grizzly Berlin Wall, and then for old time's sake we went to Lichterfelde to see McNair Barracks. She said she hadn't been back since 1958, not once. You wouldn't recognize the neighbourhood, Antoine. It's become quite respectable, only a few bars left and they no longer sell their services so garishly. The monumental gate is still there but now the stone walls around the compound are covered with ivy instead of barbed wire. Gone is the relentless roar of jeeps and troop carriers and official cars. Nothing seems urgent now. What little traffic there is proceeds in a businesslike manner, trying not to draw attention to itself.

We went to see the house on the Ringstrasse where my mother, my sister Sarah and Katya had found a brief refuge. It is now a hostel called Mennohaus, in a very respectable neighbourhood, and it serves mainly as a base for MCC workers who try to support clandestine Christian groups in East Berlin. The sight of it opened all the old wounds, though there is little evidence now that it had once been a refuge for ragged, destitute people waiting to hear what their fate would be. Uschi found a bench in a nearby park and left me to grieve by myself. It might have been almost an hour till we resumed our walk.

They were leisurely now, our walks. Thirty years ago they had not always been so. They were often occasions for Uschi to vent her exasperation with you, especially when you would disappear for two or three days. If we asked where you had been you would mumble something about taking food and clothes to someone you once knew. We didn't pry for more details but Uschi was not so easily appeased by your sullen explanations. She would set a gruelling pace through rubble-strewn streets and I would hurry to keep pace with her, and try to distract her with stories about our pranks in Russia.

I remembered one of those walks and suggested we try to find the bombed out gothic church we had stumbled upon thirty years ago. It was then a skeletal ruin among other ruins, but now it was hidden among new apartment blocks. It had been crudely restored but we recognized the two truncated towers. That day, thirty years ago, had been cold and wet and we had been walking for well over an hour when we stumbled upon it. All that remained of the nave and the lateral chapels were the walls, in places still thirty feet high. Only the apse was still partially covered by a roof. The floor of the nave had caved in under the weight of the stone vault that had fallen on it, and was littered with broken arches, carved capitals and statuary. To divert Uschi I had pretended to be fascinated by this ruin and began poking around among the debris. I tried to identify the biblical figures carved on the enormous capitals, and when I was stumped I got

Uschi to help me. She did so grudgingly at first, but my enthusiasm drew her in. We wrestled a half-buried capital upright, then squatted down so we could see the figures better. That's Joseph sold into slavery by his brothers, I said. No, he's got a harp, she said. It's Samuel anointing King David. Look, here's Abraham about to sacrifice his son Isaac. Then I found a massive wooden choir stall that had somehow survived the fire, and when I lifted the seat a grotesque face leered up at me, exquisitely carved. I was taken aback. Uschi laughed. She said such grotesques were common in old gothic churches.

It had grown darker and colder when we tired of the game. We pulled our coats more tightly around us, and Uschi's mood became sombre again. A light rain had begun and we looked for a place to sit under the roof of the apse. We found a stone slab that must have been the altar table, brushed off the debris and sat down. Uschi turned sideways and tucked her feet up on the slab, wrapped her arms around her knees and leaned her back against me. 'My mother also mysteriously disappeared, and was never heard from again,' she said, and she told me about her childhood, on a Junker estate in East Prussia. A happy enough childhood, though there were tensions in her family. She said her parents were ill-matched and were rarely together when they didn't grate upon each other. She said her father was a good man, all his tenants loved him, but he did not pretend to be a cultivated man. Her aunts and uncles regarded him as rather boorish. Her mother was more cultivated but did not get on well with the uncles and aunts either. She regarded them as pretentious provincials.

Uschi said when the Nazis came to power her father had tried to carry on as he always had, but not her mother. She was openly contemptuous, even when admirals and generals were among their guests. If she had drunk a little too much, which she often did, she would scoff at the Nazi leaders, and at Hitler too. The admirals and generals would pretend to be amused by her wit, but Uschi's father and her older brother were not amused. After the guests had left there would be a fight and things would get thrown around. Then one morning the family woke up and their mother was nowhere to be found. Neither was the family car and the old chauffeur who had been with the family for decades. That was in 1938. Uschi said they never saw her mother again, or the chauffeur. Maybe they escaped to Switzerland, or Sweden, though there were rumours that the

Gestapo had arrested her at a spa somewhere in Bohemia. If her father or her older brother knew more they never told her.

Uschi snuggled closer and we sat in silence for a long time. The massive stone walls and crumbling piers loomed above us against the open sky, and little braids of rainwater trickled down the stone shafts, faintly luminous now, caught in the low light of the declining day. 'Look,' said Uschi, 'the stones are crying. They survived eight hundred years of wars and plagues and bungling popes – but they couldn't survive us.'

Then it was my last day. I hoped we would do something together that would recall the good times we had in Berlin almost thirty years ago, that would evoke only fond memories of you. I arrived early at the tea house for my morning tea and biscuits, and as soon as Uschi had a free moment I proposed an excursion to Potsdam, to that *Gasthaus* on the bank of the Havel River where a group of us once spent a perfect summer Sunday.

On that Sunday morning thirty years ago it was Doktor Vik who had proposed the outing. He arrived unexpectedly early in the morning, and seemed even more jovial than usual. He made a few witty comments about the latest reports on the Nuremberg trials, then proposed that you and he take advantage of the day for an outing to Potsdam and the Wannsee, 'away from all this stink and rubble.' He said he knew a charming *Gasthaus* overlooking the Havel, where he was meeting a couple of 'characters' later that afternoon.

'Why don't we all go,' you said. 'We all need a reminder that somewhere in the world nature still exits.' A group outing wasn't exactly what Doktor Vik had in mind, but he could hardly object. So we all went, the five of us who had the day off – the Egyptian, you and Uschi, Max the Australian, and me.

Much had changed over the years but the *Gasthaus* itself had changed little, nestled between the river and forested parkland, geraniums spilling out of flowerboxes, a large shaded terrace overlooking the bay – though now it seemed quaint rather than surreal. There were now dozens of watercraft cruising in the bay, including ferries and floating patios that advertised their services as tour boats and party boats. Back then there had been only a few little sailboats and rowboats bobbing like toys on the water. I remembered the Wannsee, just visible beyond a headland, sparkling in the sunlight, still innocent, back then, of any association in the public mind with the infamous Conference where only four years ago Reinhard Heydrich had laid out his plan for the Final Solution.

The trip from Spandau to Potsdam, through the posh neighbourhoods of Zehlendorf, had taken us only half an hour on the S-Bahn. In 1946, from McNair Barracks, it took almost two hours, and when we arrived the terrace was already bustling with diners, couples and young families who had scraped together the means for a Sunday outing. We found a long table with a good view across the bay and settled in. We had brought two cartons of cigarettes from the PX, enough to pay for a leisurely afternoon of eating and drinking. We were all in high spirits, Uschi recalled, 'Even Antoine was laughing and babbling like the rest of us.'

The arrival of the Ami GIs had almost spoiled it. Uschi and I could laugh about it now but we hadn't found it so amusing at the time. We had finished our lunch and were well into our third or fourth litre of wine when the tranquillity of the setting was shattered by the roar of a motor launch bearing down on us. At the last moment the one at the helm threw the engine into reverse and brought the launch to a perfect standstill alongside the wharf at the foot of the terrace. They were in 'civvies,' Bermuda shorts and colourful shirts, four or five of them, accompanied by two English girls that the British had brought with them to do clerical work.

Every detail is still vivid in my memory. They stride onto the terrace, study the other diners for a minute, then pull together two tables and arrange them so they have a perfect view over the bay, blocking the view of some of the other diners. The one who had piloted the launch is a tall, rangy, sandy-haired fellow with a perfectly flat crew cut. The two girls are pretty and stylishly dressed, compared to the German diners, the other Americans are less distinct in my memory. The waiter, bowing and kowtowing, brings them their menus – two handwritten sheets tucked into red folders to make the selection appear more substantial than the resources of the kitchen permit.

Crew Cut conducts all negotiations with the waiter. He apparently imagines himself adequately fluent in German, and the others are willing to take him by his own account. He scans both sheets, then turns them over to see if anything is written on the back. He pecks at the menu with his index finger. 'You got *auf* English?'

'*Nein, leider. Nur* German.'

This is met with some grumbling but they do their best to make sense of the menus, looking for anything that resembles an English dish. 'Hunner brattin. Is that chicken?' 'What the hell is spare gel? Two legs or four?' They struggle another five or ten minutes and give up. One of the English girls can't hide the smirk on her face. 'Ask the waiter what he recommends,' she says.

Crew Cut calls the waiter, who comes on the double. '*Was du* . . .' But that's as far as he gets. 'How do yuh say *recommend* in kraut, for Christ's sake?'

The other girl gives it a try. '*Was gut schmecken?*' she asks.

The waiter shrugs and smiles. This is not going well. 'Here, pass me the damn menus,' says Crew Cut. He hands them to the waiter, but before he lets go he smacks the palm of his hand down on the stack of menus and holds it there. '*Alles. Zwei mal. Versteh?*' he says. Very distinctly. And holds up two fingers.

'*Alles?*'

'*Alles. Zweimal.*' Again two fingers.

The waiter, a little balding, chinless fellow with the air of an English butler, looks around the terrace hoping for some help from the other diners. They busy themselves with their bratwurst and *Kartoffelsalat*. He turns back to Crew Cut and repeats the order, as though it were a prison sentence. '*Alles zweimal.*'

'*Ja,* you *Dummkopf. Alles zweimal!*'

The waiter bows, takes the menus, tucks them under his arm and trots back to the kitchen. From where we sit we can hear the argument that erupts there, accompanied by crashing cookware, and soon the chef himself emerges, with his tall puffy chef's hat, a burly man like they all are, wiping his hands on his apron. He spots the Americans at the far end of the terrace and sets out toward them, an apologetic grin on his face. He throws up his arms in mock despair and cobbles together a mixture of English and German. 'Stupid vaiter,' he says, 'He not *versteh* English. He tink you order *alles* on za menu. *Alles* two times. Effry dish.' He holds up two fingers, still smiling.

Crew Cut slaps both hands down on the table and tries to restrain his frustration. '*Alles! Zwei! Mal! Versteh?*'

The chef wheels around, tucks the two fingers into his fist and marches back to the kitchen. More shouting and crashing behind us, and at last three waiters appear (the first waiter presumably out the back somewhere, sulking). Each of them is pushing a trolley piled high with dishes of food. Crew Cut and his companions pass them around, wrinkle their noses at some, nod approval at others, and pile the rejects at the end of the table. Then Crew Cut waves his hands at the rejects. '*Weg! Weg nehmen!*' he commands. '*Alles weg.*'

On the base we rarely had to witness such displays of arrogance. All of us knew our good fortune to be taken under the wing of the Amis, and we tried to overlook their faults. We would gladly have been spared this spectacle. But not Doktor Vik. He relished it. 'Behold your conquering heroes,' he intoned, 'your new Romans.' His sneer was directed more at you than at them – at your passive consent to live in a world ruled by these boors.

You shrugged. 'As conquerors go, they're not as bad as some,' you said.

'You mean the Russians? That's setting the bar pretty low.'

'The Amis don't seem much worse than the English, as I recall,' said the Egyptian. Doktor Vik rolled his eyes. It's not our place to contradict him.

The German diners had been casting furtive glances at each other. They were disgusted by this vulgar display of power and privilege but none of them dared to protest. Doktor Vik, with a sweep of his arm, gestured his contempt for them. 'Look at these Germans now,' he sneered. 'Heads down, hunkered over their plates of *Kartoffelsalat.* Like school children who've been scolded for being very naughty.'

'They should be more heroic in defeat?' you said, 'Like their *Führer,* in his bunker?'

I could barely resist clapping my hands to applaud your putdown.

At a table near the Americans a small family group – grandfather, daughter and grandson – mop up the last of their *Kartoffelsalat* with a crust of bread, their Sunday outing now spoiled. The grandson, eight or ten years old, stares at the treats piled on the Americans' table. Crew Cut looks up from his plate and notices him. He smiles. The boy smiles back. '*Du will essen, ja?*' asks Crew Cut. He selects a plate of cakes and pastries and offers it to the boy. '*Komm. Nimm. Gut schmecken.* Mmm, mmm.'

The boy's mother mumbles something to the boy and his smile disappears. He looks down at his plate but he can't resist looking up again, and now some of Crew Cut's companions are into the act. 'Hey, kid, you want more food? Here, help yourself. Good for yuh.' The boy throws a glance at his grandfather and his mother, their heads bent over their *Kartoffelsalat,* and he decides to make a dash for it. But his grandfather is too quick. He grabs the back of the boy's shirt and slams him back into his chair. Then slaps him across the face.

'Hey, what the hell!' shouts Crew Cut, 'What d'yuh hit him for?'

The grandfather glowers at him. The mother noisily throws her cutlery onto her plate, then gets up to leave and jerks at the boy's sleeve. *'Jetzt komm!'* But the boy has gone stiff as a board and slides from his chair to the ground, in what seems to be an epileptic fit.

'Jesus Christ, what're they doin' to the poor kid!' Crew Cut and his companions rush to the table, push the mother and the grandfather out of the way and take charge. 'Stick something in his mouth so he doesn't bite his tongue.' 'Stand back, give him air.' The boy begins to come out of it and Crew Cut gathers him in his arms. 'We'll take him to the clinic on the base,' he says. *'Du!'* he barks at the mother, *'Du komm mit.'* The grandfather protests and curses. 'Shut up, you Nazi bastard!' One of the GIs throws a wad of bills onto a half-eaten plate, then they board the launch and roar away. The grandfather runs to the end of the pier, shouting, *'Ich ruf die Polizei!'* Two waiters run after him, try to calm him down and take him inside the *Gasthaus.*

Uschi and I could now allow ourselves a wry chuckle at this bizarre drama. 'Thank God we don't see scenes like that anymore,' she said, 'not in West Berlin.' I paid our bill and we left. We strolled toward Potsdam and spent some time in the tourist shops, where Uschi helped me chose a scarf and a bracelet for Helena. Then we caught our bus back to Spandau. It had been a pleasant outing. Uschi and I had laughed a lot, but disturbing images intruded on our memories. Like the scene with Doktor Vik's two 'characters.' After the Amis had left, the terrace thinned out. A few newcomers trickled in and chose a table with a good view over the bay. They hadn't witnessed the spectacle with the Americans and were therefore in a better mood. Then two men arrived, whom Doktor Vik seemed to take note of. They chose the table nearest to the street, apparently indifferent to the view. They wore long coats and kept their hats on, the brim shading their eyes. After a few minutes Doktor Vik wiped his lips on his napkin and turned to you. 'I've got some business back there,' he said, 'Care to meet them?'

'Not particularly,' you said.

'Worried who might see you?' Doktor Vik aped a scowl and cast a shifty-eyed glance around the terrace.

'If I were, it's you I wouldn't want to be seen with,' you said.

He was taken aback for a moment, then he recovered. 'Ha!' he laughed. 'Me? After all my humanitarian work among the refugees?' He rose from his chair, gave you a friendly clap on the shoulder, and joined the two men at their table. There were no handshakes, they barely acknowledged each other. Doktor Vik sat down, there was a brief discussion, an exchange of envelopes, then they left, first one, then the other. Doktor Vik scrawled something on a piece of paper, folded it, and returned to our table. He handed it to you, you glanced at it, and tucked it into your pocket. Then he excused himself and left. We weren't sorry to see him go.

Our waiter brought more wine and some cheese. We waited for you to say something about those two men you hadn't wanted to meet, or about that piece of paper Doktor Vik had given you, a smug smirk on his face, but you said nothing. It irked me to witness Doktor Vik's presumption of your 'friendship,' and your complicity in his 'business,' when you clearly found it distasteful. I tried to say something agreeable to hide my peevishness. I said there was a childlike innocence about the Amis, as though they'd sprouted from the virgin American soil as naturally as a corn stalk. They bore no historical baggage on their backs.

You smiled, but you demurred. 'If they glanced over their shoulders,' you said, 'they might catch a glimpse of some baggage. The blood of their native Indians and African slaves.'

As the sun descended over the Havel, we became *gemütlich*, lulled by the warm sun and the wine. Against the slant of the late afternoon sun the little sailboats bobbing on the bay now looked like a ghostly mirage. A scene that differed little from how it might have looked a century ago, but now a feeling of brittleness hung over it. You said the Nazi invasion of Russia was not remotely similar to their invasion of France, or Holland, or Denmark. They had no ambition to colonize those countries. 'But every Russian knew that the Nazis would do to them – the inferior Slavs – what England, Spain and France had done to the American Indians – kill some and banish the rest to an uninhabitable hinterland.'

You sprawled on your chair with half-closed eyes and lapsed into a brooding melancholy. You didn't explicitly mention Doktor Vik but he didn't seem far from your thoughts. You said whenever there's a movement afoot to give the evolution of our species a nudge it's time to pack your bag and head for the mountains. There will always be those who won't or can't adapt, and they are doomed to deserved extinction. You said that was the grand vision of both the Communists and the Nazis – the Nazis by selective breeding and culling degenerate specimens, the Communists by re-inventing the working class as an autonomous machine with interchangeable parts. A metamorphosis not seen since the dawn of *homo sapiens*. 'That's what justifies the killing,' you said. 'That's why millions of obsolete human specimens have to be eradicated like weeds, so the new species can flourish. The Future will justify their evolutionary zeal. But the Amis? They tell us the way we are is just fine. All we need is to go faster, build bigger, get richer. Some people will be left behind but they still have a purpose – a few drudges to do menial tasks, and others to provide cheap entertainment. Like gladiators in ancient Rome. For the rest, there are drugs and prisons.'

'Not very inspiring,' said Uschi.

'No,' you said, 'but that's the price of Progress. Endlessly creative littering.'

'Ami capitalism is going nowhere but the dustbin of history,' grumbled Max.

You smiled and held up your hands in surrender. 'Maybe it will choke on its own abundance,' you said.

This was the old Antonii! The Antonii I remembered from our boyhood in Russia. Whimsical, teasingly ironic. The Antonii whose company I had basked in while we lay hidden under a canopy of nodding sunflowers. Yet, not quite the same. Instead of the old cockiness there was a weary resignation.

'Where do we fit in?' asked the Egyptian. 'Among those doomed for extinction?

'Maybe we are like these birds,' you said. Now that most of the diners had left, the birds – sparrows and a few finches – had become more bold. They swooped down on the recently vacated tables and began pecking at the crumbs. The waiters cursed them and flapped their towels at them but they kept coming back. 'Like these birds, we try to fly above the fray,' you said, 'but we must come down to feed on it.'

The next morning Uschi got up early so she could accompany me to the airport. One last hug before I boarded my flight to Frankfurt, the first leg of my journey home. As soon as the seatbelt sign was turned off, I turned my face to the window and stared down at the impenetrable carpet of clouds below me. I did not want to give my seatmate an opportunity to start a banal conversation that would break the spell of my time with Uschi. That brief interlude in Berlin, Antoine, a mere two years. So self contained, yet now it seems to colour all that came before and after.

June 21, 1992

From Frankfurt south to Ludwigshafen, by train, second class, the next leg of my journey. To see my sister, Sarah. Yes, Antoine, I found her too. Another miraculous reunion.

A trip to Winnipeg in 1971 had begun with the usual shopping and lunch with my granddaughter Sara, then a stop at my favourite bookstore and magazine shop to pick up a copy of *Der Spiegel* and the *Frankfurter Allgemeine*. The cover of one of the schlockier German journals caught my eye – photographs of four women, artfully arranged under a bold heading, *The New German Business Woman*. There was to be a series on this theme, apparently, and this was the second in the series. And the fourth picture? Could it be? My sister. My sister whom I had not seen or heard from since she disappeared from Berlin on a stolen bicycle twenty-five years ago. The woman pictured here was well into middle age, but in spite of the close-cropped hair I was sure it must be her. I bought the magazine and began reading. Her name, Sarah Schivelfening. That of course would be her married name. No other family names were given, no family members mentioned, living or dead, no mention of her Mennonite background, but the article did gush about her astounding rise to riches after the war – from a destitute refugee, one of the millions of *Volksdeutsche* from the Soviet Union, yes, and then there had been a 'very unpleasant time' in Berlin, yes, until one day, hardly aware what she was doing, yes, yes, there it was, in black and white, the bicycle. She saw a bicycle leaning against a lamp post, got on it and rode. West.

How many could there have been like that? (Many, it turns out, but you could not have told me that then.)

I wrote immediately. First to the editor of the magazine. The reply was prompt. He was not at liberty to divulge the address, maiden name, or any private information about the women profiled in the series. Of course, stated the letter, I would understand the delicate circumstances. These were, after all, very wealthy women. To date, the magazine had received a hundred and twenty-eight letters from various persons claiming to be the abandoned child of one or more of them. Nevertheless, my letter had been forwarded to the attorneys of Frau Schivelfening, and any further correspondence should be addressed to said attorneys.

I wrote two more letters and received no response. Then I wrote a letter addressed to her at the head office of her *Firma*. I apologized for intruding upon her private life, assured her I had no intention to insinuate myself or my family into her affairs, but I did dearly wish to know if I could now put an end to my search for my sister. And at last a brief letter arrived, written on company stationery. Yes, she was my sister, and indeed it had moved her that I had been so determined to find her, but since we had now been separated in so many ways and for so many years, we were really little more than strangers to each other, and any attempt to fabricate a relationship at this point would probably result in disappointment for both of us. She wished me a long and happy life in my new country.

This wouldn't surprise you, Antoine, neither her 'success' nor her coolness toward me. I sent one more letter, wishing her the same. I told her all I knew about our mother.

My compartment on the train was overheated and stuffy, and outside rain streamed across the window in jagged diagonal streaks. I did not expect a joyful reunion. When I wrote again to tell her I would be in Germany, she did reply, with a stiff invitation that did little to conceal her reluctance.

She was waiting at the railway station where she could easily be seen, and could see the passengers filing down the length of the platform. I immediately recognized her, and was struck by how she now resembled my Oma Enns. Her luxuriantly thick mane of golden hair, which she once proudly flaunted, was now cut short, barely covering her ears. She was very trim, almost gaunt. She wore a beige pant suit and carried a knitted brown bag slung over her shoulder. She did not look dowdy, exactly, but deliberately inconspicuous.

She didn't recognize me. She stood with her arms folded watching the passengers file by, moving her eyes but not her head. I called her name and began to waddle toward her with my luggage. She smiled and submitted to a peck on each cheek.

We took a taxi to her *Firma*, in the industrial quarter of the city. She pulled a gadget out of her bag, entered a code, and a tall steel gate rolled back to let us pass. She pressed more buttons and a uniformed security guard appeared to carry my luggage. She pointed to an office tower on our right, with narrow windows between vertical columns of concrete. 'I live up there,' she said. 'On the top floor.' She entered another code on her gadget and we rode up in a private elevator that had only one stop, the top floor. Her apartment looks onto a meagre rooftop garden, beyond that stretches an expanse of industrial rooftops, with a distant view of the barge traffic on the Rhine. Inside, the decor is severely modern, in black and white, except for three large, striking paintings on the walls of the entrance hall. Each is at least two metres tall and one and a half metres wide.

The walls radiating from the hall are curved, as though designed to hide the entrance to each room. The door to one of them was open, and I caught a glimpse of a wall covered in framed photographs. The most prominent is of a young man in his mid twenties. The others trace his childhood into his teens. If I saw any resemblance to Sarah it was subtle. His eyes seem to have a startled look, as though he were about to bolt. The other walls are covered in paintings, some quite small, others larger, and several seem to be work in progress. There is also a bed and a desk but the room doesn't look lived in.

'Looks like there's an artist in the family,' I said.

'My son. As you can see, he has talent.' She said she herself had none of our father's talent, couldn't draw a house that didn't look like a five-year-old's effort. But our father's genes seemed to have leapfrogged a generation and come out in her son.

And his father?

'He died when our son was only four.'

'I'm sorry,' I said.

We snuggled into swooping winged chairs that turned out to be surprisingly comfortable, and she popped a bottle of champagne, 'To celebrate our reunion.' I hadn't asked why she lived on the top floor of her office tower but she volunteered an explanation. 'It's convenient,' she said, 'And I have no use for a cute 19th century mansion in a posh neighbourhood. I don't *entertain*.' She asked about my family and I told her, also about Uncle Knalz, Groote Graeta, and Taunte Liese, but she was interested only in our mother. 'You have no idea who he was? That man who told her you had sent him?'

None. The first I heard of him was when I got to Paraguay.

'Well, at least she still had Katya, if no one else,' she said.

If no one else? I could have pointed out that she too had abandoned our mother, when she got on a bicycle and fled from Berlin, but I held my tongue. 'That was quite a story about you, in that magazine.' I said, 'But you didn't mention how painful it must have been to leave your family.' I let that hang in the air for a moment. Then I said, 'So you've done well, and it doesn't surprise me.'

'Puh,' she said, 'the *Wirtschaftswunder,* haven't you heard? With a little help from the Marshall Plan. Suddenly there was money, and cheap credit.' But she'd also been very lucky, she said. After her escape from Berlin she had begged and scrounged, she and the rats competing for scraps in garbage bins. In fact, she was going through a garbage bin across from a machine shop, still half buried in rubble, when she saw a stooped old man trying to tie a 'Help Wanted' sign onto a metal gate. 'Apply within.' He turned out to be the owner of the machine shop, and seemed to be struggling with the sign. So she had stepped up and told him to let her do it. She tied it to the gatepost where it could better be seen, and then she asked, 'Help for what?' 'Clerical,' he said. Then she took the sign down and handed it back to him. She could do clerical, she said.

That's our Sarah, I thought. The story about her in the magazine had described how she had rapidly made herself indispensable to her employer, how she had put the business back on its feet, and eventually she and her employer were married.

No, it wasn't love, she said, though there was respect and some affection on both sides. He wasn't as old as he looked, only in his late forties, and he'd lost his whole family in the war – his wife in a bombing raid and his two sons at the front. He was a broken man, she said. He tried to keep the business going out of a sense of duty to his employees, but his heart wasn't in it. When he saw she had a knack for business he had left more and more of the management of the *Firma* to her, and devoted himself to breeding passenger pigeons.

The shop had manufactured safes and locks of all kinds, big, heavy cast-iron things, with double and triple doors. 'After the war you didn't have to be a genius to see people were obsessed with security,' she said. 'As soon as people got a roof over their heads, they put three padlocks on their door.' So she hit upon the idea of a lock as a kind of mousetrap, with little wires and electronic sensors instead of mechanical pins and tumblers. Even before her husband died, she said, she had begun to change the *Firma* into a modern manufacturing plant. Loans were easy to get for anything that was 'modern.'

I said she was too modest. I said the story in the magazine, *The New German Business Woman,* had lavished praise upon her business acumen.

She closed her eyes and took a deep breath. 'Yes, there was that . . . that thing.'

That 'thing'? The magazine had described her as 'secretive' and 'reclusive.' The caption under her photograph was, '*Germany's mysterious Queen of Security.*'

'Those magazine people offer you celebrity,' she said, 'and they don't like it when you decline the offer.' They assumed she had something to hide, and started 'snooping around.' It was better to co-operate. She said they would have loved to hear lurid personal stuff, like her back-alley abortion, but they had to be content with rape – and stories of petty scandals the police had exposed about organized crime, thanks to her *Firma's* covert surveillance technology. That was enough to cast her as some kind of 'voodoo witch of security.'

'What were they looking for, when they started . . . snooping around?'

'They found out I'd worked for the *Bürgermeister* in that town near Danzig at the end of the war. That could make me an accomplice in Nazi war crimes.'

'For doing clerical work in a mayor's office?'

'It wasn't only stuff about street cleaning and property taxes that came across my desk,' she said. 'The *Bürgermeister* was a scoundrel. He acted as an agent for the SS at Stutthof – the slave labour camp.' She said the camp was supposed to be run like a business, even turn a profit, so the prisoners, mostly Jews, were leased to factory owners, and owners of big estates to bring in the harvest. The average rate was about 280 *Reichsmark* per week, for 100 prisoners. 'The applications for slave labour in our *Gebiet* went through my office,' she said. The *Bürgermeister* organized the delivery of the prisoners in covered troop carriers, and supplied some of the guards. 'For which the SS gave him a 10% cut.'

'And you knew about this?'

'Knew about it? I negotiated the terms of the lease. Drew up the list of applicants to submit to the *Bürgermeister.* Which he then passed on to the SS *Aufseherin* in Stutthof.'

'Maybe you could have been . . . less efficient?'

'Is this an interrogation?' she said.

I held up my hands in protest. 'You don't have to tell me anything.'

Her words now became more clipped, and the tone unyieldingly level. 'What I *could* be was corrupt,' she said, 'I became part of the *Bürgermeister's* scam.' She said he wasn't content with only a 10% cut. He had an underground network of trusted guards, including an *Aufseherin* at a Stutthof sub camp. They would cram 12 or 20 extra prisoners into a boxcar, or troop carrier, and the *Bürgermeister* would distribute them among his select 'clients' – at a third of the official SS rate. He pocketed half of the proceeds and divided the rest among his accomplices. She said these transactions could hardly be hidden from her, so she too received a share, to assure her silence. She said at first she was too afraid to refuse, and then she saw a chance to maybe do some good.

She said two of the regular applicants for slave labour had caught her eye because they had Mennonite names. Hundreds of Mennonites lived in that area, she said, been there since their ancestors left Holland. And a few had become rich landowners. One of them, Otto Franz, or Franzen, was known to be particularly brutal. His Jews didn't last long before they had to be replaced, and he was one of the *Bürgermeister's* biggest clients. The other was Werner Klaassen, who was rumoured to be more humane. She said it was even rumoured that he had once delivered lunch to his prisoners while they worked in his fields, and been severely reprimanded for it. He was *not* among the *Bürgermeister's* clients. So she had slipped a note into his receipt when he came by to pay for his allotted Jews, asking him to meet her in the waiting room at the train station later that day. When she explained the *Bürgermeister's* scam to him he said he had suspected as much. Then she proposed her own scam. He should drop a few hints to the *Bürgermeister* that he knew what was going on, and in return for his silence he should demand his fair share of cut-rate prisoners.

'So now, thanks to you, he got all his slave labour at a bargain price,' I said.

She gave me a long steely stare. 'No. He still paid the official rate for his legal Jews. The illegal Jews he got through the *Bürgermeister's* network were on no official list. So he never had to explain their *disappearance* to the SS. How many Jews did *you* save?'

I hung my head. 'I tried to save one,' I said.

'But you didn't?'

'No.'

'Hmm.'

'Did you take that risk because this Klaassen was a Mennonite?' I said.

'No. Because I heard rumours he was trying to save a few Jews. But I don't think *he* would have trusted *me* if he hadn't noticed I also had a Mennonite name. Apparently that still meant something to him. And maybe it did mean something to me too. He asked where I was from and I told him.' She said when they met again a few days later, he told her he was now on the *Bürgermeister's* list of clients, and he would pass his illegal Jews on to other farmers, small farmers he could trust, who would hide them or treat them well until the war ended.

'Were there no SS guards on the estate?' I asked. 'Was there no roll call every morning and night, to make sure all the prisoners were accounted for?'

'All the legal prisoners *were* accounted for. The illegal Jews were on no list. The *Bürgermeister* could not report his suspicions to the SS without incriminating himself.'

'And you all got away with it?'

'By the time the *Bürgermeister* got suspicious that we were scamming his scam it was too late to do anything about it. The Russians were at the door and he had to scramble to make his own escape.' She said she had managed to track down Klaassen's family after the war. They had escaped to the British Zone, but he had died two years later. She didn't know how many of the Jews he saved survived, or were caught again before the war ended.

'Did our mother know what you were doing?'

'She had a vague idea, and she was afraid I'd be caught, but she wanted to help. As you know, she was working in a factory sewing uniforms for the army. I said she could help by stealing material from the factory and sewing a few civilian outfits for men and women. She asked what kind of clothes and I told her anything that didn't have stripes. And not to worry about the size. People could be found to fit them.'

Of the three of us, Antoine, you, me, and Sarah, who would have thought it would be she who would actually do something good?

I now know that this Klaassen was probably not typical of Mennonites in Germany. Too many of them were all too willing to be complicit in Nazi horrors. What had happened to our people, Antoine? For almost 400 years they stood apart from the world. Through all the highs and lows of

European history, through the Thirty Years War, through the Enlightenment, and through all the reigns of the Great Fredericks and Kaiser Willies, they kept their faith. Then at the worst time in European history they wanted part of the 'action' and became fleas on the back of a rabid dog.

I stood up, and studied the paintings on the walls. Some were indeed striking. Some covered almost the whole wall, and there was a line of smaller paintings that called to mind Russian icons. The colours were brilliant, the blues, golds, and reds, as though they'd been done in stained glass rather than oil. Some of the figures resembled saints but without halos. They seemed to shine through a gauzy, tattered veil that shrouded them.

'Where is your son now?' I said.

She gulped down the last of her champagne, set down the empty glass on the table, and stared at it. 'In a monastery. On the Greek island of Paros. He's become a monk. He wants nothing to do with me.'

'You don't have to tell me if you don't want to,' I said.

'After that back-alley abortion, and the rape, I didn't know if I could have children,' she said. 'It took a little help from medical science. I wanted there to be at least one person in the world I could love.'

This was not the bristly Sarah of a few minutes ago. 'He wanted to be a great artist. Not just a successful artist, certainly not a rich kid with a hobby. But he was painfully shy.'

Did she go, often, to Paros, to see him?

She went, but she couldn't see him. There were only the abbot and four monks left, at the monastery. The abbot was an old Englishman. He wasn't the problem. It was her son. He locked himself in his cell when she went to see him. 'The abbot came out, dithering old fool, and said he was sorry, but my son wanted no distractions from his communion with God.' She would pace in front of the gate for hours, she said, but he wouldn't come out.

Is he still painting?

'No. All he does is pray, according to the abbot.' She said he had always been a very sensitive child, and when she heard he was bullied she took him out of school and hired private tutors. That was her first mistake. It made him even less confident among people, later. He was accepted at a couple of art schools, and some of his teachers encouraged him, but he made no friends, and lasted only a year at each. His studio was on the rooftop of one of the *Firma*'s warehouses, built to his own design, and he would spend all day there, every day, painting, or modelling figures in clay. But he was so insecure about his talent. Some days, she said, he would barge into her office and drag her to his studio to show her what he had done, other days he would come home in tears, with cuts on his hand because he had slashed ten of his canvases to shreds with an x-acto knife – paintings he had worked on for months. She said he would go for days eating hardly anything at all, and rarely bathed. 'He was only twenty-six years old but looked like a famished old refugee.'

Did he not try to show his work in local galleries?

She said she scolded and cajoled until he finally did put together a portfolio and she made an appointment with the owner of a gallery across the river in Mannheim. But the day before the appointment he backed out. The paintings were unfinished, or not his best, he said.

Then she overheard one of her engineers complaining about his wife – that she had gone to a very chic gallery in Stuttgart and spent 4,000 Deutschmark on a painting his ten-year-old daughter could have done. That gave her an idea. But first she had to get her son out of his studio, and out of the city for a few days. She saw an article in one of his art magazines about an exhibition in Munich, of painters who had been active there from 1900 until World War I, the *blaue Reiter* group. 'That's exactly when your grandfather was in Munich,' she had told him. He had always been keen to hear stories about his grandfather, so she persuaded him to go and see the exhibition. While he was gone she selected six works from among the hundred he had stashed away, and drove to Stuttgart.

Sarah said the owner of the gallery was one of those plump matrons in a flouncy outfit who call everybody 'dear.' She had flipped through the paintings, selected one and propped it on an easel. 'Hmmm. Very interesting, dear. But where did you say his work has been shown?' Then Sarah offered to buy a 12% share in the gallery, as a silent partner, and slipped a cheque for 60,000 DM under her nose. She suggested that some of the money might be wisely spent on ads and 'reviews' in two art magazines.

Was that . . . proper?

It wasn't illegal, she said. What worried her more than the legality was her son's reaction when he got a letter and a cheque from the owner of the gallery, informing him that one of his paintings had sold for 850 DM. He flew into a rage, accused her of having no faith in him, using her 'influence' to get his paintings shown. But he got over it. What she did next could *not* be forgiven.

Sarah opened another bottle, topped up our glasses, and began pacing back and forth, clutching the stem of the glass with both hands. She said it was about this time that her *Firma* had begun negotiations to install a new security system in a private residence. The *Firma* had stopped doing private residences long ago, she said – her main clients were now public institutions, the police, and the military – but this was no ordinary residence. It was a walled estate that belonged to a Collector – with a capital C – who was well known in the arts community. She said there had been two thefts recently from private collections, so the insurance companies were putting pressure on collectors to beef up their security. Her friends in the police had told her the estimated value of her client's collection, so she knew what her 'parameters' were, for a state-of-the-art security system.

What *were* these parameters, I asked.

'About 990,000 DM,' she said.

'For . . . for a security system?'

For certain people, she explained, a million Deutschmark for a security system is a token of status. And when the amount her client had spent became a subject of gossip among collectors the value of his collection would increase proportionally. She said she normally let her engineers explain the technical details of the system to her clients but on this occasion she had accompanied them to the collector's estate – even though she could only repeat what she had been briefed to say. What turned out to be a more useful negotiating tactic was her keen interest in a personal tour. When he expressed surprise at her knowledge of the gems of his collection she had casually explained that her son was a very talented young artist. He politely pretended that he'd run across his name somewhere.

She asked if she could bring him to see his collection.

'But of course,' said the Collector, he'd be delighted.

It took some persuading, she said, but her son was curious to see what a 'big collector' like her client deemed to be 'great art.' The tour began with his contemporary collection, and while she swooned over names she had never heard of a week ago, her son managed little more than dismissive grunts. She feared a disaster, the least of which would be the loss of a big contract. Then they were ushered into another room, through two sets of heavy doors, and her son came to life. The room held a small collection of medieval triptychs and icon paintings. One was a small Madonna and Child. 'Oh! Oh!' he gasped, 'That's a Kazan Theotokos.'

The Collector nodded and smiled, and explained that his Byzantine collection included works from the Third Rome as well as the Second.

'What's the third Rome,' Sarah had asked.

'Moscow of course,' said her son.

'Of course,' confirmed the Collector, grinning from ear to ear.

Sarah and the Collector left her son with the Byzantine collection and returned to the main gallery. 'What was the name of that gallery again – in Stuttgart?' he asked. He took her arm, and between fascinating accounts of how certain works had come into his possession he explained that it means nothing what someone off the street pays for a painting. But if a reputable collector should buy a painting by a little-known artist? Well, critics and other collectors would take notice.

Sarah chugged the last of her champagne and slumped into her chair.

I said, 'It sounds like this story could have a happy ending.'

'It didn't,' she said.

When she got back to her office she called the Stuttgart gallery and told the woman she wanted her to double the price on her son's paintings. 'Whatever you say, dear,' she said. Then there was another meeting between Sarah and the Collector. This time without her team of engineers. Sarah told the Collector she was pleased to inform him that thanks to an ingenious design by one of her engineers, the cost of installing his state-of-the-art security system could be reduced by as much as 20%. After a few minutes of polite haggling they settled on 22%. 'It turned my stomach, what I was doing,' said Sarah. 'But I couldn't stop. I was desperate to save him.'

So did he buy one of her son's paintings?

No, but one of his collector friends did. Then she got a call from the flouncy gallery owner, and this time there was no 'dearing.' Astounding news, she reported. A Swiss collector had bought two of the paintings for 3,200 DM, and she would be very pleased to represent her son. She proposed a vernissage, and some of the 'advance' that Sarah had paid her would be spent on a professionally designed brochure and notices in three art magazines. She would invite prominent critics and the curators of two museums who were close friends. There would be photographs of her son in his studio surrounded by his paintings, with a brief biography emphasizing her son's Russian connection – i.e., his grandfather – who had been a dissident painter in the 1920s and 30s, murdered by Stalin because he refused to prostitute his art for Soviet propaganda.

The vernissage was a big success. Photos and glowing reviews in three art magazines.

'Sounds wonderful,' I said. 'Why hadn't you thought of a vernissage?'

'What I hadn't thought of, and should have, was that my collector client might have some enemies. I should have had my friends in the police check him out. But I was in heaven. And so was my son. Yes, he was still angry that I had taken six of his paintings to Stuttgart, but how could he stay angry when galleries in Berlin and Munich now begged to show his work? We went shopping for a new wardrobe. He got his hair cut and styled. Was interviewed on television. Still a bit shy but he was gracious, he glowed. Like some of those figures in his own paintings. No, it wasn't the money. It was the attention from critics. And from people who wanted to commission large works in public places. He began talking about the power of art to bloom in a spiritual desert. Oh, it was wonderful, so wonderful to see him like that. But it lasted only three years.'

She said there was a critic with considerable influence in art circles who had a long-standing grudge against her collector client. He'd been gathering evidence of 'fraudulent practices' for a decade. When he became aware that an unknown artist's work was suddenly commanding 'astronomical prices,' it didn't take long for him to discover a 'sleazy relationship' between the collector and a security company owned by the artist's mother. His target was the collector, not her son, but her son was prominent among his examples of how the collector 'brazenly manipulated the market' while artists with 'real talent' struggled in obscurity. She said he savaged her son's work. 'Puerile religious kitsch,' he called it. The papers got hold of the story and milked it for every drop of public outrage.

Of course her son was crushed. He threatened suicide, he screamed at her that she and her filthy money had trashed his work. He could have made it, eventually, on his own merit, he said. He was *not* a fraud, a true artist, but she had made him a sick joke in the art world. Those were his kindest words, she said.

Before I left the next morning we held each other in a long embrace. There were tears. On the train back to Frankfurt I shed more tears. Sarah seemed to have few friends, and those few were also her clients. She now seemed to live in a state of emotional siege, determined to exclude any thought or feeling that might make her vulnerable. Only that fierce shaft of love for her son had made a crack in the defences of this cold Queen of Security.

Two years later I got a letter from her lawyers, informing me that she was one of 82 passengers who had drowned when the ferry she was on had capsized, only a hundred metres from the port of Paros. Another attempt to see her son. Another wasted life, Antoine, more wasted love, and she once loved you too.

A RECKONING

June 29, 1992

Oh, the years, the years, too many years, Antoine. Years of vain posturing and posing. A brave face, the model immigrant, 'successful,' a teacher, with two bank accounts and framed citations on the wall. Group portrait with *pater familias* before the fall, a new house in a new country, an ample table, carving the big bird in celebration, enough, enough. Soon they will come for me, in plainclothes, politely, in an unmarked car, but what of that. I must make my own reckoning, that I owe the living as well as the dead.

In the early 1980s, our national news media began feasting on the allegations of Sol Littman of the Wiesenthal Centre – alleging Joseph Mengele himself might be living in Canada. Then he alleged that as many as 3,000 war criminals had slipped into Canada after the war, most of them Ukrainians who had been all too eager to assist the Nazis. The Deschênes Commission, set up by our Federal Government to examine the allegations, has whittled the number down to 158, but tensions between Jews and Ukrainians are still shrill. Vladimir Katriuk, Imre Finta and Ivan Demjanjuk have become household names.

After breakfast I pour myself another coffee, open my morning paper, and there it is, on page 4 – a grainy photograph spread across the top of the page. Three young Latvians are clubbing Jews to death, women and old men, and in the background a row of Nazi officers, smoking cigarettes and smiling approval. Behind them stands another man, also in uniform but of a lower rank, leaning against the door of a Mercedes, arms crossed, a bland expression on his face. He is identified as an immigrant to Canada in the early 1950s, a retired bus driver, charged with war crimes as a member of a notorious *Sonderkommission.*

I make it through my morning classes without incident. Then I take a little longer than usual to tidy up my desk before I go to the lunch room in the teachers' lounge. I know that my colleagues will have seen that photograph. There are still five of them there, seated around the long table. Their banter seems no different than on any other day. No one mentions the story in the paper – until Jack Krutch bursts through the door. He always bursts. He's a very busy man. Union Jack, we call him, because he's a big union man, and he finds the name incredibly witty, especially since he claims to be half Irish. He is the self-appointed conscience of the teachers' lounge, committed to enlighten us and give us our marching orders on any current issue, whether it's the massacre of Tamil Tigers on the other side of the world or the exploitation of Filipino nannies on our own doorstep. The word 'fascist' leaps readily to his lips, liberally applied to our mayor, to our local RCMP constable, and to the elderly cashier at the supermarket who once packed a carton of milk on top of his fresh strawberries. He always has a backpack slung over one shoulder, and his arms loaded with books and Xeroxed copies of articles from various radical journals, for his Social Issues course. He cleared a place on the table for himself and his gear and spread the paper under our noses, opened at page 4. 'Here. You guys seen this?' He was the only one of my colleagues who made a point of tossing sneering innuendos my way, which I usually ignored when I saw they embarrassed my colleagues as much as me. 'Look. This guy says he never saw any of that stuff. Just a chauffeur, he says. Well, that's him, right there. *Respectable Canadian citizen*, it says, *good family man.* Just makes yuh wanna puke.'

He shoved the paper toward me and almost spilled my soup. 'You seen this?'

'We've all seen it, Jack,' said one of my colleagues.

The lunch room cleared a little sooner than usual. I was the last to leave. I washed my utensils, carefully scrubbed them clean and dried them, then I went down to Jack's office. The door was open and he was loudly talking on the telephone, tipped back in his chair with his feet crossed on top of his desk. I swept his feet off the desk, snatched the phone out of his hand and slammed it into its cradle. I told him if he ever again made insinuating accusations against me in the teachers' lounge, I'd tear out his tongue and staple it to the door. Then I threw the remains of his coffee in his face.

I got through the rest of my classes as best I could, then I went down to Jean-Luc's woodworking shop – Jean-Luc Kowalski, son of a Polish father and French-Canadian mother from Gravelbourg, Sask., who remained a friend throughout the coming decade when my wife and I were shunned by most of our neighbours. His blue pickup would often be shamelessly parked in our driveway. You couldn't miss it or mistake it, an impeccably restored 1952 Chevy pickup, with wooden racks that glistened under five coats of hand-rubbed varnish. He teaches Woodworking to the 'toughs' and 'dummies' who are expected to drop out the day they turn sixteen, the lowest rung on the academic pecking order, even lower than Modern Business Skills. He is one of the few people I cannot imagine ever committing an atrocity, either under Stalin or Hitler. Years ago, shortly after I first met him, he told me how satisfying he found it, teaching woodworking skills to his students. 'I've seen it happen, when they get a mortise and tenon joint just right,' he said. 'They slide the two pieces together, an' when they feel the wood yield under the pressure of their thumbs, all the tension seems to drain out of their eyes – as though at that moment they feel the world is grateful to have been touched by them.' At Christmas time, he and his class of teenaged toughs make toys out of scraps of wood, little painted trains with wheels that turn, and dolls that can actually walk, and they donate them to the Salvation Army store. He had been there in the teachers' lounge at lunchtime, and I thought I owed him an explanation. 'You don't have to explain anything,' he said.

'Maybe I have to explain it as much to myself as to you,' I said. I groped for an analogy. A village is flooded in Bangladesh, I said, and one of the villagers loses a few cows and goats, swept away in the torrent. He saves what he can, and just in time he moves his family to a village on higher ground. Here the survivors exchange accounts of what they themselves have seen. A thousand miles away, in a foreign capital, people are glued to their televisions, and the newspapers carry grim photographs of the devastation. They know. They know a third of the country is under water, thousands are dead, more thousands dying of typhus and dysentery. But the villagers know little of this. They see only the wreckage immediately around them. Not till months later, when the armies of Aid Workers arrive, can they begin to comprehend the scale of the disaster. We were like that villager, I told Jean-Luc. Though it was happening all around us, we were among the last to know the scale of the horror. But what we did see should have been enough.

When I came home my daughter Margaret was waiting for me, sitting at the kitchen table with the same edition of the morning paper, open at page 4. Helena intercepted me at the back door. 'She's very upset. Be gentle with her,' she said. Margaret had assumed the worst when I seemed to be getting off scot-free, a respected teacher in spite of my Nazi past, but when war criminals became national news she became alarmed. She wanted some assurance now that I would not be one of those, that whatever crimes I had committed, they were of a lesser order. She pointed to the photo. 'Did stuff like this happen in your village?'

'No,' I said, 'not in our village.'

'You were more moral, more humane?'

Maybe, a little. We also had less occasion. Our Molotchna Colony had been almost exclusively Mennonite, I said, and when the Germans invaded, the few Jewish *apparatchiks* that had been posted to our region had fled. And maybe there's another reason, I said. Those Ukrainian and Latvian towns not only had many Jews still living among them but also able-bodied young men. We didn't. The Soviets regarded us *Volksdeutsche* as a fifth column, and before the invasion most of our men, aged 16 to 60, had been banished to Siberia before they had a chance to collaborate. So who was left to commit atrocities? Women and children, and a few old men. They are usually less keen than young men are to beat and kill people.

'Research,' I called it, and for a time my wife Helena patiently tolerated the solitary hours I spent in the basement of our suburban bungalow. I had put cheap wood panelling on the walls, spread an old rug on the floor, and lugged down our old threadbare sofa. I put a 4x8 sheet of plywood on a pair of sawhorses to serve as a desk. Every square inch is covered with books and papers. I have lending privileges at three libraries and ten shoeboxes crammed with filing cards. In Berlin, in 1945 and '46, I had probably seen more horrors than any of you down there in the basement of McNair Barracks, but had less understanding of 'the big picture.' In Paraguay I'd had no access to libraries so perhaps I now overindulge, determined to know as much of the 'big picture' as any Union Jack could throw in my face.

World War II? There was no World War II. There was a war in the Pacific between Japan and the U.S.A., and a war between Germany and the Soviet Union. The 'war' on the western front amounted to little more than diversionary excursions by the English and Americans, nipping at the heels of the *Wehrmacht*. After the Phoney War came the hasty British retreat at Dunkirk, June, 1940, and two years later the Dieppe debacle. Not until D-Day, June 1944, did the British and Americans engage the *Wehrmacht* with any resolve. Here is a breakdown by country, Antoine, of the military and civilian deaths suffered by the major combatants (I have put Canadian and American merchant navy deaths in the 'civilian' column, though this is a controversial issue):

	Military Deaths	Civilian Deaths
Soviet Union	10,800,000	14,900,000
Germany	4,440,000	3,800,000
Poland	123,000	5,300,000
Japan	1,600,000	672,000
France	210,000	390,000
U.S.A.	373,800	1,700
United Kingdom	225,700	60,600
Canada	39,700	1,400

As with all statistics, it is not only the magnitude of the numbers but the *differences* among them that tell the tale. Calculate the total number of deaths in each country as a percentage of the population and the differences become even more eloquent:

Poland (includes 2,800,000 Jews) ... 16.1%
Soviet Union (includes 1,200,000 Jews) ... 13.7%
Germany (includes 160,000 Jews) ... 10.8%

Japan ... 3.6%
France (includes 76,000 Jews) ... 1.4%
United Kingdom ... 0.9%
Canada ... 0.4%
U.S.A. ... 0.3%

Am I angry because France, England, America, and yes, Canada, failed to contribute their fair share of corpses to the war effort? Absurd. Yet I confess I grimace when I hear the boast that England and America defeated the Nazis, or when, on the date commemorating the Dunkirk 'evacuation,' I hear Churchill's famous speech played again on every newscast, his nasal Edwardian twang about that desperate rout being their 'finest ow-wah.'

After the battle of Stalingrad, in February 1943, Winston Churchill and Averell Harriman met with Stalin and his entourage in Moscow to discuss the opening of the long promised 'second front' in the west, to take some of the pressure off Soviet forces. And Churchill, in grand Churchillian style, emphatically assured his Soviet allies that 'the British people are fully resolved to continue the struggle against these Naaazi swine.' Stalin smiled and exchanged a quick look with his entourage, who rolled their eyes at the ceiling. They knew the strategy of their western allies was to let Germany and the Soviet Union bleed each other to death, then come in and mop up the spoils.

In their letters home to their mothers and sweethearts, Canadian servicemen in England complained bitterly of boredom. For months and months now they have been in England, they complain, and then it is a year, then two years, their training completed long ago, and still they have seen no action, have yet to lay eyes on their first German. For the hundredth time they are ordered to polish their new-shined boots.

Historians now caution us that the figure for the Soviet Union – 13.7 per cent of the population – is misleading. Too low, because it is spread over the whole of the Soviet Union. Most of the dead came from the European republics of the USSR. One out of five Ukrainians was killed (20%), and one out of four Belarusians. And now an esteemed Yale historian has calculated that over a fourteen year period, 1931 to 1945, *half* of the population of Belarus and *a third* of Ukraine was either shot, starved to death, or deported. No other countries in Europe have ever suffered

such a fate. And that is the cesspool of carnage where I spent my childhood and youth. Sometimes it is not the differences but the *sameness* of
the numbers that tells the tale:

Deaths during *eight* months of the London Blitz,
September 7, 1940 to May 11, 1941: **24,000**
Jews murdered in *two* months in the town of Berdichev, Ukraine,
July 13 to September 15, 1941: **22,000**

Here is a lopsided bouquet of sixes and zeroes, Antoine, including my
own contribution to the carnage:

Total number of deaths in World War II: .. 60,000,000
Total number of Jews murdered by Nazis: .. 6,000,000
Number of Germans killed by Allied bombers: .. 600,000
Number of English killed by German bombers: .. 60,000
Estimated number of Nazis who fled to Argentina: .. 6,000
Coal consumption of all 52 Auschwitz ovens (kg./hour): .. 600
Number of *Waffen SS* who were refused entry to Canada: .. 60
Number of people I have killed: .. 6

Are you staggered by these numbers, Antoine? Are your knees beginning to wobble? Yes, I know, I know. Numbers, no matter how huge, do not
make our knees wobble, they make our eyes glaze over. They paste a veneer
of rationality upon the hideous, make it appear inevitable. There have been
times, sitting at my table at three or four in the morning, when I took a pen
in my fist and gashed a big X through them. And yet I return to them, like
an old pervert who can't resist another peek at pornography. Do I think
that unfurling these numbers like a banner somehow honours all those
dead? That a bunch of zeros following one or two crooked digits consti-
tutes a fitting monument? Or do I imagine those numbers mitigate my own
crimes? That the scale of the carnage dwarfs those 247 killed at a railway
station near Stutthof. Or is it the opposite. A grim determination to keep
the horror from fading? To keep it visceral? So I can be wracked by guilt?

There was a time when Helena would come down the stairs in her
pyjamas at two or three in the morning, lean over my back and wrap her

arms around my neck. 'Enough now,' she would say, 'Come, come to bed,' and I would kiss her arm and promise I would. But that time is past. Even before I retired from teaching it could no longer be called research. Obsession was the only word for it. Now I sit here, bleary eyed, a cold pot of coffee at my elbow, poring over survivors' accounts and statistics. Then I hear Helena stirring in the bedroom above me, hear the thump of her feet going toward the washroom, hear the door close, hear the toilet flush. Then thump, thump, thump to the head of the stairs, a pause, then thump, thump, thump, back to our bedroom. I wait till she is back in bed, then return to my research.

Doktor Vik said I needed help. Not himself, he said, it should be someone with whom I would have a purely professional relationship. First he recommended a Jungian analyst, 'a top-notch fellow,' he said, 'with a roster of patients that included television personalities and the wives of former Premiers.' Later he recommended stronger medicine. 'There are drugs now that could help you, you know.' He offered to do all the paperwork, so that it would be covered by my health insurance. What was I afraid of?

Afraid? Perhaps. I am not eager to let someone take control of my mind. I have done that too often. And after the drugs have routed my demons, what other demons might rush in to occupy the brain cells so hastily vacated? New, respectable, medically approved demons? Designer demons, called in to gentrify the neural neighbourhood? No, I have developed a perverse loyalty to my old demons. They are like children gone very wrong, but you can't disown them on that account. Or like crafty old enemies for whom you develop a grudging respect. To rout them with an assault of chemicals would be a cowardly absolution.

Apocalypse was thick in the air in the inter-war decades, not only among the literati but shouted from political podiums, leaping off the pages of newspapers, the message appropriately coarsened for mass consumption. You knew well, Antoine, how passionately bourgeois liberalism was despised then. And by the most brilliant minds of the age, whether of the Left or the Right. The Marxists and fellow travellers were matched rant for rant by fascists and proto-fascists – Heidegger, the sage of Freiburg, Carl Jung, Gottfried Benn, the Italian Futurists, Maurras and Bonnard, Drieu la Rochelle, and Yeats, Eliot, Pound – *Blut und Boden* boys, every one of them, whatever their *Blut* or *Boden* – French, Irish or German.

> *Odour of blood on the ancestral stair!*
> *And we that have shed none must gather there*
> *And clamour in drunken frenzy for the moon.*

W. B. Yeats, Ireland's greatest, most famous poet. *We are here to consider the terror that is to come,* he wrote, in the voice of Michael Robartes, one of his visionary masters. *Love war because of its horror,* he wrote, *that belief may be renewed, civilisation reborn. We desire belief and lack it. Belief comes from shock and is not desired.*

Yes, Yeats knew, better than most, the violence that was to come, could feel it in his bones, and he knew that always, when the cities lie in ruin, it is the coarsest and most brutal who are most fit to survive. And still he prayed, *Send war in our time, oh Lord,* that we may be cleansed of the modern disease and once again *gaze upon the world with ecstatic eyes.*

Stand back, Antoine, give me room to rant. When the Nazis appointed Jung president of the *Allgemeinen Ärztlichen Gesellschaft für Psychotherapie* he acclaimed Hitler as a *world-historical phenomenon,* the heroic *visionary* the whole world has been waiting for, *the truly inspired shaman,* destined to lead his people to greatness. His is the voice *which magnifies the inaudible whispers of the German soul until they can be heard by the German's conscious ear,* Jung wrote in 1938. *Hitler is the first man to tell every German what he has been thinking and feeling all along in his subconscious about German fate, especially since the defeat in the* [First] *World War. Hitler's power is not political, it is magic,* he wrote. Sounded like fun, in 1938.

'Jung! That *mamzer!* That *chazer!*' said Seymour. It was he who had inspired my 'research' into Jung. It was one of our last days together on our park bench after walking our dogs, and I had become a little annoyed by his name dropping. He seemed to know personally every politician of note and every press baron in the province. And he seemed no less on first-name terms with the 'giants' of the modern age – as though every modern idea was a Jewish *shtick* – from Marx to Freud to Einstein's theory of relativity. That's when I became testy – the only time I remember us getting testy. I was determined to let him know that my social set wasn't limited to a few hicks from the Paraguayan Chaco. As casually as I could I informed him that one of my friends was a famous psychiatrist, 'one of the top men in his field.' And then I started in on Jung. According to my psychiatrist friend, I said, Jung had delved much more deeply into the mysteries of the human psyche than Freud, had drawn upon a wealth of myth and folklore and discovered dark corners in the subconscious mind Freud had never dreamed of. On and on I went, parroting what I'd heard Doktor Vik pontificate at one of his dinner parties. 'It's not all a Jewish *shtick*,' I said. 'Last I heard, Jung's foreskin was still intact when they buried him.'

'So stick it in a jar an' pickle it,' said Seymour. 'Put it in a museum. Charge admission.' Seymour's dog had been prancing in front of him with a stick in his mouth, trying to get his attention. Seymour jerked it out of his teeth and threw it as far as he could. '*Mishegas!*'

'Look, I'll explain you,' he said. 'For us Jews all that therapy stuff is just schmoozing. It's all family. Same as you. You got a priest in the family, you go to mass. Doesn't mean you believe the stuff.'

'I thought you Jews were keen on therapy,' I said. 'You're always talkin' about it. Take Woody Allen.'

'So take him already. The *goyim* think he's a cute little yid. A yiddish Little Black Sambo. Instead of Old Swanee River you get pithy quotes from Wittgenstein. Bagels an' blintzes instead of munchin' on a watermelon.'

'Sorry. I meant no offence,' I said. Not quite true. I did.

'Jung is just Freud with better table manners,' he said, 'to make him fit company for your elegant *goyim*. Instead of sex and kaka – an' horny little *shmekels* who wanna *schtup* their mamas – you get *animus* and *anima*. An' some spooky *archetypes* that go bump in the night – that make yuh wanna pull on a pair of jackboots an' release the beast within.' He called his dog and they left.

After the war Jung hardly missed a beat. Fell in step with the new righteousness by turning his *Völkisch* racist theories upside down. *All Germans share a collective guilt for the crimes of the Nazis*, he now declaimed, *whether they were Nazis themselves, members of the army, anti-Nazis, or even refugees.* Not their *actions* but their *race* make them all culpable. The whole German people has been *demoniacally possessed*, he announced. *It is no chance that the German chief of propaganda, Göbbels, should be singled out for having a club foot, that ancient sign of the demoniacally possessed man.* And those anti-Nazi Germans who had fled to Switzerland in fear for their lives were as culpable as their Nazi pursuers. He had psychoanalyzed some of these German refugees when they arrived in Switzerland, said Jung, and he had discovered they were as *demoniacally possessed* as the Nazi leaders themselves.

Presumably the prim Swiss, even those who had been awe-struck admirers of Hitler in the 1930s, like Jung himself, were *possessed* of nothing more alarming than an occasional urge to let fly a *demoniac* yodel.

'Those were just a few bourgeois crackpots,' said Margaret. 'Most normal people never believed that stuff.'

'Too many believed,' I cried. Where were they, then, where among all that ecstatic clamour were the voices of reason and sanity? Where were the New Dealing, Lloyd George-ing bourgeois liberals? *Mishegoyim!* as Seymour would say. The New Dealers and Lloyd Georgers were reduced to petulant mumbling by the more passionate hot-gospelers on their Left and Right, now cosying up to one, now the other.

Not a single voice raised in passionate protest? Yes, one, Antoine. Coming from, of all places, the Vatican. Pope Pius XI. Among popular historians the weak-kneed opposition of Pius XII seems to have muffled his predecessor's burning cry of anguish. *Mit brennender Sorge,* begins the encyclical of Pius XI, March, 1937. Then follows, in very undiplomatic language, a denunciation of the *insidious idolatry* of *Nazi paganism,* all that whoo-whoo Nordic nonsense, the cult of the *Führer,* the *mad prophet Führer,* and the Nazi's racial theories – specifically the *hateful movement of anti-Semitism.* A translation of that encyclical was smuggled into Germany to be proclaimed simultaneously from every Catholic pulpit on Palm Sunday, March 21, 1937, before the Nazis had a chance to stifle it.

In response, the Nazis impounded the Catholic presses and imprisoned a few hundred priests, nuns, and bishops. Outside Germany, the leaders of the Western democracies hardly reacted at all – a *conspiracy of silence.* Our very own Prime Minister, William Lyon Mackenzie King had a private chat with Hitler three months later, June, 1937, and in his diary he wrote, *My sizing up of the man as I sat and talked with him is that he is really one who loves his fellow man and his country. . . . His eyes impressed me most of all. There was a liquid quality about them which indicated keen perception and profound sympathy.* Even after the *Anschluss,* after *Kristallnacht,* right up until the invasion of Poland in September 1939, Chamberlain and other Western leaders continued to fall all over each other, outdid one another signing pacts and agreements, to appease Hitler.

Again I hear Helena's thump, thump above me and hear the door to the basement open. She comes halfway down the stairs. She doesn't look at me. She sits down on the step and leans forward till her head, cupped in her hands, almost touches her knees. After a long three or four minutes she stands up and turns to face me. I can see tears on her cheek. 'You're making your remorse voluptuous,' she says. She would say that, she who has spent hours at her potter's wheel and felt the voluptuous clay writhe between her hands. She would know the sensation.

Then at the breakfast table, bleary-eyed after yet another tortured night. 'I got a call from Agnes this morning,' said Helena. She is my wife's cousin and one of her oldest friends, who now lives in Toronto.

'She's well?'

I knew Helena had told her little about the 'proceedings' against me, but others would have told her more. She would be coming to offer her 'support,' and maybe invite Helena to go back to Toronto with her, for at least a week, to get a break from all this 'stuff.'

'She's coming for a visit, arriving tonight.'

'That's not much notice,' I said.

'Her flight gets in at 9:10,' said Helena, 'I'll pick her up at the airport. It'll be late when we get home.'

'There'll be a pot of coffee waiting for you,' I said.

The next morning I busied myself making breakfast for them, chatted amiably for a few minutes, then made my excuses and left so they could talk. Aimless drives zigzagging across the prairie have become a habit. I crawl into my little brown VW and drive. The car is like my carapace and I, a tortoise huddled inside. I drive in all weather, snow and blazing heat, with only the wind and the drone of the car's tires to accompany me. There are times when the drone is a soothing lull and times when it's like the howl of demented furies, and I don't know if I drive to flee them or pursue them. Again I found myself on the edge of that coulee where I had been with Sara. The road winds down to the bottom, more like a deep canyon here than a mere coulee, a ragged gash across the flat prairie like an open wound, as though a giant's gnarled fingers had clawed through the crust of the earth, then pulled back the raw flesh to expose a tangle of internal organs, orange sandstone bluffs eroded into vertical spurs like the inside of a ribcage. The river winds far below, its course clogged by grasping green willows, a narrow rusty bridge spans a flat bed of gravel. I yield to the siren illusion that if I enter this abyss the giant's fingers will release their grip and the earth will close over me, to entomb me, or enwomb me.

On a hot summer day the road is a ribbon of glistening asphalt descending to a netherworld of drooping willows and shimmering poplars. The bottom beckons, the stillness, the peace. It would be so easy. Put the car in neutral and let it go, gathering speed. The turn at the bottom is a sharp left across the bridge. 'The heat made the asphalt greasy,' they would say, 'and there was the glare of the sun, a moment's lapse of concentration.' Causes could be found to explain it.

I held back. I drove down into the coulee with deliberate care, in second gear, yet despite my care I scraped the front fender along the steel rail of the bridge. I smelled burning rubber and stopped. I got out and yanked on the damaged fender to free the wheel, my eyes blurred by tears of humiliation. Then up the other side of the coulee, one more curve and I was again on the open prairie.

It was late afternoon when I got home. There was no sign of either of them and Helena had left no note. I made myself a sandwich and grabbed something to read. When I saw the headlights of Helena's van turn into the driveway it had been dark for hours. She took off her jacket and went into the kitchen. I followed. 'I hope you left me something to eat,' she said, 'I'm famished.' She put yesterday's leftovers in the oven and sat down at the table.

I sat down opposite her, and fumbled with the salt and pepper shakers. 'What happened?' I said. 'Where's Agnes?'

'She caught an earlier flight back.'

'And you're still here.'

'Of course.'

I reached across the table, took her hand and pressed her fingers to my mouth.

'What's this?' she said, a coy smirk on her face, 'What else you got in mind?'

I don't deserve her, Antoine.

. . .

counted on him for advice on how to mollify his superiors, though he was
too stupid to sense when that advice was ironic. I told Seymour it was
this chauffeur who had explained to me why Dupke seemed so preoccu-
pied – he was busy acquiring Swiss francs and false papers for himself
and his family, to make his escape when the inevitable would happen.

'Sounds like you were sitting pretty,' said Seymour, 'a good place to
wait out the war.'

I hated the work, and hated myself for doing it. Some of the lads I had
trained with were stumbling through the Pripet Marshes, hungry, frozen,
dying, while I ate three meals a day and sat in a warm office, covering
Dupke's ass as he planned his escape. But yes, I might have stuck with it, I
said, if it hadn't been for Liuba.

'Who's Liuba?'

A Soviet sniper, I said, whom the *Gestapo* had captured behind our
lines. I explained that snipers, whether they were male or female, had a
certain glamour among rank and file foot soldiers in the Red Army. They
worked alone, like a lone wolf, and survived by their own cunning and
instinct. After she was captured they brought her to us even though a
sniper could have little information that might be useful. I told Seymour I
'interrogated' her daily for at least two weeks, but I didn't tell him I
became fascinated by her. She was pretty, quite petite, twenty years old.
She had long black hair wound in a thick braid around the back of her
head, black eyes, and a dark complexion. I guessed she must be from one
of the 'stans. 'Turkmenistan,' she said, 'but that was way back.' She said
she'd grown up near Voronezh. Her father was a policeman, and they
lived in an apartment block with the families of other policemen. There
were always guns around, and he had taught her how to shoot when she
was just a little girl. 'Maybe because he had no sons,' she said. Later he
taught her how to take care of guns, adjust the sights, all that stuff. She
was good at it, she boasted, she had won prizes. She could hit a man dead
centre in the forehead at a distance of 200 metres. Then she raised her
hands as though she were holding a rifle, took aim at me, and pulled the
trigger. 'Pftsew.' She laughed when I quickly raised my note pad in front
of my face to shield myself.

She was lively, vivacious, her hands aflutter while she talked, her face
flitting from one expression to another, scowling, laughing, teasing, even
pensive sometimes, when she tried to take a question seriously. I didn't

tell Seymour that she began to flirt with me, but maybe he guessed. 'What are you writing there?' she demanded when there was a longish pause in my interrogation while I composed my 'report' for Dupke. She jumped out of her chair, darted around my desk and looked over my shoulder at what I had written. 'What have you said about me?' She couldn't read Roman script, so she couldn't make out a single word. 'What does that say?' She stabbed the page with her finger. I had written nothing of any consequence, mere intelligence gibberish to show to Dupke, but I pretended to read what I had written: 'The prisoner claims to have shot a colonel, four captains, and countless non-commissioned officers, but it is all a lie. She probably couldn't hit an outhouse at a distance of ten metres. The poor girl is cross-eyed.'

'I am not cross-eyed!' she screamed. She grabbed my chin and made me look up into her eyes. 'Where does it say cross-eyed?' I pointed at a line on my notepad. She grabbed my pen and crossed it out with such violence that she bent the nib. 'Oops,' she giggled.

We all knew that some *SS* officers and *Gestapo* had 'camp wives,' usually a woman plucked from the forced labour brigades and given a cushy office job. It was rare that a prisoner became a camp wife, but it did happen. I knew that was Liuba's hope, that I would save her by making her my camp wife. Her sexual advances became more explicit, and I should have told her it was not in my power to make her my camp wife, me, a lowly corporal, out of favour with my superior officer. Yes, I knew that given a choice she would as soon shoot me as make love to me, or make love to me and then shoot me, and that made her brazen but not less alluring. I tried to save her. In my reports to Dupke I portrayed her as a cruelly exploited schoolgirl, who hardly merited the status of a military prisoner.

Did she shoot anyone who came into her cross hairs, whatever their rank, I asked.

She tipped her head, left, then the right. 'Of course, the higher the rank the better,' she said, and once she was lucky to shoot a general. The story was reported in *Pravda,* with a big picture of her, holding her rifle and looking very fierce. But generals and colonels are hard to find. They stay too far back behind the lines. So mostly she shot NCOs. She said she shot a fat corporal once, who was squatting behind a bush taking a shit. Of course, at that distance nobody heard the shot. Not with the noise of all those trucks and tanks moving around. Nobody even missed him. His comrades got into the trucks and moved out. Just left him lying there in his own shit. It was more fun, she said, when there were others who noticed, when, for example, somebody is just standing there talking to his comrades and suddenly he spins around and falls down, with blood coming out of a hole in his head. You should see the others then, she said. 'They don't know where to turn. No idea where the shot came from. They run in all directions.'

Did she feel no remorse, none? No moral qualms when she popped off her victims? But from where would she have summoned moral qualms? Her whole life had been spent among people for whom killing was routine. Had she ever *not* killed, when she easily could have?

'*Blyads*. It's my job,' she snorted. 'You Germans! You're trying to kill *us*.' She turned sideways, threw her arm over the back of the chair and rested her chin on her arm. We were both silent while she sulked. Then she clapped her hand over her mouth to stifle a giggle, as though a naughty thought had just occurred to her. 'Sometimes I don't shoot them if they're very, very handsome.' Then she described one such occasion. And this I did tell to Seymour.

The Germans had retaken a town and captured a Red Army unit. This was further south, she said, where there were hills covered in trees. About half way up a big hill she saw a church steeple sticking out of the trees. The church had been burned out but the tower was still standing, and from the belfry she could see the main square of the town. Through her scope she saw a ragged line of about thirty Red Army soldiers, facing another line of about a dozen German soldiers with their guns levelled at them. One of the captured soldiers was an officer, and he stood about two paces in front the others, hanging his head. Because the Germans intended to shoot him first, she assumed. And then she saw this German officer come out of one of the buildings. 'Ooo-la-la, a real handsome blondie,' she said. He was leafing through a sheaf of papers as he approached the Red Army officer, and then he started fumbling at his belt. Liuba thought he was reaching for his pistol. Instead, he pulled out a pair of little eyeglasses, and put them on the tip of his nose, 'you know, like a professor.' He started reading something from his papers, and what happened next, she said, was just disgusting. The Red Army officer fell to his knees, folded his hands and began bobbing his head up and down. He shuffled toward Blondie on his knees, waddling like a duck. 'I swear, if I hadn't shot then,' said Liuba, 'he would have kissed that German's feet.'

So she shot him? That German officer who had been fumbling with his granny glasses? If Liuba noticed the tremor in my voice she didn't let on.

'Nooo,' she drawled, 'I told you. He was very, very handsome. I shot the Russian. Fuckin' coward.'

I called for a guard to take Liuba back to her cell. When you're in Intelligence you have access to a telephone, and when you request information people don't ask why. Liuba had told me the name of the town, and before the day was out I knew which battalion had taken prisoners in that town on a specific day, and that the name of the commanding officer was Major Friedrich von Niessen. Yes him, Antoine, no longer a captain but a major now, whose men had shot me and my two chums off our perch on that windmill – where we had gone to welcome their invasion of Russia. So long ago, it seemed, though it was less than four years.

I sent a dispatch to Major von Niessen immediately, reminded him who I was, and congratulated him on the success of his counter-offensive. Then I informed him that I was presently interrogating the mysterious sniper who had shot that Red Army officer who was grovelling at his feet. Yes, she was a Soviet sniper, not one of ours, and she had intended to shoot him too but spared him because he was so handsome. Then I wrote that I would make an official request to be reassigned to the front, to one of the troops in his battalion.

'So you could die for the *Vaterland* alongside your favourite Nazi,' said Seymour. 'That's touching.'

I let that pass. I had to request the appropriate form from Dupke himself. In the space where I was required to state my reasons for asking for a transfer I wrote that it would be a great honour to die fighting for the *Vaterland,* that there was no destiny I could more devoutly wish. I filled out the form in triplicate, one copy for Dupke, one for his superiors in Berlin, and one copy for Major von Niessen.

'You're a fool,' said Dupke's chauffeur when I told him what I had done and why. 'Sit tight till the front comes closer. After Dupke absconds, you can make your own escape.'

I didn't have long to regret my decision. Dupke's heavy footfall in the corridor put an end to my last interrogation of Liuba. He strode into the room, looked at her, then at me. 'Why are you dallying with this Soviet trash? She givin' you the hots?' Then he walloped her on the side of her head. He was breathing fast, and his whole body trembled while he pointed at her. 'Tomorrow morning – at dawn. Ffft, finished. And you,' he said, pointing at me, 'you'll be on the firing squad.' He called the guards and they took Liuba to her cell. 'You better watch your ass, boy,' he said. 'You're gettin' too big for your britches.'

I had never been assigned to a firing squad, I told Seymour. It was the guards' job. As we marched into the courtyard the sergeant handed us each our rifle and told us to line up. I was fourth in line. Liuba was already tied to the post that had been placed there for the purpose. They didn't bother with the blindfold anymore. 'Good morning, comrades,' she called, in a voice that was intended to be defiantly cheery but we were close enough to see she was shaking, and I could feel her eyes boring into me. It was a cold morning, light snow falling. I remember the others cursing the weather and blowing on their fingers.

When Dupke arrived, he looked down the line to make sure I was there, smirked his satisfaction that I was, then turned to face Liuba and snapped to attention. 'Ready, aim . . .'

'No! No!' I screamed, and jumped in front of my comrades, facing them. 'No!' I waved my free hand in front of their faces, and pushed down on the barrels of their guns.

'Fire!' But no one fired. I turned on Dupke and aimed my rifle at him. He might have expected me to shoot high above Liuba's head, or maybe he expected me to shit my pants, but he didn't expect this. He took a few quick steps back, got tangled up in his jack boots and fell over, backwards, rocking on his back like an upended beetle, arms and legs flailing the air. If I had shot then I could only have shot him in the ass. He rolled over and scrambled for cover on all fours. He tripped again and fell flat on his face, and then I was on him, the muzzle of my rifle inches from his head. 'Shoot the son of a bitch!' shouted Liuba.

Then a quiet, calmer voice behind me, the sergeant's voice. 'Lift the rifle above your head. Slowly. Then step back.'

'Shoot, you idiot!' cried Liuba.

Maybe the sergeant was hoping I *would* shoot, a convenient way to get rid of Dupke, and then he would dutifully shoot me. I felt the muzzle of his pistol on the back of my neck. I stiffened. Then the moment was lost.

A blow in the middle of my back sent me sprawling face forward, and then the sergeant's boot was on my neck, pinning me to the ground. My rifle had gone off but the shot missed. 'What a farce!' shouted Liuba, 'Look at the Master Race now! A bunch of bungling idiots.' Later, locked in my cell, I heard the sergeant yell, 'Fire.' A volley of shots, and I knew Liuba was dead.

'So why didn't you shoot that Dupke, when you had the chance?' said Seymour. 'You knew you were done for, whether you did or didn't.'

'I don't know why,' I said. 'Maybe because it would have been my first time.'

The chauffeur saved me. When he came to my cell late that night he said he had found Dupke in a state of tearful humiliation when he passed by his office. He had ordered the sergeant to muster another firing squad, for me, but then he'd changed his mind. He would shoot me himself, he told the chauffeur. *Then* his men would show some respect!

Not a good idea, he'd told Dupke. Another execution, so soon after he'd shot two deserters? Wouldn't look good to his superiors. Not good at all. There'd be another investigation, and it would all come out – that he'd shot a patriotic kid who had *asked* to be transferred to the front, so he could die for the *Vaterland*. Wouldn't look good at all. And what's the point? Just approve the transfer, he'd advised Dupke. He won't last a week at the front.

'You're right!' Dupke had said, 'Let that smart-ass shit get blown to bits at the front!'

'I gotta admit, that took guts, if not brains,' said Seymour.

To tell the rest would take more guts. When the story in our local paper was published a few weeks later it stated only the bare facts, that in the last months of the war I had been assigned to an infantry battalion known to have massacred a transport of 247 Jews at a railway station in a town called Seligenbeil, but that was enough to bring out the TV crews and press photographers from Winnipeg. They pounded on our door, pressed their faces to our picture window, goggling their eyes with cupped hands, and shouted their questions from my littered lawn. I have fared better than some. Only once was I ambushed by a photographer in my back yard, who snapped a picture of me making ape-man gestures, threatening him with my hoe. I don't know what paper he was from, or if the photo was ever published.

I knew I had to tell Seymour the rest of the story. The morning after the damning report appeared in our local paper my hands shook as I put on my coat and galoshes, took Butzie's leash from its hook by the door, and set out for the park. A dull unseasonably warm April day, half the park still covered in gritty corn snow, the other half under a thin pool of water, good weather for ducks and gulls. I sat alone on our park bench and shivered. I don't know what I dreaded more, that Seymour would appear and confront me, or that he now couldn't stomach the sight of me.

He didn't come that day, or the next. Every time there was movement at the far end of the park where Seymour and Winston usually appeared my Butzie leapt to her feet, wagged her tail and whimpered. Then she lay down again.

Then they did appear. I kept Butzie on a leash so she wouldn't bolt and start romping with Winston, and I saw that Seymour was also keeping his dog leashed. But the dogs went berserk, gasping and straining, and again we were forced to let them have their way if we wanted to avoid another scene like our first meeting, getting all tangled up by their leashes in a dreaded embrace.

We didn't sit down. We stood and faced each other.

'So? Were you there? At that railway station, Seligenbeil, near Stutthof?'

'I was there.'

Seymour turned aside so I couldn't see his face. He tilted his head back, as though he were addressing the trees. 'Two hundred and forty-seven, they say, massacred. Shot.'

'It's what they say,' I said.

'And you? You say?'

'I didn't know the number until years later. After we came to Canada. They wouldn't make a mistake about that, about the number.'

'Then about what?'

'No mistakes.' Then I mumbled something about glaring lights, the bitter cold, a breakdown of discipline. Those were the only words I could get out before my voice was reduced to a whisper. 'It's not what was supposed to happen,' I said.

'You were supposed to take them to Stutthof. To be gassed. *That's* what was supposed to happen?'

'Yes. No. That wasn't our job. The train they were on had broken down. We were supposed to guard them for a few days, till we could regroup, to be sent back to the front.'

'So instead you shot them.'

'They rushed us.'

'They were armed?'

'Some had knives and clubs.'

'You had semi-automatics.'

'Yes.'

I wanted to tell him more, I wanted to tell him what I told you in Berlin, Antoine, but only if he demanded to know more. I think he struggled but he couldn't do it. He waved his hand across his face as though he would wipe me out of his vision, out of his mind. Then he turned and walked away. At the end of the park, where the path enters the trees, he called to his dog and they disappeared. The trees closed behind them and I stared at the dark hole where they had been. My first interrogation, and by far the most painful.

LOOSE ENDS

'Are you comfortable here, Taunte Katya,' I said, after her perfunctory greeting. I had written to tell her I was coming to Russia and waited for an invitation. None came, so I didn't expect a warm welcome. That was a year ago, the summer of 1991, when Gorbachev and *glasnost* gave me the courage to apply for visas to return to the Soviet Union. I had gone first to see what remained of our Molotchna Colony, then I boarded the train to Orsk – three days before the August Coup, when Gorbachev was kidnapped by a cabal of communist hardliners and hundreds of tanks and thousands of soldiers once again prowled the streets of Moscow. In spite of *glasnost* and *perestroika* it had taken almost two years of wrangling with officials at the Soviet Consulate in Ottawa to get permission to travel deep into the Soviet hinterland, to Orsk, at the base of the Ural Mountains. I knew time was running out. I still had my driver's licence, my credit card and my passport, and my bank account had not yet been frozen, but there was no knowing how long I could count on that.

Katya was in her late 80s now. I had little hope that she would tell me anything to ease my mind, yet it was my last chance to find out what had happened to my mother – and maybe get some inkling of who that mysterious man had been who appeared at Ringstrasse 107 and said I had sent him. I tried to pretend it was a friendly visit but Katya was in no mood to be softened up with small talk. 'Comfortable!' she snorted. 'You can see yourself how I live.' She gave the four walls a dismissive wave with her hands.

She lives in a white-washed one-room cottage, with a lean-to addition opposite the entrance, barely large enough for her washstand. There are two small windows with rags tucked around the frames to keep out winter draughts. The room is immaculate. There is a white enamel basin on a white washstand, and a blue plastic pitcher next to it. A narrow shelf holds her few dishes and one cooking pot. The ceiling is of rough unpainted boards, with a frayed electric cord hanging from it, but no bulb in the socket. There is no plumbing. A small oil stove is tucked into one corner, a crude commode into another, on which stands a dented stainless-steel samovar. In the middle of the room stands a wooden table, big enough for four people but there are only two chairs. The table and chairs are a faded blue. The walls are bare except for a framed Bible verse, Romans 11:32, done in tinfoil gothic lettering on a black velvety background. On the opposite wall hangs a small *Wandtschoner,* a threadbare red and black tapestry about a metre square, depicting a hunting scene.

And then there is her bed. A single bed, with a puffy eiderdown neatly folded in half and piled high with pillows and cushions rising to a pyramid that almost touches the low ceiling. The pillows are elaborately embroidered, floral patterns in bright colours, and the cushions are trimmed in a lacy material, also of many colours. In this bare, stark room, the bed looks exotic, like the bed a Turkish pasha might provide for his current favourite. Then again, the bed looks exactly like the bed in my grandmother's room when I was a child.

There is one other prominent fixture, tucked into the remaining corner. A tall table, covered with a plain white cloth that reaches almost to the floor, with an odd collection displayed on it – a stapler, a gold-plated fountain pen, a large chrome ash tray with a black ebony bull leaping over it, a cigarette lighter, a small wooden box of paper clips, an elegantly painted wooden letter opener, one black leather glove, and a framed photograph of a stern middle-aged man with hooded eyes. It was like a shrine.

She wore a long black dress, covered by a satiny black apron trimmed in black lace. Her thinning hair was severely pulled back in a bun, held by a black comb attached to a broad black bow. She sat erect on one of the two chairs, her hands folded on her lap. There was a glass of tea for each of us on the table, and a small plate with two *zwiebak*. Whenever I steered the conversation toward my mother Katya became surly and gave one-word answers to my questions, so I asked about her son, her Pavelche – that moody little brat whom my mother had commanded us to befriend, till he became a snitch during the famine and Katya had to 'give him up' – to save him from the vengeance of our village.

Surely, I said, when she took her Pavelche away she didn't think our people would harm him, like those villagers who had stoned that other Pavlov to death, the celebrated 'boy martyr' who had snitched on his parents. She said she'd done what she had to do, took him to Voronezh and left him with a relative of her husband, a Russian woman, a widow.

I said, 'Is that his photograph on the table?'

Yes, she said, all that stuff was his. It was all she had managed to save before they cleaned out his office and put a new lock on the door. He was the director of a big meat packing plant, she said, 700 workers. He was clever, a hard worker, knew how to get ahead, knew whose back to scratch and whose not. A real *Geschäftsman*, her Pavel, not like those others, incompetent Party hacks who mismanaged every enterprise they got their hands on.

She said she used to have a small apartment in her son's office building, hot water, private toilet, even a television. After Pavel's death she sold the television and her electric stove to buy this cottage.

How had she found him after all those years, after the war, and after her release from prison? Was the widow who had adopted him still alive?

No, she was dead. A few neighbours remembered. They said Pavel had joined the army. That's all they knew.

Then how did she find him.

By looking, asking. Asking other *zeks*. *Zeks* know everything, she said. They move around, from prison to prison, camp to camp. As soon as a train load of new prisoners arrives, the other *zeks* crowd around and start asking. Anyone in your group from Kamenetz? Beryansk? Rostov? Wherever. *Zeks* have good memories, she said, and they don't have to lie. On the outside, people don't talk. *Zeks* never stop talking. Never stop asking. 'Long before my term was up I knew exactly where my Pavelche was.' But after her release she couldn't simply board a train and come here, to Orsk.

Not easy for a *Nyemtzy* traitor to get travel permits, she said. It took years till she finally got here. First she got a job as a street sweeper in front of the factory gates, and sometimes she would catch a glimpse of him leaving or entering the factory compound, in his chauffeur-driven Zil. It took another year to get a job inside the plant, another year of scheming and clawing to become a floor woman in the office building, and six more months to work her way up to the fourth floor. Where his office was. Then it was her job, hers alone, to attend to all his needs. Bring him his meals, make sure no one got off the elevator whom he didn't want to see, and clean his office after he went home.

And all those years she never let him know that ... that ...

That she was his mother? Huh! She, a *Nyemtzy* and a traitor? It would have ruined his career, if his enemies found out. What could he have done if she'd confronted him, a crazy old woman who claimed to be his mother? He would have sent her away, to an institution.

I studied the photograph more closely. A round, clean-shaven face. I could find no trace of Katya's angular features, or her husband's. 'How did he die?' I said.

'The mafia killed him.'

The mafia? 'He was on his way to a cattle station,' she explained, in a flat, expressionless voice. To do some business. In the middle of nowhere, half way to the Chinese border. There was a cattle truck blocking the road, and when Pavel's chauffeur stopped the car, men jumped out of the truck and started shooting. Then they burned the car.

A wretched end to Soviet Man, I thought. I tried to block out what Katya must be feeling. If I had to be brutal to find out what happened to my mother, so be it. 'Why weren't you and my mother on that train to Bremerhaven, with the other refugees?' I said.

She had kept her eyes fixed on the blank wall in front of her while she talked. Now she turned to face me. 'Because you sent a man to the refugee centre who told us to follow him. He said you were waiting for us. Then he turned us over to the Russians.'

Her two letters to me had not made the accusation so bluntly. I tried not to scream at her. 'I never sent that man. I have no idea who he might have been.'

She shrugged. She let her gaze drift around the room as though she had never noted its contents before. 'He knew your name, even your nickname. Called you Struvel.'

'Tell me exactly what happened.'

She shrugged, then in a flat, expressionless voice she said this man took them to a house where another man was waiting. He asked to see their papers. He glanced at them, nodded and left. With their papers. Then the first man took them to a place where a car was waiting. They said they were police. They were driven to a prison in the Soviet Sector. Interrogated. Asked stupid questions that made no sense. The policemen got angry, and when one of them hit my mother she attacked him. They were beaten some more, then put on a train. To Norilsk, a prison camp near the Arctic Circle. Where my mother died on April 3, 1949. 'So are you satisfied now?' she said.

'Is that what my mother thought? That I had betrayed her?'

'She never said so,' said Katya.

I must live with the cruel ambiguity of that statement. I broke down and wept. Then I grabbed my jacket, ran out the door, and wandered the streets of Orsk until after dark.

When I returned, Katya was sitting where I had left her. She got up from her chair, fetched a light bulb from her commode and screwed it into its socket. She poured more tea. I held my head in my hands and tried to be calm. Surely, I said, my mother could never have believed I betrayed her to the Russians. For what possible reason?

Katya shrugged. 'You were working for the Amis. You and your friend Antonii. You said he knew important people. Important people are important because unimportant people do things for them.'

'You survived. But my mother didn't,' I said. 'What did *you* have to do, to survive?'

Katya heard the cruel accusation in my voice, and I knew the accusation was false, even as I made it. 'To survive you had to become a trusty,' she said, 'somebody with a cushy job, in the kitchen. Or the laundry. Down in the pit with a pick and shovel you don't last long.' She said trusties got easier work and more food, sometimes double rations. But you had to scratch and claw at the others, who wanted the same thing. 'Your mother couldn't scratch and claw, never had to learn. I could. Had done it all my life. I gave her my extra rations, and half of the rest. Maybe it kept her alive for a while. But your mother . . . she wasn't the kind who survive.'

I had expected anger in response to my accusation, a snarling denial, but there was only sadness. 'Your mother pitied them,' she said, 'the guards, the *urkas*, all those . . . bastards. And they hated her for it. They want respect, not pity. I told her, told her many times,' she said. 'Look at their feet, not at their eyes, not with eyes like yours. But she couldn't do it.' Katya kept her face turned to the wall but I could see tears streaming down her cheek.

I could bear no more of this. I could bear her anger and spite, but not this. Her profound grief conveyed my mother's suffering more sharply than any gruesome details could have done.

I took my leave. I had a train to catch back to Moscow. I got up and put on my jacket. Katya stayed seated, her back to me. I sat down again. I couldn't walk out the door and leave her like that. We were both silent for a long time. I asked if she ever found out what had happened to her husband, Boria. The name would mean nothing to you, Antoine. In fact few people seemed to remember him. He had been one of Kommissar Kaethler's lackeys, and he was not missed when he disappeared – around the same time that my father tried to escape arrest by the GPU.

'He died,' she said, 'on a prison train, before he even got to Siberia. They put him in a boxcar with non-politicals. Thugs. One of them wanted his pocket watch. It had my picture inside the cover. He wouldn't give it, so there was a fight and they knifed him.'

'My father was arrested at the same time,' I said. 'Was he also on that train?'

'They were never . . . arrested. My Boria was told to follow your father when he tried to escape, then Kaethler sent his own goons to get them – who took them to a transit prison in Kubyansk. Kaethler had an arrangement with the director. They both had their private prisoners that they kept out of the hands of the *cheka*, so they could trade them for other prisoners. Or blackmail their families.'

How did she know this? *Zeks* told her. Such things happened all the time, she said. 'They put your father in the same cell as Kaethler's other prisoner – the *barin*, your friend Antonii's father. He knew they hated each other. Kaethler had no use for my Boria anymore, so he let the NKVD have him. But he wanted to keep your father for himself.'

Keep him for what?

'For what! To toy with him. Torment him.' She said Kaethler hated all handsome, clever people. He thought they had nothing better to do with their wit than make dirty jokes about him. 'When he became a big man in the Party he wanted your mother to grovel – to keep her husband alive.'

How long did he keep them there, in that cell, my father and the *barin*?

'Six years. Till the purge of the *kulaks*.' The prisons were full to bursting, she said, trainloads arriving everyday and not enough trains to take them east. So the director of the prison told Kaethler to come get his prisoners. People were asking questions. Kaethler and one of his goons fetched them, took them to the Dnieper Dam at Chortiza. 'His goon shot them,' she said, 'wrapped chains around them and pushed them over the wall, into the river. Then Kaethler shot his goon, and pushed him over too.'

'So those three bodies – that Antonii and I found in the river when we were boys?'

'Your father, the *barin*, and Kaethler's goon.'

So at last we know, Antoine.

'Now you should go,' she said, 'or you'll miss your train.'

A long train ride from Orsk back to Moscow, then a flight to Frankfurt and another train to a little town on the edge of the Bodensee, to see Uschi again. Interrogate her. Plenty of time to mull over the questions I was determined to ask: 'What do you know about the man who came to fetch my mother? I have a right to know.' I was angry. I had been lied to.

When I stepped off the train in Lindau, my resolve faltered. Both Uschi and Gioconda were waiting for me. Gioconda shrieked with joy and came running, careening through the crowd of disembarking tourists, tottering on high heels. She has become a little plump, and I rushed toward her with all my baggage, lest she trip and fall before we could embrace. Uschi's welcome was more restrained.

Gioconda is a widow now, and she and Uschi had bought a charming house together. It overlooks the lake, with a view of the pretty little harbour, and beyond it the foothills of the Swiss Alps. They had chosen Lindau because it is close to Munich where Gioconda's two sons live but it suits them for other reasons too. The island is tethered to the mainland by a causeway but it seems to have turned its back on the mainland, and is trying to escape.

That evening I, not they, did most of the talking. The kidnapping of Gorbachev and the standoff in front of Russia's White House were still front page news. I had been in the thick of it, but they were better informed than I was, I said. I had only the narrow perspective of what I had seen with my own eyes. I had expected a tedious three-day journey from Orsk to Moscow, but on the morning of the second day I began to notice clusters of people talking animatedly together, and I caught a few snippets of what they were saying. Gorbachev is dead? No, kidnapped, not dead, not yet. A cabal of Party hardliners have seized power. Those who boarded the train en route were grilled for information but they too had only wild conjectures and speculations. Then, in the middle of the next night, in the middle of nowhere, the train stopped. Voices outside, but we couldn't hear what they were saying. We leaned forward, put our faces to the window and cupped our hands to see out. Spotlights mounted on military vehicles scanned the windows of the train. We jerked back as a spotlight swept across our window, as though the window had been sprayed with automatic machinegun fire. Then the sound of doors slamming, and the train began to move again. And I thought how common such a scene must have been throughout the Soviet period. A train stops, voices, commands, glaring lights, and inside the passengers break into a sweat, waiting for the police to enter their compartment, demanding papers, travel permits. They rack their brains. What might they have overlooked among their papers, or their luggage, to incriminate them?

When the train stopped at Marshansk there were reports of tanks in the streets of Moscow, and hundreds of people shot. Fighter jets crisscrossing the sky, and the roads clogged with people fleeing the city. Yeltsin arrested. No, not arrested. In hiding somewhere. Some people snatched their luggage and scrambled off. Should I panic and do the same?

At the Moscow station there were no taxis. Only unmarked cars picking up people with luggage and charging exorbitant rates. Six or seven of us crammed into a mid-sized Moskvitch, and before the last passenger was fully in, one foot still on the pavement, the car bolted ahead. It swerved through the crowd and zigzagged through back streets. It was past 2:00 AM when I was finally dropped off at my hotel.

The next morning I found the Canadian Embassy and was ushered into a large room already crammed with anxious Canadians. We were assured there would soon be flights out of Moscow and that every effort would be made to get us out. Back in my hotel room I became agitated. Would these embassy people know that back 'home' I was a 'person of interest' to the RCMP? I was in the Soviet Union, so I reverted to a Soviet mentality.

'You must be exhausted,' said Uschi, but I slept little that night, and in the morning I put off the questions I had come to ask. I talked about Katya and her son Pavel. Gioconda said she couldn't believe it. She said she could believe that a mother would make the search for her lost son the consuming passion of her life, but she could not believe that having found him, having manoeuvred herself into a position where she was in daily contact with him, she would not tell him she was his mother. 'She must have deluded herself,' said Gioconda, 'created a fantasy that she dare not shatter by declaring herself, because in a part of her brain she knew that man was not her son.' Perhaps Gioconda was right.

That night, after dinner, Gioconda made us coffee, set the cups on the table, and Uschi lit the first of the many cigarettes she would permit herself that evening. 'There are things we have to tell you,' said Gioconda, 'things Uschi has to tell you.'

So it was out of my hands now.

'The man sent to fetch your mother was one of Viktor's men,' said Uschi. 'One of his sleazy agents.'

I gasped, yes, but I was not as stunned as I might have been. Over the years I had tortured myself, speculating how Doktor Vik might be involved in my mother's fate but I had tried to dismiss these speculations as absurd. 'What possible interest could Doktor Vik have had in my mother?'

'He wanted her papers,' said Uschi, 'like the document you were all issued when you crossed into the *Reich* at the end of your trek, and that document the Mennonites had issued to the refugees. He told us he needed those papers to get Antoine's woman out of Germany.'

What woman? Antoine had a woman in Berlin?

'Don't you remember how he would sometimes disappear for two or three days?' said Uschi. 'And when we asked him where he had been, he got testy. He would put together a big bag of food and clothes, and then I saw the clothes were women's clothes. If he hadn't been so secretive about it maybe I wouldn't have flown into a jealous rage.' She said you did try to explain, but she demanded to see this woman with her own eyes, and you had finally consented. But she would have to watch from a secluded distance, you had told her, because fear had driven this woman mad. She was living in a room in the British Sector, like a frightened animal. 'If she sees you she'll go berserk,' you told Uschi, 'she'll think I've betrayed her.'

Ushi said she watched you go up some crumbling stone stairs and knock on a door. She could see you talking through the door and put your ear to the door to listen. Then the door opened and Uschi saw a tall woman, old, with wild white hair. 'She dropped to her knees, blubbering and kissing Antoine's hands.' Uschi said she waited a long time there, in the dark, and when you came back you were angry. 'So are you satisfied now?'

Little by little you told Uschi this woman's story, that she had been your nanny in Russia, the only mother you knew as a child, that she had got you out of Russia when you were about to be arrested, and took you to Germany to be reunited with your birth mother. And then to Argentina. You said your mother had lost her mind, become a helpless child, and it was this woman who had fought with your rich uncle for every penny to take care of your mother – for doctors, and for your education.

Shall I go on, Antoine? 'I know that woman,' I said. 'Her name is Mary Gordon. How did she end up in Berlin after the war?'

'Apparently she had become a zealous Nazi in Buenos Aires,' said Uschi, 'Like many of the German expats there. Antoine said she was particularly enamoured of the glamorous Mitford sisters – Unity and Diana. Every week there were pictures of them in the English magazines she subscribed to. Them and that Mosley fellow, Diana's Nazi husband. Pictures of them at the Nuremberg rallies, making the Heil Hitler salute, or dining with Hitler himself, their arms around each other.' Uschi said she remembered seeing the same pictures in the German glossies. And remembered her mother jeering at them. 'Antoine said this woman was like a star-struck school girl. She tried to emulate them. She began to put on airs. Gave herself a pedigree, like the Mitford sisters – claimed to be a direct descendant of some famous Patrick Gordon, who had been Peter the Great's naval architect. Antoine said she had jokingly made the same claim back in Russia, but now she made it in earnest. He said as soon as his mother died, he left Buenos Aires for Paris. And this Mary Gordon came back to Germany, to offer her services to the Nazis.'

Uschi said when she demanded to know why that woman was so terrified you had finally told her. At first the Nazis used her to broadcast their propaganda to England, but it hadn't worked out because she would spit venom against the English, that they had been stupidly duped by the Americans and the communists in their midst, that they must ally themselves with Germany against the Soviet Union. After that she was given other assignments, until she ended up a guard at a concentration camp. At Stutthof. Near Danzig. Toward the end of the war, you told Uschi, there were several female guards there, and after the Russians liberated the camp, five or six of them were tried and hanged.

I said I remembered seeing the gruesome photos in the newspapers, six women hanging from their gallows, all in a row, and I remembered the reports about the horrible things they had done.

'But this Mary Gordon, she escaped,' said Uschi, and she was the reason you had come to Berlin, to find her and get her out. That's what your 'business' with Viktor had been about. She said you provided him with information about what you had overheard at those big meetings with Colonel Simpson, and in return Viktor would use his ratline connections to get Mary Gordon out of Germany.

'No. No,' I said. I looked at Gioconda. She stared down at the table with big eyes. I turned back to Uschi. 'So my mother was sacrificed to save Mary Gordon? She too loved him, like her own child!' I whispered, 'She too saved his life – more than once.' Maybe I didn't whisper, maybe I shrieked.

Uschi tried to salvage a few pieces of the wreckage. 'Antoine didn't know about your mother's part in Viktor's plan till it was too late.' She said Doktor Vik had got all excited when he heard the Mennonites had chartered a ship to get their people out of Germany. 'The perfect plan.' Mary Gordon would be provided with false documents, given a 'Mennonite name,' then his agents would get her through the Soviet Zone to Bremerhaven. And onto the ship that would take her to Buenos Aires. 'These Mennonites here in Berlin, they don't stand a chance of getting out,' Viktor had told you, 'But that ship in Bremerhaven is sailing on January 31st. With or without them.' He said his man in Bremerhaven would stage a dramatic last minute arrival at the dock, just before the ship sailed. Mary Gordon wouldn't have to open her mouth. His agent would present her documents, with her Mennonite name, and explain she'd been struck dumb by all her suffering. 'By the time those Mennonites get suspicious they might have a war criminal on board, the ship will be in international waters,' he chuckled. 'All they can do is hand her over to the police when they get to Buenos Aires – who don't give a shit what she did during the war.'

Uschi said she had been delighted with Viktor's plan, when you first told her. She so desperately wanted that mad woman out of Berlin, and out of your life. 'But then Antoine proposed that his agents should take all three of you – Mary Gordon, your mother, and you – through the Soviet Zone to Bremerhaven. And that's when it all came out,' said Uschi. 'Viktor said that wouldn't be a good idea. Couldn't have two women show up at the dock, both claiming to be Sonya Enns, one of whom had lost her documents.'

'He thought he was so clever,' said Uschi. She had screamed at him, 'You're mad!' But all he did was chuckle. He said there had been no time to get forged documents, so he had to 'relieve' one of the refugees at that MCC house of her documents. 'That's when Viktor told us he had sent one of his men to lure your mother out of the house on the Ringstrasse, she and that woman who wouldn't let your mother out of her sight. He brought them to a house where Viktor was waiting. He said he took their documents and instructed his man to hold them for a day, then take them back to the refugee centre.'

Uschi said you had grabbed Doktor Vik by his lapels, shook him and cursed him. And when you released him it took a few moments before Doktor Vik could compose himself. 'What's your problem?' he sneered. 'When she gets back to the refugee centre, an' tells her story, they'll just issue her new documents. No harm done.'

'But she never did get back!' I cried. 'Where did he take them? My Mother and Katya? They didn't leave with the others. And weren't there after the others had left. I went, every day, waiting for news of her. And you, you and Antoine! You knew she wasn't there.'

Uschi pinched her eyes shut and covered her ears. 'No!' she cried. 'We *didn't* know – not then. Viktor lied to us. When we confronted him, he said his man must have taken them back in time to join the others. And

they were now on their way to Paraguay. He said in the scramble to board
the ship, in the middle of the night, who's going to notice there's already a
Sonya Enns on board.'

'And you believed him?' I said.

'We *wanted* to believe him. It wasn't till you came to see me in Spandau
– and told me your mother never got to Paraguay – that's when I knew
Viktor had lied. But you said you and Viktor had become friends in
Canada. I didn't know what to think,' she said. 'And I didn't want you to
hate me.'

For days after I got home I could not face telling Helena what I had
learned – let alone confront Doktor Vik. When I did tell her she tried to
find an alternate explanation for what Katya and Uschi had told me, but
there was none.

Then I went to see Doktor Vik at his office. It was six o'clock. I wanted
to be sure we would be alone. No patients in his waiting room, no recep-
tionist. He already knew I had been to Russia, then to Germany. 'I was
wondering when you'd show up,' he said.

He has modest offices now, after his retirement, just a step up from a
storefront clinic, in a decaying downtown neighbourhood. When he
moved in about a year ago he explained that he wanted to 'keep his hand
in' by doing what he regards as clinical charity work, offering his services
to Legal Aid, for a pittance of the fee he used to command. He said
patients who try to appeal their incarceration in a mental institution
often get only a psychiatric social worker to plead their case. 'That's just
not good enough,' he says.

When I entered his office he was labelling the audio tapes of that day's
sessions with his clients. He told me to take a seat. He'd only be a minute.
I said I preferred to stand.

He has changed, Antoine, though I hadn't noticed the change until
after his father's death. He's no longer so self-assured, and seems easily
distracted. He had always been very fit, up at 6:00 AM to get his run in,
even on bitterly cold winter days. He had been an early enthusiast of the
internet but now he rarely bothered to reply to e-mails.

We had become closer since the death of his father, and I had asked his
young wife, his stylish trophy wife, if he was well. She and I had never

warmed to each other and I expected her to put me off with a shrug, but my questions brought a gush of tears and anger. 'He's become impossible.' She said he used to enjoy their dinner parties, used to enjoy what he called the 'social dynamic' among their guests, but of late he seemed bored, she said. Halfway through the main course, he would rise, apologize, complain of a headache and excuse himself. And every night, she said, he'd be up past midnight, going through his father's box of papers, or reading those morbid books about the war. She slaved for days over those dinner parties, she said, she wanted everything to be nice, and he just spoiled it. She suspected he might be medicating himself but was afraid to ask.

Doktor Vik labelled the last cassette and dropped it into a brown envelope. Then he sat down behind his desk, sighed and waited for me to begin.

Why, I said, why my mother? To get back at me? At Mennonites?

He tilted forward in his chair and placed the palms of his hands on his desk. 'Look, as it turned out, it was risky, what I did. But I didn't think I was putting her in any danger. Actually, I thought I might be saving her life. By making sure she *didn't* get on that train. It was absurd,' he said, 'to think the Russians would let a thousand *Nyemtzy* collaborators slip through their net – when the Amis had so conveniently served them up.'

'Then why did you hand her over to the Russians?'

'I didn't,' he said, 'I was double crossed.' He said the punk he had sent to fetch my mother had got ideas. When he saw Doktor Vik was going to a lot of trouble to get his hands on this one woman, a Soviet refugee – well, she must be a hot property. Either the Russians or the Amis would be willing to pay good money for her. 'So why hand her over to me, for two bottles of cognac. So cut out the middle man. Hand her over to the Russians himself.'

He said he later discovered that his man did have a Soviet contact, a SMERSH agent, who had paid him quite a lot of money for this woman. 'Must have pissed him off, when he found out your mother, and that other woman, were nobody important. By the time I found out about all this,' he said, 'your mother and that other woman were already in a transit prison in Russia.'

He said he never saw that punk again, who had double crossed him.

He disappeared. 'Would have to disappear, one way or another. SMERSH didn't like being duped by punks.'

And he'd had no inkling, what his man was up to?

'None. Well, maybe in retrospect.' He said he'd gotten in over his head when he tried to get one of his Heidelberg professors out of Germany, to Argentina. That particular caper had put him in contact with some of Gehlen's boys, 'and they played hard ball,' he said. It wasn't a very complicated plan. It had worked for scores of other Nazis, but it didn't work for the professor. 'Somebody sold us out,' he said, 'told the Amis where he was hiding.' But when the Amis came to arrest him, 'he did the Roman thing. Fell on his sword. Took a cyanide pill, before they could publicly humiliate him.'

He said that was probably when both SMERSH and the Amis started watching him. His agents might have got wind of it and decided it was more profitable to betray him than be loyal to him. He should have picked up on it but he didn't. I could believe him or not, he said.

I could believe he had glibly told himself he was 'saving' my mother, I said, and that's what made my flesh crawl. The glibness of it. That he found it so easy to play with other people's lives. As though it were his mission in life to select whose lives mattered and whose didn't. If his conscience was clear, then why, during all these years that we'd been *friends*, hadn't he told me?

'I thought Antoine had told you,' he said.

'Antoine knew? You told Antoine you were sacrificing my mother to save Mary Gordon?'

He had been calm, condescending, now he pounded his desk and exploded. 'Antoine, Antoine. Your hero Antoine! He was your *Führer*, and you were his devoted little Göbbels,' he said. 'Antoine would lead you out of the Mennonite ghetto into the Big Wide World. And when his Big Wide World came crashing down on his head after the war, you, like Göbbels, would have gladly gone down with him. Down to his bunker and swallowed a cyanide pill.'

That stung. It took me a few seconds to recover. 'He *wouldn't* let me go down with him. Not me, not Uschi!' I snarled. 'He told me to go back to my village.' I said it was he, not you, Antoine, who fancied himself a little *Führer,* a visionary who would lead his followers to a brave new future and consign the rest of humanity to the garbage dump of history. Surplus people, like my mother. 'And you were still at it,' I shrieked, 'even after the war, when your own squalid world had collapsed. You, with your network of thugs and Ratlines. Making the world safe for scoundrels. You're a sick man!'

He leaned back in his chair and slowly shook his head. 'And you? You've got a clear conscience? You think you're the only one haunted by what happened to your mother? You think I haven't lost sleep because of how it turned out? When I got your letter from Paraguay, I jumped at the chance. A chance to make amends, for at least some of what I'd done. Could you have accepted my help, if you had known?'

That's why he had been my 'friend' all these years? Why he had sponsored us, got us settled, coached my kids how to get scholarships? To keep my mouth shut? Buy me off? 'Your *help* made me complicit in my mother's murder!' I cried.

That was the shame I could no longer evade, Antoine – that maybe I *had* been bought off. There had been times when I'd had an inkling of Doktor Vik's role in my mother's death. Why hadn't I barged into his office *then,* and aggressively confronted him?

Doktor Vik tilted his chair back and took a deep breath. 'So what are you going to do,' he said, 'shoot me or just blackmail me?'

I confess that I had allowed myself a deliciously vindictive moment thinking of the field day the press would have with the story. *World-renowned psychiatrist accused of smuggling Nazi war criminals out of Germany.* That would be a front-page headline.

'You disgust me,' I said.

Then I did what I had come to do. As ceremoniously as I could I took the little stone flask out of my jacket pocket, the stone flask that had been the parting gift from Alvaro, my Guarani friend before we left Paraguay. *Diena nem met,* he had told me, *Schlaejta mensch diena vel doot moake.* A mere token of our friendship, or a potent poison to fend off my enemies? Was this the time to put it to the test? There had been other occasions, after a bleary-eyed night of 'research' down in my basement lair, when I rose from my chair and took down the box on the top shelf to make sure the flask was still there. Over the last few months it had crossed my mind – that it might serve as my cyanide pill when the time came for me to do the Roman thing.

But now I carefully pried off the stopper with my thumbs and rolled one of the three shrivelled black berries onto Doktor Vik's desk. I watched his eyes follow the berry as it rolled toward him, then stopped. After all these years it looked more like a mouldy nut. I explained that the berries were given to me by my Guarani friend, to kill the evil demons within me, or evil men who had done harm to me or my family. Then I pushed the stopper back securely with the heel of my hand. 'I'll give you a chance to do the Roman thing,' I said.

Doktor Vik reached out and nudged the berry with the tip of his finger. 'It's probably past its best-before date,' he said.

Had there been even a hint of mockery in his voice I would have lunged across the desk and jammed the berry between his teeth. But there was no mockery. He sounded almost rueful. I put my jacket on, slowly walked out of his office and closed the door behind me. I have a vague memory of fumbling for the keys to my car in the parking lot, then I remember nothing until I found myself parked in my driveway, sitting there with the engine idling.

The next morning, when I told Helena I had confronted Doktor Vik, I told her too about the shrivelled black berry. I pretended it was just a sick joke. Yes, I wanted to punish him for what he had done, but the berry was nothing more than a melodramatic gesture. And yet, I remembered that his eyes were still fixed on that berry, lying there impudently on his desk, when I left his office. He didn't look up. Might he actually have swallowed it? And if he had, would it have any more potency than a dried prune? Absurd. But in the days that followed, I imagined ghoulish scenes of Doktor Vik writhing on the floor of his office.

Then a call from his trophy wife. She'd been calling all his friends, she said, and she thought I would want to know too. He'd had a severe stroke four days ago, but was now in stable condition. He could speak, but his speech was slurred and incoherent, she said. He could move one arm and both his legs but he couldn't walk, not yet.

I held back until the following morning, then I rushed to Winnipeg, to the hospital. His wife was at his bedside. He turned his head toward me when I spoke to him and raised his good arm but he didn't speak. His wife spoke in a hoarse whisper. She had found him in the garden where he takes his morning coffee and his newspaper, still sitting in his big wicker chair, with the newspaper on his lap. The only sign that something was wrong was the empty coffee cup, tipped on its side, on the grass beside his chair.

I left Doktor Vik's room and placed myself near the nurses' station where I could ambush his doctor when he arrived. Was I family, he asked. No, just a friend. He said Doktor Vik had spent a quiet night and seemed to be stable now. He would probably recover most of his motor functions, but it would take some time. When he was released from the hospital we would all be informed how we could best assist in his rehabilitation.

I had to grab the doctor's sleeve to get his full attention. 'He's been depressed lately,' I blurted out. 'I have some reason to fear he might have taken something . . . something to do harm to himself.'

The doctor did stop then and turned toward me. 'What are you saying? Your friend has had a stroke,' he said, enunciating more deliberately than necessary. 'His stroke was caused by a cerebral embolism. All the tests, and all his symptoms, are consistent with a stroke.' Then he looked down at my hand clutching his sleeve, so I let go.

At least once a week I visit him and take him for a long drive through the country. It seems to brighten his mood a little, and has become a regular part of his rehab. He doesn't talk much but seems attentive to the passing scene. Sometimes he suddenly wheels around and looks out the back window of the car, but when I ask what he saw, or if he would like me to turn around, he seems already to have forgotten about it. When he does speak, his words are distinct but he has trouble ordering his thoughts. 'Those were good times, in Germany. They seemed to be good people there, in Heidelberg,' he said. 'Good people. That Professor Schneider. Top notch. Top notch.' He bobbed his head around, watching the passing scene. 'Not like Berlin. A bunch of riffraff. And that Uschi. A highclass bitch,' he said, 'and that Mennonite punk. Struvel.'

'I'm Struvel,' I said. He turned to study my face. 'Oh yeah,' he said.

August 14, 1992

What remains to be saved, Antoine? When Helena and I had announced that our application to emigrate to Canada had been success-ful, we felt almost instantly a distance between us and those who had decided to stay in Paraguay, or had no one in Canada to sponsor them. And as my attachment to those people became more tenuous, you were more and more on my mind. Not surprising, since I was now corre-sponding with Doktor Vik. I could never have guessed how much my life in Canada would become enmeshed with his. I expected he would be there to welcome us, explain the arrangements he had made for us, and then leave us to make our own way in a new world. But I knew that as soon as I set foot in Canada I would again have to confront the man I had been during the war and the first years of the peace. In Paraguay I had become a decent, loving human being and I did not want those few years of my youth to define who I was. I wanted to take something of my Paraguay self with me, something that could never be taken away.

When our people had been safely settled in that barren Chaco, and had begun to re-create a crude semblance of the old Russia they had lost, only then could they indulge the luxury of nostalgia and lament, and Uncle Knalz was a living archive of their fortunes and misfortunes.

During our last days together I sensed that he too felt a need to unburden himself of what he thought I should know. Helena and I had sold our tools, our horse and two cows, and whatever else we had of value, and as the day of our departure loomed Uncle Knalz would appear at our door, make a token offer to help us pack, then he'd find a chair where he would be out of our way and begin to talk.

'Everyone loved your mother, not everyone loved your father,' he said. 'And no one thought they would marry. They were too different.' He said my mother's family was 'Mennonite elite' – her father an esteemed *Ältester* educated in Germany, one uncle was a mill owner, another was mayor of one of the few villages in the Colony that claimed the status of a town. My father's father was a landless tradesman, a cabinet maker, 'more like an artisan than a tradesman,' but not elite. My mother's family had disapproved of the match.

There were still traces of Uncle Knalz's quaint mannerisms that you had mocked when we were boys, Antoine, but only traces. In Paraguay he no longer needed to be so circumspect about what to say, or to whom. He now had the manner of one who has accomplished his task and can drift into a settled retirement, absorbed in his own thoughts. When he was prodded to give an opinion about the affairs of the colony, he let his mind drift among the vast store of his memories until he found a thread that would lead him back to the matter at hand by some circuitous route. But now, sitting on his chair near the door, he needed no prodding to talk.

He said my father had a rival, that Doktor Walther from Krivoy Rog. 'They were best of friends, and they both loved your mother.' He said Walther was handsome, polished, son of a rich *khutor*, a good catch for any girl in the Colony, 'her family's first choice and their daughter's obvious choice, or so they thought.' Doktor Walther was very *korrekt*, he said, 'more Prussian than the Kaiser when he came back from his studies, in Germany. Your father was not so *korrekt*. Not the ideal suitor for a parent's precious daughter.' He said he didn't know if my mother was ever torn between them, but by the time Walther returned from his studies in Germany, they had announced their engagement. Walther had wished the couple well, then left the Colony, but he and my father remained friends. Everyone thought he would go back to Germany but he stayed in Russia, became director of the clinic in Krivoy Rog. 'He saved many lives during the typhus time.'

He and my father both hated the communists, said Uncle Knalz, and hated Kaethler, but unlike my father, Walther knew how to play their game. 'He and Kaethler each had enough information to put the other away. So they played cat and mouse.' In those days, said Uncle Knalz, some men had to make a pact with the devil, 'and you had to decide how much you could imperil your soul before it was lost. If you still had a soul.' And for Doktor Walther, that moment came when he refused to sign off on Kaethler's trumped up medical report – on those three bodies you and I found when we went skinny dipping in the river. So Kaethler orchestrated his arrest as a German spy. Wasn't hard, said Uncle Knalz. Kaethler had got his hands on some real 'evidence.' Walther ran an underground network of 'couriers' who smuggled damning reports to the West, that were published in the German press. He was taken to the Lubyanka and tortured, then given twenty years in the gulag.

'Your father was a real charmer, back then,' he said, 'but he saw, too clearly, what was happening to us, and it made him more and more bitter.'

After the Revolution the Party *apparatchiks* had recognized his talent as a photographer, and he was sent all over the country, from Kiev to Volgograd, to photograph the mighty industrial projects the Bolsheviks were so proud of. 'Lots of smoke stacks and hydro dams.' But my father took too many *unauthorized* pictures, he said – mothers with emaciated children, whole towns buried under debris after a dam had burst, mining disasters in the Donbas region. He said my father tried to go over the heads of the local scoundrels. He would send the unauthorized photographs to the responsible ministries in Moscow, and he used Doktor Walther's connections to smuggle some of his photographs to the West.

'He was a brave man,' I said. These were the images I wanted to take to Canada.

'Yes, he was brave,' said Uncle Knalz, 'but it was a complicated bravery. They confiscated his cameras, and all his other equipment, but they didn't shoot him or banish him. Kaethler protected him. Kept him under wraps on the *kolkhoz*.'

Kaethler? *He* protected my father?

'Yes, he could do that,' said Uncle Knalz. 'He had more power than you'd expect of a mere secretary of a *raikom*. Those were still the early years, before the Five Year Plan. In the Kremlin they were busy drawing the blueprint for a new socialist society, and then they'd change the blueprint. Not that it mattered much. The people who were supposed to make it happen couldn't read blueprints. So people schemed and plotted against each other, and Kaethler had an uncanny sense who to butter up, and whose career he should sabotage to advance his own.'

Why did he hate my father?

'Because he had married your mother.'

He, Kaethler? *He* had fancied himself my father's rival?

Uncle Knalz shook his head. 'No, not like that, not like a lover. Kaethler knew she was too high for him, but in his twisted way he had worshipped her.'

This information was not for everyone's ears, so when well-wishers dropped by to say their last tearful farewells Uncle Knalz would fall silent and tap his thighs with the tips of his fingers. Sometimes a farewell visit would tax my patience too, when it seemed to have an ulterior motive – like the neighbour who arrived one afternoon, her brow deeply furrowed and her mouth puckered as though she were about to burst into tears. But first she took a quick look around the room at the items we would have to leave behind. 'Ooh. Do you have to leave that beautiful lamp?' she said. 'But I guess you won't need it there. In Canada they've all got the electric.'

'So we hear,' said Helena. 'We've told Groote Graeta she could have it.'

I saw Uncle Knalz quietly get up from his chair and slink out the door. I ran after him but he waved me off. He said he'd be back.

When he appeared again the next day, Helena and I were done packing and repacking. I was waiting for him on our little sheltered porch that faced the street, opposite the school that now awaited a new teacher. We sat on two wicker chairs with an upturned box between us that served as a small table. I had saved some yerba tea that I knew he was fond of. Sipping *mate* through a shared *bombilla* had become a kind of communion ritual between us. Helena had taken our two children to the village to say goodbye to their school mates, so there were only the two of us. I filled the gourd half full with yerba leaves, laid the *bombilla* on the leaves, and topped up the gourd with hot water. I let it steep a few minutes, then passed it to him. He took a sip and nodded. It was ready, and so was he.

He said Kaethler had been a plague on my mother ever since they were school children. He would follow her around like a needy puppy, and the more she tried to ignore him the more persistent he became. At school he would watch her, and if she broke the point of her pencil he would jump up and offer her his. He would hide her mittens, then find them and solemnly present them to her. Uncle Knalz said at first her classmates thought it was laughable, but when they saw it was driving my mother mad they tried to protect her. Taunte Liese would run after him and beat him with her book bag. And when my mother pleaded with him to leave her alone he would fold his hands and hang his head, but with a coy smile, grateful that his devotion had been recognized. My mother's older brother gave Kaethler a bloody nose, and finally a thorough beating, but that only proved how much he was willing to suffer for his devotion.

Then something happened, said Uncle Knalz, when they were both in their mid teens. Kaethler changed. If he saw her on the street, he would turn up his nose, with a pained look on his face. As though he'd discovered that my mother was common clay after all, not some goddess to be worshipped. 'But maybe you don't need to know the details,' he said. 'There are some things a foolish old uncle shouldn't tell his nephew.'

'I want to know,' I said.

'You might have to plug your ears.' He took a long draft on the *mate bombilla*, and a wry smile flickered across his face that he couldn't suppress. He said shortly after they were married – he and his wife, and my mother and my father – all four of them had made a Sunday excursion to a pretty little island up the river, to celebrate their married bliss. That was before the civil war. He said storm clouds were already gathering on the horizon, but in the Colony it was still a sunny time. They had brought provisions for a picnic, smoked sturgeon, a bottle of Georgian wine, a selection of pastries. They spread their blanket on the ground and spent an idle afternoon talking and eating. 'Our own little Deschenay sir Lerb,' my father had said, or something like that. He said it was the name of a famous French painting.

Uncle Knalz said he didn't remember how Kaethler's name had come up. Back then Kaethler was more to be pitied than feared. People often made fun of him. Uncle Knalz said it was his wife who had jokingly said, 'Whatever did you do to that poor man, Sonya, to turn him against you?'

My mother had blushed and covered her face, but my father had laughed. Maybe he'd drunk a little too much wine. 'Go ahead, tell them, Sonya,' he said. 'It's a very funny story.'

So my mother told. She said she had done as she always did in the spring – took a basket and went to pick wildflowers at the edge of the woods by the river. After the beating her brother had given him, Kaethler wasn't so bold anymore, though he continued to stalk her at a distance. So she was startled when she heard him behind her. He stood there, holding a bouquet of wildflowers in one hand, the other hand on his heart, bobbing his head like a doting imbecile. She said she turned her back and began walking away but he darted in front of her, offering his bouquet to her, bobbing and smiling. So she stopped, set her basket on the ground and lifted her skirt, high, exposing her panties. Then she touched herself. She said Kaethler took a step back, almost tripped, shielded his eyes and began to blubber. He threw the bouquet down, grabbed a handful of dirt and threw it at her. Then he ran away. My mother said she felt ashamed, but she knew she had to do it.

Uncle Knalz said they had all burst out laughing.

I sat stunned for a moment, staring at him. Then I too burst out laughing. My mother, a model of propriety, always perfectly poised. Was this an image of her I needed to take to Canada? Why not. I poured more hot water on the *mate* and we each took a good long sip.

'Later, of course, it was not a laughing matter,' he said. When Kaethler became a big man in the Party he took revenge. Demanded respect. He made sure my mother knew her husband's life was now in his hands. And my father knew it too. Uncle Knalz said it's not easy for a proud man like my father to live with that, to know he owes his life to a sick man's fantasy about his wife. And to know that everybody else knew. It made him feel dirty, 'slathered in Kaethler's slime,' he said. My father, who had once been the best of company, witty, charming, full of stories, became belligerent and rude. Some people became afraid to be seen with him. And the more reckless he became, the more blatant his provocations, the more unhinged Kaethler became. My father was supposed to cower, not defy him.

Uncle Knalz said Kaethler would never directly confront either my father or my mother. It was always he, Uncle Knalz, who would be called into Kaethler's office, to hear him vent his frustration. 'Does she think her asshole husband is some kinda hero – with his stupid pranks?' He snatched a sheet of paper off his desk and waved it in Uncle Knalz's face – another memo from the GPU in Donetsk, instructing him to take the 'necessary measures' to silence my father. 'What's she thinkin, huh? That I'm gonna put my head on the block, to save her husband's ass? Huh? Huh? That smartass prick. Looky me, looky me, I'm smarter than every-body else! Drawing dirty pictures of us. Tellin' jokes about us. Ha-ha-ha. Very funny. Tell her next time he gets frisky, she should shove her big tit in his mouth, an' shut him up.'

Uncle Knalz said my father, in a fit of rage, had once told him the only way he could feel clean would be to kill Kaethler. 'What he did was almost as desperate. But you know that story.'

Yes, I knew. We all knew the story. In the mid 1920s the Party had stepped up its anti-religion campaign, and troops of students toured the countryside performing little skits depicting lecherous priests and nuns, and in every *oblast* they distributed large lithographed posters satirizing biblical figures. Kaethler had dutifully mounted one on the door of our old church. It showed a very pregnant Virgin Mary blushing sheepishly under her halo, her hands resting on her swollen tummy, with a caption at the bottom, '*Hey, tovarish. Which way to one of your modern Soviet abortion clinics?'* A few days passed and there was muffled excitement in the village. 'Go. Go see for yourself,' people whispered. Someone had sabotaged the poster. With a few simple strokes he had turned the Virgin Mary into Mother Russia, wearing the traditional *kokoshnik* instead of a halo. He had parted the robes that covered her swollen tummy to expose a pudgy foetus with a big black moustache on its oversized head, unmistakably the head of Stalin. And peeping around Stalin's buttocks, another little foetus with a round cabbage head. Unmistakably the head of Kaethler. The caption remained the same.

Uncle Knalz said the old church stood just beyond the village, so for three or four days Kaethler didn't know it had been sabotaged. No one dared tell him. When he saw our people skulking to the church and returning with their hands clapped over their mouths he didn't know they were laughing. He assumed they were outraged by the scandalous blasphemy of the poster.

Then Boris, Katya's husband, appeared at Uncle Knalz's door to inform him that Comrade Kaethler wanted to see him, immediately. At his house, not at his office.

'You seen it? You seen what he done, that smartass prick?' Kaethler fumed. 'He's finished! It's out of my hands now. He's red meat for the GPU!'

Uncle Knalz had come directly to our house, he said. He found my mother and father sitting side by side on a cot, exhausted, waiting for the axe to fall. They had done all the crying they could do. My mother rested her head on his shoulder, held his hand in both her hands and pressed it to her cheek. Uncle Knalz said there was no point in raging at my father's desperate act. He said, 'Knalz, you don't have to tell me it was stupid – what I did.'

I watched Uncle Knalz lean forward in his chair and press the heels of his hands into his eyes. 'And your mother, six months pregnant. With you,' he said.

Uncle Knalz said he had wanted to say something, anything, that might redeem my father's reckless act. So he told them not only people from our village but others too had seen the sabotaged poster before Kaethler tore it down. Including two of Kaethler's comrades from the *obkom*. 'Maybe they were too squeamish to tell him they had seen him pictured there, in that . . . embarrassing position.' And God help him, said

Uncle Knalz, before he could stop himself a twitchy grin snuck up on his face. My father had stared at him for a moment, then burst out laughing. Uncle Knalz looked at my mother. She closed her eyes and covered her mouth with her hands.

Uncle Knalz told my father that the defaced poster made a good story, and a story travels fast and far. By the time Kaethler had torn down the poster, the story would have spread through all the surrounding *oblasti,* and in every town and village where that poster was still displayed, it would now have to be torn down. 'By defacing one poster you sabotaged a thousand,' Uncle Knalz had told my father. 'What you did will give courage to others. To resist.'

'Thank you Knalz, for saying that,' my father said.

Uncle Knalz said he didn't know what devilry had come over them, all three of them, laughing at a time like that. He said maybe it hadn't sunk in yet, during those early stages of Bolshevik terror, how fatal such an act would be. They still thought, then, that the chaos and killing could not go on. But then came Stalin, and it got worse. 'Who could imagine that communist gangsterism would last for decades.'

My father had already packed a change of clothes and some food – bread, a sausage, some dried fruit. His only chance was to flee. 'I need a horse and a saddle, Knalz,' my father had said. 'Not a good horse. Any old nag that will take me as far as Krivoy Rog.' He said he knew Doktor Walther had been known to hide a few criminals among the cleaning staff at his clinic till some arrangement could be made for their escape.

Then all three of them knelt down and prayed for God's guidance and mercy. 'But your father never got to Krivoy Rog.'

'How did Kaethler die?' I said.

'Doktor Walther killed him.' Uncle Knalz said in the summer of 1943 the Germans had already told our people to get ready to be evacuated, and he was scrambling to help people get the provisions they would need for the trek. Then a man appeared at his door, hobbling on crutches. He had a long mangy beard and wore dirty, ill-fitting civilian clothes. And a filthy bandage was wrapped around his head like a turban, caked in dried blood. When he said who he was, Uncle Knalz quickly pulled him inside and shut the door.

Walther leaned his crutches against the wall and walked on two good legs to the chair Uncle Knalz had placed for him at the kitchen table.

While Uncle Knalz poured him a glass of tea Walther began to unwrap the turban around his head, then vigorously scratched his scalp. There was no sign of a wound on his head. He was not talkative, he simply explained that he had been released from prison to tend the wounded at Stalingrad and then Kursk. A slaughter, he said, on both sides, and the Germans were now in desperate retreat. Uncle Knalz said he answered a few more questions, then he said, 'Where's Kaethler? I heard he was working for the Germans. He and I have some unfinished business. If he escapes to Germany it'll be too late.'

Uncle Knalz said he didn't ask, too late for what? – maybe because Walther wouldn't tell him, maybe because he was afraid he would. He told Walther he'd make some inquiries, and find out where Kaethler's *Sonderkommando* had been operating. Walther said he'd wait.

Uncle Knalz said he didn't know what happened till a year later, at the Gronau refugee centre. Frau Kommissar and her two grown children had staggered into the camp, destitute, in rags, and immediately she began to wail and beat her breast. '*Och,* such a horror.' She said her husband had known, before anyone else knew, that they had to get out of Russia. But how? No help from the Germans. That was their thanks for everything he had done for them, and for the Mennonites. Her husband broke down then, she said. Afraid to leave the house. 'At night he woke shrieking, tormented by nightmares, and all day he sat shivering by the stove, in the dark, with the blinds drawn.' Then this man had appeared, she said, filthy, on crutches, with a bloody bandage wrapped around his head, knocked on their door and demanded to speak with Herr Kaethler. Her husband had approached the door, she said, still in his nightshirt and wrapped in his blanket. He had peered over her shoulder, and he seemed to recognize this strange man. 'Leave us,' her husband had said. She didn't want to go, but the man was a cripple, hobbling on crutches, what mischief could he do?

So she took the children and went across the street, where people were already loading their things into trucks and wagons. It wasn't long, then the strange man came out on his crutches, squinted at the light, and hobbled down the street, around a corner and out of sight. She told the children to wait and rushed back to the house. Blood everywhere, and her husband slumped across the kitchen table with his throat cut.

Uncle Knalz sat quietly for a time. 'Kaethler was an evil man,' he said, 'but he was no longer worth getting blood on your hands.' He said Frau Kommissar and her two children left the Gronau camp after less than a month. They weren't welcome there, in spite of their loud proclamations of piety. He said he didn't know if they were still in Germany or were repatriated to Russia and didn't care.

Throughout my childhood and youth I had treasured an image of my father as a hero, but you had some misgivings. You said before my father sealed his doom with that reckless act he should have made sure the reverberations would be felt beyond our little *oblast,* all the way to the Kremlin. 'He should have rallied your people instead of scaring them off,' you said. He should have seized the sabotaged poster and carried it like a banner, leading our people on a protest march to Moscow, joined by others en route.

They would have been slaughtered before they left our *oblast,* Antoine. It might have made a good story, and perhaps it would have rated a brief item at the end of a newscast in the West.

Can we now shame our people for not being more heroic? 'The best we could do was to pour a little sand into the machinery of the Bolsheviks, and try to keep our faith,' said Uncle Knalz. Did we do better when we were put to the test, Antoine?

Uncle Knalz rose from his chair and thanked me for the *mate.* He had told me all he could to take with me to Canada. And what image of Uncle Knalz himself could I take with me? I remember how he would drop in on us when I was still a young lad in Russia, supposedly to visit with my mother and my Oma Enns. He would begin to talk in his usual musing manner. 'Ran into young Jasch Ewert last week,' he would tell my mother. 'You know – grandson of that Peter Ewert whose family came here from Prussia in 1876. That was in Bismarck's time, German Unification and all that.' Then he might glance at me out of the corner of his eye before he continued. 'A lot of our people emigrated then,' he would say. 'That's how it was with the Mennonites. Whenever nationalism reaches fever pitch, our people start lookin' for another country. Usually happens when our host country gets belligerent toward its neighbours. First thing they do is revoke our exemption from military service.' Uncle Knalz pondered that for a moment and shook his head. 'People could read the signs. Here, in

Russia, there were already signs in 1906, but we missed them.' And again he cast a glance at me to see if I was listening.

Later, during the German occupation in our villages, his 'lessons' became more stern. Captain von Niessen's company had moved out and *Sturmbannführer* Rösler's military and civilian administrators had moved in. Rally time. My mother hadn't been there, at the rally, neither had Uncle Knalz and Taunte Liese, so I gave her my report of how stirring the event had been, the singing and the speeches – especially the speech of Herr Doktor Stumpp, the world famous expert on the history of *Volks-deutsche* in Russia and the Ukraine. I told my mother how he had praised our people, who so bravely, so faithfully had kept our German culture and language in spite of decades of repression.

The next day Uncle Knalz dropped in on us to give us *his* report. He and a small delegation had met with Doktor Stumpp after the rally to convey some of their concerns about the disturbing news they had heard, about what the *SS Einsatzgruppe* had been up to in our region. He said he had thought they would stand a better chance of getting a hearing from Doktor Stumpp, a civilian who was outside the military chain of command. He said he had explained, as politely as he could, that it was ill-advised to treat our Ukrainian neighbours as enemies, who, given half a chance, would welcome the Germans as their liberators, as we *Volks-deutsche* had done. (He said he didn't need to mention, explicitly, the deportation of young men and women to the Ruhr as slave labour in munitions factories. Or the Jews.)

The Herr Doktor had allowed they perhaps had a point, that most Ukrainians were no doubt grateful to be relieved of the communist yoke. But it was their very eagerness to be led – by a stronger and more gifted *Volk* – that made these Slavs untrustworthy. That's what had made them a ready cohort of those clever Jewish Bolsheviks. Huh! Just imagine. He and his staff had barely settled into their new quarters when one of these Slavs had come swaggering into his office. A big flat-faced oaf, one of these nationalists, *narodniks*. Waltzed in and plopped himself down on the edge of the Herr Doktor's desk. 'Hey, comrade,' he said, 'this time we're gonna fix those Russkies good, *ja?*'

'What? *We* are going to fix the Russkies? *We? We?*' Doktor Stumpp had to laugh. For centuries all this Slav had shown the Russkies was his bare buttocks. 'Here, *bitte schön*, comrades, my pleasure. *Zum Ekel.*'

But this wasn't a good time to launch a protest, Stumpp explained. He himself did not doubt the delegation's good faith, but they must know how touchy some of these *SS* people get about this. 'I have to tell you,' he said, 'I had quite an argument with a particular *Sturmbannführer* who wanted to lump your people in with the Slavs. As for the Jews, you better keep your opinions to yourself.'

'In times like these,' I heard Uncle Knalz tell my mother, 'some people put their head in the clouds, or stick it in the sand.' They both threw me a quick glance.

If someone had told me then that Uncle Knalz was trying to be both a father and a mentor to me I would have laughed in his face. I wouldn't laugh now.

September 12, 1992

The proceedings against me are proceeding, Antoine, but my lawyer said he still had a small arsenal of legal delays. My next hearing was scheduled for the coming Monday. This time I would be interrogated by both the RCMP and the Immigration people. The issue for them was whether or not I had lied about my *Waffen SS* record when I entered Canada. I had two days to brace myself.

Another hot, humid night, impossible to sleep, but I probably wouldn't have slept anyway. I heaved myself out of bed and sat there a few minutes in a sweat. 'I'm going down to the basement, where it's cooler,' I told Helena. I do have an old couch down there, but I didn't lie down. I stared at the litter of papers and filing cards on my desk. With a sweep of my arm I brushed a stack of them onto the floor, then went back to the kitchen and took a can of beer out of the fridge. I thought I heard rain, so I went to the living room and stood in front of the picture window. Down the street, toward town, big luminous drops streaked through the glow of a streetlight. I stood there in my boxer shorts, with my beer, watching the light. I unlocked the front door, opened it, and felt the cooler night air on my body. I stepped out and let the rain fall on my bare chest and shoulders. Sweat washed into my eyes. All the houses on our street were dark except for the two that leave the porch light on all night. The only sound was of a car now and then, speeding along our main street. I could see the glare of headlights as they passed through the intersection at the foot of our street. More traffic than usual at this late hour, so it must be a Saturday night.

I stepped off the porch and walked down to the curb. I inhaled the sweaty smell of hot asphalt, cooled by the first big drops of rain but still warm under my bare feet. I finished the last of the beer and ambled down toward the main street. It seemed to me that something should hold me back but nothing did, and that pleased me. I stood in the middle of the intersection, in the middle of the square of traffic lights, covering all four cardinal points of the compass. I watched them going through their cycle, dutiful sentinels unperturbed by the late hour, by the rain, or the empty street – red, green, yellow – over and over. Then a car honked and swerved to miss me. Idiot. Plenty of space for him to pass.

Then all was quiet again. The unblinking neon signs above the shops brooded vacantly, unheeded, unremarked, their futility reflected in blind picture windows. Still a few of the older houses here, holding their own among the newer rectangular blocks. It was raining harder now, prickling my bare shoulders. Another car honked and swerved. It stopped, and someone shouted out the window, 'Get off the road, yuh fuckin' pervert!' The car sped away. I gave them the finger, but I was more puzzled than angered by their behaviour.

A dog barked, and that set off the muffled barks of other dogs guarding their darkened property. Somebody turned on a light in a window above a row of shops. Then another light further up the street. A corner of a curtain drew back and I saw the silhouette of a head. The curtain closed, the light went out. Big drops of rain smacked my skull and shoulders, but they felt good. 'Go back to bed,' I shouted at the windows. 'No need for you to lose sleep because evil once stalked the earth. Not stalked, ran rampant. But that was in another country.'

I felt obliged to rise to the occasion, now that I had rousted them from their beds. The floodlit square of wet asphalt seemed like a stage set, and I an actor called upon to do justice to his lines. The scene called for a crowned figure in a white toga, standing at the centre of a semicircle of flaming torches, not an old man in his boxer shorts standing in the rain, barefoot and bare-chested, but I did my best. 'You, you boy-scout canucki schmuckies!' I raged, 'Still spouting the same moral maxims that a prissy schoolmarm once placed on your tongue like a sacramental wafer. You have but a child's notion of those times.'

More dogs barked, more lights came on, and the rain had begun to pelt. 'Fools, fools,' I shouted. 'Those were not normal times,' I cried, 'they were *full* times. Full of feverish hopes and fears, a last chance to ride the wave of history to glory, or perish in the attempt. A time when all the famous chefs, in the famous kitchens of high learning, had cooked, stewed, seasoned and whipped up a gastronomic feast that made half of Europe drool. How can you, you with your meat-and-potatoes morality, presume to judge?'

A pickup truck swished by me, stopped, and backed up, slowly. I recognized it. Jean-Luc's '52 Chevy, but it was not Jean-Luc. It was his young son, and his girlfriend. 'You OK, Mr. Enns?'

I stared at him and shrugged.

'You want us to give you a lift home?'

When I said nothing, and did nothing, he took my arm and led me to the passenger side and I got in. His girlfriend moved toward the driver's side to leave as much space between us as she could. Jean-Luc's son politely introduced us. 'This is my dad's friend, Mr. Enns. My girlfriend Cindy.' We nodded to each other.

The front door was unlocked but I stood patiently behind Jean-Luc Jr. while he rang the bell, and waited for my wife to answer. The porch light came on and the door opened. 'What happened?' she said.

'Well, ah, Mr. Enns – he was getting wet, out there, in the rain.' He was too discreet to say more in my presence. Helena ran to fetch my bathrobe. She led me to the kitchen and sat me down at the table, then she went back to get the full story from Jean-Luc Jr. I heard them talking quietly, heard Helena's muffled cries, then Jean-Luc Jr. left.

'We should see a doctor,' said Helena, but I shook my head. She cautiously prodded me with questions. I shrugged and tried to play down the whole incident. She fetched a towel, removed my robe, and dried me off.

When I came down to a late breakfast that morning, Jean-Luc Sr. had already arrived. He and Helena were at the kitchen table drinking coffee.

'Whew. We needed that rain,' I said.

He said, 'I hear you had a rough night.' He tried to sound cheery. 'Been sleep walkin', have yuh? Had a great aunt used to do that. When they were still on the farm. Sometimes they'd find her in her nightie, feedin' the chickens. Or she'd be all dressed up in her Sunday best, sittin' in the car, waitin' to go downtown. At three in the morning.'

I was grateful to him for trying to take the edge off my humiliation.

Late that afternoon my daughter Margaret arrived, with her suitcase, and moved into the room that had been Sara's room on weekends and holidays. I tried to be helpful in the kitchen, helping Helena prepare a modest dinner. I sliced an onion, peeled a few potatoes and set the table. Margaret's eyes followed my every move. We tried to converse normally till we had cleaned up the dishes and sat down to another cup of coffee.

'What were you doing out there, in the middle of the night, papa?'

'Giving my neighbours a history lesson.'

'Couldn't you have saved it for the Mounties?'

'They've got their own version,' I said.

'Tell me everything, papa,' she said, 'I have a right to know.' Margaret, my daughter, who had never wanted to know, who had averted her face and held up the palms of her hands to fend me off, 'Please. Spare me the details.' She was worried about her mother now, afraid that by herself Helena would not be able to deal with me. And perhaps she was worried about me too, out of filial affection. Our son Neil was in Hong Kong, negotiating a merger between two big banks. He would be of no help.

'What do you want to know?' I said.

'They say 247 Jews were shot – at a train station near Stutthof. Men, women and children. Is it true you were there?'

'I was there.'

'Did you shoot at them, papa?'

'I shot. I can't swear I shot over their heads.'

Margaret and I sat on opposite sides of our kitchen table, Helena leaned against the frame of the doorway that led to the front hall, as though to fend off any unwelcome intrusion. Soft evening light flooded the kitchen, and two late summer roses bent their heads over the rim of a vase standing on the window sill. Near the back door my dog Butzie slept on her mat. An assortment of serving bowls, plates and vases decorated the room, Helena's work, and these gave the kitchen an agreeable clutter. In this unthreatening setting they hoped I could tell them something they could hang a shred of hope on. I told Margaret what I had wanted to tell you, Antoine, when we were in Berlin, but it never seemed to be the right time. Back then it was you who wanted to be spared the details.

I told Margaret how I had made contact with Major von Niessen and got assigned to his company – yes, the same von Niessen whose company had invaded our village almost four years ago. I said when I had tried to explain it to my RCMP interrogators at my first hearing, they weren't interested. 'We have that on record, Mr. Enns. Try to stay focussed on the night of January 28th, 1945.' They had no interest either in how our battalion had been slaughtered in the *Heiligenbeiler Kessel*, and that the whole of Army Group Vistula was being reshuffled because of all the casualties we had suffered. And that was why we, a small remnant of Major von Niessen's company, had been pulled back and ordered to guard a transport of Jews – stranded there, in that train station, for a variety of reasons – a shortage of rolling stock, mechanical breakdowns, and Polish partisans blowing up the lines. And also because Stutthof was already operating at full capacity. The Jews who were already there could not be gassed and disposed of fast enough to accommodate the new arrivals from the east.

'So you had no choice, papa,' said Margaret. She put her hand on top of my folded hands. 'You asked to be sent to the front, not to guard Jews.'

No, we had no choice, I said, but we had no complaints either. It was supposed to be a brief respite for us to lick our wounds, before we were sent back to the front.

I told her that among our company there were several young recruits, some even younger than I was, most of them eager to do their duty. There was a larger group of seasoned veterans, who had a more chastened sense of duty and discipline, and then there was a third group, who were no better than thugs – who had only recently been assigned to Major von Niessen's command. They too were hardened veterans, but as they themselves boasted, they were veteran shirkers, who had survived by manoeuvring themselves into positions well behind the front lines. Their leader was a *Feldwebel*, the highest rank of non-commissioned officer, and he had earned the loyalty and trust of his men for keeping them out of trouble. He had the hearty beer-hall charm that readily wins the admiration of certain kinds of men. He was tall, trim, and could even be called handsome except for his flared, up-turned nose, so pronounced that it might more properly be called a snout. We others called them the Augsburger troop, because both the *Feldwebel* and his 'second in command' came from the city of Augsburg. They functioned almost as a unit unto themselves, often in open contempt of Major von Niessen, who seemed too embittered or indifferent to discipline them. None of us were eager to be sent back to the front, to face more Russian artillery, but especially not the Augsburger troop – who were determined to wait out the war guarding that small trainload of Jews. And it was they who had come on duty that night when the Jews tried to make their escape, when they charged us with kitchen knives and clubs.

'That's enough now,' said Helena, to Margaret. 'He can tell you more tomorrow.'

Margaret drove me to Winnipeg for my hearing. The RCMP had taken my passport and driver's licence, and I felt quite relaxed during the drive. Margaret seemed to think I would need the next two hours to prepare myself mentally for the grilling I could expect, and did not press me to tell her more about what happened that night. My dear Margaret. I was moved by her kindness after so many years of bitter quarrelling between us. I chatted almost wistfully about how I had become Major von Niessen's *Offiziersgehilfe*, his batman, and I allowed myself the boast that the Major could not have wished for a more dutiful personal attendant. I would bring him his breakfast, make his appointments and remind him to keep them, and I would make excuses for him when there was an appointment he didn't want to keep. Yes, I said, the Major had changed – no longer the confident, gallant Captain he had been in 1941. There was little left of that aura of casual authority. He went days now without shaving, sometimes slept in his clothes, couldn't get past noon without a couple of nips from his bottle of brandy. *'Ja, ja, mein Freund,'* he said, the first time we had a chance to have a private talk, *'so steht die Sache nun.'* Germany had made a mess of it, he said, the Nazis had made themselves odious, even more odious than the communists. There was now little left for sacrifice to save.

After my hearing, and after my lawyer had given me a little pep talk, Margaret was waiting for me. 'So how did it go?' she asked, once the traffic had thinned out beyond the airport. I said my interrogators had asked questions and I had told them more than they wanted to know. Then they and my lawyer discussed precedents, both in Canada and in the United States, debated which were relevant, which not, while I sat quietly and tried to pay attention. 'Everybody was polite,' I said.

'You seem pretty calm. Tell me what happened. If you want to.'

'What happened in there, or back then?'

'Whatever. Start with in there.'

I said I had tried to describe the railway station and the town where it all happened, but my interrogators became impatient, couldn't see the 'relevance' of it. 'Try me,' said Margaret, 'We've got at least two hours before we get home.'

I said the station was incongruously large compared to the squat, drab town that clustered around it. Most of the inhabitants had fled, except for a few stubborn old men, so we had a choice of sleeping quarters. Our supply of coal was running low, so we used the empty houses for firewood. We started by breaking down tables and chairs, then we tore out the stairs, and finally the floor boards. Major von Niessen turned a blind eye. The Augsburgers regarded this work as a great indignity. They complained that it was 'Jew work,' that the Jews should be pressed into service to provide our firewood.

It was a 'terminal' station, I said, an example of flamboyant age-of-rail architecture, a huge cavernous shed closed at one end and open at the other. A glass roof arched over the whole structure, with small diamond-shaped panes held aloft in a net of steel brackets, and supported by a tangle of struts and heavy girders. More than necessary, it seemed to me, as though the architect had lacked confidence in his calculations and doubled their number just to be safe. The closed end of the station was a solid concrete wall, the open end was spanned by a glass curtain wall, hanging from the glass dome to the level of the concrete walls that supported it. Many of the glass panes were broken or had fallen out.

There were two sets of tracks, separated by a narrow platform and connected by a catwalk. The main platform ran the length of the station between the track beds and a row of offices and storerooms. The station had functioned mainly as a supply depot, and some of the storerooms were still stocked with flour, canned meat, and potatoes, to feed the army at the front – though the supply lines had long ago been broken. There was a cafe with a large kitchen, where four German cooks, assisted by about a dozen Jewish *kapos* prepared our meals. Full rations for us, half rations for the Jews – which was at least twice as much, I explained, as prisoners were 'entitled' to. The Augsburgers resented this largesse, as they called it. At the end of each day, the head cook would hand Major von Niessen a form, authorizing the requisition of specified quantities of flour, potatoes and canned meat from the storerooms. The Major hardly glanced at the form before he signed it. But when I tried to explain this at my hearing, my interrogators began to drum on their desks with their fingers.

The train that had brought the Jews to the station – and was now disabled – consisted of only eight box cars. There was no locomotive. The Jews were behind wooden barricades at the closed end of the station, but they were allowed to huddle inside the boxcars for warmth. They had to go in shifts, which meant more work for us guards. Four guards were always posted on the catwalks, and six more at the open end of the station. Because of the intense cold, each watch lasted only two hours. The Augsburger troop grumbled but usually took their turn like the rest of us.

Flood lights had been suspended from the lower girders, I said, again twice as many as necessary. They flooded the whole length of the platform in a blinding light, leaving the cavernous upper structure in almost total darkness.

'I can see why the Mounties became impatient,' said Margaret.

You have to picture it, I said.

It was a beautiful fall day now after that cleansing rain. Most of the harvest was in, almost no activity in the fields that so recently had been swarming with combines and trucks. 'It's hard to talk about what happened on a grim cold night when it's such warm sunny weather here,' I said. Then I must have fallen asleep in the car, or into a half-sleep. I had already become drowsy toward the end of my hearing. While my lawyer and my interrogators debated legal niceties I began to muse upon the word 'framed.' Yes, I was being framed, but not maliciously, not because the evidence was deliberately misconstrued. My 'case' was being framed like a picture is framed, to define what belongs in the picture and what doesn't. Only when a picture is framed can it be judged, only then is it possible to determine what it is a picture *of*. To me it seemed that my story was like a mural that goes on and on, around corners, over walls, and spreads across the ceiling.

The car stopped, and Margaret turned the engine off. I hadn't realized we were already home. Helena was waiting. Another pot of coffee and another debriefing at the kitchen table. Again I felt their hope as a weight pressing down on me, their hope that after my interrogation I could tell them the evidence against me was not as damning as they feared. But instead of sparing them the gruesome details, I felt a perverse compulsion to rub their noses in the squalor. As though, to spite my need for their love, I was determined to challenge its limit.

I told them that twice each day, morning and evening, we had to march the Jews across the catwalk, in batches of forty or fifty, to their 'public lavatory' on the far side of the tracks. We made them line up close to the edge of the platform, and watched over them while they defecated. Men, women and children, squatting as close as they dared to the edge. Then a group of *kapos* shoveled their shit off the platform onto the track bed below, ready for the next batch – for which the *kapos* got extra rations. I said sometimes the old ones, weak and exhausted, lost their balance and fell into their own shit, or toppled backwards off the platform into the shit on the track bed. Then two or three others had to jump down and help them back up, trying not to get covered in shit themselves.

The Augsburgers especially resented this smelly toilet duty, I said, and they complained to the Major that according to regulations, prisoners are entitled to only *one* lavatory break per day. The Major said those regulations applied only to prison camps, and this wasn't a prison. But the Jews took much too long, so the Augsburgers tried to speed up the evening toilet break. 'No shitting!' shouted the *Feldwebel*, 'Pee only! If you shit, we'll rub your face in it.'

After two or three weeks, standing there in the freezing cold, gagging on their stench, I too began to hate those Jews. Not *my* fault that they were prisoners. Not *my* fault that they were Jews. I too shouted at them to hurry up, and jammed the butt of my rifle into the backs of the laggards. Yes, in the beginning there had been times when I felt compassion, when I saw a young Jew help an old one, hold on to him to steady him, so he wouldn't fall off the platform. Or when I saw a man cradling a child in his lap, bobbing his head up and down as he sang a lullaby. Then I did long to go among them and speak courage to them. Hold on, hold on a little longer, I wanted to tell them, the war is almost over. But toward the end, those moments became rare.

'Oh god! Stop, papa,' said Margaret. She stood up from the table, turned her back to me, braced her arms against the kitchen counter and stared out the window above the sink. I must stop this. I must not wallow, must not plead. I clasped my hands in front of me and locked my fingers together tightly. The facts then, just the facts. It is a fact that Major von Niessen summoned the Augsburger *Feldwebel* to his office and ordered him and his troop to inspect the brake lines and coupling mechanisms of each boxcar. He told them where they could find hammers and axes to chop off the ice, and blow torches to thaw out the lines. It is a fact that the *Feldwebel's* truculent scowl suddenly lit up into a big grin. I was there. I saw it. He snapped to attention, saluted the Major, and shouted, *'Jawohl, Major!'* It is a fact that the order was carried out with alacrity, in spite of the bitter cold, even though some of them had to crawl on their stomachs under the carriages of the boxcars. Hours of banging and cursing, and the hiss of scalding steam where gobs of ice had encased the cold metal. If the boxcars hadn't been disabled before, they were now.

'I'm not sure I'm getting the point of all this,' said Margaret.

The point is that the Augsburgers deliberately vandalized the brakes and the couplings, I said. The point is that the *Feldwebel* had correctly understood that was exactly what Major von Niessen had wanted them to do – but wrongly understood that he wanted the train disabled because he was a shirker like them, so he could wait out the war in safety, far from the front. After the *Feldwebel* reported the job was done, Major von Niessen dismissed him and ordered me to send a telegram to Stutthof, stating that repairs to the box cars were underway, and would take a few more days to complete. Welding equipment was available in the town, and two of his men were skilled in the trade. When the repairs were done, they could send out a locomotive to move the prisoners out.

The Major saw the blank look on my face. 'Yes, yes, it's a lie,' he said, 'but we have to put them off a while longer or we'll be ordered to march the prisoners to Stutthof on foot.'

I understood what that meant, I told Margaret. It meant a long trek in bitter cold. It meant the old and feeble would collapse from exhaustion, and we would have to shoot them. The rest would be gassed when they arrived.

In a few days, a locomotive did come chugging into our station, and the Major came up with another stalling tactic. The Jews' best hope was that in the next few weeks, or less, the Red Army would advance to within twenty or thirty kilometres of us and we would beat a hasty retreat – leaving our prisoners to be liberated by them.

'Did you tell the Mounties that?'

I did. They were sceptical. Too bad it didn't work out that way, they said.

'Why didn't it?'

We got sloppy, and they tried to escape. Because of the bitter cold we had split our night watch into two groups, each of us taking short two-hour shifts. One group stood watch while the other warmed up in the waiting room. Four of the older veterans were in my group, including our *Unteroffizier,* the rest were young recruits like myself. That night our shift began at 2:00 AM, in relief of the Augsburger group. We shuffled onto the platform, still rubbing the sleep out of our eyes, while the Augsburgers shouted at us to hurry up. We shouldered our rifles and began to take our positions when one of our boys thought he caught sight of something moving among the girders, in the darkness above the floodlights. We shaded our eyes with our hands and tried to peer through the glare of the lights. Then others spotted him. 'There! There he is!' I saw him too, in his striped prisoner's uniform.

He was magnificent, I told Margaret. I saw him leap from girder to girder, high above our heads, saw him run along a narrow crossbeam, leap, catch another, and swing his body onto it. Then we lost him in the maze of girders, then a brief glimpse, moving toward the open end of the station. Before the war he must have been a circus performer, I said, and he must have been captured recently because he was still so strong. I was like a child, dazzled by his daring attempt to escape. I could hardly restrain myself from cheering him on. You would have cheered too, Antoine. Like an enraptured child, I invested his performance with the hope of us all, as though our common fate hung upon each leap and lunge, as though his daring deed would save us all, if he made it. Or something like that, I said.

Then we lost him again, somewhere in the glare of the lights. I looked back at the other Jews and saw some of them looking up, shading their eyes, but if they saw him they gave no sign. The others had their eyes on us.

We had an open VW *Kübelwagen* parked on the platform, the German version of a Jeep, I said, equipped with a powerful searchlight. The Augsburger *Feldwebel* ordered it brought forward. He beamed the searchlight back and forth, up and down, but he couldn't find the elusive Jew, tucked out of sight among the maze of girders. He began to curse, his sweeps and tilts became more erratic. Then, 'There he is!' someone shouted. Not up in the roof among the girders but scrambling down the steel lacing of the glass curtain wall that spanned the open end of the station. He was halfway down, almost there, but the search light froze him, pinned him against the glass panes – spread out, like a spider caught in his own web, a striped black and white spider against the dark glass.

The *Feldwebel* jumped off the *Kübelwagen*. 'Hold your fire, boys!' he shouted, 'This one's all mine.' He stepped forward, a few metres in front of us, all of us with our eyes fixed on the Jew. And now he took his time. He flexed his fingers and slowly raised the rifle to his shoulder. He would not be rushed. He would relish the moment. Then I charged and slammed the butt of my rifle as hard as I could into the *Feldwebel's* neck, and watched him sprawl forward onto his face. And then, as they say, all hell

broke loose. I heard a clatter, heard running feet, heard shouting. 'The
Jews! The Jews!' and then I heard shooting. I turned around to see a wall
of Jews bearing down on us, with clubs and kitchen knives. I fired. I know
I fired my first volley over their heads. I fired again, and now they were
almost upon us. I charged into their midst, yelling at them, amid the roar
of the guns. 'Back, you fools!' I shouted, 'Not now! Wait! Wait!' and while I
yelled I jabbed at their chests and faces with the butt of my gun. Then I
felt a wallop on my shoulder, I spun around and fell, and bodies fell on
top of me. Jewish bodies.

I still see that wave of humanity bearing down on me, I said, and I
knew each one of them wanted to crush my head and every bone in my
body. I remember gasping for breath, and I have a vague memory of
bodies being pulled off me. I remember voices but they were muffled and
distant. I remember some things vividly, I said, but not coherently, and
maybe I only imagine I remember. I said I remembered a bright red and
white gash on the side of a Jew's head, from his mouth to his ear, where I
had struck him with the butt of my gun, and I remember the roar, all
those guns reverberating in that hollow glass shell. But not much more,
until I woke up in a hospital bed with a very sore shoulder where a bullet
had been removed. It was in a nearby town but I don't remember the
name, if I was ever told it.

'Maybe all your shots went over their heads,' said Margaret, snatching
at phantoms.

'Many nights I have tried to imagine it was so,' I said. 'It's possible, but
not likely, and it no longer seems to matter as much as it once did.'

Margaret sat down again and put her hand on my locked fingers.
'Papa, they can't deport you for this,' she said. 'Yes they can,' I said. 'I was
there. I shot.'

Did I tell the truth, Antoine? How else could I have lived with myself all
these years if I had not construed the story as I told it to Margaret? There
are no known witnesses that can either prove or disprove my story, and
how can I presume to remember exactly what thoughts flashed through
my head during those few seconds? Maybe I began inventing the story the
moment I regained consciousness, lying in my bed in the clinic. Maybe
before I regained consciousness. The human mind is capable of vivid

delusions without the aid of our will. And yet, the Augsburgers would not have fired on me, and would not have demanded my execution when they learned I was still alive, if there were not some truth to my story.

The second time Major von Niessen appeared at my bedside it was at daybreak. By then I could move my right arm without too much pain in the shoulder where the bullet had been. There were two men with him, one a young corporal, the other a gaunt old Lutheran pastor. The corporal had brought a pickaxe and a spade, the pastor had brought a Bible. Major von Niessen told the corporal to leave the tools by the door and dismissed him, then he asked the pastor to wait outside. He sat down on the edge of the bed and told me I was very lucky to be alive. 'Some of the bullets that the Jews took, who fell on top of you, were meant for you,' he said, 'because the Augsburgers thought you had killed their *Feldwebel*.'

'Did I?' I said.

The Major shrugged. 'Who knows? Some of the others say he was trampled to death by the Jews, after you knocked him down.' He said the Augsburgers were now demanding I be put in front of a firing squad. 'I told them I'd take care of you myself.' Then he told me to get dressed. He had brought civilian clothes and a wool coat in a burlap bag.

I remember a dull day, but no fresh snow. We walked through the town in single file, the pastor in front, hands folded, eyes cast down, then me, carrying the pickaxe and the spade, then the Major. It was a silent procession through a silent town. I tried to keep my head up and my eyes straight ahead, but nevertheless I saw soldiers, already awake, watching in open doorways. Some spat on the ground as we passed, a few made the sign of the cross.

Beyond the edge of the town a footpath led to a cemetery, where I assumed I would be shot. But we walked past the cemetery. We came to a river. There was a boat and the Major told us to get in. He checked if anyone had followed us, then he got in himself. The pastor and I rowed. When we reached the other bank the Major asked the pastor which way. 'Upstream,' he said, 'around that headland.' We rowed around the headland.

There was another path here and we followed it for about ten minutes until we came to what looked like a burned out hunting lodge. 'Dig here,' said the Major.

The ground was frozen. It would have been slow going even if I'd had the full use of my right arm. 'Help him,' the Major ordered the pastor.

'I refuse,' he said. 'What you're doing is a sin. The worst sin.'

'So be it. Help him,' said the Major.

The pastor took the pickaxe and started hacking at the frozen ground. After we had hacked through the crust the digging became easier. When we finished, the pastor fell on his knees and began praying, moving his lips, silently, his eyes pinched tight shut. I stood facing the Major. 'Turn around,' he said.

'*Nein, mein Kapitan,*' I pleaded.

'Turn around,' he said, and I heard the click of his Luger behind me. Then the shot, and I too fell to my knees.

We laid the Major's body in the grave and covered it. The pastor spoke the appropriate words and then we stood there, bareheaded, for a long time. I placed the Major's cap at the head of his grave, but the pastor took it and put it under his coat. He said, 'If they find the grave they'll dig it up. Then no one will know where they put him.' He said he would notify the Major's family and after the war they could recover his body.

There was a small sleigh for hauling firewood. We dragged it overtop of the grave to hide it. The pastor shook my hand and gave me a sausage and half a loaf of *Schwarzbrot.* He said I should take the major's Luger and the green box of bullets. 'God be with you,' he said, then we parted. He walked north toward the Baltic coast, I walked south into the forest.

September 28, 1992

In the end I still had four stalwarts faithfully supporting me, Helena, Margaret, and my two old friends, Jean-Luc and Brumtup. I got at least one phone call from each of them every week, to see how I was 'holdin' up.' My fiercest defender left the country over a year ago. My granddaughter, my dear Sara. She has now spent a year as a nurse in a Palestinian refugee camp in the West Bank, 'If you can call it a medical clinic,' she wrote in her last letter, 'when there is no medicine.' She says thousands of children die every month from malnutrition and diarrhoea in Gaza and the West Bank.

During her second year at university, she had become 'political,' as she put it, and the issue that had politicized her was the Arab/Israeli conflict. Helena and I became aware of it she old us she and her friend had been barred from all their classes for repeatedly disrupting their three-hour evening class, 'Women in the Third World.' The professor was a young woman with a popular following on campus, a well known activist for women's rights who often appeared on the local television news. According to Sara, her lectures were a glitzy performance that shamelessly pandered to her 'groupies,' unabashed or unaware that she might be offending a small group of students in her class. There were only four men in the class, two of them had Arabic names, as did two of the women. One of the women was more 'Western' than Dolly Parton, said Sara, but the other wasn't. She came to class wearing an elegantly embroidered hijab and matching caftan, and her presence clearly rankled the professor. She seemed to take the hijab as a personal affront, and perhaps, said Sara, it was intended as such. Her name was Nouria Jabari. Sara said she sat near the front of the classroom, stone faced, rarely spoke or asked questions, but the professor's wry comments and witty asides became more and more pointed.

It was Sara who first began to challenge the professor's 'glib' analysis of Islamic culture and society, and that emboldened Nouria and two of the men to become more vocal. And then Sara herself showed up in class wearing an elegant head scarf.

That's my Sara, I thought. Fearless defender of the underdog. But it also troubled me.

Apparently the class then divided into two factions, the 'groupies' vs

the Arabs and a few of their supporters. The sessions became chaotic
shouting matches, and eventually the professor called Security and Sara
and Nouria were forcibly taken from the room. Later there was a 'hearing' in the dean's office where Sara and Nouria were confronted by the
professor and two of her 'groupies,' and a few days later Sara and Nouria
were informed they'd been suspended for the rest of the semester.

They became good friends, and Nouria introduced her to her other
Muslim friends. Soon Sara began to learn Arabic, and she told us she'd
made a few stabs at reading the Q'uran. 'Are you planning to convert?'
joked Helena. 'Not yet,' said Sara. But it began to worry me. She has her
father's features, bold blue eyes, fair hair that curls over her forehead in
girlish bangs, a face that can flit from a radiant smile to a scowl in an
instant. She might be called petite if there was something dainty about
her. But she is more like her mother was at that age than either of them
would admit, and I wanted to save her from becoming shrill.

Before the end of her third year she switched from Liberal Arts to
Nursing, and when she graduated she spent a year at a hospital in downtown Winnipeg where she got a closeup look at how our indigenous
people are treated. 'The cops pick them off the street and drop them at
the ER like a sack of potatoes,' she told us. But her ambition was to sign
on with an NGO and get a posting to a refugee camp in the Middle East.
It took a year of writing letters, endless phone calls, and finally she was
summoned for an interview in Toronto.

At our last meeting there were many hugs and tears. 'I love you,
grandpa,' she said, 'and it breaks my heart to abandon you, at a time like
this.' I assured her I would not feel abandoned, that she must not
squander this opportunity on my account. I said I was proud of her, of
her passion to 'do some good' in the world. That was true, but not the
whole truth. I could not dismiss the undertone of anti-Semitism in her
passion, and I knew it had been planted there by her fierce loyalty to me.
*The iniquity of the fathers shall be visited upon the children to the third and
fourth generation.* That hurts, Antoine.

During those last months before she left for the Middle East we had
some bitter arguments. I said she could never become a 'real' Muslim, that
the rituals and feelings of devotion that are instinctive to a Muslim would
always remain 'studied' for her, no matter how sincerely she observed
them. I told her she was shackling herself to the most rigid, most cultur-

ally barren, most oppressive of the three Abrahamic faiths, especially, of course, oppressive to women. And I couldn't resist throwing in her face a recent report in our news media of the public stoning of an Iranian woman accused of adultery. Sara said she expected crap like this from her mother but not from me, parroting anti-Muslim propaganda in our mass media. Did she really need to remind me? For every story about a stoning in Iran, these same media reported twenty stories about an enraged, jealous husband in Texas or Los Angeles, or Winnipeg, who had brutally murdered his wife and then murdered her children as well. Was I really so ignorant, she cried, to think that her friends, and *their* friends, weren't disgusted by those stonings? Just as disgusted as I was by the wife murderers in Texas?

Apparently there are some Iranians who aren't disgusted by it, I said.

'Pooh. There are a million rednecks in the States who think those wife murderers are heroes. The bitch probably got what was comin' to her, they tell each other, once they get a few beers in them. Then they go home and tell their own wives the same thing. If you think things are so wonderful here, you should talk to some of our native women,' she said.

'Yes, of course my Muslim friends hate the Jews,' she said. 'Their Jews are not like your Jews, grandpa. When they picture Jews they don't picture famous violinists, scientists and writers. They see a deranged, fanatical settler in the occupied territories, or a teenaged kid at a check-point with an AK47 – or whatever toys they've got now – amusing his comrades by humiliating a Palestinian mother.'

Her last letter is five pages of her dense, small script, describing in graphic detail the hunger, squalor and despair in the camp, and all the checkpoints and regulations thrown up by the Israeli government to frustrate the efforts of relief agencies. And then there is one shaft of light. The letter has a photograph tucked into it, of Sara and a young man with their arms around each other, and a note scrawled on the back. 'I've got a new friend, grandpa. He's a doctor at the clinic. And he's a Jew. Can you believe it? Well, a half Jew. His grandfather was a rabbi in Brooklyn.' And then she adds, 'A lot of Jews here hate what their government is doing to the refugees,' as though that would be news to me.

May God bless you, dear Sara.

. . .

My friend Brumtup kept issuing invitations to Helena and me to come and spend a few days with him. The last time we went I took care that our visit would not include a Sunday, as it had usually done before my public disgrace. It used to be a happy reunion, meeting my old Paraguayan friends after the Sunday service, also my former colleagues from the printing shop where I had spent my first five years in Canada. But for Brumtup and his wife as well as Helena and me that would now be very awkward, now that I was a stain upon the reputation of Mennonites across Canada. So we arrived on a Wednesday, and planned to return home on Friday.

After lunch on Friday, Brumtup and I adjourned to his basement, to his 'office' where he conducted the business of his small construction company. We talked about Paraguay, how the colony now seemed to be thriving, we talked about Russia and the state of the world generally, and then I asked him, 'If a Nazi war criminal were to make a regular appearance at your church, make a formal confession of his crimes and ask for the congregation's forgiveness, do you think your people could forgive him?' I smiled. I pretended the question was just a matter of academic interest, but Brumtup saw through the pretence.

'God can forgive you, if you bare your soul to Him,' he said, 'And if God can, we must.'

I have no doubt that Brumtup and his family could forgive me. And given his high standing among his people, maybe a few others would try their best to forgive. After all, they're a brotherhood of Christians. They would have to love me. But I knew that if I began attending Brumtup's church many of his congregants would defect, and Brumtup would be left with a half empty church.

Can you picture it, Antoine – me, trying to wriggle back into the Mennonite fold?

So many dead, all the people in my *krasnyi ugol*, my 'beautiful corner.' My mother, Uncle Knalz, Ohm Isaac, Taunte Liese, those men and women whom I have now come to venerate. And you dead too, Antoine.

After I visited Uschi in her tea room in Spandau, 1975, we exchanged one or two long letters every year for a while, which eventually dwindled down to a short letter and a Christmas card. Then came the news. She wrote that an American journalist who had covered the war in Vietnam had tracked her down. He had told her that after the fall of Saigon he had gone back to report on the new regime, and had tried to find you. It took him two years to discover what had happened to you, then six more years for him to track Uschi down in Berlin. He said when he returned to Saigon he had gone to the rooming house where you were living when he had left, where he found your former landlady. She had kept your 'personal effects' in a wicker basket. There were two white shirts, a black tie, and a pirated 1943 issue of the *Nouvelle Revue Française* that included one of your short stories – about the errant son of a noble family who had gone to Argentina to live among 'savages' on the *pampas*. And there were two letters that Uschi had sent you, letters you never answered. No return address, but the letters mentioned Berlin and McNair Barracks. Your landlady said she didn't know what had happened to you, if you had got out, if you were still alive.

Uschi said she and the journalist had both wept when they talked about you. He told her when he first met you in Saigon you were a waiter in the officers' mess. There seemed nothing remarkable about you, yet there was something that drew certain people to you, especially people who had become disillusioned with the conduct of the war. He said his own disillusionment with the war came when he'd been embedded with an American unit and had witnessed their 'successful' operations against the Viet Cong in the villages to the north. Then you quit your job, he said, and became like an ascetic monk. You lived on whatever your small following of devotees provided – enough for a roof over your head and money for food and opium.

Yes, opium. He told Uschi that during the two years before the Americans left you had spent much of your time in an opium den, patronized by people who had been 'friendly' to the American occupation and knew what fate awaited them when the Americans would pack up and leave. One of them was a Chinese businessman who had provided various services to the Americans, who was well connected, and well known to the journalist. And he had promised to get you out when the time came – since you seemed indifferent to your own safety. He told the journalist he and a few others had hired a boat to escape with their families to Singapore, and he would take you with him.

A year later, when the journalist returned to Vietnam, he had tracked this businessman down in Singapore, and got the story of how he had tried to save you. He said he had dragged you out of your opium den and stuffed you into his car, along with his family. The boat was waiting in a secluded cove, moored to a wooden wharf, and a small crowd had already gathered, pleading to get onto the boat. The owner of the boat and his pilot had to fire their guns over the heads of the crowd to drive them back.

The businessman had got his family on board, and you too, Antoine, but there was an hysterical woman among the crowd, with a large child clinging to her back. 'Take the boy! Take the boy!' she screamed. Then there was a cloud of dust on the road beyond a fringe of forest, and then they saw the jeep – with three soldiers and a big gun mounted on it. The gunner had already begun to fire at the boat, and the woman still scream-ing, 'Take the boy! Take the boy!' Then you jumped off the boat, grabbed the woman and child and pushed them on board. 'Take her instead,' you shouted, then cast off the line. The boat charged out of the cove under a spray of bullets. The businessman said he saw you turn and face the jeep, and when it came to a stop one of the soldiers got out and shot you with his pistol.

In her letter to me Uschi wrote that you had left a brief note for her when you disappeared, saying you were going to the far East. The note included a quote from some English poet:

> Go from me. I am one of those who fall.
> Has no cold wind brushed your face at all
> In my sad company? Before the end,
> Go from me, dear my friend.

Uschi said it almost sounded like a suicide note. It frightened her, and enraged her. She said after you got Mary Gordon safely out of Germany you seemed to withdraw, from everything and everybody, as though you had accomplished your task – had repaid that monster woman for her fierce love when you were a motherless child in Russia, and then again in Argentina. 'As though there was no one now whose love was worth living for,' she wrote. 'That's what hurt the most.'

Adieu, mon frère. Can I forgive you, I, who stand in need of forgiveness myself? Would my mother forgive you? Yes, she probably would, empow-ered by her unshakeable faith in goodness and mercy. Could God forgive you? If God can, I must?

. . .

I took my dog Butzie for our last walk in the park. We have grown old together, though I hardly noticed until recently. Age creeps up on dogs more suddenly. She is still eager for her walks, and eager for new scents, but she has become more contemplative, content to lie at my feet and rest her head on her paws. But on this, of all days, our park bench has been usurped. Two men in identical tracksuits sit sprawled on our bench – the bench to which, for years, Seymour and I had a proprietorial claim. There are Nike logos on their jackets, matched stripes running down their sleeves and pant legs. They are in their thirties, maybe early forties, and one wears a green headband.

They belong to the 'new people' in our town, most of them engineers and geologists who began to move in after an international corporation developed a potash mine near us. They have brought their 'culture' with them. There is now a fitness gym in our town, a proper bicycle shop, a new shoe store, and joggers are a common sight. Construction has begun on a new wing to our school, and the selection of wines at our liquor store is much improved.

The two usurpers leisurely let their gaze drift around the park, the way men do when they're talking about 'work.' They don't need to look at each other while they talk, and can allow long pauses in their conversation.

'Why'd they pick Philadelphia? Doesn't sound like a fun place, for a convention. Especially not in winter,' said the one with the headband.

The other one shrugged. 'Maybe because it's got more class than Vegas.'

'Don't see the point of it, myself.'

I slowed my pace and Butzie stared at them as we passed, but they took no notice. We made a circuit of the park, and still they showed no inclination to leave. Unlike the older residents, the 'new people' don't seem scandalized that their town may have harboured a war criminal for almost thirty years. They don't see me. I am debris left over from another age, for the proper authorities to dispose of. We come from different worlds. They can no more look into my past, if they were ever so inclined, than I can look into their future.

I turned off onto a narrow path through the trees, then like a spoiled child I sat down in a huff under a towering elm. The ground was damp and the leaves had already begun to fall, a splotchy brown carpet on the grass. Butzie stuck her nose in my face, as though a scent might explain my unusual behaviour. I gave her head a rub and told her to lie down. She sniffed out a spot, circled twice and lay down.

I sat legs crossed with my hands on my thighs. I kept my eyes fixed on the ground and took deep breaths to calm myself. I gave Butzie's head another rub, then I too lay down on my back and gazed up at the sky through the branches above me. I watched the clouds shaping and reshaping themselves into various figures, and for a brief moment I thought I saw my people up there among the clouds – my mother, Uncle Knalz, Groote Graeta, Ohm Isaac, all of them sitting in the ample lap of Abraham and looking down on me. It seemed a forgiving look. I relaxed. I let my hands ruffle the leaves at my side and began to feel strangely buoyant, like a swimmer might, floating on his back. I began to move my arms and legs like I'd seen Canadian children do, playing in new-fallen snow, moving their arms up and down and their legs in a scissors motion. They call it making angels. And indeed, when they get up and look down they see the imprint of a winged angel on the snow. My green angel was a bit messy, the outline not as sharp as the angels children make in the snow, but I was content with it.

Time now for Butzie and me to go home. After my last hearing the police had bent the rules a little and let Margaret drive me home, but now they would be waiting for me. I did not wish to alarm them unduly by a long absence. They would be polite, and Helena would be stoic. She would have served them coffee and cookies. Margaret would be there too, doing her best to restrain her instinctive aversion to policemen.

As I passed our bench, the two men in track suits were still talking about work. 'Think I'll take the wife an' kids this year. Make it a holiday,' said the one with the headband. He seemed to have warmed to the idea of a convention in Philadelphia.

'What's to do in Philly – for a holiday?' said the other.

'Lots of stuff. Lot of history. They got a Ben Franklin museum, a whole museum just about one guy. And of course, they got the Liberty Bell.'

'What happened there?'

'I dunno. Somebody rang it.'

GLOSSARY

Blyads. Russian expletive, roughly comparable to 'fuckin'ell.'

Einsatzgruppe C. The SS paramilitary death squad active in the southern Ukraine.

Khutor. Owner of a large Russian estate.

Kolkhoz. Soviet collective farm, usually consisting of the people and former property of one village, but sometimes as many as four or five villages. Managed by a Director, usually not a local man, in spurious consultation with brigade leaders, local commissars, and the workers' union.

Komsomol. Soviet youth organization, combining the functions of boy scouts, ideological vigilantes, and volunteer labour brigades.

Hiwi. Slang abbreviation of 'Hilfswillige,' literally a 'volunteer,' the usual designation of a captured Soviet soldier who 'volunteered' to change his allegiance and serve the German *Reich*, to avoid probable death in a German POW camp. Normally it required some ingenuity to persuade a German officer of one's sincerity.

Mishegoyim. Crazy goyim (often applied to ignorant gentiles).

NEP. New Economic Policy, 1921-28, permitting private ownership of redistributed land and livestock, replaced by Stalin's Five Year Plan of forced collectivization.

Nyemtzy. Derogatory Russian/Ukrainian term for German colonists, comparable to 'Kraut.' It derives from the Russian word for "mute".

NKVD. Soviet secret police agency, successor to the GPU and OGPU, forerunner of the KGB.

Raion, Volost, etc. Municipal administrations, comparable to District or County.

Urka. A prisoner in the Soviet Gulag, usually a non-political, i.e. a thug, with authority to terrorize other prisoners. Roughly comparable to a *kapo* in the Nazi concentration camps.

Volksdeutsche Mittelstelle. A paramilitary branch of the SS, responsible for the welfare of ethnic Germans (*Volksdeutsche*) in territories occupied or claimed by the *Reich*. It provided some order to the evacuation of *Volksdeutsche* refugees from Russia, the Ukraine, and the Baltic countries. In practical terms, this often meant they stole land and supplies from Poles and Ukrainians and distributed it among the ethnic German refugees.

Zusammenbruch. 'Collapse.' The chaos that followed the German surrender.

SOME LESS WELL-KNOWN
HISTORICAL FIGURES

Denikin, Anton Ivanovich (1872-1947). Leader of the White Army and later escaped to France, succeeded by Pyotr Wrangel.

Dyck, Peter (1917-2004) and Elfrieda (1914-2010). Born in Russia, immigrated to Canada in 1927. Married in 1940. They represented the Mennonite Central Committee (MCC) in Germany after the war, establishing and managing refugee camps, and organized the evacuation of Mennonite refugees to Paraguay. Probably two of the most highly esteemed figures of the post war period by Russian Mennonites.

Dzhugashvilli, Iosif Vissarionovich. aka, Joseph Stalin.

Froese, Otto, and Werner Klaassen. Their names appear in Gerhard Rempel, "Mennonites and the Holocaust," *The Mennonite Quarterly Review* (October 2010), 507-549.

Makhno, Nestor (1888-1934). Leader of an anarchist movement (Makhnovtze) in the southern Ukraine during the Russian Civil War. His Black Army fought both the Reds and the Whites, then joined with the Reds to defeat the Whites, then were betrayed by the Reds. Makhno escaped to Paris after 1921. Mennonites regard Makhno as a murderous terrorist, but some historians in the 1960s pictured him as a romantic Robin Hood figure.

Mozorov, Pavlov. The celebrated 'boy martyr,' as he is described in the novel.

Schneider, Dr. Karl (1891-1946). Chairman of the Department of Psychiatry at the University of Heidelberg, 1933-45, and a leading figure in the Nazi euthanasia programme, much loved by his students. Committed suicide after his arrest by the Americans.

Stolypin, Pyotr (1862-1911). Prime Minister and Minister of Internal Affairs, one of Imperial Russia's greatest statesmen, who tried to implement much needed agrarian reforms. Assassinated in the Kiev Opera House by a leftist revolutionary, Dmitry Bogrov, but perhaps with the complicity of the Tsarist secret police and extremist rightwing elements opposed to his agrarian reforms.

Stumpp, Dr. Karl (1896-1982). Highly regarded ethnographer and historian of ethnic German settlements in Russia and the Ukraine. Headed a *Sonderkommando* during the Nazi occupation to register ethnic Germans, and also provided the SS with very useful information about Jews in southern Ukraine. Nevertheless, he had a successful academic career in Germany after the war.

ACKNOWLEDGMENTS

My wife, Linda, has been a steady presence at my side through every stage in the writing of this novel, through all the many revisions. I also owe a huge debt of gratitude to my publisher, Jonathan Seiling, for his brazen confidence in the merit of my novel, and to John Rempel and Ernie Regehr for bringing my manuscript to his attention. And another huge debt of gratitude to Elias Mina who designed the covers of the novel.

Then there are the many people of my parents' and grandparents' generation whose stories of the Great Trek and life under Soviet Communism I absorbed from the time I was a child, then the people I later interviewed who gave me the confidence of their often painful memories, and those who allowed me to read their family memoirs.

Among less known published sources, I'm indebted to *Up From the Rubble* by Peter and Elfrieda Dyck, *Tiefenwege,* the diary of Jacob A. Neufeld, and his later memoir, *Path of Thorns,* also *Das Ende von Chortitza* by Gerhard Fast, *Gibt der Wahrheit die Ehre!* by Karl Fast, the prison letters of Abram Tertz (Andrey Sinyavsky) in, *A Voice from the Chorus,* Lev Kopelev's memoir, *The Education of a True Believer;* also, *A Woman in Berlin: Eight Weeks in the Conquered City,* by Anonymous, and Marlene Epp's oral history, *Women without Men.*

Among the many academic histories, I'm particularly indebted to *The Nazi Doctors: Medical Killing and the Psychology of Genocide* by Robert Jay Lifton, and *Bloodlands: Europe between Hitler and Stalin* by Timothy Snyder.

ABOUT THE AUTHOR

Erwin J. Wiens was born in Edmonton and grew up on a farm in the Niagara fruit belt. After graduating from the University of Waterloo, he spent two years in Newfoundland where, in the late 1960s, the National Film Board and Memorial University had launched a pilot project using film in community development. He received his MA from the University of Waterloo and his doctorate from the University of Ottawa, followed by teaching positions in English Literature at Queen's University, the University of Ottawa, and Heritage College in Gatineau, Quebec. Some of his poems have appeared in *Queen's Quarterly* and *Bridges: An Ottawa Anthology.* In 1990, he toured the Soviet Union, where he visited the former Mennonite colonies in southern Ukraine, distant relatives east of the Urals, and two elderly survivors of the gulag.

Manufactured by Amazon.ca
Bolton, ON

24672198R00226